WINNETOU

KARL MAY
WINNETOU

Translated and abridged
by David Koblick
from the original 1892-93 edition of Winnetou I

Foreword by Richard H. Cracroft

Washington State University Press
Pullman, Washington

Washington State University Press
PO Box 645910
Pullman, WA 99164-5910
Phone 800-354-7360; FAX 509-335-8568
wsupress@wsu.edu
www.publications.wsu.edu/wsupress
© David Koblick, 1989
© Foreword, Board of Regents of Washington State University, 1999
All rights reserved
First printing 1999

Library of Congress Cataloging-in-Publication Data

May, Karl Friedrich, 1842-1912.
    [Winnetou. English]
    Winnetou / by Karl May ; translated and abridged by David Koblick from the
original 1892-93 edition of Winnetou I ; foreword by Richard H. Cracroft.
      p. cm.
    ISBN 0-87422-179-X (alk. paper)
    1. Apache Indians—Fiction. I. Koblick, David, 1916- . II. Title.
PT2625.A848W7413   1999
833'.8—dc 21   99-18364
                                                CIP

Cover painting: "The Gift," ©Keith Powell, P.O. Box 788, Grand Coulee, WA 99133.

ACKNOWLEDGMENTS

Much of the biographical and statistical material in the Introduction was obtained from *Karl May—Ein Popstar aus Sachsen* (*Karl May—A Popstar from Saxony*) by Klaus Farin, and is used here with that author's gracious consent. Thanks to Mike Morrow for pointing me in the right direction, and to Alex Kuo for giving me a push.

INTRODUCTION

By David Koblick
Steyr, Austria

The Horatio Alger fable of the poor but hard-working lad who starts as a shoeshine boy or dishwasher and ends up a millionaire has its real-life counterpart in the life of Karl May, whose beginnings were even less auspicious than those of Alger's youthful protagonist. May was born in Ernstthal, Germany, on February 25, 1842, with the odds well stacked against him; he was blind for the first four years of his life.

Karl was the fifth child of a poverty-stricken small-town weaver. Nine more children followed, but few of them lived to see their first birthday. The May family's constant state of deprivation—there was never enough to eat—marked Karl indelibly. Still, his father had high hopes for him, and brought home every sort of printed matter for the boy to read, even a 500-page German atlas to study and copy, although it was 40 years out of date. In this way he amassed an enormous store of information, supplemented with folktales told him by his grandmother.

May entered school at seven, and due to exceptionally high grades was able to start studying for a teaching credential when he was only fourteen. But he was expelled three years later for pilfering six candles he had intended to give his parents as a Christmas present. He was able to resume his studies elsewhere, however, and passed his final examinations and obtained a position as a teaching assistant. That lasted twelve days; his landlord complained to the school superintendent that the nineteen-year-old stood too near his wife while giving her piano lessons. He was dismissed.

His next job was teaching underage workers in a textile mill, children who were obliged by law to attend school after their 10-hour workshifts in the mill. When Karl went home for Christmas vacation, he took with him his roommate's watch and smoking utensils. He was arrested and sentenced to six weeks in jail, and on his release was forbidden to teach.

That ended his dream of a teaching career. Twenty-one years old—what should Karl May do now? He turned to petty swindling and confidence trickery, and in 1865, after several episodes involving the impersonation of officials, received a four-year prison sentence.

Released early for good behavior, he returned home to Ernstthal. His reputation had preceded him, and the townspeople regarded him mistrustfully. He resumed his false identity career, first passing himself off as a police lieutenant from Wolframsdorf and impounding a "counterfeit" 10-thaler note and, as stolen property, a watch that took his fancy. Then he assumed the role of a Dresden attorney's representative bringing fictitious news to a master baker and his sons about a legacy left them by a relative who had emigrated to America. He was on his way to a notary, he said, to officially register the inheritance. It was, of course, all a pretense—he was only looking about for any pilfer-prone money. He disappeared with 30 thalers, but was soon found and rearrested. A second four-year sentence resulted—the first year in solitary confinement. May was released on May 2, 1874; he was 32 years old.

During those years in prison he had read omnivorously and started writing, putting down on paper his fantastic dreams of grandeur, adventure, and superheroic deeds, with himself as daring-doer. He had sent stories to several publishers, but all were rejected. Ten months after his release, a small publisher of the German equivalent of "dime novels" sought him out; Heinrich Gotthold Münchmeyer, journeyman carpenter turned publisher, had read some of the rejected manuscripts May had written in prison.

There had been great changes in the world outside. Prussia had fought and won a war against France and begun unification of the many independent German states. The war had impoverished the populace and many had emigrated, most of them to the United States (two million in the last quarter of the 19th century)! Berlin's population had doubled to over a million, and although an ever-greater percentage of the people lived in grinding poverty, illiteracy gradually was being eradicated.

Hardbound books were an extravagance and comparatively few could afford them, but cheap, soft-bound booklets with stories set in exotic locales unknown to insular Europeans were for many an escape from daily drudgery. Münchmeyer set May to work as a writer of adventure tales and as editor of the weekly, *The Observer*. May's pen raced across the paper, and three new periodicals were founded to absorb the output—entertainment journals to "bring sunshine into the homes and hearts of their readers." His initial first-person adventures, *From a World-traveler's Files*, appeared here, and the first mention of the name Winnetou is found in his 1875 western story, *Old Firehand*. However, Münchmeyer was rather tight-fisted with money, although he presented May with a piano as a Christmas gift. May left him after 18 months and became a freelance author.

After being presented in weekly installments with the title *Captured at Sea,* May's first full length novel, *Old Sureband,* was published *in toto.* Now other periodical publishers knocked at his door, and many of May's narratives were printed by them in installments, often without payment. Many of his tales appeared in *Deutscher Hausschatz,* a Catholic family magazine.

On a visit to his sister's house, May met, and later married, nineteen-year-old Emma Pollmer, a local beauty who, besieged by other suitors, had taken refuge in her grandfather's house. (Although the marriage would last 22 years, May wrote rather wistfully in his autobiography, *My Life and Strife,* in 1910: "My wife had never read one of my books; the purpose and content of my writings were unknown to her." He divorced Emma in 1903 and married the widow Klara Plöhn, who would have great influence on his further writing career, not all of it positive.)

Personal problems still cropped up after he met Emma Pollmer. In January 1878, the elder Pollmer's only son, after a beer-hall brawl, had fallen beneath a carriage-horse's hooves and was killed. The elder Pollmer did not believe his son's death had been an accident and coerced May into conducting an investigation. May did so, resuming his old habits by faking an appointment by the government and stating his authority superseded that of the district attorney. May interrogated witnesses about the death of his in-law. They became suspicious and reported him. He was imprisoned for three weeks for "usurpation of authority"—unjustly as it turned out, for he was not in violation of the paragraph cited in the conviction, as attorney and May-researcher Claus Roxin later determined.

In 1881, May had started writing a cycle of Oriental novels. These were printed in installments by several periodical publishers over the next decade, but it was a demanding life, and payment often was hard to come by. It was not until 1892 that fortune again began to smile on him; the first six green-and-gold-bound *Collected Travel Novels* were reprinted from the previously published installments by the Freiburg publisher Fehsenfeld. May was penniless at the time, and had to beg the publisher for an advance.

The rest is history. This slight, sickly, eccentric jailbird became the most-read author writing in the German language. The reading public practically snatched each new "travel narrative," as he called them, as it fell from the presses, and readers began to believe that May really was the world traveler depicted in his books—a man of superhuman strength who spoke 1,200 languages and dialects, and could deduce the nationality and state of health of a horseman by his steed's hoofprints.

Karl May's most popular work, *Winnetou I*, was written in 1892. In 1895, 100,000 May novels were sold, and he began to receive an annual stipend of 60,000 marks. In 1900, distribution of his travel narratives reached the million mark, and since then there is no end in sight; compare 9 million copies of May novels published in 1945 with 25 million in 1965, twenty years later. In the 1970s that number doubled, counting only those published by the Karl-May-Verlag (founded in 1913 by May's agent Euthar Schmid) whose total production to date has surpassed 100 million. Twenty-five million copies of May's novels have been published in the German language by a dozen other publishers under license from the Karl-May-Verlag. The publishers make minor alterations in each annual edition and apply for a new copyright date; the original editions are by now, of course, in the public domain.

Translations into at least 30 European languages, mainly without purchase of translation rights, began to appear at the turn of the century. In the Dutch-Flemish area about 55 publishers have May titles on their lists. In Lithuania, 300,000 copies of the *Winnetou* series (there are three volumes) were sold in 1986-88. Editions of several hundred thousand are published annually in Hungary and the Czech and Slovak republics, and when Bulgaria lifted a ban on May's books in 1977, the initial edition of 300,000 sold out on the first day.

Karl May began to believe his own legend: "I really am Old Shatterhand and I am also Kara ben Nemsi, and I have experienced all that I relate." His fictional character, Kara ben Nemsi, roamed Arabia. His narratives covered the world—many in Europe, but also the Near East, Mexico, South America, the Pacific Islands. . . His special adventureland was the post-Civil War American West; he visited the United States for the first time late in his life, in 1908. May's dozen or so novels located there, inspired by the writings of James Fenimore Cooper, glorified and ennobled Native Americans, and reviled and condemned the palefaced interlopers who had stolen their land, massacred their people, laid waste to their settlements, and driven them to retaliate with the same cruelties practiced by the whites. Although he sometimes erred in historical and ethnic areas, May's admiration for Indian culture and customs was an early denunciation of racism.

May's other and earlier extra-European journey had been a 15-month tour through the Orient in 1899-1900, when he was 58. That confrontation with reality, visiting the localities where his heroes—*he himself!*—had performed such valiant deeds, must have been a great shock. It brought him home to Saxony a completely changed man. From then on he began to demolish the legend he had spent a quarter-century fabricating, and his final writings were rather milktoasty *romans à clef.* After a decade of legal and editorial mudslinging, Karl May died on March 31, 1912.

Gone but not forgotten. There is to this day hardly a German-speaking household whose bookshelves do not hold a goodly assortment of May's 73 novels. To the hundreds of millions already published, add another million or so annually. The total of May's published works surpasses those of any other German writer.

And they are read, devoured, and discussed in bars, schools, youth clubs, and even universities where many doctoral candidates in Germanistics take the May phenomenon for their theses and respected professors of literature occasionally digress from teaching Goethe and Schiller to remark, with both admiration and distaste, on this prolific author of *Schundliteratur*—trash novels, penny dreadfuls.

Every summer more than a million Karl May fans congregate at the many open-air theaters where events from his novels, mainly those involving Old Shatterhand and the Apache Chief Winnetou, are reenacted by players dressed in Western and Indian costume. The Karl May Association, one of the largest literary clubs in Germany, is a reservoir of May devotees and researchers, and the Karl-May-Verlag also deals in sideline sales of costumes, wigwams, posters, stickers, feather headdresses, tomahawks, and other Indian and Western memorabilia.

In 1962, the May novel *Der Schatz im Silbersee (The Treasure in Silver Lake)* was filmed, with Pierre Brice as Winnetou and Lex Barker as Old Shatterhand. It was the biggest box-office hit since the end of World War II, and reinvigorated the languishing German film industry, pulling in over three million paid admissions in its first run. Lex Barker, who had played Tarzan in the early 1950s and had had a featured role in Fellini's *La Dolce Vita*, made a perfect Shatterhand. The movie was filmed in low-budget Yugoslavia with the sound-track dubbed in German where necessary. Seventeen more Karl May novels were made into films in the next six years, eleven of them starring Brice and Barker as Winnetou and Shatterhand. May novels set in the Near and Middle East also were filmed in the 1960s, though the story lines often departed radically from the originals. No new May films were made in the 1970s or later, although all of the old ones appeared, and still appear occasionally, on German, Austrian, and Swiss television. Pierre Brice made a personal appearance before thousands of screaming Winnetou fans as recently as 1996, when he was 67 years old, and in 1998 was featured in a two-episode made-for-TV "Old Winnetou" revival.

Karl May *fan*aticism never ebbs. In the mid-1980s, a poll of Leipzig (in former East Germany) high school students asked for the titles of their ten favorite books. Four May novels were on the list: *Winnetou I* in first place, *Der Ölprinz (The Oil Prince)* fourth, *Der Geist der Llano Estacado* in eighth place, and number ten, *Der Schatz im Silbersee*. May's popularity appears to be everlasting.

xii   *Winnetou*

The list of Karl May fans or at least avid readers has included Konrad Adenauer, Albert Einstein, Hermann Hesse, Adolf Hitler, Fritz Lang, Heinrich Mann, Albert Schweitzer, Max Schmeling, Erich Honecker, and Franz Josef Strauss. The names Helmut Kohl and Arnold Schwarzenegger are found in a long list of contemporary readers, as are the Archbishop of Munich and the Bishops of Mainz, Osnabrück, Eichstatt, and Passau.

A final note: This translation is based on an original 1892 edition of *Winnetou*. In the writing style of his time, Karl May was given to including numerous passages—frequently at great length—of description, exposition, and philosophizing, which often divert the reader from the continuity of the plot, and always slows the action. Where these passages are integral to the story, I have left them in; where they have little or nothing to do with what is happening, I eliminated them. I assure the reader, nothing vital is omitted.

FOREWORD

By Richard H. Cracroft
Brigham Young University

I

For over a century, Karl Friedrich May (1842-1912) has made the Wild West of North America as meaningful to the *Bürger* of Stuttgart, Salzburg, and Zürich as it is to their counterparts in Santa Fe, Des Moines, or Buffalo. Thanks to Karl May, whose volumes of exciting adventures in the American West and Arabia can be found in the home libraries of many European families, smoke signals, hairbreadth escapes, peace pipes, amazing feats of strength, uncanny woodsmanship, and pinpoint accuracy with firearms are as familiar to quick-drawing European youths as to their war-whooping American cousins.

Europeans—not all of them young—continue to read the astonishing adventures (*Abenteuer*) of Karl May, who maintained the falsehood, even to his second wife, Klara, and to closest friends, that his travel novels (*Die Reise-Erzahlungen*) were autobiographical, that he had indeed roamed the American West as Old Shatterhand and the Arabian desert as Kara ben Nemsi.

Today, nearly a century after his death, legions of fans, happily overlooking his delusions, continue to enjoy television reruns of Old Shatterhand/Winnctou films, and a million devotees flock each summer to the popular Karl May Festival at Bad Segeburg, Germany. The result of this long-standing love affair between fantasy-hungry Europe and the imaginative May has established and perpetuated May's singular image of the American West among a readership which never seems to weary of the adventures of Germany's famous counterparts to Natty Bumppo and Chingachgook (or the Lone Ranger and Tonto)—noble Old Shatterhand and his blood brother Winnetou, *der rote Gentleman* (the red Gentleman) and noble "High Chief of the Apaches." These two indefatigable adventurers continue to satisfy the romantic *Drang nach Westen* (The Urge to Go West) and the *Freiheitssehnsucht* (Yearning for Freedom) which have characterized the Teutonic peoples since the Rhine and Danube rivers first flowed out of *ur*history.

A gifted storyteller with a fertile imagination, *"Karl der Deutsche,"* influenced by American and German predecessors in rendering the American West as literature, created in his Old Shatterhand/Winnetou tales a German saga which, as the first-time American reader soon discovers in David Koblick's lively translation of the exciting first volume of the *Winnetou* trilogy, continues to excite the Germanic imagination even as it startles the American reader with its Teutonization of a region which North Americans have mistakenly laid claim to as their sole property.

II

In *Winnetou,* May launches Karl (Charlie), a brilliant young German who finds himself in St. Louis as a tutor to a well-to-do German immigrant family, on a lifetime of never-ending summer adventures in the Wild West. Mr. Henry, a (true-to-life) weapon maker, sees Karl's amazing potential as a *Westmann* (May's untranslatable name for a westerner, frontiersman, mountain man, or adventurer), and fits him out with his two powerful trademark weapons, the double-barreled "Bear Killer" (*Bärentöter*), and "Henry Rifle" (*Henrystutzen*), the latter a secret weapon that carries 25 rounds. Mr. Henry then secures his young apprentice a position with a surveying crew of a westward-expanding railroad.

No ordinary greenhorn, as friends and enemies soon learn, Karl (called "Charlie" by his American companions) soon becomes acquainted with the crudity of the American and exerts his German wisdom and remarkable strength to teach a few Teutonic manners. He also meets Sam Hawkens—of German ancestry (naturally)—who has some years of experience as a *Westmann.* Hawkens, a comic-relief figure, undertakes to educate this greenhorn in the ways of the West. Karl, of course, is an amazingly adept pupil. Although he admits to being a greenhorn, it becomes apparent that this educated German greenhorn is far superior to the common Yankee variety; indeed, Karl seems to have sprung, full-blown, from the Rhine legends.

Amidst this surveying and western schooling, which includes an introduction to tracking, capturing, and taming wild mustangs, hunting buffalo, and grappling with a grizzly bear, Karl and his companions are captured by Kiowa Indians and Karl must demonstrate his extraordinary strength and endurance. However, it is after felling Rattler, the white trouble-maker, with one blow from his lightning-fast, dynamite-packed fist, that Karl is christened "Old Shatterhand."

"So there I was," says the newly named *Westmann,* "baptized again without my consent with that fighting name [Old Shatterhand], the name I have carried from that day to this. It is common in the West for men to have such names." May's works are full of descriptions of such "customs."

Further tests of Shatterhand's mettle come in a knife duel with the strong man of the Kiowas, and in a successful run-and-swim-for-life struggle against the chief of the Mescalero Apaches, a triumph that earns him the blood-brotherhood of Winnetou and launches a friendship which will last over fourteen adventure-packed years. Under Winnetou's tutelage, Shatterhand enters "Indian School," where he becomes adept at Indian life and proficient in the Navajo and Apache languages and dialects.

Shatterhand is a remarkable linguist. In language twists unique to May, Shatterhand is able to foil miscreants because of his astounding linguistic knowledge. In *The Black Mustang* (1896), for example, he trips up an Indian spy on the shibboleth of the English tongue. As he explains to the captured villain, "Your language reveals your disguise. I know exactly how an Upsaraoka and every tribe speak the language of the paleface. You are not a Crow Indian, but a Comanche."

Another time Shatterhand, who knows more languages than a Vatican guide, overhears two Chinese coolies plotting a payroll robbery. After bringing the two to justice, he remarks, "They didn't realize that Old Shatterhand had also spent time in China during his . . . world travels, and had an excellent command of Chinese" (*The Black Mustang*).

May himself modestly claimed, "I speak and write: French, English, Italian, Spanish, Greek, Latin, Hebrew, Romanian, Arabian (six dialects), Chinese, Turkish, and the Indian languages of the Sioux, Apache, Comanche, Snakes, Utahs, Kiowas, besides the three South American dialects of the Katschumany [Kechumaran]. I won't count Lapplandic" (quoted in *Der Spiegel*, September 12, 1962, p. 65). He had obviously applied himself during his years in prison.

Amidst this mixture of adventure and brilliance, there is, of course, little place in Shatterhand's life for a lady love. Indeed, there is only one woman in May's Winnetou tales—Nsho-chi, the beautiful sister of the young chief. She falls in love with the blond superman, who, although a miscegenist, holds out hope for her suit if she will be educated in the white man's ways. En route to enter a white school in St. Louis, she and her father, Chief Inshu-chuna, are murdered by the evil Yankee, Santer. This cowardly act not only relieves Shatterhand of an embarrassing hindrance, but drives him and Winnetou, now the High Chief of the Apaches, through two more volumes of adventures as the grief-stricken pair track down the wily villain (*Winnetou II, III*). So completely does May avoid the female in his works that most readers sooner or later must come to grips with German critic Paul Elbogen's assertion that May's works evince a "childish connection with sexual stimulation" and suggest a condition of "ideal homosexuality" (quoted in *Der Spiegel*, 62).

In reality, Shatterhand has no time for women. His is a virile, dedicated, hard-fighting, masculine life. But it is also a Christian life, and

Shatterhand often resembles a celibate, holy knight in search of the Grail. His gentle, tolerant, and forgiving nature make him the kindliest Christian "between the Mississippi and the Rocky Mountains." He shuns killing, shoots only to maim, and consequently must spend much of his time dodging old enemies whom he had wounded in earlier adventures. Through all of the tales, May preaches an orthodox Christianity that thrilled many ministers of his day, who often saluted him for his positive influence on their congregations.

Wrote one convert family: "We are poor and can give you only our thanks. Since we have read your works, we are no longer Social Democrats" (*Der Spiegel*, 65).

Shatterhand prays, keeps the Sabbath, listens to warnings from a small "voice," which is "most certainly the voice of my Guardian Angel" (*Old Surehand II*, 1895), freely proclaims his belief in God and Jesus Christ, and eventually brings about the conversion and deathbed baptism of Winnetou, who, after hearing Shatterhand sing May's poem, "Ave Maria," whispers in his white brother's ear: "Charlie, I believe in the Savior. Winnetou is a Christian. Farewell!" and dies in his grieving sidekick's arms (*Winnetou III*).

Shatterhand's almost militant Christianity frequently lands him in trouble. His kindly Christian treatment of African-Americans brings the Ku Klux Klan on his trail, although May's portrayal of Negro Bob, a recurring figure in his westerns, is stereotypical, showing Bob as eye-boggling, simple, illiterate, but good-hearted. It is, however, Old Shatterhand's Christian embrace of the Native American, as embodied in Winnetou, that is May's central theme.

III

May saw himself as the enlightened German minstrel of the *Götterdämmerung* of the Native American. Like Cooper, he tinged his tales with nostalgic laments about the vanishing Indian race. While he packed his books with authentic if eclectic anthropological detail and drew upon an extensive library of source materials, his "factual" descriptions of Native American language and folkways ultimately dissolve before the dreaming power of his vivid and idealistic imagination, and his Indians become a patchwork of assorted anthropological facts and romantic idealization. The result is not literary realism, but a highly original and unusual native who falls somewhere between Cooper's romantic Indian and the Noble Savage of Jean Jacques Rousseau.

As Old Shatterhand represents the highest ideal of the German nation, so Winnetou embodies the nobility to which the Native American

can rise, assisted by enlightened whites. Shatterhand's "first meeting" with Winnetou, he reports, "made a deep impression on me," and he strikes the tone of the nobility, mutual affinity, and equality of the two heroes which he will sustain in all of their adventures: "[Winnetou's] features, even nobler than his father's, were unlined, the skin a dull light brown with bronze highlights. His height was the same as mine, and as I later learned, our ages also matched . . . We exchanged a long searching gaze with each other as if there were no others present."

Unlike the naturally noble savage of Chateaubriand or Rousseau, Winnetou is noble because of his willingness to embrace the best of European (read "German") culture and blend it with the finest traits of his own race. It is Winnetou's ability to read, write, and discourse, as well as his rejection of barbarous savage customs, which ennobles and endears him to Old Shatterhand, his equally noble (if somewhat patronizing) side-kick and blood brother.

Indeed, during Shatterhand's temporary imprisonment in the pueblo, he (and the North American reader) is surprised and astonished by the Apache chief, who "was wearing a white linen robe, and carried no weapons. A book was under his arm, and I could read part of the title '—OF HIAWATHA' in large gold letters. This son of the 'savage' race of Indians could not only read, but had a taste for classic literature, in this case Longfellow's epic poem celebrating noble and romantic characteristics of his race. Poetry in the hands of an Apache Indian!"

Although May apparently attempted to model Winnetou on some of the Apache chiefs—especially Cochise—Winnetou emerges as an *Edelmensch* (a noble person) and is essentially untouched by his surrounding culture. Where other Apaches utter authentic Apache words, gleaned by May from ethnographical studies, encyclopedias, and other reference sources, Winnetou (not an Apache name) speaks in unaccented English and High German; and where other savages indulge in authentically grounded barbarisms (which Cooper calls Indian "gifts"), Winnetou cultivates the manners and discourse of a refined and genteel Christian.

May allows Winnetou to use *Howgh*, that one word that he claims is common to all Indian tribes. "*Howgh*" is, says May, "an Indian word of affirmation and means nothing more than 'amen,' 'so it remains,' 'it shall be so.'" Thus Winnetou invariably ends every deliberation with *Howgh, ich habe gesprochen* (Howgh, I have spoken), after which the other natives will reply, *Uff uff*, another ubiquitous term which registers, says May, "admiration, astonishment, scorn or surprise—depending on the context." (In this WSU Press edition, however, the translator uses *Ugh*, rather than *Uff*, since the former expletive is familiar to American readers). These two phrases, *Howgh* and *Uff uff,* are integral to the perceived German-Indian idiom, and are, along with *Hände hoch!* (Hands up!), essential German Wild West speak—ask any native speaker of German!

IV

Original as he is, May is nevertheless indebted to James Fenimore Cooper and, more immediately, to such German writers as Charles Sealsfield, Friedrich Gerstäcker, Friedrich Armand Strubberg, Balduin Möllhausen, and Nicolaus Lenau for a considerable "western" literary heritage.

In *Winnetou III,* when an old mountain man chides Shatterhand for being a greenhorn, he tests the hero's western savvy by asking, "Surely you have read Cooper?" to which Shatterhand responds, "But of course." Cooper's Leatherstocking Tales, much published and widely read in German countries, fashioned very early in the century the German and European image of the American frontier, an image which May would augment with his own romanticized view of the West.

That German vision of the American Indian and the West was also influenced by the works of Charles Sealsfield (Karl Postl, 1793-1864), a contemporary of Cooper. Sealsfield, who made five visits to the United States, recounted for rapt readers heroic histories of the settlers of Mexico, battles with the Indians, the way of life of American ranchers, farmers, and frontiersmen, and, importantly, conveyed to the German people— hungry for excitement, adventure, and freedom—a description of an ideal life of independence in the brave new western world.

Friedrich Gerstäcker (1816-72), whose work was artistically inferior to Sealsfield's, wrote more than 150 widely read volumes which had a great influence upon German emigration to America. He spent six years in the U.S. and probably knew more about the frontier than any other German writer. Gerstäcker became increasingly critical about many aspects of American life, which may have contributed to May's own cynicism concerning the Yankee, who is generally a villain, along with Mormons and half-breeds, in his works. Gerstäcker's novel, *Flusspiraten des Mississippi* (*River Pirates of the Mississippi,* 1848), remains a favorite of German youth, in part because of its exciting story and coarse realism which borders on literary naturalism, the influence of which may be seen in May's lurid treatments of death on the frontier.

"Armand," or Friedrich Armand Strubberg (1806-89), lived for a time in a Texas palisade and, in imitation of Cooper's Leatherstocking, told the tale of a boy who became a great hunter in the West. If Gerstäcker knew more about the frontier, Strubberg knew more about Native Americans than any other 19th century German writer. Strubberg's Indian is a real and embattled one "who had lived through a century of shame and dishonor, one broken in strength, retreating ever farther to the West" (Preston A. Barba, "The American Indian in German Fiction," *German-American Annals* XI [1913-14]). Although Strubberg suffered at the hands of thieving Indians, he remained aware of the injustice they had undergone at the hands of the whites, and, like May, sides with the Indians, whom he portrayed realistically, but with a tendency to idealize.

Balduin Möllhausen (1825-1905), often called "the German Cooper" (Barba, 165), was the author of many western tales, notably *Das Mormonenmädchen (The Mormon Girl)*, and was one of May's favorite writers. In 1851, Möllhausen accompanied Prince Paul of Württemberg on an expedition to the Rocky Mountains; he left the expedition for a time to accompany hunting parties of a band of Omaha Indians. He later joined Lt. Whipple in 1853-54, serving as an artist-topographer on an important expedition to investigate routes for a transcontinental railroad through to the Pacific. In 1857 he explored the Colorado River with Lt. Ives (Barba, 160). His accounts had a direct influence on May, whose Old Shatterhand begins his western experiences as a surveyor for a railroad.

Another influence on May was Nicolaus Lenau (1802-50), whose penchant for constructing a "moody, dreamy fairytale world" (Karl Heinz Dworczak, *Karl May: Das Leben Old Shatterhands* [1950], 172) contrasted with bitter feelings about American realities and probably helped to firm up May in his belligerent attitude towards the Yankee while promoting May's own fairytale-like fantasies.

V

Still, Karl May's West, although influenced by these spiritual precursors, emerges with idealized characteristics all of its own. Old Shatterhand not only possesses Atlas-like strength, amazing intelligence, and every Christian virtue, but, of course, German blood as well.

Klaus Mann, the brother of Thomas Mann, would write in 1940: "There is hardly a single detail in [May's] 'American' stories . . . that is not a total and ludicrous misrepresentation. Atmosphere and landscape, gestures, words and actions are thoroughly un-American. Un-American are the villains—who, for some mysterious reason, are usually presented as Mormons or *Americans;* un-American are the noble heroes; utterly un-American above all is the self-righteous narrator, Old Shatterhand-Karl May" (*Living Age*, CCCLIX [November 1940]).

Mann might well have substituted "German" for "un-American," for Old Shatterhand symbolizes May's estimation of the ideal virtues of late

19th century Germany. It is through this Teutonic hero's eyes that the Wild West is seen—and distorted: "Karl May has, according to his statement, attempted to glorify the Indian character. But in reality, he has idealized in Old Shatterhand . . . the character of another people: The Germans" (*Der Spiegel*, 63).

As "the perfect Germanic hero—a *Goodwill* ambassador of the Wilhelminian Empire, ready to save the Indians through the German being" (*Der Spiegel*, 63), and eager to teach the Yankees much-needed lessons, Old Shatterhand rides through the West as enlightened "Germania," victorious over mean-spirited Yankee bigotry and Indian anti-white prejudice, and his heroes remain, even in the Wild West, as "pious as the catechism, as proletarist as the law book and as German as the National Hymn—supermen" (*Der Spiegel*, 54).

Consequently, Old Shatterhand, a.k.a *Karl der Deutsche*, discovers a German or a German-speaking connection in every adventure, in every straight-shooting companion. Even the comic Sam Hawkens, Shatterhand's first western mentor, soon confesses that, *jawohl*, he is a German, and Shatterhand points out that he and Hawkens often converse *auf Deutsch*, because Sam "held his German fatherland lovingly in his heart." So thoroughly has May transplanted German customs and thinking to the American West that readers may come away with the impression the U.S. is somehow a German fiefdom.

May's heroes hear German music and songs wherever they go—songs with "German inwardness and depth of feeling—such songs as are only written by Germans" (*Satan und Ischariot*, 1896); they take a stand as Germans on the slavery question; they read German newspapers such as the *Anzeiger des Westens* (*Western Review*), which Shatterhand accurately praises as "the most influential foreign language newspaper in the whole West" (*Weihnacht im Wilden Westen* [*Christmas in the Wild West*], 1893); and they drink German beer, for, *natürlich*, as one German *Westmann* remarks, "where the German goes, there will always be a brewery" (*Unter Geiern* [*Among Vultures*], 1886).

May's writing responds to a period of national pride. His blend of factual information and imaginative detail tapped into the pan-German nostalgia for the romantic and exotic while it stirred a sense of nationalistic glory. The *zweites* (second) *Reich,* under the Hohenzollerns and Bismarck, was ushering in a new era for a unified Germany which had recently avenged itself on France in the Franco-Prussian War (1870-71), after French servitude following the Thirty Years' War (1618-48) and during the Napoleonic conquests (1800-14).

Immersed in American western literature as he was, May heard the nationalist call to arms which crescendoed over Germany throughout much of the 19th century and inspired August Heinrich Hoffman von Fallersleben (1798-1874) to pen the stirring *Das Lied der Deutschen* (Song of the German People):

Deutschland, Deutschland über alles,	(Germany, Germany above all else,)
Über alles in der Welt	(Above everything in the world.)
. . .	. . .
Deutsche Frauen, deutsche Treue,	(German women, German loyalty)
Deutscher Wein und deutscher Sang	(German wine and German song)
Sollen in der Welt behalten	(Shall in all the world retain)
Ihren alten schönen Klang	(Their old and ringing refrain.)

VI

Karl May's imaginative view of the Wild West, perpetuated now for over a century, stirs the soul of the modern German and European reader. May presents them with a well-defined cultural heritage in a region which continues to excite and refresh their imagination.

May's West is not, however, a region familiar to the American or Canadian reader. Accustomed to having their North American heroes at the forefront in the winning of the West, readers of the *Winnetou* saga are subjected to seeing Germany's finest, represented in Old Shatterhand, and Winnetou, the noble Apache, jousting with the best that other, albeit clearly inferior peoples, can offer. In May's scenario, this noble Teutonic/Indian duo emerges triumphant over the inferior Yankee/American—thereby inverting and subverting an almost sacrosanct myth and causing May's western books to ring strangely and falsely in the North American ear.

May undertook to ground his noble *Westmann* and his remarkably un-savage Indian in a body of textbook-derived anthropological facts, which initially ring true enough to the North American ear—but then he strangely distorts the drama with manifold imaginative twists. The result is a highly romantic, idealized, Teutonized West in which Old Shatterhand and Winnetou move about, lending assistance and bestowing moral admonition where needed, defending the oppressed, restoring order, avenging murders, and rescuing captives from unenlightened savages and degenerate Americans. The American reader scratches his head in bewilderment!

Europeans, from Thomas Mann and Adolf Hitler to Albert Schweitzer and Albert Einstein, have been thrilled by Karl May's depiction of the American West. During the occupation of Germany after World War II, the U.S. State Department urged U.S. personnel in West Germany to become familiar with May's works, so as to better understand the German view of Americans.

Karl May made no attempt to deal with the historical or anthropological realities of Western American life. He described his vague, idealized hopes for the future in *Winnetou's Heirs* (1909), his last book about the West. In it he relates a mythic dream in which "the last of the redskins unite with the whites to form a new German-Indian race which will create and work in the spirit of the noble Winnetou" (Dworczak, 116). Throughout his career, from his first western book to his last, May bewailed the retreat of the Native American before the greed of American geographic, economic, and cultural imperialism, while evoking the poignant and romantic pathos of a "Last of the Mohicans" motif.

This yearning for an idealized union of the red and white races is symbolically depicted at the end of nearly every adventure as the two heroes, emblematic of all that is best in their respective races, temporarily part—Shatterhand to some other rendezvous, and Winnetou to govern his tribe or pursue a renegade Indian or white to his just punishment.

Intones Winnetou at a typical separation: "The Great Spirit commands that we separate. He will bring us together at the right time, for Old Shatterhand and Winnetou cannot continually be separated . . . Love will join us once again. *Howgh!*"

Then, hand raised in a dramatic farewell, the noble Winnetou rides into the horizon, ending another adventure of the two heroes of the West. Says Old Shatterhand: "A press of his hand for me, a loud, resounding shout to his horse ["Hi-ho *Iltschi*"?], and he gallops away, his long, glorious hair trailing behind him like a mane. I watched until he disappeared. Will you find the enemy? When will I see you again, you dear, dear Winnetou?" (*Winnetou II*)

In this excellent English translation of *Winnetou*, many North American readers will meet Old Shatterhand and Winnetou for the first time on the (German) frontier. Happy trails!

Howgh! Ich habe gesprochen!

SELECTED REFERENCES
IN THE ENGLISH LANGUAGE

Ashliman, D.L. "The American West in Twentieth-Century Germany." *Journal of Popular Culture* II (1) (Summer 1968): 81-92.

Barba, Preston A. "The American Indian in German Fiction." *German-American Annals* XI (1913-14): 143-75.

Billington, Ray Allen. *Land of Savagery, Land of Promise: The European Image of the American Frontier in the Nineteenth Century.* New York: W.W. Norton, 1981.

Cracroft, Richard H. "The American West of Karl May." *American Quarterly* XIX (Summer 1967): 249-58.

_____. "The American West of Karl May," M.A. thesis, University of Utah, 1963 [170 pp.].

_____. "May, Karl Friedrich (1842-1912)." *The New Encyclopedia of the American West*, edited by Howard R. Lamar. New Haven: Yale University Press, 1998 [686-87].

_____. "Siegfried in a Coonskin Cap." *The American West* I (Summer 1964): 32-33.

_____. "World Westerns: The European Writer and the American West." *A Literary History of the American West*, edited by Thomas J. Lyon, *et al.* Fort Worth: Texas Christian University Press, 1987 [159-79].

Mann, Klaus. "Cowboy Mentor of the Führer." *Living Age* CCCLIX (November 1940): 210-21. Also as, "Karl May, Hitler's Literary Mentor." *Kenyon Review* II (4) (1940): 391-400.

Stadler, Ernst A. "Karl May: The Wild West Under the German Umlaut." *Missouri Historical Society Bulletin* XXI (July 1965): 295-307.

Walker, Ralph S. "The Wonderful West of Karl May." *The American West* X (6) (November 1973): 28-33.

Wechsberg, Joseph. "Winnetou of der Wild West." *Saturday Review* (October 20, 1962): 52-53, 60.

Wittke, Carl. "The America Theme in Continental European Literatures." *Mississippi Valley Historical Review* XXVIII (1) (June 1941): 3-26.

KARL MAY
WINNETOU

PROLOGUE

Alas, the red race is dying! From the Land of Fire to far above the Great Lakes of North America, the smitten giant lies prostrate, struck down by a pitiless fate, a destiny inexorable. With wily ferocity he fought the futile battle to survive, but his strength had gradually failed. Now he breathes his last, the shudders that time and again seize his naked frame signaling the imminence of death.

Is he himself to blame for his own demise? Has he earned it, does he deserve it? If it's simple justice that every living thing is entitled to life, and if that applies to the whole as well as to each individual part, then the red man has a right to exist no less than has the white man. He should have been given the opportunity to live in his own fashion, to develop and maintain a society in harmony with his environment.

Of course, some assert that the Indian doesn't possess the characteristics necessary to create a society. Is that true? I say NO! I omit a long dissertation, simply consider these facts: The whites had *time* in which to develop—from hunters to herdsmen, and onward to agriculture and trade, manufacturing and industry. But this development took place over many decades, centuries, millennia. The red man started later; he hasn't had that time. Should he ascend from his primitive state to a higher level in one giant leap? This was what white society demanded of him, without realizing that the attempt must fail, and lead to his destruction.

It is a cruel law of Nature that the weak must yield to the strong. But isn't it also true that the eternal Wisdom that gave us this law is at the same time Love eternal? Couldn't the law have been mitigated in the case of this dying red giant, so that the race would be allowed to survive?

The first "palefaces" to arrive on these shores were greeted not merely with hospitality, but with almost divine veneration. What did the Indians receive in return? Indisputably, the land whereon they lived belonged to them. It was taken from them. The rivers of blood that flowed in the taking, and the unspeakable cruelties practiced, are common knowledge to anyone who has read the history of the Spanish Conquistadores.

On this model the bloodshed and cruelty continued. The white man came with sweet words on his lips, but with a sharp knife in his belt and a loaded pistol in his hand. He promised love and peace, but gave hate and strife. The red man had to fall back, step by step, always in retreat. From time to time he was given guarantees regarding "eternal" rights to "his" lands, and shortly after evicted from them. Territory was "bought" from him, paid for with useless trinkets, or more often with nothing at all. The insidious poison "firewater" was given to him, together with smallpox and other diseases which decimated many tribes and depopulated entire settlements.

When the Indian dared to assert his rights, he was answered with powder and ball, and again he had to retreat before the superior numbers and weapons of the whites. Resentful, embittered, he revenged himself on every paleface he encountered, and in consequence began to practice the same cruelties and carry out the same massacres taught him by the white man. Initially a proud, daring, valiant, upright, truthloving huntsman, loyal to his fellow-tribesmen, he became through no fault of his own a slinking, lying, mistrustful, murderous redskin. The white man is to blame for that transformation.

Yes, the Indian is terminally ill, and we stand by his deathbed, waiting to close the lids over his eyes. To stand by while death approaches is a solemn chore, a thousand times more solemn when an entire race is dying. And many questions arise, these in particular: What would this race have accomplished had it been granted time and space in which to develop its strength and talents? What unique capabilities have been lost to mankind through the destruction of this folk?

But of what use are such questions in the face of death which cannot be averted? What use recriminations, when it is too late to bring the dying giant back from the brink? My laments change nothing, I can only grieve. I? Yes, I! who have learned to know the red men over many years, and among them one who lives forever in my heart and in my thoughts. He, the best, most loyal and devoted of all my friends, was a true representative of the race from which he sprung, and even as it perishes did he perish, his life extinguished by an enemy's murderous bullet. I loved him as no other human, and still love the dying folk whose noble son he was. I would have given my life to save his, just as he had risked his own for me a hundred times. But it is only his body that has died—his spirit will continue to live in these pages as he continues to live in my soul, he, Winnetou, the High Chief of the Apaches. Here will I build for him a well-earned monument. And if the reader, seeing it in his mind's eye, comes to a just conclusion about the race whom this chieftain so truly typified, I shall feel richly rewarded.

Radebeul, 1892.

CHAPTER ONE

D o you know what the word "greenhorn" means? It's an angry
and contemptuous designation for the one to whom it's applied. A greenhorn is one who's still *green*, that is to say, newly arrived and inexperienced in the basic knowledge he needs to cope
with the customs of the country. A greenhorn doesn't get up when a
lady enters the room; he greets the master of the house without first
bowing to the mistress and her daughters. Worse, he loads his weapon
backwards, first the wadding, then the ball, and last the powder.

A greenhorn speaks either pure and affected English or else no
English at all; if the former, it pains him to hear Yankee- or back-
woods-English spoken. He mistakes a raccoon for a 'possum, and a
birch tree for a pine. He smokes cigarettes and despises tobacco-
chewers. If a ruffian boxes his ears, he takes it to court instead of
throwing a punch in return, or shooting the brawler down on the
spot.

A greenhorn takes with him a bath sponge, a scrub brush, and a
pound of soap for a day-trip out on the prairie. He writes down a
hundred Indian words and expressions, and when he meets his first
red man finds he's left the list at home. He buys gunpowder, and
when he tries to use it, finds that he's been sold powdered charcoal
instead. He sticks his Bowie knife in his belt so that when he bends
over it stabs him in the thigh.

A greenhorn is—well, a greenhorn. And back then I was one of
them. But of course I had no inkling that this derogatory term could

be applied to me! No, for a greenhorn's prime characteristic is that he doesn't realize he is one. On the contrary, I believed myself to be an exceptionally clever and experienced young man. I had studied hard, learned much, and passed all my examinations with ease. The fact that life itself is the real teacher whose students are being tested daily, hourly, had never crossed my youthful mind.

The restrictive conditions and limited opportunities in my home-land and an inborn thirst for action had induced me to cross the ocean to the United States, where conditions and opportunities for an ambitious young man were much more favorable. I had soon found good situations in the Eastern states, but I felt the romantic Wild West drawing me. I had earned enough in short but well-paying positions to let go; I arrived in St. Louis well-outfitted and filled with cheerful courage. There I had the good luck to find quarters with a German couple, and a temporary position as their children's tutor.

Through this family I met a certain Mr. Henry, a gun maker. An eccentric fellow, he worked at his trade with the dedication of an art-ist. A sign hung outside his workshop on which he had proudly let-tered "MR. HENRY, THE GUNSMITH." He was a great humanitarian, although outwardly he seemed to give a completely opposite impres-sion. He had few friends aside from the Webers with whom I lived, and treated his customers in such a brusque and offhand manner that they continued to come to him only because of the high quality of the weapons he made. He had lost his wife and children in a dreadful happening of which he never spoke, although I gathered from re-marks dropped by others that they had been killed in the course of an attempted robbery.

Though rough on the outside, Mr. Henry was a kind and gentle man at heart. I'd often seen his eyes grow moist when I spoke of my home and my people, with the emotion that still grips me when I think or speak of them. Why this older man took a liking to me, a brash young stranger, I couldn't imagine. Although he knew that my given name was Charles, he started calling me "Bud" in a friendly way, meaning no derogation. Ever since I'd been at the Webers, he came by oftener, sat near while I taught the children, and finally in-vited me to visit him at his shop. I knew such an invitation wasn't extended to just anyone, and I hastened to take advantage of it. Mr. Henry was often put off by my European reserve, and I remember the sullen mood in which he once received me, not even responding to my polite "good evening."

"Where were you hidin' out yesterday, Bud?" he growled at me.

"At home."

"And the day before?"

"Also at home."

"Hmmph! I find that hard to believe. Young birds like you don't loll around in the nest. They fly about and stick their beaks in everywhere, to see what's goin' on. Everywhere—I'll bet you've been in every shop and tavern in the town. Everywhere 'cept where you belong."

"Oh? And where do I belong?"

"Right here, understand? For a long time there's been somethin' I've wanted to ask you."

"Why haven't you asked it?"

"Because I haven't wanted to till now."

"So, ask away!"

He looked me full in the face and shook his head disapprovingly. "Hmmph! As if I have to ask a greenhorn's permission before he'll let me talk with him."

"Greenhorn?" I repeated, feeling deeply insulted. "I assume, Mr. Henry, that you spoke that word without thinking."

"Don't flatter yourself, sir! I said it deliberately. You are a greenhorn, and what a greenhorn! It's true that you have the contents of many books in your head—it amazes me what you people over there have to learn. A young man like you knows how far away the stars are and how much air weighs, air he can't even grasp. And because he knows those worthless things, he thinks he's a clever fellow. But get involved in life, real life, as I've been for some fifty years, and you'll learn what genuine knowledge and cleverness consist of. What you know now is worth nothin', nothin' at all. And what you can do now counts for even less. You don't even know how to shoot!"

He spoke in such a disparaging tone and with such conviction that I realized immediately the point of his tirade.

"I can't shoot?" I replied with a smile. "Is that the subject you've been leading up to, the question you wanted to ask me?"

"Yes, that's it! What do you have to say?"

"Put a good firearm in my hand, and I'll give you my answer."

He put down the rifle barrel he was working on, got up from the workbench, stood closer, and regarded me with amazement.

"Put a firearm in your hand, Bud? My weapons are handled only by persons who know and have respect for them."

I inclined my head. "I have such knowledge and respect."

He didn't respond at first, just looked at me sidelong for a moment, sat down and resumed work on the rifle barrel. About a quarter-hour went by before he spoke again. "Now tell me the truth, have you ever had a gun in your hand?"

"Many times."

"Aimed and fired it?"

"Of course."

"And hit what you were aimin' at?"

"Naturally."

Mr. Henry put down his work. "The devil! You must've been shootin' at a barn door! I can't believe that a greenhorn and bookworm like you knows how to shoot." He pointed to the wall behind me. "Take down that old gun and show me how you hold it. It's a bear-killer, the best I've ever had in my hands."

I took down the gun and put it to my shoulder.

"Hello!" Mr. Henry sprang from his chair. "You handle that weapon like it was a walkin'-stick, and it's the heaviest gun in my shop! Are you really that strong?"

In answer, I put the gun in my left hand, and held my right arm straight out. "Go ahead, swing on it," I said. Mr. Henry gripped my forearm and lifted his feet from the floor. My arm stayed horizontal.

"Amazing!" he cried. "You're even stronger than my Bill!"

"Your Bill? Who's that?"

He hesitated. "He—he was my son, who—no, I don't want to talk about it. He's dead, and that's it." An expression of deep sadness came over his face. "You've got his same bearing, almost the same eyes, and the way you move your lips . . . " Then, in a normal tone of voice: "But your strength, that's a wonder to me, for somebody who's had so much to do with books. I always thought bookworms were weak and spindly. You been active in sports?"

"Yes, I have."

"Boxin'?"

"Not much—boxing's not so common over there. But I was quite good at wrestling and gymnastics."

"Ridin'?"

"That too."

"Fencin'?"

"I've had some lessons."

"Bud, stop your braggin'!"

"Want to have a go at it?"

"No, that's enough. I have to get back to work. Sit down again." He returned to his workbench, and I did as he asked. Conversation following was mainly in monosyllables—Mr. Henry seemed to have something on his mind. Presently he stopped working, and asked, "Have you studied mathematics?"

"It was my favorite subject."

"Algebra, geometry?"

"Of course."

"Surveyin'?"

"I liked that especially. Often I took my instruments and went on surveying trips just for the fun of it. But I don't claim to be a professional surveyor by any means."

"Very good, very good."

"Why are you asking, Mr. Henry?"

"Because I have good reason to, understand? One which you needn't know about at present. First, I have to know whether you can really shoot a gun."

"So, try me out!"

"That I will, you can count on it. What time in the morning do you start your tutorin'?"

"About eight o'clock."

"Then come here about six. We'll go out to the firin' range where I test my guns."

"Why so early?"

"Because I don't want to wait any longer to prove to you that you're still a greenhorn. Enough for now! I have much more important things to do."

He finished with the rifle barrel, put it away, and took a many-faceted metal piece from a box. He began to file a corner. I saw that each of the flat faces had a hole in it. He worked with care and concentration, and seemed to have forgotten my presence. The piece he worked on was evidently of great value to him, so I asked: "Is that part of a weapon, Mr. Henry?"

"Yes," he answered, as if just realizing I was still there.

"I've never seen a firearm with a part like that," I said.

"I'm sure you haven't, but you will. My name will be on it, it will be called the 'Henry'."

"A new invention?"

Brusquely. "Yes."

"Please excuse my curiosity. Is it a secret?"

He took a long time before answering, looking through each of the holes and turning the piece this way and that. Then: "Yes, a secret. But I trust you to keep it, even though I know you're a real greenhorn. It's goin' to be an automatic carbine, a multi-loader with twenty-five rounds."

"Impossible!"

"Hold your tongue! I'm not stupid enough to work on impossibilities! Here, watch closely." He explained how the mechanism would work, a ratchet rotating the chambers one by one to line up with the single barrel, each chamber holding a cartridge. "The steel alloy is also my secret, and the part is shaped so that it loses heat quickly. I've been workin' on it for many years, and now at last I think I've solved the final problems. I already have a good name as a gunsmith, but the 'Henry' will make me famous, and bring me more customers."

"And a guilty conscience to boot!"

He stared at me in surprise. "Guilty conscience? How so?"

"Every murderer has, or should have, a guilty conscience."

"The devil! Are you sayin' that I'm a murderer?"

"Not yet. But you'll be one soon, for an accessory to murder is just as guilty as the murderer himself."

"What? Are you sayin' I'll be an accessory to a murder?"

"To only one? To mass murder! Think about it! When you've perfected a gun with twenty-five rounds, and many of them get into the hands of unscrupulous villains, then murders will be committed everywhere, on the prairie, in the mountains! The poor Indians will be shot down like coyotes, and in a few years there will be no Indians left at all! Do you want to have that on your conscience?" He glared at me and didn't answer.

"And," I continued, "if just anybody can buy these murderous weapons, there will be thousands of them sold in a short time. The wild mustangs will be wiped out—and the buffalo, and other animals whose meat the red man needs to live. Blood will flow in streams, both human and animal blood, and soon there will be no living thing on either side of the Rocky Mountains."

"Damnation! Did you really just come over from Germany?"

"Yes."

"And you've never been here before?"

"No, never."

"So—an absolute greenhorn! You talk as if you're the great-grand-father of all the Indians, and have lived here for thousands of years! Listen, I have no intention of openin' a factory to make these guns— I work alone, and don't want any employees. Each 'Henry' will be my own manufacture, and I'll have to know a man well before I'll sell one to him. Does that make you feel better? Now go on home, I'll see you tomorrow."

I didn't know then how important this evening would be for me, and it never crossed my mind that the old gun Henry called a bear-killer, and the Henry-carbine too, would play such vital roles later in my life. I looked forward to the next morning, for I was really quite a good marksman, and was eager to surprise the old man with my skill. I was there at his shop promptly at six. Henry was already waiting.

"Welcome, Bud! You're wearin' an expression of victory. Think you can hit that barn door I spoke of yesterday?"

"I hope so."

"All right, let's go. I'll carry a lighter gun and you carry the bear-killer. I'd rather not lug such a load." He hung a double-barreled rifle over his shoulder and I took the heavy old gun. We walked a short way to the firing range.

Henry loaded both weapons, and shot twice at a fair-sized target already in place. He nodded to me, and I stepped forward with the bear-killer. Now of course I didn't know this weapon, but my first shot clipped the edge of the black bull's eye. My second shot was within it, and my third was dead center. I had the feel of it now, and suc-ceeding shots all went through the center hole that the third bullet had made. Henry's astonishment grew from shot to shot. When I took the rifle and had the same success, he could keep silent no longer.

"I can't believe it! Either the devil's on your side, sir, or else you're a born Westerner! I've never seen a greenhorn shoot like that!"

"It's not the devil, Mr. Henry," I laughed, "just lots of shooting practice, back home in Germany."

"Well, with that kind of marksmanship for a start, we'll make a real Westerner out of you! How would you like that?"

"Why not?"

"And you said you could ride, too?"

"If necessary."

"If necessary?" he mocked, "not as well as you shoot, eh?"

"Pff!" I dismissed his mockery, "riding isn't hard. Getting up in the saddle is the difficult part. But after I'm up there, there's not a horse that can throw me."

Mr. Henry looked at me searchingly, not sure whether I was serious or just joking. I kept a poker face.

"As you say, gettin' up is the hard part, because you have to do it yourself. Gettin' off is easy, the horse does the work—all you have to do is fly through the air."

"Well, I'd like to take a try at it."

"So you will. It's only seven o'clock—we still have an hour's time. Come along, we'll go see Jim Horner, the horse-dealer. He has a roan horse that will suit you just fine."

We went to Jim Horner's. He had a large corral, with stalls around it in a half-circle. Horner came out, greeted us, and asked our pleasure.

"This young man claims that no horse can throw him," said Mr. Henry. "What do you say to that, Mr. Horner? Would you let him climb onto your roan?"

The horse-dealer measured me with a shrewd eye, and satisfied, nodded his head. "Looks like he's built strong and supple. Anyway, young people don't break their necks as easy as older ones. If he'd like to try out the roan, it's all right with me." He called out an order, and presently two handlers led a saddled horse from one of the stalls. He was restless, rearing and trying to pull away. My old Mr. Henry became uneasy, and asked me if I wanted to reconsider.

I said no. Firstly, I was confident, perhaps even cocksure. Secondly, it was now a matter of pride. I was handed a whip and a shiny pair of spurs. It took several tries—the horse objected violently—before I succeeded in gaining the saddle. I was hardly seated, my feet not yet in the stirrups, before he began to buck and rear. As that didn't dislodge me, he tried to scrape me off along the corral fence. I'd had time to reach the stirrups then, and I pulled him away with spurs, whip, and reins. Now began a fierce battle between horse and rider; how long it lasted I couldn't say, it could have been five minutes or fifty. I was not really an experienced horseman, and managed to hang on by brute strength and sheer determination not to be unseated. My thigh muscles finally won the battle, and the roan stood still, stiff-legged, blowing foam, and dripping with sweat.

Mr. Horner was a little concerned about his horse, but after the roan had been wrapped in blankets and led away, he turned to me and said, "My compliments, young man. I thought you'd be thrown in the first few seconds. There's no charge, and any time you want to come and give the roan another riding lesson, you're welcome to do so."

"Thank you, Mr. Horner. It would be a pleasure," I replied.

Mr. Henry had not said a word since I'd dismounted, just shaken his head in wonder, or perhaps in concern. Now he clapped his hands together and cried: "This greenhorn is like no other greenhorn I've ever seen! Bud, where did you learn to ride?"

"I must confess, I've never really learned. But one other time, on a dare, I rode a wild Hungarian plains stallion that nobody else could stay aboard. So I thought I could ride the roan the same way."

"It's amazing! Well, I've seen you ride and I've seen you shoot, and that's enough for one day."

We parted. A few days later Mr. Henry came by the Webers. It was afternoon, he knew I was free then. "Would you like to take a little walk with me?"

"Where to?" I asked.

"To visit a gentleman who wants to meet you."

"Meet me? What for?"

"Well, let's say he's never met a genuine greenhorn."

"All right. I'll give him the privilege."

We walked along several streets where I'd never been before, and came to a small building with a large glass entrance door. On it in gold letters were the words "SURVEYING OFFICE." We entered. Within, seated at desks, were three gentlemen who greeted us cordially, Henry as an old friend and me with open curiosity. Maps and plans lay about on the desks, and an assortment of surveying instruments were lined up along the wall.

It wasn't clear to me for what purpose my friend had made this visit. He wasn't delivering guns nor soliciting business, only engaging in friendly conversation, which soon turned into a discussion of the maps and instruments. That suited me fine, as now I could join in, and perhaps learn something about American surveying standards and practices. Henry seemed to take a great interest in the art, and little by little I was drawn so deep into the conversation that I found myself explaining the use of the various instruments, and answering questions about cartography. I was a real innocent, because it didn't occur to me what was happening here.

I was in the midst of a lengthy discourse on surveying methods using polar and rectangular coordinates, perimeter measurement, the repetition procedure, and trigonometric triangulation, when I sensed that no one was paying much attention, and that the three gentlemen were nodding covertly to Mr. Henry.

I got up from my chair, indicating to Henry that I wanted to leave. He didn't object, and we were bid adieu even more affably then we'd been received. After we'd turned the first corner and couldn't be seen from the surveying office, Henry stopped, put his hand on my shoulder, and looked into my face with an almost glowing expression on his.

"Sir, man, youngster, greenhorn, Bud—you've made me very happy! I'm really proud of you!"

"Proud? Why?"

"Because you've greatly exceeded my recommendation, and even the expectations of those gentlemen!"

"I don't understand."

"Easy to explain. You said the other day that you knew a little about surveyin', and to see if you were just braggin', I took you around to visit those surveyors, good friends of mine. As I said, you did me proud!"

"Bragging? Mr. Henry, if you think I'm capable of that, I'll not come to visit you again!"

"Now, now, young sir, you wouldn't deny an old man the pleasure of your company, would you? More and more I see your resemblance to my son Bill. Have you been back to Horner's corral?"

"Every morning."

"Ridin' the roan?"

"Yes."

"What will become of that horse?"

"He's for sale, but I doubt that any buyer will get along with him as well as I do. In this short time he's gotten used to me, and Mr. Horner say he throws off everyone else who tries to ride him."

"That pleases me, pleases me greatly! It seems that he'll let only greenhorns ride him! Come, let's go this way. There's a dinin'-house down this street where they serve good food and drink. We've got to celebrate the outstandin' way you passed the examination!"

Mr. Henry's words and actions were beyond my grasp—he was a different person. This solitary reclusive man wanted to eat in a *dining-house*! And he'd said "examination"—what was that supposed to mean? From that day on he visited me daily and acted toward me as if I was an old friend that he was about to lose.

At the same time the Webers' attitude toward me also changed. The children were sweeter, and their parents more solicitous than before. About two weeks after the "examination," Mrs. Weber told me to be sure to stay for dinner that evening, as she had also invited Mr. Henry and a couple of other gentlemen, one of them a famous Westerner by the name of Sam Hawkens. Being a greenhorn, I'd never heard his name before, but I looked forward to meeting a genuine Westerner—and a famous one, to boot.

I was a house guest, so didn't have to wait for a dinner bell to ring—I walked into the dining room a few minutes before the usual dinner time. To my astonishment, I saw that the room was prettified and decorated as if for a festival. Little five-year-old Emmy was alone in the room, and she quickly pulled her finger out of the blackberry-jam jar, licked it off, and wiped it on her long blonde pigtail. I was still looking around in bafflement when she ran to me, pulled my head down to hers and whispered:

"*Your farewell dinner.*"

My farewell dinner? Impossible! Where had the child gotten such a ridiculous idea? I gave her an amused smile. Hearing voices in the front room, I went in to greet the dinner guests, who had all arrived at the same time. Mr. Henry introduced me to Mr. Black, a young, rather stiff and formal young man, and to Sam Hawkens, the Westerner.

The Westerner! I must admit that as I looked at him for the first time with open curiosity, his appearance was not at all what I'd expected. Truthfully, I didn't know how a Westerner was supposed to differ from the Americans I had met so far. The figure he cut was one I had never seen before; later I met many similar types, although Sam Hawkens himself was unique. He gave the impression of one whose

manner and appearance would be the same whether he was standing here in this lovely parlor or trekking through the wilderness.

Looking out from under the brim of an old felt cap were a pair of
small, sharp eyes set in a full-bearded face. What skin the beard didn't
cover was brown and leathery. A large nose stuck out from the center of this countenance, one which could have doubled as the pointer
of a sundial. But the eyes were by far the principal feature; they were
observing me as attentively as I was observing him. I soon learned the
reason for his interest.

He was wearing an old leather coat which had been patched an
uncountable number of times, and covered his short body down to
the knee. Two skinny legs clad in leggings stuck out from under the
coat, ending in a pair of decorated, but scratched and soiled Indian
boots.

This famous Westerner was carrying a rifle whose homemade
stock made it look more like a club than a firearm, though he cradled
it lovingly in the crook of his elbow. At this moment I couldn't imagine a more absurd caricature of a prairie hunter; it wouldn't be long
before I learned to know the real worth of this little man who stood
before me, this Westerner Sam Hawkens.

When he had looked me over to his satisfaction, he turned to the
gunsmith, and asked in a high, almost childish voice:

"Is this the young greenhorn you were tellin' me about?"

"Yes," nodded Mr. Henry.

"Well! He looks all right to me. Hope old Sam Hawkens looks all
right to him, too, heeheehee!"

With that peculiar giggle, which I was to hear again a thousand
times, he turned to the dining room door, where the Webers had just
appeared. They welcomed the guests, and we all entered the dining
room. To my surprise, Sam brought his rifle with him, and looked
around for a place to put it. He leaned it in the nearest corner, and
said:

"A Westerner never lets his gun out of his sight. Even here among
friends, a man gotta be ready in case an enemy shows up. That brave
Liddy of mine is always nearby."

So he called his weapon Liddy! I found later that almost all Westerners named their guns, and treated them as living things. Before we
sat down, Sam had another surprise in store. He removed his felt cap,
and his stringy hair came with it, leaving a smooth, blood-red

baldness. The lady of the house shrieked, and the children's mouths fell open. Sam turned and said calmly:

"Don't be shocked, lady and gentlemen—it's nothin' to be afraid of. I had my own hair until I met up with a couple dozen Pawnees, and they took it away from me, together with my scalp. It was a devilish disturbin' feelin' for me to have a naked head, but I survived, heeheehee! So I went to Tekama and bought myself a new scalp, a wig. Cost me three stacks of beaver skins. But the new scalp is more practical than the old one, 'specially in summer—I can take it off when I sweat, heeheehee!"

He hung the cap on his rifle barrel, put on the wig again, and took off the leather coat. Under it he wore a leather vest, and he had a knife and two pistols stuck in his belt. Before we all sat down, he looked at me, then at Mrs. Weber, and said:

"My lady, before we eat, shouldn't we tell the greenhorn what this is all about—if I'm not mistaken?" That expression of Sam's, "if I'm not mistaken," I would also hear many, many times. Mrs. Weber nodded, indicated the other young guest, and said:

"Perhaps you don't know yet, Charles, that Mr. Black here is your successor."

"My—my successor?" I asked in confusion.

"Yes, indeed. We're celebrating your departure tonight, and we had to employ a new tutor."

"My—my departure?" Stupidly, I could only repeat the bewildering word.

"Yes, sir, your departure," she repeated, smiling. "We really should have given you notice, but we have liked you and enjoyed your company so much that we wanted you to learn about your new good fortune here in the company of all concerned. We're sorry to see you go, but our blessings and our best wishes go with you when you leave tomorrow morning."

"Leave—tomorrow—where to?"

Now Sam, who was standing next to me, put his hand on my shoulder, and said with a smile, "Where to? With me, into the Wild West. You passed your tests with honors, heeheehee! The other surveyors are leavin' tomorrow, and can't wait for you any longer; we all hafta leave together. Dick Stone and Will Parker and me, we've been hired as guides—up the Canadian River and into New Mexico. Didja think ya were going to stay here and be a greenhorn forever?"

At last the scales fell from my eyes. Everything had been prearranged! I was to go with a surveying party, probably to lay out a route for the planned cross-country railroad. What a joyful surprise! I didn't even have to ask for details, for my good old Mr. Henry came to me, took my hand and said:

"I've already told you why I like you so much. These are wonderful people you've been stayin' with, but a job as a children's tutor ain't for you. No, Bud, you've got to go out West, the West is where you belong. I applied to the Atlantic and Pacific Company and let 'em check you over without your knowin'. You passed, as Sam said, with honors. Here's your contract—all you have to do is sign it."

He handed me the document, and continued, "You'll be ridin', so you need a good horse. I've bought the roan for you, the horse you broke yourself. And you've got to have a weapon; I'm givin' you the bear-killer, that heavy old gun with which you hit the bull's eye every time. What do you say to that, sir?"

I couldn't speak for a few moments, and when I found my voice again, tried hesitantly to refuse the gifts. These good people had agreed between themselves to overwhelm me with happiness, and they would have been deeply hurt had I rejected their gifts, their blessings, their good wishes. We all sat down to dinner, and I was content to let the conversation turn to other subjects. It wasn't until after we'd eaten that I learned a few details about the expedition starting next day.

The rail line was to run from St. Louis through the Indian Territories, New Mexico, Arizona and California to the Pacific Coast. This long stretch had been divided into sections for each of several teams to explore and survey. The section assigned to our team, a party chief, three other surveyors and myself, lay roughly between the Canadian River and the source of the Rio Pecos. Sam Hawkens and the other two guides were to bring us to the first camp, where we'd hire other brave Westerners to travel with us for protection against marauding Indians.

I found that Mr. Henry and Sam Hawkens had between them procured everything I'd need in the way of outfitting, down to the smallest item. All that remained was for me to meet the other members of the party, who were waiting for us at the home of the chief engineer. Sam Hawkens and Mr. Henry and I walked over to his house, and there were introductions all around.

Early the next morning, after I'd said good-bye to the Weber family, I went to the gunsmith's shop. Mr. Henry cut short my fervent thanks, shaking my hand energetically and interrupting my outpouring with these words:

"Hold your tongue, sir! I'm sending you out there into the West so that my old gun will have a chance to put in a word or two. When you return, come visit me and tell me all the things you've been witness to and what you've experienced. Only then will we know whether you still are what you are today—a greenhorn who denies that he is one!"

Then he pushed me out the door. But before he closed it, I saw that his eyes were brimming with tears.

CHAPTER TWO

I t was near the start of the glorious North American autumn, and we'd been on the job almost three summer months. Although many of the other surveying parties had already returned home, we had not yet finished surveying our assigned section. There were two reasons why.

The first was the circumstance that we had especially difficult country to cover. The railroad was to run through prairieland, roughly following the upstream course of the southern Canadian toward the area of its source, then into and through the valleys and passes of northern New Mexico. But our section lay between the Canadian and New Mexico, and before we could survey we had to explore, to determine the best route. This involved time-consuming rides, strenuous climbing, and the taking of many trial measurements for comparison, before we could decide exactly where rails would be easiest to lay.

Compounding the difficulty was the fact that the area was also quite dangerous—Kiowas, Comanches and Apaches were all about, and none of these tribes wanted a railroad driven through terrain which they considered theirs. We had to be constantly on guard, which of course impeded progress and made our work exceptionally difficult. We hesitated to hunt, for shooting would have alerted the Indians to our presence and task, so we often had to wait for supplies we needed to be brought from Santa Fé by oxcart.

The second reason for our slowness was the composition of our surveying party. I mentioned that in St. Louis I'd been greeted with friendliness by the chief engineer and the other three surveyors; I anticipated good relationships and cooperation. I was soon disillusioned—my colleagues were real Yankees who saw in me, the greenhorn, an inexperienced "Dutchman," and they used that last word as invective. They all wanted to earn their pay without working too hard for it, and soon saw that as I worked steadily and never complained, they could shift the dirtiest and most difficult tasks on to my shoulders.

Mr. Bancroft, the chief engineer, was more educated than the others, but it turned out that he was a brandy-drinker. Several kegs of this destructive beverage had been brought from Santa Fé, and since then Bancroft spent more time with the brandy than with the surveying instruments. I, and the other three surveyors, Riggs, Marcy and Wheeler, chipped in to pay for the liquor; they also drank a fair amount. I had no taste for it, but it was impossible for me to do everyone's job, and the work suffered.

The rest of the company consisted of a dozen "Westerners" who were waiting for us when we arrived at the first camp. Being a greenhorn, I'd expected to meet men of upstanding character who knew the western plains and mountains, who would help us to make and break camp, assist with daily chores, and protect us in case Indians appeared. Without exception, they turned out to be men of low moral caliber. They slept till noon, spent the afternoons jabbering and gambling, and the evenings drinking and brawling. As for helping us with daily tasks—I think the twelve laziest sluggards in the United States were gathered here for a reunion.

So, discipline was non-existent. Bancroft was the man in charge, but no one heeded him. When he gave an order, the others either ignored it or else laughed in his face. Then he would curse a streak and return to the brandy cask. Riggs, Marcy and Wheeler worked with me now and then—at least two men are necessary for almost every surveying procedure—but for all these reasons progress was slow. In order for any progress at all to be made I had to take the reins, but without being too obvious about it, and without giving anyone a direct order.

Fortunately, in the persons of Sam Hawkens, Dick Stone and Will Parker, I had three willing and knowledgeable companions, good men who helped with daily tasks and stood by when needed. Sam especially took it upon himself, when time and opportunity permitted, to give me theoretical and practical lessons in everything that one should know and be able to do to cope with life in the Wild West.

"That's the way, youngster! Now you've got the hang of it!" For several weeks Sam had been training me to throw a lasso, even letting me use his horse and himself as targets. I was quick to pick up the technique, and now was able to rope any moving or stationary object whether afoot or on horseback.

"You're learnin' fast," Sam continued. "If you keep practicin', then in six or seven years, with all the other things I'm teachin' you, you'll be a real Westerner, if I'm not mistaken. Nobody will call you 'greenhorn' again." He spoke in earnest and I took it the same way, although we both knew the friendship and humor behind his words.

Then one day Sam took me aside and said, "I s'pose sometimes you're wonderin' how I became a Westerner, learned all the things I know about these plains and mountains, about Indians, huntin', trappin', stayin' alive and suchlike. You might think I was born and bred to this life, but to tell the truth—now don't fall over in amazement—I'm a German immigrant just like you."

My mouth fell open—I was speechless. Sam went on.

"Well, not an immigrant exactly—I was born in Arkansas—but my father's father came over from the old country long ago. I spoke only German till I was six. When my folks died I was twenty. That's when I decided to become a Westerner."

Sam smiled through that bushy beard and shook his head.

"Still got those German feelin's racin' around in my blood, I guess. That must be why I took to you right from the start."

In spite of all the hindrances to our progress we were within a week of reaching the end of our section and meeting up with the next surveying party. In order to check in with them it would be necessary to send a message, and Bancroft decided that he would make the trip himself, taking with him one of our guides. This was not the first time for an exchange of messages—we had been keeping in intermittent contact with both the party ahead and the one behind since we'd started.

Bancroft decided to leave on a Sunday morning. He wanted to have a farewell drink, and invited everyone to join him. I alone was not included, and Hawkens, Stone and Parker politely refused. As I could have foretold, the drinking continued until Bancroft was no longer in condition to ride, and all the others were just as drunk as he was. Bancroft retired to his tent, and the others crawled behind bushes to sleep it off.

What should be done? The message must be sent, and all these men would surely be sleeping until late in the afternoon. If I took it upon myself to go, I knew no work would be done during the four days it would take me to ride there and back. While I was talking to Sam about it, he pointed to the west and said:

"Looks like you ain't gonna hafta go, Bud. You can give the message to the two men ridin' toward us."

I turned and saw two riders, white men. In one I recognized an old scout from the other party, who had brought us messages and progress reports several times before. Next to him rode a younger man I didn't know, not dressed in western gear. I walked toward them, and they reined in their horses. The younger one asked my name, and then regarded me with a friendly expression.

"So you're the young German gentleman who does all the work while the others lay around on their lazy backsides! My name is White, and I'm the chief engineer of the next section." He dismounted, gave me his hand, and swept our campsite with his eyes. Except for the guides and myself, not a man was on his feet. He glanced behind bushes and at the brandy cask, and shook his head.

"Drunk, all of them?" he asked.

I nodded. "Afraid so. Mr. Bancroft was about to leave for your camp, but wanted to have a farewell drink. The rest joined in, and—" I turned toward the tent. "Shall I wake him?"

"Hold it! No, I want to talk to you privately. Who are those three men standing nearby?"

"Sam Hawkens, Will Parker and Dick Stone, our three scouts."

"Ah, Hawkens, the matchless little hunter. A capable man—I know of him. They can come with us, over here to the side, out of earshot." I motioned them forward.

"You came yourself, Mr. White," I said. "Is it important news you bring us?"

"No news—I only wanted to see what was really happening here, or not happening, as the case seems to be. And I wanted to speak with you in particular. We're finished surveying our section, but you're not nearly finished with yours."

"Well, the difficulty of the terrain is mainly to blame, and we've also been slowed down by—"

"I know, I know," he interrupted. "I know all about it, unfortunately. If you hadn't been working, Bancroft would still be at the starting point."

"That's not the case, Mr. White," I protested. "Please don't think that I was the only one doing any work—"

"Stop! It's good of you to defend this crew of boozers, but remember that messages have been going back and forth between us, and I've been kept informed of the general situation. Now I'd like to hear some details, and if you're too kind-hearted to tell tales on your fellows, why I'll put my questions to Sam Hawkens, and to Stone and Parker."

I kept silent then; the guides answered all his questions. He asked to see our drawings and the daily log, and I brought them to him. He examined them carefully, noting that almost all the entries were in my hand, and the sketches initialled by me. Sam let slip that I kept a personal diary in a sardine can under my shirt, and White asked to see it. What could I do but hand it over? I begged him never to let anyone else know the contents. For it was a narrative of my private thoughts, not only about the work we were doing, but about the West, what I was learning from Sam and the others, and my daily impressions about everything. Of course the other members of the team, and the twelve drunken "Westerner" assistants, weren't referred to in a very complimentary fashion.

We walked back into the camp area, and Mr. White banged on the dinner gong until all the members of the company staggered out from behind their bushes. Bancroft was in bad temper at being awakened, but I politely explained to him that Mr. White from the next section had arrived; the two had never met before. The first thing Bancroft did was to offer White a tot of brandy, but this triggered a bitter verbal attack by White which Bancroft listened to for a few moments in astonishment, then interrupted by going up to White and taking his arm. White shook him off.

"Mister, you want to tell me your name again?"

"My name is White; you've already heard it."

"And who are you?"

"I'm the chief engineer of the next section."

"Has anyone from here given you any orders?"

"No."

"Well, then! My name is Bancroft, and I'm the chief engineer of this section. Nobody from your section is going to give me any orders, least of all you, Mr. White."

"It's true that we're both at the same level of authority," answered White calmly, "but when one of us sees that the other isn't carrying out the duties for which both of us are being paid, it's his duty and responsibility to make the one concerned realize his shortcomings. It looks to me like you're spending your days and nights around the brandy keg. I count sixteen men here, all of whom were dead drunk when I arrived two hours ago."

"Two hours? You've been here that long?"

"To be sure. I've looked at your records, and learned how you've been spending your time, in idleness and drunkenness. While one man on the team, the youngest of all of you, has been doing all the work."

Bancroft turned to me and hissed threateningly, "That's what you've been telling him, you malicious liar, you damned traitor!"

"No!" White broke in, "the young gentleman defended you and had nothing but good to say about you. I'd advise you to ask his pardon for calling him a liar and traitor."

"Ask his pardon? I wouldn't think of it!" Bancroft sneered, "This greenhorn doesn't know a level from a measuring rod, and yet claims to be a surveyor. The reason we haven't made progress is because he does everything backwards, and now instead of admitting it he slanders the rest of us—"

That was as far as he got. I had been patient for months, and let these men think of me as they pleased. Now the moment had come for me to show them that their thinking was in error. I gripped Bancroft by the arm, painfully enough so that he left the sentence hanging, and said:

"Mr. Bancroft, you've drunk too much brandy and haven't had a chance to sleep it off. I'll assume that you're still drunk, and don't know what you're saying."

"Me, drunk? You're crazy!"

"Yes, drunk indeed. Because if I thought you were sober, and said those abusive words deliberately, I'd punch you in the face. Now, are you still going to deny that you're drunk?"

I still held his arm tightly. Surely he had never believed that he would have cause to be afraid of me. Yet now I saw fear in his eyes. He was by no means a weakling, but the expression on my face must have frightened him. He didn't want to say that he was still drunk, yet didn't dare to stand by the accusations he'd made. He turned for help to the leader of the twelve rogues posing as Westerners who were hired to assist us.

"Rattler, are you going to stand there and let this kid hold me by the arm? Ain't you here to protect us?"

This Rattler fellow was tall and broad, as big as I was and probably as strong, a raw mean character and Bancroft's favorite drinking partner. He didn't care much for me, and was glad to have the opportunity to give his dislike free rein. He came over quickly, held me by the arm the same way I was holding Bancroft, and answered:

"No, that I can't stand for, Mr. Bancroft. This brat is still wearin' his first pair of long pants, yet he talks big to grown men, shames 'em and lies about 'em. Take your hand off Mr Bancroft, young 'un, afore I show you what a greenhorn you are!"

He shook my arm as he threw this challenge. I liked this better, for he was a stronger opponent than the engineer. If I taught him some manners, it would carry more weight than would a moral and physical victory over Bancroft.

"Me a brat, a greenhorn? I'll have an apology from you too, Rattler, or I'll knock you flat on your back!"

"You will?" he laughed. "You're not only green, you're stupid! I'll—"

He spoke no further, for I swung my fist and hit him on the side of the head so hard that he fell like a sack and lay there in a daze.

There was dead silence for a short moment; then one of Rattler's crew cried out:

"Hey, you devils! Are we gonna just watch while this Dutch beggar beats up on the boss? Let's get 'im!"

He sprang at me. I greeted him with a boot to the stomach, a quick way to put an attacker out of action, if one is firmly balanced on the other foot. As he bent double, his descending jaw met my ascending fist, and he laid himself down next to Rattler. I jumped back a step or two, pulled both revolvers from my belt and called out, "Who's next?"

Rattler's whole band held back, none of the rest of them having a deep desire to revenge the defeat of their two mates. They looked at each other uncertainly, and I gave warning:

"Listen carefully, you men. Whoever takes a step toward me or reaches for a gun will get a bullet through his head! Think whatever you want about greenhorns in general—but let me tell you that there's one greenhorn here who can take on twelve so-called Westerners like you any day!"

Sam Hawkens walked to my side and said:

"And I, Sam Hawkens, will warn you too, if I'm not mistaken. This young German greenhorn is under my personal protection. Whoever even touches a hair of his head will get a hole through his frame, and I'm dead serious, heeheehee."

Dick Stone and Will Parker also planted themselves next to me, to show unmistakably that they were on the same side as Sam. That impressed our opponents, who turned away mumbling curses and threats into their beards. A few of them picked up their two dazed comrades and led them off, staggering.

Bancroft thought it prudent to disappear into his tent. Mr. White had watched the whole episode with eyes wide in astonishment. Now he shook his head and said without artifice:

"Sir, that was appalling! I would never want to get on the wrong side of you. To see you lay low a sturdy tree-trunk of a man with one blow, and another one two seconds later! I've never seen the like of it! They ought to call you 'Shatterhand'!"

This suggestion seemed to tickle Sam Hawkens no end. He giggled with joy. "Shatterhand, heeheehee! A greenhorn, and he's already got a fightin' name, and what a name, if I'm not mistaken! Shatterhand, Old Shatterhand. A name like Old Firehand, another Westerner, strong as a bear. Dick, Will, what d'ya think a' that for a name?"

I didn't hear their answer, for Mr. White had taken me off to the side and was speaking to me confidentially.

"I like you exceptionally well, sir. Would you want to come along with me?"

"Want to or not, Mr. White, I may not."

"Why?"

"Because my duty keeps me here."

"Pshaw! I'll take the responsibility."

"That's of no use to me, if I can't be responsible myself. I was hired and sent to help survey this section, and don't feel that I can leave until the work is done."

"Bancroft and the other three can finish up."

I laughed scornfully. "Yes, but when? No, I have to stay."

"But consider—it could be dangerous for you!"

"Why?"

"Do you need to ask? You must realize that all these men now hate you like poison."

"Maybe so; but I'm not afraid of them. They're sure to have more respect for me now, after that little set-to; none of them will want to take me on. And I have Hawkens, Stone and Parker on my side."

"As you will. You would have been of great help. Will you at least ride part of the way back with me?"

"Yes, but when?"

"Now."

"You want to leave right away? You had something of importance to tell Bancroft."

"Yes, I did, but I can tell you just as well. I wanted to warn him about the redskins."

"Have you seen some, then?"

"Not directly, but we've seen their tracks. This is the time of year when the buffalo and wild mustangs move south; the redmen leave their settlements to hunt for meat. We're not afraid of the Kiowas; we've come to an agreement with them about the rail line. However, the Comanches and Apaches haven't been told about it yet, and so we'd rather not be seen by them. I'm not too concerned any more— we've finished our section and will be on the way home. But your crew should also finish, and leave as soon as possible. This area will become more dangerous day by day. So that's all I had to say. Saddle your horse, and ask Sam if he'd like to come with us."

Of course Sam would like to come.

I really wanted to work that day. But it was Sunday, and I thought I deserved a day of rest. I went to Bancroft's tent, and told him that Sam and I were going to accompany White for a way along his return route.

"Go! Go to the devil, and may you break your necks!" he answered, and I had no inkling that we'd soon be close to making his farewell wish come true.

We rode along in the beautiful autumn morning, talking about the ambitious railroad project and other things we had on our minds. White gave me information on how best to approach and connect with his section, and pointed out pertinent landmarks. At midday we stopped to water our horses and ourselves, and eat a frugal meal. White and his scout rode on, and Sam and I stayed for a time beside the stream to rest and talk.

Before we turned back, I knelt and cupped my hand to scoop up a last swallow of water. In the shallow water at the very edge of the bank I saw what looked like a footprint, and I called Sam's attention to it. He examined it carefully and said:

"Mr. White was right to warn us about Indians."

"Do you mean to say that's an Indian sign, Sam?"

"Sure is; it's the print of an Indian mocassin. Does that give you a strange feelin', Bud?"

"No. Should it?"

"Ah! You must think or feel somethin'."

"What should I think, except that an Indian has been here?"

"You're not afraid then?"

"It doesn't occur to me to be afraid!"

"Not worried even a little bit?"

"No. Why, should I be?"

"You don't know the redskins."

"I hope to get to know them. I think they'll be just like other humans, namely enemies of your enemies and friends of your friends. And as it's not my intention to treat them as enemies, I assume that I have nothing to fear from them."

"Spoken like a greenhorn! However you make up your mind to treat the redmen, it'll turn out entirely different from the way you plan. Whatever happens doesn't depend on what you intend. You'll learn that, and I can only hope that the learnin' don't cost you your life."

"How long ago do you think this Indian was here?"

"About two days ago. We woulda seen his tracks in the grass if it was sooner; the grass has straightened up again."

"A scout, do you think, or a spy?"

"A scout after buffalo meat, yes. As I don't think the local tribes are on the warpath right now, he probably wasn't a spy. He wasn't 'specially careful, so he was probably young."

"Why do you think so?"

"A careful brave doesn't leave a print under shallow water like this one did, a print that'll stay in the soft wet bottom for a long time. He must have been a red greenhorn, like you're a white one, heeheehee."

We could have ridden back the same way we'd come, but it was part of my job to check the area on both sides of our proposed route, so we branched off for a way and took a parallel course. It led us into a broad valley. The slopes on both sides were lined with bushes; higher up, it was densely forested. The valley ran bee-line straight; we could see to the end of it, about a half-hour's ride away. We'd only gone a short distance when Sam reined in his horse and gazed attentively ahead of us.

"Hi-ho!" he said, "there they are, the first ones."

"What?" I asked. I looked far ahead and saw about two dozen dark specks, moving slowly at the end of the valley.

"What?" Sam repeated my question. "You do see somethin' out ahead, don't ya? Take a guess, what is it you see?"

"A guess? Hmm. I'd take them to be deer, if I didn't know that deer seldom travel in herds of more than ten—you told me that. Anyway, as tiny as they seem from here, they look rather larger than deer."

"Deer, heeheehee!" he giggled. Yes, you're right about that, they are rather larger than deer, much larger!"

"Don't tell me, Sam. They're buffalo!"

"Right, they're buffalo, bison actually—real bison on the way south, the first I've seen this year. Now you know how right Mr. White was. Bison and Indians. Of the Indians we saw only a footprint, but here are the buffalo, the bison, life-size. What d'ya say to that, if I'm not mistaken?"

"Let's ride faster! But without spooking them—I want to get a closer look at them!"

"Only look at them?" Sam's small sharp eyes peered at me.

"Yes. I've never seen bison except in pictures, and I'd like to observe them up close."

My zoological interest Sam couldn't grasp at all. He clapped his hands together and declared:

"Observe, observe! You greenhorn, after all I've been teachin' you! We're not gonna observe 'em, we're gonna hunt 'em! Buffalo means food, meat, hides, leather! But mainly meat, fresh meat, insteada that jerky they been sendin' us from Santa Fé! A piece of buffalo haunch — ah, a piece of that buffalo haunch is somethin' I'm lookin' forward to!" He paused and considered. "The wind's in our favor, that's good.

We'll ride on the southern, shady side; then the buffalo won't see us too soon, before we're ready for 'em."

He rechecked his Liddy to make sure it was loaded and ready to fire. I followed suit, checking my bear-killer. When Sam saw this, he pulled up his horse and asked:

"You wanna take part in this too?"

"Naturally!"

"That'll be nice. Ya could get y'rself stamped flat in the wink of an eye! A buffalo ain't no canary bird, y'know. He's a very dangerous animal."

"But I only want to—"

"Be quiet and listen!" Sam interrupted, in a tone he'd never used with me before. "I don't wanna have your life on my conscience, and if you've never had any experience with buffalo, you'd be ridin' into the jaws of death, sure death. So observe all ya want, so long as ya keep over to the side and out of my way. Just do like I tell ya—no backtalk, understand?"

If there hadn't been such a good relationship between us, I would certainly have come back with a sharp retort. But I kept silent, and rode slowly behind him in the shadows cast by the forest above. Sam resumed speaking, now in a milder tone:

"I count twenty head. But there was a time not long ago when herds of a thousand and more thundered across the savannah. I've even seen herds numberin' *ten* thousand. They were the Indian's basic food, but the whites took it away from 'em. The red man killed so that he could live, but the whites rampaged through the herds like mad dogs in a chicken run, killin' only for the thrill of it, just to watch the blood flow. It won't be long before there'll be no more buffalo at all, and a little while later no more Indians." He paused in thought. "And the same thing's happenin' with the wild horses. There used to be herds of mustangs too, a thousand head or so. Now if you're lucky, you might see as many as a hundred runnin' or grazin' together."

We'd been nearing the buffalo herd meanwhile, and we halted about four hundred paces from them; they'd taken no notice of us, but continued to graze slowly up the valley. In the forefront was an old bull whose gigantic build I beheld with amazement. He was surely two meters tall and a good three meters long. At the time I didn't know how to guess a bison's weight; today I'd estimate his at close to fifteen hundred kilograms, well over a ton and a half—an astounding mass of flesh and bone.

The bull had found a mudhole and was wallowing in it with evident enjoyment. "That's the herd-leader," whispered Sam, "the most dangerous of them all. Anybody who fixes to meet up with him better first sign his last will and testament. I'm goin' to take that young cow at the right rear. Notice where I place my ball, behind the shoulder-blade at an angle, so it goes straight into the heart. That's the best sure shot, except into the brain through the eye. But only a crazy man would try to take a bison from the front, so's he could shoot him in the eye! Now you ride your horse into the bushes, and keep outa sight. I'm goin' to circle 'round, and when they see me and start runnin', there'll be a wild stampede right by this spot. But don't you move from here till I get back—less'n I call to you."

Sam waited until I'd concealed myself in the bushes, and then rode slowly and quietly away. I felt strangely exhilarated. I'd often read how bison were hunted, the details weren't new to me; but there's a great difference between reading descriptions of such hunts and being there on the scene in person. Today, for the first time in my life, I was actually seeing real buffalo. The game I had hunted in Europe—quail, chamois, mountain goat—were as nothing compared to this gigantic and dangerous beast.

One would assume then, that I was content to obey Sam's command to keep out of sight; on the contrary, a thrill of daring flashed through my veins. Before, I'd only wanted to observe the animals, to listen to them; now I felt an almost irresistible urge to take part in the hunt. So, Sam was going to shoot a young cow, was he? Bah! I thought, that doesn't take courage; a real man would go after the largest, strongest bull!

My horse had become exceptionally restive, moving uneasily from side to side. He too had never seen nor smelled a buffalo before. They evoked fear in him and he wanted to run; I had a difficult time holding him in check.

And I was thinking: should I, or should I not, take after that bull? Thinking calmly now, not excitedly, just weighing the two words *yes* or *no*. A few moments later the decision was made for me.

Sam had approached to within three hundred paces of the herd before spurring his horse into a gallop, past the mighty bull in his mud-wallow and toward the cow he'd indicated. She raised her head but didn't run, and then he was upon her. I saw him swivel in the saddle and shoot as he passed her. She swayed and her head sank, but I didn't see her fall, for at that instant my eyes were drawn in another direction. The giant bull had sprung from his wallow and was racing toward Sam Hawkens.

What a mighty animal! That enormous head with its short but thick curved horns, the shaggy, matted mane on neck and chest, an extremely dangerous creature! And the desire to pit my human knowledge and cunning against his violent animal strength rose up in me and spilled over . . . as my roan shot out of the bushes and tried to turn away, to the left. I pulled him hard right and galloped toward the bull's course, intending to cut him off before he reached Sam. He heard me coming and turned to meet me, lowering his head to engage both horse and rider with his horns.

I heard Sam let out a yell, but had no time to glance in his direction. I wasn't well positioned for a shot, and was having trouble controlling my horse, who was rushing in fear and panic directly toward those threatening horns. By brute strength I was able to pull him slightly to the side as the bull's head came up in a mighty toss, and we were past him, my leg grazing his flank. The roan slipped in the muddy bull-tracks, and I pulled my feet out of the stirrups just in time, jumping clear as he fell.

How everything could have happened so quickly is still unclear to me today—but a moment later I was standing there boot-deep in mud, my gun still held tightly in my hands. The horse had risen and the bull turned and sped to have another go at him, presenting his flank to me. I raised the bear-killer—now I'd have my first chance to use it in earnest—and aimed where Sam had told me to, behind the shoulder-blade. One more leap and the bull would have reached and impaled my roan. I pulled the trigger, and the bison stopped in his tracks, whether from shock at hearing the shot or because it had struck him in the heart, I didn't know. I immediately let go with the second barrel; he slowly raised his head, let loose a roar that vibrated through my whole body, swayed to and fro for a few moments, and collapsed on the spot.

I would have taken a moment to jump for joy over this narrowly-won victory, but I had more pressing things to do. Back on the right slope my horse stood riderless, and I saw Sam Hawkens galloping toward me along the left slope, closely followed by a buffalo steer not much smaller than the one I'd just shot. Now I know that the bison, once provoked, goes after his provoker with single-minded perseverance, and can run a fair distance as fast as a horse. He exhibits courage, cunning and endurance one would not have given him credit for.

So it was with this steer, hard on Sam's heels. Trying to elude him, Hawkens was making sweeping turns, tiring his steed, who wouldn't be able to hold out as long as the buffalo. So Sam needed help and needed it urgently. I didn't even take time to check if my bull was really dead or not; I quickly loaded both barrels of my bear-killer and ran toward the left slope.

Sam saw this and turned his horse to meet me. That was a mistake, for the steer was so close behind him that the horse was now targeted within reach of those deadly horns. I saw how the bull sank his horns into Sam's steed, lifted horse and rider high, and continued to stab furiously with that massive horned head as they fell to the ground.

Sam yelled for help. Although I was still a good hundred and fifty paces distant, we couldn't afford an instant's delay. If I'd been closer it would have been a surer shot, but any hesitation might have spelled death for Sam. And even if my ball just hit the bull anywhere, I hoped it would distract him from my friend. I stopped short, aimed at the spot behind his left shoulder blade and pulled the trigger.

The buffalo lifted his head sidewise as if he was listening, and slowly turned in my direction. He saw me and came running toward me, but with less speed than he'd shown earlier; that gave me time to reload the expended barrel with feverish haste. I was ready with it when the animal was about fifty feet away. He'd slowed to a walk—I must have hurt him badly—but was still advancing like inevitable Fate. I kneeled and lifted the weapon; this movement caused him to halt and raise his head so he could see me better, bringing those malicious eyes directly in front of my gunsights. I sent one ball into his left eye and one into his right. He trembled for a moment and then fell to the ground.

I jumped up to run to Sam, but saw that he was already running toward me.

"Hey, Sam!" I called. "You're alive! You're not injured?"

"Not at all," he called back, lowering his voice as he came within earshot, "—well, my right hip does hurt a little from the fall, or maybe it's the left, if I'm not mistaken."

"And your horse?"

"He's done for. He's still alive, but the buffalo ripped him up the side. We'll have to shoot the poor *caballo* to keep him from sufferin'. Is the buffalo dead?"

"I hope so. Let's look."

We did, and assured ourselves that he was indeed dead. Sam gave a deep sigh, and said:

"Yep, that brutal old ox really kept me busy! A cow woulda been a little more gentle with me. Well, I guess you can't expect oxen to act ladylike, heeheehee."

"What gave him the wild idea to take after you?"

"Din't you see how it happened?"

"No, I was pretty busy myself."

"Well, I was still gallopin' when I shot down the cow, and before I could stop I ran right up against this ox. That made him mad and he took a swipe at me. I quick gave him the shot I still had in my Liddy, but it didn't seem to calm him down, only riled him more. He kept on rushin' us—I couldn't even stop to reload; I just threw Liddy away, 'cause I needed both hands to rein and guide the horse, if I'm not mistaken. The poor nag did his best, but it wasn't good enough."

"Probably because you made that last fatal turn. You should've kept on riding a big sweep, and the horse might have been saved."

"Saved, would he? You talk like an old hand, not the kind of talk you'd expect from a greenhorn."

"Well, even greenhorns know how to think."

"Yep, I guess—if you hadn't been here, I'd be lyin' over there ripped open like my poor nag. Let's take a look at him."

We found him in sad condition, intestines hanging out from a long slit torn in his belly; he lay there snorting in pain. Sam picked up his gun, reloaded it and gave him the *coup de grâce*, then unfastened the saddle and bridle, saying:

"Now I'll have to saddle myself. But not for long!"

"What do you mean? Where will you get another horse?"

"That's easy to answer. I'll just catch me one."

"A mustang?"

"Right. The buffalo are here, startin' to move south. That means the mustangs are nearby; we'll soon see 'em."

"Can I go along? I'd like to see how you catch one."

"Sure, you have to learn how to do it, too. But now let's take a look at that old bull. Maybe he's still alive; when they get that old, they're pretty tough to kill."

The bull was dead. Now, as he lay there still, one could better gauge the enormous mass of him. Sam eyed him from one end to the other a few times, screwed up his face, shook his head, and said, "I can hardly believe it! You shot him in the exact right spot and at the exact right angle, didn'cha? You know what you are, Bud?"

"No, what am I?"

"Stupid and careless!"

"I've never thought of myself as having those failings."

"Well, think about it now. I gave ya an order to keep clear of the buffalo and stay hid in the bushes. Why didn'cha?"

"I don't know myself."

"So! You did somethin' without even havin' a good reason for it. Wouldn't ya call that careless?"

"We-e-ell, maybe there is a reason."

"Tell me!"

"The fact that you gave me an order; I hate to take orders."

"So, even though I did it to keep ya out of danger, you're so stubborn that ya rushed right into it anyway!"

"I didn't come out West to avoid danger, but to meet whatever dangers there are."

"Okay. But you're still a greenhorn and hafta know how to take care of yourself. If you didn't wanta stay put like I said, why didja take after that giant bull instead of a cow?"

"Because it seemed more . . . gallant!"

"Gallant! This greenhorn wants to play like a cavalier, if I'm not mistaken, heeheehee!"

Sam laughed so hard he had to hold his belly, and continued, still laughing:

"Cavaliers don't last long—they get et by buzzards. If a Westerner does somethin' like you did, he doesn't first ask himself whether it's 'gallant'. He decides what to do dependin' on whether it's *useful* or not."

"Well, that's the case here."

"How come?"

"I picked the bull because he has much more meat on him than a cow has."

He looked me in the face for a long moment, and then cried: "More meat? This young man shot the old bull for his meat, heeheehee! I'll bet you even thought I wasn't very 'gallant' because I picked out a cow to shoot, right?"

"No, not at all—I just thought it would be braver to cut out a big strong bull."

"And eat bull-buffalo meat? Let me set you straight—this bull is a good twenty years old if he's a day. He's made of hide and hair, bones and muscles and gristle. And whatever meat is on him ain't really meat any more, 'cause it's as tough as leather. You could fry it or boil it all day long, and it would still be too hard to chew. Every plains hunter knows that, and he shoots a cow rather than a bull, because a young cow's meat is tender and juicy. So, add that to the things you're learnin'. Learnin' somethin' new every day, ain'cha?"

He shook his head and continued, "I was too busy to watch and see what happened. What exactly did happen with you and the bull?"

I told him in detail. When I finished, he opened his squinty eyes wide, shook his head again, and said:

"Go fetch your horse. We'll load him with the meat, whatever we take with us."

It was said more like a request than a command, and I did as I was told. I was really a little peeved at Sam's attitude; he'd heard my story without comment. I'd expected at least a word or two of approval, but he'd only shaken his head. Well, I hadn't killed the bull just to win praise; I went and got my horse.

I led him back to where Sam was kneeling by the buffalo-cow he'd shot. He'd skillfully stripped the hide from a rear quarter and was cutting off the haunch.

"So," he said, "that'll do for me, you, Will and Dick. If the others want some meat too, they'll just hafta ride out here and fetch the rest of the cow."

"If it isn't already eaten by vultures and coyotes."

"You're catchin' on. We'll of course cover the carcass with bushes and branches, and weight them down with big rocks. Then only somethin' as big as a bear could get at it."

We cut some thick branches from the nearby thicket, fetched some stones, and did as he said. We loaded the buffalo haunch on my horse. Then it occurred to me to inquire:

"What'll we do with the bull?"

"Him? What can we do with him?"

"Can't we use any part of him?"

"Nothin' at all."

"What about the hide?"

"Are you a tanner? It's a smelly, dirty job."

"But I've read about buffalo hides being cached—and picked up later in a good state of preservation."

"Oho, you've read about it, have ya? Well then, it must be true, like everythin' you read about the Wild West, absolutely true, heeheehee! Of course there are plainsmen who shoot bison just for their hides; I've done it myself. And lotsa that buffalo-slaughterin' I told ya about was done by professional hunters an' skinners who sold the hides to fur traders. But it takes a lot of time and know-how to make a good buffalo robe, and we're not here for that reason; we don't wanna load ourselves down with that heavy, smelly hide."

CHAPTER THREE

E ven though we had to walk, it took little more than an hour to get back to camp, as it wasn't far from the valley where I'd shot my first, or rather my first two, buffalo. It caused a stir when we arrived on foot, and without Sam's horse. Questions were fired at us from all sides.

"We were huntin' buffalo, and my horse was gored by one of 'em," answered Sam.

"Huntin' buffalo! Where, where?" they shouted in chorus. "A half hour from here. We brought a haunch; you men can go fetch the rest of it."

"We sure will," shouted Rattler, who acted as if nothing had occurred between me and him, "where's the place?"

"Just ride back along our trail and you'll find it; you've got enough eyes among ya, if I'm not mistaken."

"How many in the herd?"

"Twenty."

"And how many didja kill?"

"One cow."

"That's all? Where'd the others go?"

"Away. You can go lookin' for 'em. I didn't take time to watch where they went, and didn't ask 'em neither, heeheehee."

"But just one cow! Two hunters, and only one buffalo shot out of twenty!" said one of the men with a sneer.

"Well sir, do better if you can! You prob'ly would've shot all twenty of 'em. By the way, when you get there you'll see two more, twenty-year-old bulls shot by this young man here."

"Bulls, old bulls!" the cry went up, and one of them yelled, "Only a stupid greenhorn would shoot twenty-year-old bulls!"

"Go ahead and laugh, mesh'shurs. But take a good look at those bulls—he saved my life by shootin' 'em."

"He did? How come?" They were curious to hear what had happened, but Sam refused to continue.

"I don't wanta talk about it. He can tell ya himself if he feels like it. But you'd better fetch the rest of that meat 'fore it gets dark."

Good advice. The sun was fast descending, and in a short while it would be evening. I'd been silent throughout, and as they saw I wasn't going to tell the story, they all mounted their horses and rode off. All of them—nobody wanted to stay behind, for they didn't trust one another.

In any company of honest and honorable men—hunters, Westerners, plainsmen—game shot by one of them belongs to all, by unspoken agreement and common consent. Such sense of fellowship was absent among this bunch of louts. From the conversation when they returned I gathered that they'd fallen upon the cow's carcass like madmen, each trying to hack off the largest, choicest chunk of meat for himself.

While they were gone we unloaded the haunch and saddle from my horse, and I led him off to tether, giving Sam enough time to tell Stone and Parker about our adventure. When I walked back I heard Sam's voice; the tent was between us, so they didn't know I was within earshot.

"You can believe me, it was just like I'm sayin'—the lad took on the biggest, strongest bull and shot him down like an old experienced buffalo hunter! Sure, I made like it was downright stupid damfoolish, and bawled him out proper; but I'm really gettin' to know what kinda man he is."

"Me too," Stone put in. "He's goin' to be a crackerjack."

"And real soon," I heard Parker say.

"Right!" said Hawkens. "He was born to the West, really and truly born to be a Westerner. And those muscles of his! Didja see him pull our heavy ox-cart outa the mud yesterday, all by himself and not even askin' for help? But wait a minute—I want both you men to promise me somethin'."

"What?" asked Parker.

"Don't let him know what we think about him."

"Why not?"

"Because it might go to his head."

"Oh, no!"

"Oh, yes! Right now he's a modest fella, he don't have his nose in the air. But it's always a mistake to pat a man on the back too much—you kin make him think he's better than he is, turn him into a blow-hard. So keep callin' him a greenhorn; after all, he still is one. Even though he has everythin' needed to become a real Westerner, he still don't have the experience. That'll come little by little as time goes by."

"Didja even thank him for savin' your life?"

"It didn't come to mind."

"No? You shoulda thanked him, Sam. He'll think less of you if you don't."

"Makes no difference to me what he thinks, no difference at all, if I'm not mistaken. Naturally, he takes me for an ungrateful rascal, but that's not the point. The main thing is that he stays the way he is now, doesn't get arrogant. What should I 've done, hugged him and kissed him?"

"Ho!" shouted Stone, "Kiss you! A man could maybe risk huggin' you, but kiss you? Never!"

"That so? Why not?"

"Why not? Didja ever look in a mirror, Sam, or see your charmin' face in clear water? That face, that beard and that nose! Anybody, man or woman, who gets the crazy idea to plant a kiss on your lips—if they could even find 'em—is either sufferin' from sunstroke or they musta lost their mind completely!"

"So! Hmm-mm. That sounds real friendly. So I'm an ugly old bas-tard, am I? What d'ya take yourself for, a handsome prince? Don't you believe it! I swear, if just the two of us was in a beauty contest, I'd get first prize; you'd draw a blank, heeheehee! Well, enough of that—we're talkin' about our greenhorn. No, I didn't thank him and I'm not goin' to. But when we roast our haunch, he gets the tenderest, juici-est piece; I'll cut it for him myself. And you know what I'm goin' to do tomorrow?"

"What?" asked Stone.

"Show him how to catch a mustang."

"You're goin' after mustangs?"

"Yep. I hafta have a new horse. You gotta lend me yours for the hunt, Dick. Buffalo showed up today, so mustangs oughta be nearby. I think we'll ride back to that prairie area where they surveyed day before yesterday. If they're around, that seems like a likely place to look for 'em; lots of juicy grass."

I stopped eavesdropping and backed off, circling around so I could approach the three scouts from another direction. I didn't want them to know that I'd heard what I wasn't supposed to hear.

They'd made a fire between two forked branches driven into the ground, forced a strong, straight bough through the buffalo haunch for a spit, and bridged the forks with it so the haunch was directly above the fire. Sam began to turn the spit with what seemed to be artistic skill, and I had to smile at the rapturous expression on his face.

When the others returned with their meat they also built a fire, but their grill-party wasn't peaceful and friendly like ours—everyone wanted to do his own roasting. They quarreled over priority and position on the spit, and the result was that many had to eat their meat either half raw or half burnt.

Sam handed me the best cut; it must have weighed a good three pounds, and I ate it all. I wasn't a glutton. On the contrary, I usually ate less than others, always leaving a little space in my stomach. But I'd had a hard day, and needed to refuel. Anyone from more civilized parts would be astounded at how much meat a hard-working Westerner or plainsman can put away at a sitting.

Besides inorganic foodstuff, a human being needs to eat certain amounts of proteins and carbohydrates, and if he lives in civilized areas, normally eats them in the right proportion. But out West, where a man may not be in an inhabited area for months, he is nourished almost entirely by meat, which contains almost no carbohydrate. So he must eat enormous quantities of meat to supply his body with sufficient carbohydrate. He just has to accept the fact that he's getting an oversupply of protein. I once saw an old trapper put away about six pounds of meat, and when I asked him whether he'd had enough, he answered with a grin:

"It hasta be enough, 'cause I don't have any more; but if you wanta give me a piece of yours, you won't hafta wait long to see it disappear."

While we ate I heard the "Westerners" talking about Sam's and my buffalo hunt. When they saw the two bulls, it seemed they got a different idea about my "stupidity" in shooting them.

Next morning I started to gather my surveying gear to go to work. But Sam came up and said:

"Leave your instruments, Bud. There's somethin' more interestin' to do today."

"What?"

"You'll see. Saddle your horse—we're ridin'."

"Just going for a ride? Work comes first!"

"Bosh! You're workin' long and hard enough. Anyway, I think we'll be back by noon, and after that you can measure and figger all you want, for all I care."

I told Bancroft I'd be gone till noon, and we rode out. Sam kept silent as we rode, and I didn't tell him that I already knew his intentions. The ride took us back over the same stretch we'd last surveyed, and we arrived at the prairie Sam had described.

It was a good two miles wide and twice as long, and lined with wooded hills. A broad creek ran through it, so there was enough moisture to foster a heavy growth of lush grass. We stopped, and Hawkens swept the area with an exploring gaze; then we rode on, northward along the creek. Suddenly he let out a hiss, pulled up his horse, dismounted, and splashed across the shallow creek to a spot where I could see the grass had been trampled down. He checked the surrounding area, came back, mounted again, and led the way, but no longer northward, rather westward away from the creek, so that in a short time we reached the western edge of the grassland. Here he dismounted again and carefully tethered his horse, giving him enough rope to graze. Not a sound had passed his lips since that hiss by the creek, but now an expression of satisfaction spread over his bearded face like sunshine bathing a clump of trees.

"Get down, Bud, and tether your horse. We'll wait here."

"Why tether him?" I asked, although I well knew the answer.

"Well, 'cause otherwise you might easily lose him. Many times I've seen a horse bolt on such an occasion."

"What sort of occasion?"

"Can't you guess?"

"Mustangs?"

"What gave you that idea?" he asked, and looked at me suspiciously.

"Well . . . I read about it."

"Read what?"

"That tame horses sometimes run off with wild mustangs if they're not tied fast."

"The devil! Nothin' surprises you, 'cause you've read about everythin' already. Better if you didn't know how to read!"

"Why, did you want to surprise me?"

"I sure did!"

"With a mustang hunt?"

"Right!"

"But that's no surprise. A surprise has to come with no warning beforehand—and you've told me about mustangs being nearby when buffalo are sighted. Anyway, you need a new horse."

"Hmm . . . you're right. Well, listen, the mustangs were already there."

"Those were their tracks by the creek?"

"Right. They were through here yesterday, the scouts were. Let me tell you, these animals are real smart. They always put out sentries, ahead and to the side. They have officers just like in the army, and the general is always the strongest, most experienced and bravest stallion. When they graze or when they're on the move, the stallions are always around the outer edge of the herd, the mares next, and the colts and fillies in the center. That's how they try to protect each other. Now, you know how to swing a lasso, and I've showed you a few times just how to rope and hold a mustang. Do ya still remember how?"

"I sure do."

"Think ya could rope one?"

"Of course!"

"Well, sir, you'll have a chance to do so this mornin'."

"Thanks! I won't try it."

"No? Damnation! Why not?"

"Because I don't need a horse."

"What are ya gettin' at?"

"Well, it's not the way I imagine a brave Westerner to be."

"How should he be, then?"

"You told me about pothunters yesterday, about white men who shoot buffalo by the hundreds just for sport, not for their meat. I take that to be a crime—against the animals and against the Indians who depend on them for food. Do you agree?"

"Yep, I agree. Whatcha tryin' to say?"

"It's exactly the same with horses. I don't want to rob any of these noble mustangs of their freedom. I'd do it only if I needed a horse, and I don't need one."

"That's an honest answer, Bud, straight and honest. Every man should think the way you do, think, talk, and act. But who says that you have to rob a mustang of his freedom? I showed ya how to throw a lasso, and this is just an examination to see how well you learned. Rope one, and then let him go. Okay?"

"That's different. Yes, I'll go along with that."

"Fine. In my case it's another story. I need a horse, and I figger on gettin' one and breakin' him. Now, I've told you this before and I'll tell you again. Sit tight in the saddle and keep your horse reined back at a standstill when the rope pulls taut. If you don't, you'll get un-horsed for sure and the mustang will run off, draggin' your horse by the lasso right along with him. Then you'll be a plain foot-slogger just like I am now."

He opened his mouth to continue, but suddenly fell silent and pointed to twin hills above the prairie's north end. Between their wooded slopes a lone horse had appeared, a single horse. He walked slowly forward, not grazing, turning his head from side to side and raising it as if he was sniffing the air.

"See him?" whispered Sam. He kept his voice low from excite-ment; even had he spoken normally, the mustang couldn't possibly have heard him. "Didn't I say they were comin'? That's a scout, sent out ahead to see if all is well. A sly stallion. See how he looks and sniffs in all directions! He won't smell us, 'cause the wind is in our faces; that's why I picked this spot."

Now the mustang broke into a trot. He ran toward us, then a short way to the right, to the left, turned suddenly and disappeared be-tween the hills where we'd first caught sight of him.

"Didja see the way he moved?" asked Sam. "How he used each bush for cover, so he wouldn't be seen by a possible enemy? An In-dian scout couldn'ta done it better."

"Right—I'm really amazed."

"Now he's gone back to tell the general that all is clear. But he's wrong about that, heeheehee! Watch, they'll all be comin' out in ten minutes at the most. You know how we're goin' to work this?"

"Well, no."

"You ride back quick to the prairie exit where we came in. I'll ride to the other end and hide among the trees. I'll wait till the whole herd is out on the flat and then ride out toward 'em. They'll all stampede in your direction—then let yourself be seen, and they'll turn back toward me. We'll keep 'em runnin' back and forth between us till we've picked out what looks to be the best two, and we'll catch 'em. I'll choose the best of those two, and we'll turn the other loose. Does that plan sound all right to you?"

"How can you ask? I know nothing about mustang-hunting, at which you're a master. So of course I'll do whatever you say."

"Yeah, you're right. I've had many a wild mustang under me, so I guess you could call me a 'master'. So, start off! Time's a-wastin', and we wanta be in position when they show up."

We mounted again and rode off in opposite directions, Sam to the north and I south, to where we'd entered the grassland. The heavy bear-killer was an unnecessary hindrance to the job at hand, and I'd just as soon have left it behind. But I'd read, and heard it from Sam too, that a careful Westerner parts with his weapon only if he's absolutely sure that he has nothing to fear, and will have no occasion to use it. That was not the case here; an Indian, or perhaps a beast of prey, could appear at some unexpected moment. So I just made sure that the gun hung securely by its sling and didn't slap against my leg.

Now, hiding in the shadow of the trees nearest the grassland, I waited tensely for the horses to appear. I'd tied the end of my lasso rope tightly to the saddle-horn, and placed the loop and coiled slack ready to grab and throw.

I was now so far from the end of the flat that I wouldn't be able to see the mustangs when they first came out of the woods, only after Sam had driven them in my direction. I hadn't been waiting longer than ten minutes when I saw in the distance a cluster of dark dots, which quickly grew larger as they rushed toward me. First the size of sparrows, then cats, dogs, calves, until they'd gotten so near that I could make out their actual size. They were the mustangs, coming at me in a wild stampede!

What a magnificent sight, these splendid animals! Their manes waved above their necks like flags, and their long tails streamed behind them like feather-plumes. There must have been three hundred head, and the earth shook under the thunder of their hooves. A big white stallion was in the lead.

I couldn't pause for reflection—now was the time for me to show myself. I rode out into the open, and the reaction was instantaneous—the white horse reared, and the whole herd stopped short behind him. There was a fearful snorting and they turned as one, the white horse arrowing through them to lead the herd in the opposite direction. I followed them slowly, for I knew Sam would soon be driving them toward me again.

I'd seen the herd for only a few moments, but I thought I saw a mule among them, right close to the leader. A smaller animal, with large head and long ears, it was easy to spot, and a few minutes later, when Sam drove the herd toward me again, I took a closer look. Sure enough, there was a mule, light brown with dark stripes along its spine. Not as elegantly proportioned as a horse, a mule is nevertheless a handsome animal, with some qualities that outshine a horse's— more patient, surer-footed on steep mountain paths . . . although much more stubborn, too. Mules, half horse, half donkey, are usually bred in captivity; this one must have somehow escaped from service to humans, and joined the herd. I decided to catch it for Sam.

Here they came again, Sam so close behind them that I saw him plainly through the dust. Now we had them hemmed in ahead and to the rear, and they started breaking away to either side, split into two groups. I saw that the mule was still with the leaders in the larger group, running close alongside the white stallion. I followed them, as did Sam. He shouted to me:

"Right through the middle, me left, you right!"

We spurred our horses and rode into the midst of the herd at the same time, well before they could reach the shelter of the trees. They turned again and tried to run between us; we blocked them by moving quickly toward each other, and suddenly we were in the center of total confusion, the mustangs rearing and turning in every direction. The stallion and the mule separated from the others and galloped away side by side. We turned and kept pace with them, Sam now whirling his lasso. He yelled again:

"Still a greenhorn!"

"Why?"

"You're chasin' the white one, that's why! Only a greenhorn would do that, heeheehee!"

I answered him but he didn't hear me, for his laughter overrode my words. So he thought I was after the stallion, did he? I let him go on alone, and rode off to the side, where leaderless mustangs were still snorting and milling about in panic and fear. I saw Sam throw his lasso, and the loop settled around the mule's neck. Now, as he had so carefully told me, one must stop dead, turn his horse, and pull back so as to take up all the slack in the rope. Sam did this, but he was a second too late; his horse hadn't quite turned nor planted himself solidly before he was jerked off his feet by a violent pull from the lassoed mule. Sam Hawkens somersaulted through the air, his leather coat flapping, and came to earth, a luckily-placed low bush cushioning his fall. The horse quickly regained his feet and ran toward the mule, who had stood fast, the rope's tension choking off its wind. Now it could breathe again and it galloped off across the prairie, taking Sam's unresisting horse with him, for the end of the rope was tied to the saddlehorn.

I hurried to Sam to see if he was injured. He was on his feet when I got there, and shouted excitedly:

"Thunder and blazes! There goes Dick Stone's nag and that blanky mule! Without even sayin' goodbye, if I'm not mistaken!"

"Are you all right? No bones broken?"

"No! Get off quick and let me have your horse!"

"What for?"

"I wanta catch those runaways, dammit! So get down!"

"Out of the question! Might be another Hawkens somersault, and then both horses would be gone for good."

With these words I turned and galloped off after the roped-to-gether animals, who were by this time a good distance away. I reached them quickly, however, because the horse was no longer going willingly, but showing the mule a little of his own contrariness. I saw that I wouldn't need my own lasso, because all I had to do was take the one that linked them together, and both animals were in my grasp. I let them run on, gradually pulling on the rope and cinching the slack on my saddlehorn, all the time steering us all in a sweeping arc back to where Sam was standing. By then I had pulled both of them within a few feet of my own horse, and I jerked the lasso tight to cut off the mule's wind; it sank slowly to its knees and fell over, its legs kicking.

"Hold tight!" yelled Sam, and ran to the mule's side.

"Now let go!"

I let go of the lasso; the mule gasped, shook its head and struggled to its feet. Sam had jumped on its back as it arose, and it stood motionless for a long second, as if posing for a painting. Then it began to buck and run, jumping forward, back, and to the side, trying to unseat Sam, who held fast with his knees and two handfuls of hide.

"It can't throw me off!" shouted Sam, "but it's sure goin' to try to run me off! Wait here for me—I'll bring it back tame as a kitten."

He'd no sooner said the last word when the mule threw itself to the earth and tried to rid itself of Sam by rolling over him. As Sam jumped to the side to keep his ribs from being broken, I also jumped off my horse, grabbed the slack rope which still lay on the ground, and wound it twice around the sturdy root of a bush sticking out of the ground nearby.

Not a moment too soon; the mule had shed its rider and was off like a shot, but the rope held and jerked it to the ground again. Sam had retreated a few yards, and was feeling himself all over for possible injuries. He made a sour face.

"Let the beast go. Nobody's goin' to tame it, if I'm not mistaken."

"Not on your life! I'm not going to let an ornery mule make a jackass out of me, a mule whose papa wasn't even a gentleman! Watch out!"

I flipped the rope off the root and jumped on the mule's back as it arose, just as Sam had done. But I had an advantage that Sam didn't have—my legs were long enough to squeeze the mule's ribs together, and that ability was decisive. The mule tried to throw me as it had with Sam, but I hung on, taking up the rest of the rope and pulling the loop tight around its neck. Each time I sensed that the beast was about to throw itself to the ground to dislodge me, I pulled it tighter. This manipulation, together with constant pressure on the mule's ribs, kept it on its feet.

It was a wicked battle, stubbornness and strength on both sides. I began to sweat from every pore, and so did the mule; droplets of sweat from both of us flew through the air as it bucked and kicked, and foam flecked its jaws. But after a long while its movements grew weaker, and at last it stopped still, drawing deep sighing breaths—stopped still not as surrender, but because it was simply too weak to continue the battle. I also drew deep, deep breaths; I felt as if all my muscles were torn, and my tendons stretched to their limit.

"Damnation! What kinda man are you? You're stronger'n the mule! If you could only see your face, you wouldn't know it was you!"

"I believe it."

"Your eyes are bugged out, your lips swelled up like sausages and your cheeks are real blue!"

"That's because I'm a greenhorn who doesn't want to give up. An expert mustang-hunter, on the other hand, ropes his horse to a mule and sends both of them off for a stroll."

Sam's face fell, and he spoke with entreaty:

"Please say no more about it, Bud, 'specially to the others. Even the most experienced hunter sometimes has a bad day. You had two good ones, today and yesterday."

"I hope to have more days like these. But you—how do your ribs feel, and the rest of your bones?"

"Don't know for sure. I'll stroke 'em and count 'em again when we get back. Right now I feel like they're jumpin' around inside of me. I've never had a beast like that between my knees before. Hope you got it to understand who's the boss."

"Of course—see how peaceful it is now. Why don't you put your saddle on and ride it home."

"Maybe with me ridin', it'll start to buck again."

"I doubt it, it's had enough. It's an intelligent animal, and I'm sure you'll take to each other."

"Well, I hope so. I had my eye on the mule from the beginning. You were goin' for the stallion, which I thought was pretty stupid."

"What makes you think I was after the stallion?"

"What then?"

"I was chasing the mule, too."

"You were?"

"Of course. Even a greenhorn knows that a white horse is of no use to a Westerner. Anyway, same as you, I liked the looks of the mule as soon as I saw it."

"Well, if that's the case, I gotta admit you're gettin' to be a good judge of horseflesh—and muleflesh!"

"Sam, I hope that my judgment of manflesh is just as good! Now bring over your saddle and gear; as soon as you do I'll dismount slowly and carefully, and we'll put it on together, you on one side, me on the other."

The mule gave no trouble, just stood shivering while we saddled and bridled it. And when Sam mounted, it acted as docile and obedient as if it had never been a free-runner.

"It's had an owner before," said Sam, "somebody who was a good rider, and who treated it well. We'll never know how or why it ran wild. Know what I'm goin' to call it, or rather, *her?*"

"What?"

"Nancy. I had a pack-mule named Nancy a long time ago, so I'm used to the name. 'Nancy' and 'mule' sorta go together, way I reckon."

"So, you've got a mule Nancy and a weapon Liddy!"

"Right! A coupla nice names, ain't they? And now I'm goin' to ask you again, real sweet, to do me that favor."

"Sure. What favor?"

"Don't say anythin' about what's happened here. I'd be real grateful."

"Nonsense! I don't ask for gratitude for doing a favor for a friend. I would have kept silent without your asking."

"I just don't wanna hear that bunch back at camp laugh when they hear how Sam Hawkens got his lovely new Nancy. I'd never live it down. If you don't say anythin'—"

"Enough, Sam, enough!" I broke in. "You're my teacher and my friend. I think of you as I would a—a favorite uncle. No more need be said."

I reached out and we shook hands. His eyes grew moist.

"And I would do anythin' for you, Bud, anythin'! Should you ask me, for instance, to eat this mule of mine here before your eyes, hide, hair, and all, I'd do it! Or, if ya wanted me to—"

"Hold it!" I laughed, "Let Nancy live for the time being, and let's get back to camp. I still have work to do."

"Work? If what you've done here this mornin' wasn't work, then I don't know what else to call it."

I roped Dick Stone's horse to mine with the lasso, and we started back. The mustangs were long gone. The mule obeyed its rider willingly, and as we rode Sam sang out happily:

"She's had trainin', this Nancy, good trainin'! I can feel it comin' back, everythin' she once learned and then forgot when she was with the mustangs."

"How old do you think she is?"

"Not more'n five. I'll look her over more closely later and I can tell exactly. I got you to thank for this animal, not myself. I've had two bad days, and you've had two good ones. Didja ever think you'd learn both buffalo-huntin' and mustang-chasin' in only two days, one after another?"

"Why not? Here in the West a man has to learn everything he can as fast as he can, if he wants to get along and stay alive. I hope to learn other kinds of hunting and many more things."

"Hm-mm, yes. We'll just hope that you come through all right like yesterday and today. Yesterday 'specially, your life was hangin' by a hair—you were takin' big risks. Don't forget what you just said, that you still got lots to learn. In the future, don't trust y'rself too much! Y'know, as dangerous as buffalos are, there's another animal still more dangerous to hunt."

"Which one?"

"The bear."

"The black one with the yellow nose?"

"No, the black bear is a good-natured, peace-lovin' fella; you could teach him how to dance and juggle, and other tricks. No, I mean the grizzly, the gray Rocky Mountain bear. You've read so much about everythin', you must've read about him, too."

"Yes, I have."

"Well, be happy if you never meet up with him! When he gets up on his hind legs he's more'n eight feet tall. He could bite off your head with one bite, and when he attacks he flies into a rage and won't stop till his enemy is torn to bits."

"Or until his enemy wins the fight."

"Oho! You're not payin' attention! We're talkin' about the mighty, unbeatable grizzly bear, not about a little raccoon."

"I know. I don't mean to underestimate him. But unbeatable, unconquerable—I don't think so. There's no animal in the world that can't be conquered by humans, not even the grizzly bear."

"Is that somethin' you read?"

"Well, yes, I read it, but I also know it—simply said, humans are more intelligent."

"Hm-mm. I think it's the fault of those books that you're so light in the head. You seem to be a good lad otherwise, if I'm not mistaken. But I believe you'd go up against a grizzly bear just like you did yesterday against them bison."

"If I couldn't do anything else—yes."

"Anythin' else! What d'ya mean by that? You could cut and run, couldn't ya?"

"Well, wouldn't that be cowardly, to run away?"

"Cowardly has nothin' to do with it. It's not cowardly to run away from a grizzly. On the contrary, it's plain suicide *not* to run away from one."

"That's where our opinions differ. If he takes me by surprise and there's no time to run, I'd have to fight for my life. And if he attacks a comrade of mine, I'd feel it my duty to come to his aid. Those are two cases where I couldn't run. Besides that, I can imagine a daring Westerner taking on a grizzly even when he doesn't have to, just to test his courage."

Sam was shocked speechless. We rode silently for a good five minutes before he spoke again.

"It's plain impossible to talk sense to you! I just hope to God you never meet a grizzly!"

"Well, you probably don't have to worry about that now," I said, trying to pacify him, "there are no gray grizzlies in this area. Or are there?"

"Why not? Grizzlies are found everywhere in the mountains. They follow the creeks and rivers, and sometimes even go far into the prairie. God help whoever meets one! Let's not even talk about it any more."

We arrived at camp, which had been moved a considerable distance forward, as during our absence Bancroft and his three surveyors had finally decided to show what they could do, working to make up for lost time. Our arrival caused a little excitement.

"A mule! A mule! Where dja get it, Hawkens?"

"It was sent to me," answered Sam with a straight face.

"Impossible! How?"

"Special delivery mail, for five cents. You wanna see the envelope?" Some of them laughed, others snarled. But he'd made his point, and there were no further questions. Sam joined Dick and Will, and I started working with the surveyors. By late afternoon we'd gone so far that by next morning we would reach the valley where Sam and I had had our buffalo adventure. I asked him that evening whether they might still be around to interfere with our work. He shook his head emphatically.

"Not a chance, heeheehee! Them bison are just as smart as the mustangs. The sentries have warned the herd, and they've all gone off in another direction. They'll avoid that valley for a long time."

CHAPTER FOUR

When morning came we moved our camp to the upper end of the valley. Hawkens, Stone and Parker had gone on ahead to look the area over, Sam wanting to break in his newly-acquired "Nancy." Some of Rattler's crew helped with the move, while I and the rest of the survey party worked, covering a fair distance by midday. Rattler himself, with a few malingering comrades of his, kept out of sight until lunchtime.

We had reached the area where Sam and I had had our buffalo adventure, and we looked for the carcass of the old bull. It was no longer there. From the spot where it had lain a broad track of flattened-down grass led into the nearby trees and bushes.

I heard Rattler's voice behind me. "Can't believe it! I looked at both bulls when we fetched the meat, and I would've sworn they were both dead. But this one must still have had a little life in him."

"You think so?" I asked him.

"Sure. Looks like he crawled. Dead buffalos can't crawl."

"Maybe he was dragged."

"Yeah? By whom?"

"By Indians, for instance. Sam and I saw a moccasin print not far from here."

"Still talkin' like a greenhorn! If Indians were here, why would they drag him away? Nah, he dragged himself into the trees and probably died there. We'll see in a minute."

He and his men walked off, following the trail of flattened grass. Maybe he thought I'd come along, but his sneering remarks grated on me, and I turned to go back to work. Anyway, I wasn't really interested in what had become of the old bull's carcass.

I had just picked up a measuring rod when I heard a chorus of shouts and screams of fear. Two or three shots rang out, and I heard Rattler yell:

"Climb a tree, quick, climb a tree! He's not a climber!"

One of Rattler's men burst from the trees and ran toward me, his face contorted in deadly fear.

"What is it, what's happening?" I called as he ran past.

"A bear, a giant bear, a grizzly!" he panted, not stopping.

At the same instant a louder scream came from the trees.

"Help! Help!" He's got me! Ahhh-hhh!"

A human being screams that way only when he's looking into the jaws of death. Those cries for help had to be answered, and by me. But how? I'd left my bear-killer at the tent, for it was a hindrance while working, and we had the Westerners to protect us. In the time it would take me to run for the gun, the bear would tear the man apart. So I had to go to his aid as I was, with just a knife and the two revolvers in my belt. What pitiful weapons with which to fight the gray bear!

These thoughts flashed through my mind in less than a second. Before the last scream had died away, I was running full speed through the bushes to where the trees began, there where the bear had dragged the bull's carcass. He'd come out from there too, but dragging the bull had obliterated his tracks, and we'd missed seeing them.

It was a terrible moment. Behind me the yells of the surveyors, running to the tent for their guns. Ahead the shouts of the Westerners, the agonized screams of one of them suddenly ceasing. I reached the spot, and now I heard the growls of the bear, and near the partly-stripped carcass of the buffalo, saw him standing erect and tearing the flesh and clothing from the lower limbs of the one who hadn't climbed fast enough, still holding a tree's lowest branch in a death grip.

The man was dead or dying, it was too late to rescue him. But there arose inside of me a violent reaction to this scene of violence. I picked up one of the rifles discarded by the men as they fled; it had already been fired. Holding it by the barrel, I sprang over the buffalo and with all my strength clubbed the grizzly on the back of his enormous head. Ridiculous! The stock splintered and the rifle came apart in my hands, but the blow diverted the bear's attention from his victim.

He turned slowly toward me, not with the rapid motion one would expect in a beast of prey, and measured me with his beady eyes, as if deciding whether or not to leave his mangled victim. That short instant of delay saved my life, for it gave me time to pull my revolver and shoot him three or four times in those eyes. Unsportsmanlike? I was balanced between life and death.

I immediately jumped far to one side and drew my Bowie knife as the blinded bear sprang directly onto the spot where I'd stood a second earlier. I was away, and with snorts of pain and rage he began to search for me, tearing up the ground and underbrush in a wide circle all around.

Finally he gave some thought to his injuries rather than to the one who had caused them, sat down panting and grinding his teeth, and lifted his paws to his sightless eyes. In a flash I was next to him, and stabbed him twice between the ribs with the Bowie. The knife hadn't found his heart; he reached for me, but again I was away, and he resumed his search with redoubled rage and violence, continuing for a good five minutes. He was losing blood, and was obviously weaker.

Again the bear sat and pawed at his eyes, giving me the opportunity to knife him twice more in the ribs and spring away, and this time my stabs were lethal. He staggered forward a few steps, sank to the ground, tried to rise again but hadn't the strength, fell slowly over on his side and lay still.

"Thank God!" cried Rattler from his tree. "But are you sure the beast is dead? He could still be dangerous!"

"Come out of your trees," I answered, "he's dead all right."

"No, no, not yet! First check to see if he's really dead!"

"He's dead."

"You can't be sure. You don't know how hard it is to kill a grizzly—they live forever. Look him over sharp."

"For you? Come down and look him over yourselves. You're all experienced Westerners and I'm only a greenhorn."

With that I stepped to the tree where their dead comrade hung from a branch. His face was distorted, his open eyes stared at me glassily. The flesh had been torn from his body from the waist down, and his internal organs were visible. I suppressed my horror and turned away.

One braver than the rest came down from his tree and hesitatingly approached the dead grizzly. Not until he had satisfied himself that the bear was dead, and assured his fellows of that fact, did the rest of them descend from their trees. They took down the mutilated body of their friend with difficulty, for his arms still held a death grip on the branch. Rattler knelt by the bear, drew his knife, and said:

"Well, we turned it around! The bear wanted to eat us, but now we're goin' to eat the bear!"

"It would have been better," I said, "if you'd tried to use that knife on him while he was still alive. Now, don't touch him!"

"What? You telling me not to bother cuttin' myself a steak?"

"That's just what I'm telling you."

"By what right?"

"By accepted custom, Rattler. I killed the bear."

"The hell! Don't try to tell me that a greenhorn could kill a grizzly with a pocket knife! We shot at him as soon as we saw him. It just took him a little while to die."

"And then you ran for the trees."

"First we pumped bullets into him. That couple of needle-pokes you gave him didn't do him in—our guns did. The bear is ours, and we'll do whatever we damn well want with him!"

"I'm warning you—don't touch him!"

As in spite of my warning Rattler gripped a fold of bear-hide and started to cut it away, I reached down, grabbed him by the waist, lifted him high and threw him so hard against the nearest tree that something cracked—either Rattler or the tree. While he was flying through the air I drew my second, still-loaded revolver. Rattler got up, shook his head, and came at me with the knife he still held.

"Hold it right there!" He stopped. "Drop that knife or I'll shoot it out of your hand! I'll give you three seconds! One—two—"

Rattler still held the knife, and in the next second I would have put a bullet through his hand, but at that instant a loud voice was heard:

"What's happening here, men? Are you crazy? Why would white men be at each other's throats, for what reason? Leave off!"

We all turned toward the voice, and saw a small, lean figure step forward—a man dressed like an Indian, with sun-browned, almost

Indian features, but for all that a white man. He carried a rifle and a knife; he came up and stood between me and Rattler.

"You have strength in those arms, sir! To throw a man that size through the air is no mean feat. It was delightful to see." He nudged the bear with his foot and continued. "This is the rascal we were trailing. Unfortunately, we've arrived too late."

"You were trailing him?" I asked.

"Yes. We came across his tracks yesterday and followed them back and forth, up and down—a bear never walks a straight path—and now when we've finally caught up with him, we find that the hunt is already over."

"You keep saying 'we', sir, but you seem to be alone."

"No, there are two others with me."

"Where are they, and who are they?"

"I'll tell you that as soon as I learn who you are. You know that one cannot be too careful in this region; you meet more evil men than good ones. I hope and trust you are the latter kind." His gaze passed over Rattler and his friends.

"We're a surveying party, sir," I explained, "one Chief Engineer, four surveyors, three scouts, and twelve guards to protect us from attack."

"Hmm-mm. From what I saw, you for one don't seem to be a man who needs protection. So, you're surveyors, eh? Just what are you surveying?"

"We're laying out a route for a railroad."

"That will pass through this area?"

"Yes."

"So—you've bought this land?" He asked this question earnestly, his eyes piercing. He already knew what the answer was.

"I was hired to work with this crew as a surveyor," I said, "and I know nothing about the business details."

"I see. However, I'm sure you know what the facts are. The land you're standing on is hunting grounds. It belongs to Indians, the Mescalero clan of the Apaches, among others. I know for certain that this land has not been sold, nor has the right to survey it been granted."

"What's that to you?" Rattler broke in. "Don't put your nose in other people's business, stick to your own." He sheathed his knife, and seeing that, I stuck my revolver back in my belt.

"That's what I'm doing, sir, for I am a Mescalero Apache."

"You? Don't make me laugh! It's plain to see that you're a white man."

"Don't judge by my skin-color, rather by my name. I am called Kleki-petra."

Rattler had obviously heard the name before. His lip curled and he said sneeringly, "Ah, Kleki-petra. Now I remember hearin' about you—a white schoolteacher turned Apache native, teachin' 'em all the paleface secrets."

Kleki-petra ignored the remark. He turned to me and spoke.

"Now that I know who you are and what you're doing here, I can tell you who my companions are. Better yet, present them to you in person." He called out a few words I didn't understand.

Two impressive figures stepped out from behind nearby trees and slowly and deliberately approached us. They were Indians, immediately recognizable as father and son.

The older one was about average height, but powerfully built. He had a noble bearing, moving his body with elegance. His head was uncovered, but an eagle feather marking him as a Chieftain was fastened in his hair. He wore a leather jacket, leggings and moccasins with little decoration. A knife was in his belt, and he carried a twin-barreled rifle, the stock covered with silver nailheads. A pipe and a small medicine bag hung from a thong around his neck.

The younger one was dressed similarly, though his garments bore rather more ornamentation than did those of his father. His moccasins were embellished with porcupine quills, and his leather jacket with patterns of red stitching. Like his father, he carried a knife and double-barreled rifle, and his medicine bag hung from a beaded leather thong. His head was also uncovered and displayed no feather, but the long blue-black hair cascading down his back was interlaced with snakeskin. His features, even nobler than his father's, were unlined, the skin a dull light brown with bronze highlights. His height was the same as mine, and as I later learned, our ages also matched. My eyes absorbed all these details in an instant, but that first meeting made a deep impression on me, one which I've never forgotten.

We exchanged a long searching gaze with each other as if there were no others present, and for an instant I saw a spark flash deep within those black eyes before he turned away.

"These are my friends and companions," said Kleki-petra, indicating first the father, then the son, "this is Inshu-chuna, High Chief of the Mescaleros, acknowledged as Chieftain by all the other Apache clans. And here stands his son Winnetou, who in spite of his youth has performed more brave deeds than have many older warriors in an entire lifetime. His name is known and respected from the savannahs to beyond the Rocky Mountains."

That speech seemed rather effusive at the time, though not exaggerated, as I later learned. But Rattler laughed scornfully.

"So the young redskin has performed great deeds, has he? I can imagine what kind—prob'ly robbery and pocket-picking."

That was a deadly insult, but the three acted as if they hadn't heard it. They went to the bear; Kleki-petra knelt down to examine it. There was dead silence during the two or three minutes it took him to do so. Finally he rose, and said, "The bear was killed by a knife, not by a bullet." Of course he'd overheard our quarrel, because he'd interrupted it at the critical moment.

"Hell you say!" growled Rattler. "What does a schoolteacher know about bear-huntin'! When we skin him we'll see for sure if it was a knife or bullet. I say it was a bullet. A greenhorn only knows how to use a knife to peel apples."

Then Winnetou knelt and felt the bloody spots where my knife-thrusts had found their mark, stood up and spoke for the first time, asking:

"Who attacked this animal with a knife?" To my amazement, he spoke pure unaccented English.

"I did," I answered.

"Why didn't the young paleface use his rifle?"

"I didn't have it with me, only hand-guns."

"But there are rifles lying about."

"They're not mine. I only had time to try one, and it had already been fired by its owner, who then dropped it, ran and climbed a tree."

"When we came near we heard a terrible scream. Where did it come from?"

"There." I indicated the dead man, lying on the ground a short distance away.

"Ugh! Squirrels and skunks run and climb trees when danger threatens, but brave men should fight. Men gain strength to match their courage, strength to conquer the fiercest beast. The young paleface had such courage. Why is he called 'greenhorn'?"

"Because I've only been here in the West for a short time, and everything is new to me."

Winnetou shook his head. "The palefaces have strange ways. A young man who attacks and kills a fierce grizzly with a knife is slighted with the name 'greenhorn'. But those who climb trees and howl with fear are held to be capable, experienced men, and are honored with that name I've heard them called, 'Westerners'. The red men do not make such an error. A brave is a brave and a coward is a coward."

"My son has spoken the truth," spoke Inshu-chuna. "This brave young paleface is no longer a greenhorn. Those who ran in fright should not insult him with that name, but rather respect him for his courage. But now let us go to their camp, and find out why the palefaces are here in our hunting-grounds."

What a difference between my white companions and these Indians they despised! And what courage they displayed, taking my side even though it might antagonize a half-dozen others. They still didn't know how many were in our party altogether, and they were only three.

When we came out into the open, Inshu-chuna at once saw the survey stakes. He stopped and turned to me.

"What are these? Are the palefaces measuring this land?"

"Yes."

"Why?"

"To build a trail for the fire-horse."

His eyes lost their calm, pensive look, and his expression and attitude changed suddenly from friendliness to anger.

"Are you one of these people?"

"Yes."

"And you help them measure?"

"Yes."

"Do they pay you for doing so?"

"Yes."

His eyes swept over me with a look of contempt, and his voice was also scornful as he said to Kleki-petra:

"Your teachings ring true, but they're often false. Today we meet a young paleface with a brave heart, with honest face and eyes. And when we ask him what he does here, we find that he has come to steal our land and be paid for doing so. The faces of the white men may show good or they may show evil, but inside they are all the same."

I felt deeply ashamed, and couldn't think of a word to say in my own defense. The Chief was right, it was just as he had said. How could I be proud of my profession, my knowledge?

We approached the camp; the chief engineer and the three surveyors emerged hesitantly from their tents. They were surprised to see Indians accompanying us, but first asked about the bear. Rattler answered quickly:

"We shot him. We'll have bear steaks tonight."

The red men looked at me to see how I'd react. I of course knew the custom that game one kills belongs to all, but this was a special case.

"I say that I killed him with my knife, and you'll have bear steaks only with my permission. When Hawkens and the other two scouts return, they'll either verify my claim or prove me wrong. Until then the bear stays like he is, unskinned and unbutchered."

Rattler, standing next to me, drew his revolver. "I'll be damned if I'll let you tell me what to do! C'mon, men. We're going back in there and cut up that bear, and nobody'd better try to stop us!" He hadn't yet taken a step toward the woods before I spoke again:

"Go tend to your dead mate, but don't touch that bear until I say you can!" Bancroft stepped back, shocked by my words.

"Who's dead?"

"It's Rollins," said Rattler. "It was prob'ly this greenhorn's fault. Rollins could maybe have got away if the damn greenhorn hadn't showed up and made the bear ragin' mad."

This was so far from the truth and such an unjust accusation that I saw red. I grabbed his gun with my left hand and struck him in the face so violently with my right that he staggered back and fell a good ten feet away. Just as he'd done in the woods, he got up with drawn knife and came at me again. But now I knew his style, and I was ready for him. I threw his gun down, warded off the knife with my now-empty left hand, and struck him again with my right, this time a calculated blow that stretched him out cold at my feet.

"Whew!" said the surveyor Wheeler. "That was Shatterhand!" I didn't react to the remark; I was watching Rattler's mates for their reaction. They were restless and obviously angry, but no one said a word and no one reached for his gun.

"Mr. Bancroft," I said, "you'd better take Rattler in hand or else pay him off. If he keeps picking fights with me, there'll be another dead man here, and I'm dead serious. It will be either him or me."

Bancroft tried to treat it casually. "Oh, I don't think the situation is that serious."

"It *is* that serious, Mr. Bancroft," I replied. "Here, take his knife and revolver, and please don't return them to him until he's gotten over the rage he'll be in when he comes to. I value my skin, and I'm telling you that if he comes at me again with gun or knife, I'm going to shoot him down. and I'd be within my rights to do so." I looked at Rattler's crew again, a long sharp stare. "That applies to anybody, not just Rattler."

There was silence for a moment, then Inshu-chuna addressed the chief engineer. "From what has been said, you must be the one who gives the orders here. Is that right?"

"Yes," Bancroft answered.

"Then Inshu-chuna must talk with you."

"What about?"

"You will soon learn. But men must sit when they talk."

"Are you inviting yourself to be our guest?"

"No, that is impossible. How can Inshu-chuna be your guest when you are here on his ground, in his forest, his valley, his prairie? I say the white men may sit, and we will talk." He turned his head. "Who are the other palefaces coming toward us?"

"They are scouts, part of our group."

"Then they may also sit with us."

Sam, Dick and Will rode up, dismounted, and looked at Rattler lying there on the ground without saying a word. They didn't seem to be surprised by the presence of Indians, but when they heard who two of them were, they became instantly alert.

"Who's the third one dressed like a Indian?" Sam asked me, leading me aside.

"His name is Kleki-petra; Rattler called him a schoolmaster."

"The schoolteacher Kleki-petra! Yes, I've heard of him, if I'm not mistaken. He's a mystery, a white man who's been with the Apaches for a long time, teachin' 'em languages and all the white man's tricks.

Glad to finally meet up with him, heeheehee! Besides your friend Rattler takin' his siesta, anything else interestin' happen while we were gone?"

"Well, ye-ess. I did what you warned me yesterday not to do."

"Don't know whatcha mean—I warned ya against lotsa things. Which one was this?"

I answered with the one word: "Grizzly."

"Whaa—aat! There was a grizzly here?"

"Not here in camp, there in the woods; he dragged the bull's carcass away. Rattler and some of his men thought the bull had dragged himself, went to look, and tangled with the bear—that is, they ran and climbed trees."

"Did they all get away?"

I shook my head sadly. "No. Rollins—he's dead."

"And you—what did you do? Stayed clear, I hope."

"Noo—oo. Like I just said, I didn't take your advice. I did stay clear until I saw my chance, and then I was able to stick my knife between his ribs a couple of times."

"You went at him with a knife? Are ya crazy? Why didn'cha use your gun, the bear-killer?"

"Didn't have it with me, and there was no time to go for it."

"Goshamighty! So what happened then?"

I told Sam the details, finishing with the quarrel between me and Rattler over who had really killed the bear.

"Seems like we missed all the fun," Sam said. "C'mon, Dick and Will! I've gotta have a look at that grizzly and see what this greenhorn's been up to!" They walked off toward the trees.

Winnetou, his father and Kleki-petra had seated themselves in the grass, and Bancroft sat down facing them. They hadn't begun to talk yet, apparently waiting for the three scouts to return. Sam emerged from the trees a few minutes later and came back to camp, Dick and Will following shortly after.

"That was real stupid, to shoot and run! If you don't wanta fight a grizzly, you don't waste a second shootin', you just get far away fast. Shootin' at him just makes him mad. Rollins sure looks awful! Now, who killed that bear?"

Rattler, who meanwhile had come to, growled, "I did!"

"Well, if all of you shot at him, looks like all the shots missed 'cept one."

"That musta been mine!" crowed Rattler.

"Could be," said Sam. "The only fresh bullet mark we could find was where a piece of his ear was nipped off—mighta been your rifle that did it. His eyes are shot out, but don't look like rifle fire. There's four knife holes in that bear, two near the heart and two right smack into it. Who went after the bear with a knife?"

"I did," I said softly.

"Just you?"

"Nobody else."

"Well then, the bear is yours. But bein' as we're all one big happy family, the meat is for everybody; you decide how it's divvied up. But the pelt—that's yours alone. What d'ya say to that, Rattler?"

"Go to hell!" Rattler shambled off to the chuck wagon where the brandy cask waited, and turned the spigot. I saw what a generous glassful he'd poured, and knew he'd drink himself into a stupor.

Now that the bear question had been disposed of, Bancroft asked the Indians what they wanted to talk about. Inshu-chuna spoke:

"Inshu-chuna, High Chief of the Mescalero Apaches, tells you that you must stop measuring Indian land and return to your own."

"We can't take orders from you," replied the engineer, but placatingly.

Anger flashed across the chief's face, but only for an instant. He composed himself, and said:

"I will ask my white brother a few questions, and expect that he will answer them truthfully."

"Ask away."

"Does he have a house in which he lives?"

"Yes."

"And a piece of land around it?"

"Yes."

"If a neighbor wanted to build a path across this land of my white brother's, would he allow it to be done?"

"No, of course not!"

"The land beyond the Rocky Mountains, and the land east of the Mississippi belongs to the palefaces. What would they say if the Indians came there and wanted to build an iron road?"

"The red men would be chased away."

"My white brother has spoken the truth. Now I ask that he make an honest judgment on what I have to say. The palefaces come here to this land which belongs to us. They round up the mustangs, they slaughter our buffalo, they search for gold and precious stones. Now they even want to build an iron road, a trail for their fire-horse. Along this road more and more palefaces will come, attack us and overrun us, and take away that little of our land and possessions that now is left to us. What can you answer to that?"

Bancroft was silent. After a moment Inshu-chuna continued:

"Have we fewer rights than you? Your people speak of love, yet they steal from us and dispossess us—is that love? In return, we should act honestly toward you—is that fair? Didn't this entire land once belong to the red men? It has been taken from us, piece by piece. And what have we received in return? Misery, poverty, hunger! You drive us ever further back, and press us ever closer together, so that in a short time we will suffocate and die.

"Why do you do this? Out of need, because you have no room? No, out of greed, for in your lands there is still room for many millions. But each of you wants a whole mountain for himself, a whole forest, a whole prairie. For that you ask that we let ourselves be turned out of our houses and driven away. Where to? We have been pushed from place to place, further, ever further. Now we live here in these lands, and we believed we could rest at last and breathe freely. But the white man comes again, to build an iron road.

"Do we not have the same rights that you have in your house, on your land? If we applied our laws to the white man, then we must kill all of you. But we wish only that your own laws apply to us as well. Do they? No! Your laws have two faces, and the one they turn to us is the evil one, the one that condemns us and works to your advantage. You want to build an iron road here. Have you asked our permission?"

"I don't take that to be necessary."

"Why not? Is this land yours?"

"I think it is."

"No, it belongs to us. Have you bought it from us?"

"No."

"Have we given it to you?"

"No, not to me."

"Nor to anyone else. You were sent here to measure the land for an iron road. Did you ask those who sent you if they had the right to pass through this land? No, you did not. Inshu-chuna forbids you to continue your measuring." He rose to his feet, as did Winnetou. Kleki-petra remained seated.

All this was spoken in flawless, educated English, although with a slight accent Winnetou's English didn't have. The point-by-point logic was unassailable, and Bancroft obviously didn't know how or what to answer. He threw up his hands, turned to me and started to speak, but I stopped him with a gesture.

"I cannot help you, Mr. Bancroft. I am here as a surveyor, not as a judge of right and wrong. Do as you think best—I can only survey, not discuss how or why we come to be here."

The chief had been watching and listening. "Further discussion is pointless," he said, "it is enough that Inshu-chuna has said that you must stop surveying, and depart from here tomorrow, back to where you came from. Inshu-chuna and Winnetou will return when the sun has touched that mountain,"—he pointed—"to hear your answer. If you have decided to go, we will mark you as friends and brothers; if you stay, then is the tomahawk raised between you and us. I am Inshu-chuna, High Chief of the Apaches. I have spoken."

The two walked slowly down the valley, and we watched them until they disappeared around a bend. Bancroft went to Kleki-petra, still seated on the grass, and wordlessly spread his hands in a questioning gesture of helplessness and uncertainty.

"You must decide, sir," that one answered. "I think the same way as does the chief. A major criminal act is being perpetrated against the red race, though as a white man I know full well that the Indians' resistance is futile. Should you depart tomorrow, then the next day others will come to continue your work. Still, I must warn you that the chief's words were spoken in earnest; do not take them lightly."

"Where have they gone?"

"To fetch our horses. We tethered them and went on foot when we saw that we were nearing the bear." He stood up and walked a little distance away, and I followed him.

"I want to tell you, sir," I said, "that although I cannot make decisions here, I feel in my heart that Inshu-chuna is in the right. When I was hired for this job, no mention was made of ownership of the lands we were to survey—the subject was never brought up."

Kleki-petra smiled. "I sensed that you are an honest and straightforward young man, and I am witness to the fact that you are also a brave one." He paused. "I also sensed some instant affinity between you and Winnetou when first you saw each other, a flash of . . . of . . . it can't be called friendship; you have nothing in common except perhaps your youth. But it pleases me greatly; I hope one day you do get to know each other."

"Yes, I felt something pass between us, too," I murmured, "and I would be honored to have Winnetou as a friend. But tell me, sir, how did a white man come to be an Apache, accepted and obviously trusted by a High Chief such as Inshu-chuna?"

"I can tell you in a few words. I was a young university professor with excellent prospects, a fulfilling career ahead of me. But I saw what white civilization was doing to the Indians, the race who once roamed this land from sea to sea. And I gave up my white heritage to come and live with them, and teach them some of what I knew, knowledge which might help them resist the barbarity and duplicity of the white invaders, the palefaces who were driving them ever westward, who slaughtered them and stole their hunting-grounds. Pure chance led me to the Apaches."

He paused, and for a minute or so seemed lost in thought.

"That was more than thirty years ago, and I have never looked back. They didn't accept me at first, but little by little I won their confidence and trust. Winnetou is my pride, my joy. He has been my student and protégé from the day he was born, and I would give my life to save his."

Kleki-petra looked down the valley and his face lit up. I turned and saw Inshu-chuna and Winnetou approaching, mounted and leading a third horse. We walked toward them, passing Rattler, who leaned against the chuck-wagon and stared at us with red, hate-filled eyes. He'd been working at the brandy cask.

The Indians dismounted. They, Bancroft, Kleki-petra and I faced each other in a rather wide circle. Inshu-chuna spoke:

"Has my white brother decided whether he will go or stay?"

The chief engineer had decided to give only a conciliatory answer, hoping to gain time.

"Even if we wanted to leave immediately," he said, "still we must stay here in obedience to the orders we received. But I will send a message to Santa Fé and ask what I should do—then I can give you my answer."

"Inshu-chuna cannot wait. I must have your answer now."

Rattler staggered up and joined the group, holding a glass filled with brandy. I expected him to approach me, but instead he went up to the Indians and said with thick tongue:

"If the Indians drink with me, then we'll do what they want and break camp, otherwise not. The young one can be first. Here's your firewater, Winnetou!"

He held out the glass. Winnetou stepped back with a gesture of refusal.

"What! You won't drink with me? That's a damn insult, you cursed redskin! Here, if you won't drink it, then lick it up!"

He threw the contents of the glass in Winnetou's face. That was a deadly insult, an action Winnetou reacted to with lightning speed. He drove a fist into Rattler's face, knocking him backward a few stumbling steps before he fell. He rose slowly, and I got ready to take part in whatever was going to happen. But Rattler only glared at Winnetou, then spun about and returned to the chuck wagon.

Winnetou wiped his face, still expressionless, as was that of his father. One could not see what emotions seethed within him.

"Inshu-chuna asks for the last time," said the chieftain, "will the palefaces leave this valley?"

"We cannot," answered Bancroft.

"Then we will go. There is no peace between us." The three went to their horses, as from the wagon Rattler shouted:

"Go, go, you damn savages! But first the young 'un will pay for that punch in the face!" He lifted the rifle he'd snatched from the wagon and aimed it at Winnetou.

I leaped toward Rattler, and at the same instant Kleki-petra sprang to shield Winnetou. The rifle cracked as I reached and slammed Rattler to the ground a split-second too late.

The bullet had struck Kleki-petra near the heart, a lethal wound. Son and father knelt by him, Winnetou cradling his head, and watched helplessly as blood gushed from the hole in his chest. His eyes were open, he was still alive and conscious, and he looked straight at me, standing above the three of them. The words he had spoken to me only moments before, "I would give my life . . ." rang in my memory.

"Stay by him—be his friend—ahh-hh, Winnetou, my son, Winnetou . . ." He lifted his hand to me, and I reached over Winnetou's shoulder and took it in mine. The two Indians turned their faces to me in astonishment. Kleki-petra's hand became limp and I let it fall. A last weak spurt of blood, his eyes closed, his head sank—he was dead!

Winnetou laid Kleki-petra's head tenderly in the grass, rose, and looked questioningly at his father.

"There lies the murderer," I said. "He's yours—do with him what you will."

Inshu-chuna looked at me grimly, and said one clipped word: "Firewater!"

"I am your friend, your brother," I said, "take me with you."

Inshu-chuna spat in my face. "Scabby dog! Stinking coyote! If you dare to follow us, Inshu-chuna will kill you, you thief who takes money to steal land!"

Had anyone else done and said that, I would have reacted violently. But now I felt ashamed and disheartened. How could I comply with Kleki-petra's last wish if the Apaches rejected me?

The whites, Bancroft, the scouts and the others, stood by silently, waiting to see what the Indians would do. They took no further notice of us. They lifted Kleki-petra's body, sat it upright in his saddle and tied it securely, then mounted and rode off, one before, one behind. No further words of threat or revenge were said, not one backward look was wasted on us. And yet—the unspoken word, the uncast glance, left a feeling of fear and terror hanging in the air, much more than if the word had been spoken and the glance cast.

"That was pretty awful," said Sam Hawkens, "and it's goin' to get awfuller, if I'm not mistaken. There lies the cause of it all, still out cold from brandy and your fist. What are we gonna do with him?"

I didn't answer. I saddled my horse and rode away. I wanted to be alone, to marshal my thoughts and plans, and try to smooth over this last terrible half-hour, at least externally. I rode for many hours, returning sweaty and weary, feeling beaten in both body and spirit. It was very late, the camp was still.

CHAPTER FIVE

D uring my absence Rollins had been buried, and Sam and a few of the men had dragged the grizzly's carcass into camp. The next morning I saw that Sam had skinned it, although there'd been no butchering done. He came over as I was washing up, apparently a little put out, but only a little.

"Where was you off to last night, Bud? We all waited for you to come back so's we could get a taste of that bear. I didn't want to cut him up without your say-so, but I did help him off with his overcoat, heeheehee! Hope you don't mind."

I shrugged. "No, I don't mind."

"Now it's up to you how the meat gets divvied up. There's enough for bear steaks for all of us, today, tonight, and for a few days more, if I'm not mistaken."

"Carve it up any way you want," I said, "the meat belongs to everybody."

"Well, let me tell you a secret. The paws are the best part—even better than steaks from his haunch or ribs. There's nothin' tastier, but as you can guess, not many people ever get to find out how delicious bear-paws taste. Now the meat, and the paws too, tastes even better if you let it stand for a few days. Trouble is, we don't have a few days; I think the Apaches will be back real soon. So we'll cut 'im up and eat 'im fast as we can. And of course you'll start with a tasty front paw, all right?"

"All right."

Sam started to butcher the bear; several fires had been made, and the others crowded near, each of them snatching his piece of paw or steak and taking it away to be roasted. Hawkens saved one paw for me, although it was much too much for one man. Anyway, although I was really hungry, I had no appetite, as contradictory as that may sound. Yesterday's events weighed heavy on my heart, the murder scene imprinted on my brain like a brand. Kleki-petra had died to save Winnetou, as he had said a few moments earlier he would willingly do. And his last words to me: 'be his friend'—a dying wish I would gladly obey. But how, when Inshu-chuna had spat in my face, and Winnetou had ignored me?

I sat a little apart, thinking these thoughts and paying no attention to the others or to the passage of time, until Sam came up to me with the roasted bear-paw on a slab of wood.

"Whatsamatter, Bud? Come down to earth, and have somethin' good to eat."

"I'm not hungry."

"You oughta be—it must take some energy to do all that heavy thinkin'. Here, just take one bite, and I promise you'll eat it all." He handed me the meat and I took a bite. It *was* good! Sam went on talking while I ate.

"I know there's lots to think about. It grates on me too, what's happened here. But death is always around the next bend; every square mile out here has drunk its fill of blood. This time I think more blood's goin' to run besides Kleki-petra's."

"More blood! Last night you asked me what should be done with Rattler, that drunken killer. Well, I'm asking you: What will be done, and what will happen to us because of him?"

"We talked about it last night."

"So, what's the verdict?"

"Verdict? You mean, we oughta try him and sentence him?"

"I mean just that."

"Do you now! And how do we do it? Send him to San Francisco or Washington in chains, charged with murder?"

"No, we can try him right here!"

"Ha! You mean the Law of the West; an eye for an eye like in the Bible, right? Well, forget it. We got no right to set up a court here, and anyway, Rattler is already sentenced, if I'm not mistaken."

"What do you mean?"

"I mean the Apaches will take care of him. I'm worried that they'll wanna take care of us at the same time, in fact I'm sure they will. They consider us all just as guilty as Rattler. When they do come, there'll be lots of 'em, a warrior-party."

"So, what should we do? We ought to leave before they come back, but we still need about five days to finish our section."

"Hmm-mm. Far as I know, ain't no Apache village nearby, but maybe there's a camp; it'd help to know if there is or not. I'd guess the nearest Mescalero settlement would be south, 'bout three days heavy ridin' from here. For Winnetou and Inshu-chuna four days—totin' the body will slow 'em down. Three days to ride back, this time to the end of the section, with a party of braves—that makes seven days! So, you could finish surveyin' and we could break camp and high-tail back to St. Louis with two days to spare. That's if my figgers are right, heeheehee!"

"And if they're wrong?"

"You wanna finish surveyin', that's a chance you'll hafta take. You wanna be safe, we'll leave right now!"

"I just think it unlikely that two high-ranking Indians would range so far from their settlement without warriors for company. So they might be back to take revenge sooner than we think."

Sam shrugged his shoulders. "You could be right. Only way to know for sure is to track 'em, see where they go and how far. And that's what I'm gonna do."

Will and Dick protested to Sam that he shouldn't ride alone, that they would both accompany him, but with a nod he indicated Rattler and his gang, and said, "You're needed here."

"It's dangerous to ride alone," said Parker.

"I'm takin' this greenhorn with me."

Bancroft walked up at that moment, and Sam had to explain what he was talking about. Bancroft grew red in the face.

"We need him to help finish the surveying!"

"Well, I need him worse—him and his bear-killer. There's four of you, and if you all work, you can get the job done by the time we get back—with good news or bad."

"What do you mean by that?"

"I mean Apaches are right behind us—that's bad—or we've got two or three days to pack up and get out—that's good."

Bancroft didn't answer, just looked grim. Sam went on:

"If there's two of us and we get jumped, there's a chance one of us could escape to ride back and warn ya." He paused. "And another good reason for takin' Bud along is to get him out of Rattler's neighborhood for awhile. You know that lad has it in for him, and will sure as hell start trouble again soon as he has a few drinks."

Nothing more was said for a minute or two while Bancroft thought it over. Finally he nodded.

"All right, he can go with you. When will you leave?"

"Sooner the better. Soon as we cut and roast a couple of bear steaks we'll be on our way. We don't wanna take time to make a fire while we're trackin'—it'd attract attention, anyway—and we won't have the chuck wagon with us, heeheehee."

While Sam and I broiled the meat, I asked him which horse he was going to ride.

"No horse."

"What then?"

"What a question! Think I'm goin' to ride an alligator or a bald eagle maybe? I'll ride my mule, my mule Nancy."

"Think that's wise?"

Sam cocked his head at me. "All right, Bud, out with it."

"Well .... I read that out here a man's life may sometimes depend on the horse he's riding. A horse's—or a mule's—neighing or snorting might betray a man's location to an enemy, maybe an Indian, that he was trying to hide from. And—"

"You read, you read!" Sam broke in. "If I wasn't a Westerner myself, I'd go back East, meet all those fancy people, and sit around and read all about Indians and about life out here in the Wild West. I bet whoever wrote what you read was never west of the Mississippi."

"Why do you think that?"

"I'll tell you why. Because a hand that's spent some time yankin' on a horse's reins, pullin' a trigger, grippin' a knife and swingin' a lasso is no longer fit for scribblin' words on a piece of paper. If he's really a Westerner he's forgotten how to write, and if he ain't, then he's writin' about things he don't understand."

"Well . . . I know of someone who's learning about hunting and tracking, and all the things a man has to know to be able to cope with life out here—a man who intends to go home some day and write about it."

"Yeah? Who's that?"

"Can't you guess?"

"You don't mean yourself?"

"Yes."

"Damnation! Why, Bud? Why d'ya wanna do it?"

I hesitated, asking myself why, trying to compose a short, easily-understood answer.

"Because I want to be a teacher for my readers, to tell them things I know that they don't know, and at the same time earn a living, make money by my writing."

"Hell! A teacher for your readers! Your readers won't learn anythin' from you, 'cause you're only a greenhorn, a greenhorn who doesn't know anythin' himself!"

"But, Sam, I'm learning, learning from you. And you can be sure I'll give you credit for what I've learned—I'm going to put you in the book, too. That should make you happy."

Hawkens jumped to his feet. "Happy, because you put me in the book? You mean to write about everythin' I do, put down everythin' I say?"

"No, not everything. But be sure I'll write about you with admiration and respect, just the way I feel about you right now. My readers will learn what an experienced scout, hunter, tracker, and all-around Westerner you are."

Mollified, Sam sat down again, and no more was said about my writing career. We finished broiling the bearmeat, wrapped it in leaves, saddled up and were ready to go. A last confab with Dick and Will about what to do if we didn't come back, or if only one of us returned, or whatever else might occur, and we started off.

We left in the same direction the two Apaches had taken, down into the valley and along the edge of the forest. Tracks in the grass could still be seen—they were obvious even to me, the greenhorn. They led northward, although we should be searching for the Apaches to the south. As we turned a bend we came to a clearing which looked as if it had been burned over. Here the trail curved in a wide sweep toward the south, the clearing becoming green again and opening out into flat prairieland tilted upward at the far end. Here too the tracks were easy to follow; the Apaches had apparently ridden around us.

When we came to the crest of this tilted prairie, a broad, level, grassy flatland lay before us, which seemed to extend southward forever. Although about 18 hours had passed since the Indians rode this way, their tracks ran in a straight line across the flatland. Sam shook his head and growled:

"I don't like this beeline-straight trail, not at all."

"Why not?"

"Well, as an old savannah-runner, I find it fishy. When two Indians leave such a plain trail, you better believe that they did it with somethin' unfriendly in mind. Like a ambush, maybe, 'cause they know for sure that we're goin' to follow."

"Hmm!" I hmmed.

"What?" asked Sam.

"I don't think there's a trap waiting for us."

"Got it all figgered out, have ya? Okay, tell me why not."

"Well, look. They want to get to their own people—they want to lead them against us as soon as possible. But they have a body with them—in this heat! Those are two good reasons for them to push ahead as fast as they can, for otherwise the body is going to putrefy, and also they'll be too late to catch us. So they wouldn't waste time covering their tracks or ambushing us."

"Hmm!" grunted Sam in his turn.

"Anyway, as long as we're here in the open we're okay. We can ride slower and more carefully when we reach the trees."

"Hmm!" grunted Sam again, sneaking a sidelong glance at me, "the body—you think they'd keep it with 'em in this heat, not bury it somewhere along the way?"

"No, no! The dead man was a highly honored person, and would have to be buried with all the Indian rituals. What they'd prefer best of all would be to bury the murderer at the same time. So, they'll try to preserve the body and hurry to capture Rattler and the rest of us. As I know them, that's what we can expect."

"As you know 'em! You're out here in Apache country for the first time! How do you know so much about Apaches?"

"From those books that you're so set against."

"Well!" Sam shook his head. "Let's ride on."

We came to a place where they'd stopped—grass was trampled down in a rough circle—and from then on the trail was triple; now they were riding side by side.

The prairie gradually narrowed to a strip of meadow with a scattering of bushes here and there, and a half hour later we reached a place where the bushes were thicker, and scrub oaks and beeches lined a small clear stream. We checked the area carefully, not approaching until we were convinced that the redmen had departed long before. We found a flattened patch of grass. It looked as if the Apaches had dismounted and made a litter for Kleki-petra's body, for oak branches had been chopped off, and twigs and foliage lay scattered about.

We rode on, and saw that it wasn't a litter, but a drag-sled they'd made, for now they were riding single-file, with a line drawn through the grass on each side. As there was plenty of room between the widely-spaced trees to ride abreast, I tried to think of a good reason not to, and finally it came to me.

"Sam," I said, "they built that drag-sled not only to make it easier to haul the body, but also to be able to split up without our noticing."

"Where'd ya get that idea?" he laughed. "Come to ya in a dream?"

"No, not in a dream—I'm wide awake."

"Then it's from somethin' you read in a book."

"It's not in the books—I worked it out myself. Of course the books helped; they teach you how to analyze evidence and come to a likely conclusion, like a detective."

"So tell me!"

"Well, why do Indians ride single file?"

"Nyah," Sam grunted, "it's true, most times so's anybody followin' won't know how many of 'em there are. But in this case I think it's only because of the dead man. One rides ahead to break trail, then comes the horse pullin' the drag-sled, and behind him the other rider, to make sure the sled holds together and the body don't slide off."

"Could be. But remember, they're in a hurry because they want to get back to us and Rattler, and finish us off. So one could ride ahead to muster the Apache warriors."

"Well, I don't believe it. I tell you that there's three horses makin' these tracks we're followin' right now."

Why should I argue with Sam? Indeed, I could be wrong. Yes, I probably was, because he was an experienced scout and I was only a greenhorn. So I said no more, but kept a sharp eye on the trail. We camped when it got dark, and started again at dawn.

An hour later we came to a wide flat watercourse, now completely dry, one of those ravines that drains the mountain snow-melt in spring and is dry the rest of the year. Between the two low banks were pebbles and gravel on a bed of fine sand. Less plain but still visible, the trail led across the ravine at an angle.

As we rode slowly across, I carefully examined the sand and detritus on both sides. If I had guessed right, here would be an ideal spot for one of the Apaches to turn off. He could ride up- or downstream for a short way, letting his horse step only on the hard pebbles, and disappear without leaving a trace. If the other continued on his way with the sled-horse behind him, one might take the tracks of two horses to be the tracks of three.

Back then I didn't have the sure eyes, the sharp senses and the experience I gained in later years. But what I was later able to state and prove, now I could at least suspect. That the small round depression I saw in the sand near the far bank was made by the rim of a horseshoe. Sam wanted to ride on, but I held him back.

"Ride upstream with me a ways, Sam," I said.

"What for?"

"For nothing, if I'm wrong—but maybe I'm right."

Staying near the bank of the dry gully-bed, we walked our horses slowly upstream. We hadn't gone more than two hundred yards when we saw fresh horse-tracks emerge from the watercourse and head southward across the grass.

Sam's small eyes seemed to retreat into their sockets, and he made a long face.

"What didja see back there that I didn't?"

"In the sand—a print of what I guessed was the rim of a horseshoe. But don't feel bad, Sam; it was very small, and I could have just as easily been wrong about it. Let's go back to the other trail and see if it's now being made by two horses."

We rode back and looked carefully, and sure enough, found that from here on only two horses were leaving tracks. Sam coughed a couple of times, scrutinized me mistrustfully from head to toe, and shook his head.

"It just flusters me," he said, "when I can't make head or tail of somethin'! A greenhorn comes out here to the West who's never seen the grass grow or heard a cricket chirp, and on his first scoutin' trip he makes old Sam Hawkens blush with shame. When I was as young as you are now I was ten times as smart. And now when I'm a little older I feel ten times as stupid."

"No, Sam, don't think that's so! It isn't that I'm smarter than you about the West—I just used logical reasoning to come to a conclusion. Logic—that's the key."

"What d'ya mean, the key to a lock?"

"No, I mean the key to drawing a conclusion."

"That I don't understand—it's too high-fangled for me."

"Well, I went at it like this: If Indians ride single file, they want to mislead possible trackers. The two Apaches rode single file, so that was their intention. I followed that idea and came to the right conclusion. You understand that?"

"Sure. That's easy enough."

"Look," I said, thinking to pull his leg a little, "I'll give you another example of logic. Your name is Hawkens, right?"

"Right!"

"A hawk is a kind of falcon, and falcons eat field-mice. Is that correct?"

"Yeah, if they can catch 'em, they eat 'em."

"Now you follow these facts to their logical conclusion. The falcon eats field-mice. Your name is Hawkens, meaning falcon, so it follows that you eat field-mice."

Sam's mouth fell open. He glared at me for a long moment and then exploded.

"Dammit, Bud, are you makin' fun of me? That's a insult! To say that I eat mice, and miserable field-mice at that! I've got a good mind to—"

I smiled placatingly and held up my hand to interrupt his tirade. "No, no, Sam, I'm not making fun of you—you know I have the greatest respect for you. You'll just have to get used to my sense of humor. I apologize if I've hurt your feelings, and I'll make it up to you in another way."

"How?"

"I'll make you a present of my grizzly bearskin; you know, the 'overcoat' you helped him off with."

Instantly his small eyes gleamed.

"Hi-ho, I accept! Thank you kindly, sir, thank you! Hooray!—you know what I'm goin' to do with it?"

"No, what?"

"A new huntin'-jacket, a jacket of grizzly-leather. What a sight that'll be! I'll tan it, cut it and sew it myself; I'm a top leather-worker. Look at the one I have on now, how well I've sewn and patched it!"

He indicated the prehistoric rag he was wearing, innumerable patches of leather sewn one upon the other, so that the entire jacket had become as thick and stiff as a board.

"But," he added in great delight, "I'll give you back the ears and teeth, and the claws I've already pulled. I don't need 'em for the jacket, and anyway, they're your vict'ry symbols. I'll make a necklace for you out of 'em—I know how to do that kind of work, too. Would you wear it?"

"I sure would!"

"Okay—both of us get pleasured, each in his own way. Now for all I care, you can say that I not only eat field-mice but rats too. And about those books—I guess they're not so bad as I thought, a man could learn a lot from 'em. You really goin' to write one?"

"Maybe several."

"And you're goin' to put me in 'em?"

"Not unless you want me to."

"Yes, sir, I do want you to! That's all I ask, please put me in your books."

"Good, it'll be done."

"But now, in those books, if you're goin' to tell about all the travelin' we did together, please leave out the part about my not see-ing this track branchin' off from the other one—it'd put old Sam Hawkens to shame before all your readers. If you'll just leave out that part, then I don't care if you tell 'em that I eat field-mice. Don't mat-ter to me what people think about what I eat, but if they take me for a Westerner who overlooks an Indian's trail, well, that would trouble me greatly."

"But, friend Sam, I can't do that," I said.

"No? Why not?"

"Because I have to describe everybody I write about exactly the way he is. So I'd rather leave you out entirely."

"No, no, I want to be in the books, in the books without fail—so I guess it's better if you tell the truth. If you tell the truth about my mis-takes, it'll be a warnin' example to your readers, who 're just as stu-pid as I am, heeheehee. Agreed?"

I nodded in assent. "Agreed."

"Then let's ride on."

"Which trail do we follow, the one branching off?"

"No, this one here, Winnetou's trail."

"Why do you think it's his?"

"Because the one who's hurryin' on ahead to assemble his warriors must be the Chief, Chief Inshu-chuna. What we wanna know is whether Winnetou made camp or not—that's important."

We rode on. About an hour before midday Sam called a halt.

"This is far enough," he said, "no sign that he stopped to rest; he rode the whole night through. Sure, they were both in a great hurry, and we can figger they'll be back on the attack before the five days we need are over. So let's us hurry too, if we wanta get back to camp to warn the others. We hafta have a serious powwow with Bancroft."

CHAPTER SIX

We rode back the same way we'd come, making better time because we were no longer tracking. When we reached the
where the Apaches had made the drag-sled, we stopped to rest and
refresh ourselves and our mounts.

Everything we'd had to say to each other had been said and we
felt no need to keep watch, so we stretched out silently in the grass
and shut our eyes for a short nap. We'd ridden long hours and I
should have been tired enough to sleep, but I couldn't stop thinking
about Winnetou and the impending encounter with him and his
Apaches. Sam was asleep as soon as he'd closed his eyes, as I could
tell by the rhythmical rise and fall of his chest under the leather coat.

Nancy was tethered out of sight among the trees and bushes, and
was munching contentedly on tender leaves. My roan, which I hadn't
yet named, stood nearby and cropped grass. Suddenly from the mule
came a short bray, a strange warning sound I had not heard from her
till then. Sam was instantly awake and on his feet.

"I heard my mule snort while I slept. There's a man or a animal
comin' this way. Where is she, where's Nancy?"

I pointed. "There, in the bushes."

We moved quietly toward her until we could see her through the
foliage. She was wiggling her long ears and her tail swept back and
forth. When she sensed that we were near she calmed down, and her
ears and tail were still. We continued on beyond her and peered
through the bushes and low branches. We saw six mounted Indians,

one behind the other, coming from the north, the way we were headed, and following the trail we and the Apaches had made the day before.

The leader, a small but muscular man, kept his head bowed and his eyes on the trail. All of them wore leather chaps and dark homespun shirts, and they all carried rifles. I could see knives and tomahawks, and their faces glistened with grease, over which blue and red stripes were painted.

I turned to run for my gun, but Sam grabbed my wrist and said in a normal tone, "What luck, Bud! This'll solve our problem."

"What do you mean?" I whispered. "And keep your voice down, they'll hear us."

"I want 'em to. They're Kiowas. The one leadin' is Bao, a brave warrior, but sly like his name, which means *fox* in their language. Now there's Kiowa Apaches and other Apache clans, cousins of the Mescaleros; but these Kiowas are a completely different tribe, from a different area. This tribe's chief is named Tangua. I know him well, though I can't say he's a friend of mine; I know him too well to call him friend, heeheehee. They're wearin' warpaint—must be an advance party, scouts probably, as there's only six of 'em. I don't know who they're on the warpath with, but it ain't us, that's for sure. Could be any tribe, even some other Kiowa clan or even their buddies the Comanches, 'cause they fight and steal from their own red brothers just like they do from the palefaces. Now just stay still, and don't say nothin' till I give you the word." This long explanation was spoken somewhat hastily.

The Kiowas were coming nearer. How six Indians, especially bandits like these, were going to solve our problem was unclear to me, but Sam must have a reason for saying so. For the moment, I was content to believe that we had nothing to fear from them. But now they saw our return trail overlaying the old one, and surmising that men were hiding in the bushes, wheeled away to take cover. Sam quickly stepped out into the open, made a trumpet with his cupped hands, and emitted a high-pitched vibrating sound I had never heard before. The Indians reined in their horses and looked back, and I stepped to Sam's side. He repeated the cry and made a hand signal, both of which they must have understood. They must also have recognized Sam's unmistakable figure, for now they came toward us in a gallop, as if they were going to run us down. We stood there calmly, and the six pulled up at the last moment, jumped from their horses and encircled us.

"How is it that we find our friend Sam here on the path of his red brothers?" asked Bao, the leader. He spoke fair English, but with a strange accent.

"We meet," answered Sam, "because Bao has followed my trail."

"We thought that your trail was the trail of the dogs we are searching for."

"Which dogs does my red brother mean?"

"The Apaches of the Mescalero clan."

"Why do you call them dogs?" asked Sam. "Is there war between them and my brothers, the brave Kiowas?"

"Yes! The war-tomahawk is raised between us and those scabby coyotes!"

"Ugh!" said Sam, using that Indian ejaculation I had never heard from him before, "I am happy to know that! Will my red brothers sit with us? I have somethin' important to tell them, somethin' that will help them against their enemies."

At first Bao did not reply to this invitation to sit and talk, but instead transferred his attention to me. "I have not seen this paleface before. He is still young. Is he one of the white man's warriors? Has he already earned a name?"

Had Sam spoken my German name, it would have made no impression. Instead he led up to the name White had coined for me.

"This young paleface is my dearest friend and brother," rang his answer. "He is a strong warrior among his people, and has just come across the Big Water. In his land are no buffalo and no bear—he had never seen these animals—but two days ago he killed two buffalo to save my life, and yesterday fought the gray bear of the Rocky Mountains and killed him with only his knife."

Bao spoke and signed a few words to his men. "Ugh, ugh!" they cried in admiration, and Sam continued exuberantly, "His bullet never misses its mark, and his fist has so much power that he strikes his enemy to the ground with only one blow. Because of this the white men have given him the name 'Old Shatterhand'."

So there I was, baptized again without my consent with that fighting name, the name I have carried from that day to this. It is common in the West for men to have such names—often men who are close friends for years do not know each other's real names.

Bao held out his hand to me and spoke with a smile, "If Old Shatterhand allows, we will be his friends and brothers. We love warriors such as he, who strike an enemy to the ground with one blow. You will always be welcome in the tepees of the Kiowa."

What he really meant was: We can use rascals who are strong like you are, so come along! If you help us steal and rob, you can lead a pretty good life with us.

I answered him in the same formal, dignified speech which I later became quite adept at using:

"I love the red men, for they are sons of the Great Spirit, who also numbers the palefaces among his children. We want to be as brothers, and stand together against all our enemies."

Bao's greasy, color-smeared face displayed a crooked smile, and he replied in kind: "Old Shatterhand has spoken well. We will smoke the peace pipe with him."

We all sat down in the grass by the streambank. Bao produced a calumet which gave off a sickly-sweet odor even before being lit. He filled it with a mixture of ingredients I couldn't identify, none of which looked like, or at a short distance smelled like, tobacco. He lit the pipe, stood up, took a long puff, blew the smoke toward the sky and toward the ground, and said:

"The Great Spirit lives there above us, and here on the earth grow the fruits and animals he has given to the Kiowa warriors."

Then he took four more puffs, blew smoke toward each of the four cardinal points, and continued:

"In these lands live red men and white men who have unjustly taken the fruits and animals for themselves. But we will search for them and take back what belongs to us. Bao has spoken!"

What a speech! Altogether different from other peace-pipe speeches I'd read about or heard since then. This Kiowa was saying in plain words that he considered the entire plant and animal kingdoms on earth to be the property of his tribe, and that it of course followed that robbery was not only a right, but a duty.

Bao, the fox, handed the reeking peace-pipe to Sam, who likewise took his six puffs and blew in the six directions, the while I wondered how he was going to respond. His speech was noncommittal.

"The Great Spirit doesn't look at the skin color of his children, but at their hearts. The hearts of the Kiowa warriors are brave and true. My heart is bound to them like my mule is bound to the tree where

I've tied her. That's how it will be bound for all time, if I'm not mistaken. I, Sam Hawkens, have spoken."

A genuine Sam Hawkens speech, greeted by a chorus of "Ugh! Ugh!" from the six Kiowas, although I doubted if any of them except Bao had understood a word of it. Unfortunately, it was now my turn; Sam handed me the pipe and I slowly puffed and blew the six obligatory smoke-clouds, trying simultaneously to compose a speech and to identify the pipe's burning ingredients. I guessed beet-tops, hemp, and powdered acorns, and then it came time for me to speak.

"The sunshine and the rain come from heaven, and from heaven comes all good things, all blessings. The earth takes the warm sunbeams and the wetness, and gives in exchange the buffalos and the mustangs, the bear and the deer, the pumpkin and the corn, and also the plants which the clever red men mix together to make *kinnikinick*, whose smoke coming from the peace pipe is a symbol of love and brotherhood."

Somewhere I'd read the Algonquin word for that peace-pipe mixture, and also that it was used by many other tribes. I hoped Bao and the others would be impressed by my using the word. In truth, my speech so far had been even less specific than Sam's, but I was just getting into stride, and felt more words bubbling up inside of me. I continued, unable to stop:

"In the west rise the Rocky Mountains, and the Great Plains stretch away to the east. The Great Lakes are in the north, and south is the Big Water. If the land lying between these four borders were mine, I would give it all to the Kiowa warriors, for they are my brothers. In this year may they hunt and slay ten times as many buffalo and deer as there are Kiowas; may their ears of maize grow to the size of pumpkin squash, and the squash grow twenty times as large. I, Shatterhand, have spoken!"

I stole a quick look at Sam; his mouth had fallen open, and his small eyes were round in wonderment. Bao had been whispering a translation of my words to the other warriors, and now their greased and painted faces glowed as if they had already received all the good things I had wished for them. No one, especially no paleface, had ever granted them such spoken abundance. They responded with a chorus of "Ugh! Ugh!"

Now that the formalities were over and the braves in a good mood, Sam began with a question:

"My brothers say that the war-tomahawk is raised between them and the Mescalero Apaches. This is the first I heard about it. When was the peace first broken?"

"As many days ago as there are fingers on three hands," answered Bao. "If my brother Sam was in this area then, he would have heard of it."

"Right. But the tribes have been at peace till now. Why have my brothers gone on the warpath?"

"The Apache dogs killed four of our braves."

"Where?"

"At the Rio Pecos."

"But your tents are not there, are they?"

"No—the pueblos of the Mescaleros are there."

"Why were your warriors there?"

Bao didn't pause for a moment to frame his answer, just came out with the barefaced truth:

"A band of our warriors set out by night to raid the Apaches and take some of their horses. But the stinking dogs were awake and resisted us—they killed four of our brave men. So now there is war between them and us."

So the Kiowas wanted to steal some horses, but were caught in the act and some of them killed. That the Apaches were in the right, trying to protect their property, didn't occur to Bao, and I was getting ready to point this out when Sam shot me a warning glance, and asked another question:

"Do the Apaches know that your braves are on the warpath?"

"Does my brother Sam think that we will warn them? We will take them by surprise, kill as many as we can, and take away as many of their horses and as much of their goods as we need."

I could keep silent no longer, although I tried to ask my question diplomatically, so as not to make them angry.

"Why do my brave brothers want the horses of the Apaches? I have heard that the Kiowas already own more horses than they need." That was pure guesswork, I had heard no such thing, but it brought the true story from Bao's smiling lips.

"My young brother Old Shatterhand has just come over the Big Water, and does not know how the people here live, nor how they think. Yes, we have many horses. But the palefaces came to us and wanted to buy them, to buy more than we can spare. Then they told us about the herds of Apache horses, and said they would pay the same price in goods and firewater for an Apache horse as for a Kiowa horse. That is why our braves set out to bring back some Apache horses."

So that's where the trail led! That's who was guilty of the killings, past and future! White horsedealers, who incited the Kiowas to steal and who paid with whiskey and brandy. I took a deep breath, preparing to embark on a tirade, but Sam put his hand on my arm just in time to stop me.

"My brother Bao," he asked quietly, "leads a scoutin' party?"

"Yes."

"How far behind are your warriors?"

"They are one day's ride behind us."

"Who's leadin' them?"

"Our brave Chief Tangua himself."

"How many warriors does he have with him?"

Bao hesitated a moment before replying. "Two hundred."

"And you think you can surprise the Apaches?"

"We will fall upon them before they know we are there, like the eagle surprises the rabbit!"

Sam slowly shook his head. "My brother is wrong; the Apaches already know that they will be attacked."

Bao sprang to his feet. "How can that be? Are their ears so long that they reach to the tents of the Kiowas?"

"It is so."

"I do not understand my brother Sam."

"Yesterday we saw two such 'long ears' who had been listenin' at the tents of the Kiowas."

"Ugh! Two long ears! Two spies, then?"

"Yes."

There was silence for a good minute. Then Bao spoke:

"If what our brother Sam says is true, then Bao must ride back quickly to tell Tangua. We will need more than two hundred warriors if the Apache dogs know that we are coming."

"My brothers the Kiowas have not thought carefully. When Inshu-chuna, the Apache chief, saw that four of your warriors had been killed, he knew that you would want to take revenge, and so rode to your camp and crept near your tents to hear your plans."

"Ugh! Ugh! Inshu-chuna himself?"

"With his son Winnetou; those were the two 'long ears' I spoke of. Kleki-petra was also with them then."

"Ugh, Winnetou too! If we had caught them, how we would have laughed to take the Apache dogs prisoner. But now they will gather many of their warriors to fight us. I must ride to tell Tangua, so that we can also bring more braves with us. Will our brothers Sam and Old Shatterhand ride with me?"

Sam only nodded.

"Then quickly, let us ride!"

"Wait," said Sam, "I have more to tell you."

"You can tell me as we ride."

"No, I must tell you now. We will ride together—not to Tangua, but to our camp."

Bao showed his teeth and spoke a few words to the others, who immediately drew their knives. Sam remained motionless, and following his lead, so did I, although my mind was troubled.

"What does my brother Sam mean by that?" asked Bao angrily, a question I was also silently asking. I was puzzled and uneasy.

"Listen, brother Bao, to what I have to tell you," said Sam, "Do you want to capture Inshu-chuna and Winnetou alive?"

"Yes, yes! How can we do that? And when?"

"I thought in five or six days, but now I think sooner."

"Where?"

"At our camp."

"Where is your camp?"

"You'll see when you ride with us—and I'm sure you will ride with us when you hear what I tell you now."

Sam related the whole story. Meeting the Apaches, the murder of Kleki-petra, our tracking Inshu-chuna and Winnetou, and the certainty that they would return to take revenge. Then he put in an additional twist:

"Yesterday it surprised me to see the Apache chief, his son and Kleki-petra ridin' alone without braves, and I thought they were huntin' buffalo and that their warriors were nearby. But now I believe that they were comin' back from spyin' on you. By this time Inshu-chuna will be at their camp gatherin' his braves, and as soon as Winnetou arrives with Kleki-petra's body, they'll return to our camp at top speed."

"Now I must ride," said Bao, "to tell our chief Tangua."

"Wait—there's more," said Sam. "The Apaches now have two battles to fight. Revenge on us for the killin' of Kleki-petra, and a battle with the brave Kiowas, who only want to revenge the killin' of their four warriors. They'll sure send a large party against you and a small one against us, and the chief and his son are sure to be in the small one sent to wipe us out. But they'll prob'ly number not more than fifty braves. And Bao! The large party won't find your two hundred warriors, 'cause they'll be hidin' by our camp, waitin' to surprise Inshu-chuna and Winnetou and their small party of fifty Apache braves."

Bao's face lit up with the dawn of understanding. Sam continued: "Now you see why I want to show you where our camp is, and then you can ride quickly and tell Tangua what I have said."

I was beginning to see a logical pattern in Sam's plans, although my mind still stumbled over several details. The Kiowas would protect us from the Apaches, but how could we protect the Apache chief Inshu-chuna and his son Winnetou from the Kiowas? Sam knew in what high regard I held Winnetou, and that I would fight to keep him from harm, for I had told him of the strange current that had flowed between us when we met, and of the wordless promise I had made to the dying Kleki-petra.

We all mounted and rode, not following a trail this time, but as speedily and as directly as possible. I tried to attract Sam's attention, to say a few words of protest or to hear from him a few words of explanation, but he deliberately ignored my surreptitious signals and rode close by Bao's side.

We reached camp at dusk and our arrival accompanied by six war-painted braves caused quite a stir. Luckily no shots were fired, and when Sam explained the Kiowa presence, and that their main force would be on hand to protect us from the Apaches, there was general rejoicing; we would be able to finish our surveying.

The six Kiowas were fed—there was still bear-meat a-plenty—and they rode off immediately afterward. They'd be riding the whole night, in order to bring the message to Tangua as soon as possible. Now I could learn in detail what Sam had in mind. He led me aside, away from the others.

"You don't look very happy, Bud," he began, "an' I can guess why. But I couldn't take a chance on explainin' my idea to you till Bao was gone."

"So, explain," I said, not very warmly, "it better be good. It looks like you're letting Winnetou, his father and the others fall into a trap."

"Yep, that's just what I'm doin'."

"And then what happens?"

"Well, first let's go back a ways to where I started thinkin' it over. I finally figgered Inshu-chuna and Winnetou weren't on a bear-huntin' trip, but had already called out their braves to get ready for a battle. So the Apaches must be nearer than we thought, and it's a good thing we tracked those two, to know that they split up and Inshu-chuna galloped ahead. Now I figger they could be back day after tomorrow, and two hundred Kiowas will already be here waitin' for 'em, and—"

I broke in. "I'm going to warn Winnetou about the Kiowas!"

"F'r God's sake, no!" Sam burst out. "They'll keep out of sight till the Kiowas leave, and we'll have them on our necks anyway! No, they have to be captured—Tangua will be sure to take 'em alive—and then we hafta free 'em. Without bein' caught at it, heeheehee! That way we get their thanks 'stead of their revenge. Though we'll have to turn Rattler over to 'em; there's no way out of that, if I'm not mistaken."

"You're sure this'll all work out just the way you planned?"

Sam came close, looked me full in the face, and raised his shaggy eyebrows. "Bud, I'm not even sure the sun's goin' to rise tomorrow—but this is the way it'll hafta be; there's no other way I kin see to keep the Apaches from wipin' us out, no other way of gettin' back on their good side. To do that, we have to set 'em free from Tangua, so they can get away and bring help to get *us* loose from Tangua. That's how old Sam's figgered it."

I was silent, trying to see the situation from all angles. Sam was right, I couldn't think of a good alternative. But I was resolved that come what may, I would not let Winnetou be harmed, even though I knew I might have to put my own life on the line. I held out my hand to Sam in assent, and said no more. He went off to confer with Dick and Will, and I tried to get some sleep.

"Old" Sam, he called himself. In spite of his leathery face, what I could see of it through that forest of a beard, in spite of his mountainous nose, scarred arms and calloused hands, he couldn't have been more than forty. But the adjective "old" had nothing to do with age here in the West—it was used in a positive sense, good old fellow, old prospector, an old friend—and in my own case, "Old Shatterhand"! Then there were others Sam had mentioned at my christening, Old Firehand, Old . . . . I must have dozed off at that point.

Up early the next morning, and under the pressure of danger I and the rest of the surveying crew covered twice as much ground as we'd ever done before in a single day. Rattler and his crew seemed rather subdued; they worked also, moving our camp ahead to keep up with the survey. There was little conversation and no drunkenness, and that night we all slept soundly. We all worked just as fast the next day—until noon, when our work was rudely interrupted by the arrival of some two hundred Kiowas.

They'd found us easily, following our survey stakes from the earlier campsite where Bao had left us. All of them were fitted out for war—fierce expressions on their painted faces, rifles, knives and tomahawks . . . they could have wiped out our entire party in seconds. Their leader was Tangua, the chief Sam had described to me, and he looked to be the fiercest of them all, with piercing vulture's eyes and a violent bearing which boded ill for Inshu-chuna and Winnetou, should they be captured.

He came as our friend and ally, but his attitude to us was anything but friendly. He spoke no word of greeting, only made a sweeping gesture to his braves without dismounting, upon which they immediately encircled us. Then he rode to our wagon and lifted the rear flap to see what was inside. It apparently was interesting, for he dismounted and climbed into the wagon for a closer look. If they stole from their red brothers, I thought, they wouldn't hesitate to steal from us. But I kept silent.

"Oho!" said Sam softly, standing by my side, "looks like he already figgers us to be his captives and our property his own. I'll soon change his mind about that."

"Easy, Sam," I said, "we're a little outnumbered."

"Outnumbered in numbers, mebbe, but not in brains. Come over to the wagon with me, and I'll show you what I mean." We walked leisurely over, empty-handed so as not to excite the encircling braves by carrying weapons. Sam spoke loudly through the closed wagon-flap.

"Does Tangua, the great chief of the Kiowas, want to go to the happy huntin' grounds before he's ready?"

Tangua stuck his head out immediately, and regarded us for a moment with those glittering eyes before answering. "What does paleface Sam mean by such a question? Tangua has many years to hunt and fight before he goes to the eternal savannah, where he will be honored forever as a great chief." To my surprise, his English was flawless.

Sam shook his head. "Many years? Only a minute."

Tangua threw back the flap, hand on tomahawk. "Is Sam making fun of Tangua? Will Sam send Tangua to the next life?"

Sam held up his empty hands and smiled. "No, Tangua will be his own enemy and blow himself to pieces, unless he leaves the wagon and listens to me."

Tangua jumped down and took Sam by the arm. "Blow himself to pieces? Why does Sam say such words?"

"Only to warn his brother Tangua, whose death waits inside the wagon."

"Death inside the wagon? Tangua saw only good things!"

Sam moved away from the wagon, and Tangua moved with him. I stood a little apart, listening carefully. "Have your scouts told you why we are here?" Sam asked.

"Yes, to mark a trail for the fire-horse."

"That's right. And the trail will cross rivers and climb hills, and go through forests and along cliffsides."

"Tangua knows that. What has it to do with his death?"

"More than you think. We must make the way easier for the fire-horse, and so we use gunpowder to blast away stumps and rocks and even cliffs. But not the same gunpowder you use in your rifles—this is giantpowder, many times stronger, and in- side the wagon is a great amount of it, enough to blow Tangua and us and all the Kiowa warriors into hundreds of pieces."

"Ugh! Ugh!" blurted Tangua, stepping back in shock, "was Tangua near this powder?"

Sam nodded. "So near that if I had not called out to warn him, Tangua would now be on his way to join his fathers. But he would be in many pieces, with no scalplocks, no medicine bag, and so could not be honored as a great chief, there in the evergreen savannahland."

An Indian who enters the happy hunting grounds without the medicine bag he carried in life, without scalps of the enemies he'd killed, would be despised by the hero-warriors who had preceded him. As Sam spoke, one could almost see Tangua's face grow pale under the warpaint.

"Then Tangua must tell all his warriors not to go near this danger- ous wagon."

"Yes, you must tell them! You see how Sam worries 'bout the well-bein' of Tangua and his brave Kiowas. He does so because he considers them to be his brothers, who will protect him and his friends from Inshu-chuna's Apaches. But Tangua should also treat Sam as a friend. He came with no word of greetin', no smile of friendship. Now is the time for Tangua and Sam to smoke the pipe of peace, Tangua for himself and his warriors, Sam for himself and the other palefaces."

This was a long speech for Sam, whose language when he spoke with the Indians was completely different from the way he spoke with white men. Tangua protested:

"Sam has already smoked the calumet with Bao, my scout!"

"Only Sam and this paleface next to me, none of the others. If Tangua doesn't want to smoke with Sam, then I must doubt that he considers us to be brothers."

It was evident that Tangua didn't want to commit himself to being our friends and allies. He made a gesture of negation.

"Tangua must first talk with his warriors." He led his horse away, and we saw Bao and a few of the others gather around him.

"If he wants to talk it over before smokin' the calumet, it's a good sign that he has bad intentions, if I'm not mistaken," Sam said to me. I'd kept silent during the whole exchange, but now I had to speak.

"But he calls himself your friend and brother!"

Sam laughed in derision. "Friend! The word means nothin' to these Kiowas. You're a friend so long as you got nothin' worth stealin'. But we've a wagonload of things they'd kill to get their hands on—food, brandy, guns, tools—and you can be sure that Tangua saw all them things afore I scared him off with the 'giantpowder' story. We're gonna be robbed, no doubt about it."

"Now?"

"No, for the moment we're safe. How everythin' else is goin' to turn out, I don't know, but we'll just have to change our plan accordin' to the way the wind blows. Here comes Tangua again."

I was about to say that I didn't know Sam's plan in detail, so wouldn't know how to change it, but kept silent as Tangua came up. "Tangua has spoken with his warriors," he said, "and we have decided to smoke the calumet as brother Sam suggested, he for his people and me for mine."

And so it went, the same smoke ritual as with Bao, this time without my participation. Which was just as well, that mixture had made me slightly ill. I had a vague idea that Tangua had agreed to this temporary truce, for that's all it was, because he needed our help and advice for the upcoming encounter with the Apaches. As it turned out, my guess was close to the mark.

CHAPTER SEVEN

N ow that there was a temporary state of neutrality between us and the Kiowas, we, meaning the surveying crew, could continue to work toward the end of our section. We wanted to get as far as possible before the Apaches arrived—in fact, Bancroft hoped to be able to finish before then, so he could pack up and head back to avoid the impending conflict. That is, if Tangua let him leave without first confiscating all those "good things" he'd seen in the wagon.

I of course had resolved to stay on the scene come what may, for Winnetou's life was my main concern. Sam came out to where I was driving stakes, and said:

"Tangua wants to have a powwow, to plan exactly how we're goin' to trap the Apaches."

"When?"

"Right now."

"Well, I want to be in on it because I have my own plans to work out. But we're moving ahead real fast now—I don't want to stop for a powwow. Can't he hold off till tonight?"

"He says, and he may be right, that the Apaches could arrive tonight, or even sooner, and he wants to be ready for 'em. But you don't really hafta be there; I'll tell you exactly what's decided, and then you can figger out how you want to play it."

"If I'm not at the powwow to put a word in, what they decide might not include details I need to be able to protect Winnetou and his father!"

"Leave it to Sam Hawkens, Bud. I give you my personal word that Winnetou and Inshu-chuna will be taken alive. It's somethin' I'm sure of, 'cause I know Tangua wants it too." He patted me on the back, grinned at me through the beard, and walked off.

I'd explained to Bancroft and the other surveyors that if we weren't through when the Apaches came, our bunch would be in the crossfire, and might not get through the mixup with whole skins. On the other hand, if we finished before then, we could save ourselves and hopefully some or all of our supplies and survey gear. So we all continued to work with renewed energy and efficiency. Naturally I said nothing about my own resolve to remain.

We quit only when it became too dark to see graduations on the levelling rod. It was a good half-hour's walk back to camp, and the powwow was just breaking up. Sam took me aside.

"Firstly," he said, "nothin's goin' to happen to your Apache friends. They'll be grabbed and tied up before they realize the Kiowas are here. We know for sure they're comin' from the east, cause they'll be followin' our stakes from the place they saw us last. And we're almost sure it'll be tomorrow night."

"But you can't be absolutely sure of that, you can only guess."

"Well, it's somethin' we have to know, and we can only find out if we send somebody back to listen for 'em, and return quick to warn us they're comin'."

"But they'd soon see the spy's tracks and be warned that—"

"Yep, if the spy was a red spy, an Indian spy, they'd be on the lookout. But if the tracks they see are a paleface's tracks, why that's just what they'd expect to find!"

"I see. And I guess the paleface spy is named Sam Hawkens."

"Good guess. And I'm gonna let 'em see not only my tracks, but me too, without lettin' on that I know I've been seen. It'll be an advance party of one or two braves, and if I just ride off out of sight leisurely-like before high-tailin' back here to say they're comin', then they won't suspect a trap."

"But that advance party will follow you, see the Kiowas, and gallop back to warn the others!"

"Oho! You think old Sam hasn't got it all figgered out? The Kiowas will be well hid and well away from camp, in a circle 'cept for an openin' to the east. When the scouts spy on us, all they'll see will be the same people that Winnetou and his father saw, goin' about their business. And they'll see us by the light of a few bright campfires."

"Then they'll ride back and tell the main body that all's clear and they can attack—is that it?"

"Right! But we'll hide a coupla spotters in the bushes on both sides of the stake-line, and when they tell us the scouts have left, all of us palefaces hafta melt away into the woods and let the fires die down. The Apaches 'll find a deserted camp. Not here, up ahead, where Dick and Will found a perfect place for everythin' to happen just the way I got it planned."

I felt a few scattered drops of rain, and Sam clapped his hands in glee. "That's a stroke of luck for our side, heeheehee! A good rain will wipe out all the Kiowa tracks around this camp; the grass'll spring back up, if I'm not mistaken. Now let's get movin', and pitch a new camp up ahead."

"Now? At night? In the rain?" For now it began to rain steadily.

"We hafta leave this campsite so it just looks like we were the only ones here. The rain'll do that for us. You're already staked out half-way to the new location, and I've got Rattler's crew so a'scared of what's gonna happen that they're doin' exactly what I tell 'em—they're breakin' camp right now."

I looked around and saw that it was so. They'd even gathered fire-wood, covered it with canvas to keep it dry, and were carting it to the new campsite a couple of miles ahead. Dry firewood was one of the most important details of Sam's plans, as he explained to me.

Wet and exhausted, we finished about midnight, and even keyed up as we were, nobody seemed to have trouble getting to sleep. The rain had stopped and the sun was out when we arose next morning. A quick breakfast, and we, the survey party, backtracked to where we'd left off and began working west again toward the new campsite. Sam Hawkens had disappeared and didn't show up until late after-noon, by which time we'd reached camp again and stopped work for the day, tired and sweaty. The Kiowas were still keeping out of sight, but we knew they had the camp and the stake-line to the east under close observation. Sam motioned to me and Dick and Will, and we all walked off to one side.

"Guess you know," he said, "I was back along the stake-line quite aways."

"Did you see their scouts?" I asked, "and did they see you?"

"See the scouts? I did better than that, much better. I saw the whole troop, not only saw 'em, but listened to 'em."

"Overheard them talking? How did you get that close without getting caught? And what did you find out?"

"I'll tell you the whole story, but first I've gotta tell the Kiowas. Get your gear together and stay close to camp." He jumped the small stream by the camp and vanished into the woods.

In camp we waited anxiously for his return. We neither saw nor heard him coming, but suddenly there he was in our midst, saying laconically, "Don't you boys have eyes or ears? I bet even a elephant could take you by surprise."

"You don't make as much noise as an elephant," I laughed.

"No, I don't," answered Sam, suddenly serious, "I just wanted to show ya that you can get pretty close to men, even Indians, without lettin' 'em know you're there. That's just the way I did it when I was at the Apache camp today."

"Tell us what you overheard, Sam!" I asked, burning with curiosity. All the others had gathered round, also curious, for their lives hung on what Sam had to say.

"Well, I'll tell ya! But I hafta sit down, I'm real tired. My legs are used to straddlin' a horse—or a mule, in my case—and I've been there and back on foot. On foot for about the last twenty hours, if I'm not mistaken. If I was a soldier, I'd pick the cavalry over the infantry, that's for sure."

He sat down near me, looked around at the others one by one, and said: "The fun begins tonight!"

"Tonight!" I blurted, half surprised and half glad that the decisive moment was almost upon us. "That's good, good to know when to expect them, although I wouldn't call it fun! What else did you hear?"

"Hm-mm. You sound like you can hardly wait to get into the hands of the Apaches," grunted Sam chidingly, but went right on. "You're right, anyway. It's good that we're no longer up in the air, and while we don't know exactly what's comin', at least we know when it's comin'. It ain't pleasant to wait for somethin' to happen that might turn out different from what you expected."

"Different from what's expected? What do you mean?"

"Easy, Bud, easy. What I overheard won't make sense unless I tell you what happened first. I left here while it was rainin', didn't hafta wait till it stopped, 'cause the heaviest rain can't get through this coat of mine, heeheehee! Went almost to the campsite where we met Winnetou and Inshu-chuna, but then I had to hide 'cause I saw three redskins nosin' around. Figgered they were scouts. They looked around awhile, but couldn't find anybody's tracks in the dark and rain. Dunno what tracks would've told 'em, anyway. The rain eased off, but it was still wet out in the open, so they sat down under a tree and waited. A good two hours, and I was waitin' too, under another tree, waitin' to see what was gonna happen next."

Sam paused and looked around at us for comments, but nobody said a word, so he went on: "Here come a troop of braves. It was just startin' to get light, and I could see they wore war-paint. Like I figgered, it was Winnetou and Inshu-chuna, leadin' about fifty braves, like I also figgered. The scouts reported to the chief, and went on ahead, the troop followin' slowly and old Sam Hawkens bringin' up the rear. Wish I always had as good a trail to follow like those damn survey stakes.

"They were movin' slow and careful 'cause they didn't know when they'd catch up with us. I stayed pretty close, and could see 'em makin' signs to each other, but nobody talked. They went only about three or four miles, then stopped, tied their horses and disappeared in the woods."

"And then's when you overheard them?" I asked.

"Yep. Like clever trackers they lit no fires, but old Sam is just as clever, and could get closer in the dark without bein' caught, crawlin' on my belly like a snake. Got close enough to Inshu-chuna and Winnetou to hear what they were sayin'."

"Could you understand everything?"

"'Course I could! How could I tell you what it was, then?"

"I mean, they surely didn't speak that Indian-English gibberish we use when we talk with them," I put in questioningly.

"'Course not! They talked Mescalero Apache, which I have a middlin' good hold on. It ain't a speechifyin' language, just as few words as they need to say what they wanta say. And from them few words I found out where we stand."

Sam paused. "So, out with it!" I urged him.

"Well, firstly, they plan to take us alive."

"Not kill us?"

"Oh, yes, they wanta kill us, but not right away; they figger to kill us little by little. They wanta take us to the Mescalero pueblos on the Rio Pecos, tie us to stakes and torture us slowly till we're dead."

Amid exclamations of shock and anger, Sam continued: "They got special treatment planned for Mr. Rattler, who's sittin' there so quiet like he ain't got a care in the world. Yep, he's gonna be spitted, staked, poisoned, stabbed, shot, broke on a wagon wheel, hung upside-down, one nice thing after another, but never enough to kill him, 'cause they want him to last a long time—and then they'll put him in the same grave with the man he shot, Kleki-petra, and bury him alive."

"Migod! Is that what they said?" blurted Rattler, his face white with shock.

"That's what they said, and you got it comin', if I'm not mistaken. With one pull of the trigger you put all of us here in the same spot."

Rattler jumped to his feet. "I'm not stayin'! I'm leavin' right now! They're not goin' to get me!"

Sam held up a warning hand. "Better not take a step outside of camp. I tell you that the Apaches are pretty close, somewhere inside the ring of Kiowas, and they'd catch you right away. You just gotta take a chance that you'll come out alive after it's all over—the Kiowas might save ya from the Apaches. But don't even count on that too much, heeheehee."

Of course none of them knew of the plan Sam had, to try to earn the Apaches' gratitude by setting Inshu-chuna and Winnetou free, hoping that they would return with a larger force to overrun the Kiowas, and incidentally to save us from being robbed of all our instruments and provisions. But the question of our surveying through lands the Apaches and other tribes believed to be their hunting grounds would still have to be resolved. Our situation was too complicated to even guess in advance how it was going to end.

Sam went on: "When I'd heard enough, I wanted to come back right away and tell you and the Kiowas about it, and get set for the Apaches. But at night it's hard to move without leavin' any trace, so I just stayed under cover till mornin'. Watched 'em awhile longer, but saw they were really waitin' for night like they said they would, so I made a big detour around 'em and here I am. All this happened about six miles back along the stake-line. But while I been talkin', and knowin' how Apaches think, I'm sure they've moved up close and are watchin' us right now. Now everybody should go about their business like they ain't got a care in the world," he warned, for some of the men had jumped up in alarm, "just take it easy, make a few campfires, and stay where you can be seen." The conference was over, and Sam drew me and Dick and Will aside.

"Didn't you let them see you, like you said you would?" I asked. "You said that was part of your—"

"I know, I know," answered Sam, "it warn't necessary." There was a shrill bird-cry. "Listen! That's a Kiowa spy, sittin' up in a tree. Told 'em to give me that signal when they see Apaches on the savannah. C'mon, Bud, let's gather some firewood."

I picked up my rifle and started to follow him.

"Halt!" ordered Sam. "Leave your gun here. I know that's not what I told you 'bout always havin' it with you, but this is an exception, for a good reason. We don't want the Apaches to think we suspect any danger. We wanta make it look like we're just pickin' up wood for the fire. Then they'll know we're settlin' in here for the night."

We walked out among the bushes along the edge of the forest and started to gather fallen branches. Apaches could have been hiding behind some of those bushes, and were, as a matter of fact. Winnetou told me much later that he had been watching from behind a bush not fifty paces from us. Today I would have known someone was there, partly by instincts I've since learned to sharpen, partly by close observation that doesn't depend solely on good eyesight, but also on attention to details like insect sounds and mosquito swarms. But then I was still a greenhorn.

We made several trips and gathered more wood than we'd normally need for one evening's camp. But Sam said, "We'll leave 'em wood aplenty, so when they see we're not there, not asleep in the tents, they can build the fires up high to look for us. You stack it around handy, Bud, I got somethin' else to do."

The evening meal was cooked and eaten, and we yawned and stretched and were off to bed, or so it would look to anyone watching. The fires were left to die down. It had been dark for about two hours when Sam reappeared, silent as a shadow.

"Two scouts are comin', one on each side," he whispered, and then began to talk louder, just small talk, motioning for us to join in. We went out and sat by the fire's glow and kept jawing, not casting any suspicious glances at the bushes round about. A half hour went by, and Sam finally said, "They've gone back by now, to say it's time to attack. The Kiowas are ready for 'em, and it's time for us to go. Rouse all the others, but quietly." Dick and Will silently entered the tents to wake the others, but I held on to Sam's arm.

"Sam, there's no way to avoid some bloodshed that I can see," I said, "but I'm still going to see that Winnetou and his father are captured without injury. Can I depend on you to help?"

"Sure you can. How d'ya figger to do it?"

"Well, we have to get to them before a Kiowa brave does. So we stay here when the others have gone."

"All right. What then?"

"I'll take care of Winnetou. You, Stone and Parker take care that no Kiowa gets to Inshu-chuna."

"Just one for you, and three of us for the other one? That don't seem fair, if I'm not mistaken."

Parker and Stone joined us. "There's just us four here now," said Will, "all the rest are with the Kiowas."

I told them what I wanted. "I can lay Winnetou low with one punch, if he's not expecting it. Then no Kiowa will have any reason to chop or cut him. But you three have to crowd around Inshu-chuna when the Kiowas attack, so no Kiowa tomahawk or knife can get to him. I know they want to take him alive, but they wouldn't hesitate to injure him during the capture."

"Okay, okay," Sam whispered. "Now let's get away from the fires. But not too far away—we gotta stay pretty close, and come in at the same time as the Kiowas."

We slipped off into the dark under the trees, and not a moment too soon, for the whole fifty-strong Apache troop ran in with wild war-cries. It didn't take long, however, for them to discover that the camp was minus all its palefaces. Inshu-chuna shouted one word which must have meant "fire!", for they piled on armloads of the abundant firewood we'd left handy, and the entire area became bright as day.

They were all afoot; they'd left their horses behind, expecting no mounted opposition. In fact, they expected no opposition at all, figuring to take us completely by surprise. But now Winnetou, displaying that quick analysis of a situation which I later came to respect and admire, shouted one word which I took to mean "Away! Away quickly!"

He and those surrounding him and his father started to run, away from the bright fires, but I was there before him. Three or four long strides brought me to the circle of braves running with him, and I swept them aside left and right. Sam, Dick and Will were right behind me. Not five seconds after Winnetou's shouted order to retreat, he and I stood face to face. We looked at each other for a long instant before his hand flew lightning-fast to his belt, to draw his knife. But my fist was already swinging toward his jaw. It landed—he staggered and fell to the ground. I turned and saw the three scouts holding Inshu-chuna fast.

The Apaches were howling in rage, but their voices were drowned out by the bellowing of two hundred Kiowas, racing into battle from all directions. We four had been the first to break through the circle of Apaches, and now we stood in the very center of combat. Two hundred to fifty, four to one! I spun like a top, striking as many Apaches as I could reach, some as they came at me, some as they fought the outnumbering Kiowas. I knew that those I could lay low would not be killed in the mêlée, although their eventual fate was of course out of my hands.

In five minutes it was all over. Only five minutes! But in such hand-to-hand fighting, five minutes is an eternity. Chief Inshu-chuna lay tied tightly on the ground, Winnetou lying next to him, still unconscious, but also bound. Not a single Apache had escaped; none had attempted to escape, for it wouldn't have occurred to any of these valiant warriors to desert their chief. Many of them were wounded, as were many of the Kiowas. Four of the Kiowas and six Apaches were dead. That hadn't been part of our plans nor the Kiowas' plans, who wanted to capture as many live Apaches as possible, but the Apaches' fierce resistance had compelled the Kiowas to use their weapons with greater force.

All the other Apaches were also bound—not a difficult job, for three Kiowas could hold a prisoner while the fourth tied him. The bodies were moved away, and as the Kiowa braves were attending only to their own wounded, we whites tried to examine and bandage the injured Apaches. With scant cooperation from them, as with good reason they considered us to be allies of their enemies the Kiowas. Fortunately, although some of their injuries were bloody and unsightly, none were life-threatening.

I wondered how the prisoners were going to spend the night. Tangua stood before me, and answered my unspoken question.

"These dogs are not yours, but ours, and I will decide what is to be done with them!"

"What then?" I asked.

"We should let them live until we have brought them to our village. But now we want to attack their pueblos, and we cannot take them along. They will die here, on the torture-stakes."

"All of them?"

"All of them."

"You said the Apaches are yours, but you are wrong," I said.

"They are mine!"

"No," I went on, "prisoners belong to those who have captured them. Take those that you and your warriors have overcome, but those we have conquered belong to us."

"Ugh! Ugh!" shouted Tangua, enraged, "you want Winnetou and Inshu-chuna to be your captives?"

"Exactly."

"And if Tangua does not allow it?"

"You must allow it." I spoke quietly but emphatically.

Tangua drew his knife, drove it into the ground to the hilt, and spoke through clenched teeth, "Try to take a single Apache and this knife will drive into your heart the same way."

It was said in deadly earnest, and I would have at least made a retort showing him that I wouldn't be intimidated, but Sam shot me a warning glance, and I kept silent. Tangua glared at me for a full minute, then withdrew his knife and walked away.

The bound Apaches lay on the ground around the fires, where they could be easily watched. But Tangua wanted to show me openly that he considered all of them his property, so he gave orders that they be bound to trees, upright. That was done, and not gently; the Kiowas used unnecessary violence, trying to inflict as much pain as possible. None of the captives let out a sound, or even grimaced. Winnetou and Inshu-chuna were handled with especial violence, fetters tied tight enough to draw blood.

Bancroft, Rattler and the others had slowly trickled back into camp after the sounds of battle ended. They spoke neither to us nor to the Indians, merely entered the tents in silence. We four remained in the open, lying by a fire not far from the trees where Winnetou and Inshu-chuna were bound. None of the Kiowas lay near us, and none spoke to us, for they'd heard the exchange between Tangua and me, and though we were not prisoners, did not consider us to be friends. It was as if the earlier peace-pipe ceremony was no longer in effect.

The camp gradually became quiet. Intermittent conversations died down, and except for a few sentinels posted by Tangua, the Indians slept. The campfires' faint glow diminished, and all was still. But the four of us were awake and alert, and now we spoke in whispers. It must have been midnight, or shortly after; there were still many hours of darkness during which we could try to free Winnetou and Inshuchuna.

"All four of us can't leave this spot together," whispered Sam, "one man could do it, or maybe two."

"I'm one of them," I immediately whispered back.

"Easy, Bud. The job is dangerous."

"I know it."

"And you want to lay your life on the line?"

"Yes."

"Well, you're a brave lad, if I'm not mistaken. But whether we get away with it will depend on who does it. If somethin' goes wrong, we don't get another chance."

"I understand that."

"You're still too new—you don't know how to move without bein' seen or heard. If you got caught, it might be the end for all of us. Be reasonable." It was a word I had never heard Sam use before. "Let me and Dick go."

"Let me at least try."

"Try? How can you do that? It's a yes or no job."

"I'll creep over to see if Tangua is asleep. If I get caught I can just say I was checking to see if the sentries were alert."

Sam hesitated a moment. "All right. But what's your tryout goin' to prove?"

"If I get there and back with no trouble, that you can take me with you to set Winnetou free."

"Hm-mm. If you make it, then we'll talk about it."

"Fine! Now can I leave?"

"Yes. But take care! If you do get caught, you'll be plantin' the idea, not now but later, that we cut Winnetou loose." I started to crawl away, but Sam grabbed my pants leg. "Use every tree and bush for cover. Stay where it's darkest. Move by feel when you can't see." He let go. I moved my knife sheath around to the side and crawled away.

I'd lied to Sam. I had no intention of checking to see if Tangua slept. No, I wanted to prove to Winnetou, by putting my life in jeopardy to free him, that I was really his friend, not the contemptible paleface land-thief he and his father thought I was. And I wanted to do it myself, alone, without Sam's help. I realize now how foolhardy I was then, how I was risking not only my own life but all our lives, including Winnetou's.

I'd read about stalking and spying, and heard some details from Sam and others in the months I'd been on this grand tour; now was the time to test whether what I'd read and heard had sunk in. I lay in the grass and wriggled slowly behind the nearest bush. It was about fifty paces to the trees where Winnetou and his father were tied. I should have moved supported only by my fingertips and boot-tips, but then I didn't have the necessary strength and endurance in my fingers and ankles that one gains by long practice, so I crept on knees and forearms. Before I put my arm down I felt over the intended spot to make sure there was no twig that might crack or dried leaf to rustle. It was slow work, but I kept moving.

The two Apaches were tied to trees on one side of a strip of grass. On the other side of the strip, about four or five paces away, a Kiowa sat watching them, his back against another tree. This was going to make my task difficult, if not impossible, un- less I could distract his attention.

I'd crept about halfway, and it had taken about half an hour. Think, half an hour for a distance of twenty-five paces! Just to the side I saw a patch of something slightly lighter than the near-total dark around me. I crawled a couple of feet sideways to investigate; it was a shallow depression filled with coarse sand, evidently deposited there in spring when the little stream overflowed. Although I'd rather have had pebbles, I stuffed a few of handfuls of sand in my pocket and crept onward.

Another half hour, and I'd reached a spot behind Winnetou and Inshu-chuna, perhaps four paces behind the trees to which they were tied, trees almost as thick as a man's body. I lay still, debating my next move, and watched the watcher. It was too dark to see whether his eyes were closed, but now and then his head nodded, so I guessed he was not entirely alert. Behind him and to the side I saw what looked like a bush, slightly darker than the dark background.

Keeping Winnetou's tree between me and the Kiowa, I crept up until I was directly behind it. Before I could free him I had to know how he was tied, so I felt carefully around the trunk and touched his feet and calves. He must have felt my hand, and for a moment I feared he'd react by sound or movement and betray me.

How little I knew Winnetou! Much later, when we spoke about his release, he told me of the thoughts that had raced through his mind. He'd assumed it was one of his Apache scouts or messengers who hadn't been with the raiding party, and who had now slipped in to free him. Feeling my hand, he expected to be cut free, but wouldn't have reacted, mainly because he had no intention of escaping before his father was also cut free.

I felt that his ankles were tied with rawhide, and a rope around the tree-trunk held them fast. So, two cuts were needed. Now I ran my hand carefully upwards, and felt his hands, pulled back around the trunk and tied similarly. A third knife-cut.

I cut the two lower bonds, but lying flat as I was, couldn't reach his hands to cut them loose without raising my body a bit; I needed two hands, to make sure I was cutting rawhide and not Winnetou. Now was the time to distract the guard's attention. I pulled out a handful of sand and tossed it toward the bush.

The sand rustled through the bush, and the guard turned his head and looked that way, but soon resumed his position. Another handful, and this time he rose and examined the bush cautiously; it could have been a small animal or poisonous snake. In those few seconds when his back was turned, I stood up, cut Winnetou's hands loose, and felt around the trunk for other bonds. There were none, but I felt the long hair cascading down his back, and on an impulse, seized a thin lock of it with one hand, cut it off with the other, and dropped to the ground again.

Why did I do that? It was an instinctive act, not a reasoned one; my subconscious mind must have inspired it. But now I held material proof that I was the one who had freed Winnetou.

To my relief he made not the slightest movement, but stood against the tree as before, his hands behind him. I wound the lock of hair into a ring and pocketed it. So that the Kiowas wouldn't know how he'd gotten loose, I gathered the cut pieces of rope and rawhide, crawled slowly over to Inshu-chuna, and repeated the same steps I'd taken with Winnetou. This time I saw, with my ever-sharper night vision, that the Kiowa's head was resting on his chest, so I tossed no sand, nor did I cut off a lock of hair. As his son had done, Inshu-chuna remained motionless.

Now I must make haste. I dared not be in the vicinity when the two Apaches disappeared and the alarm was raised. I crawled slowly away in another direction, where I concealed the cut bonds in a bush, poured the rest of my sand over them, and crept back to our place near the burned-out campfire. My three companions had been beside themselves with fear for my safety.

"D'you know how long you've been gone?" whispered Sam. "More 'n two hours. What took you so long?"

"Took a half hour to get there and a half hour to get back," I whispered in answer, "and I stayed there an hour."

"Why so long?"

"I watched Tangua the whole time," I lied, "to make sure he was sleeping. He hardly moved at all, so that convinced me he was really asleep."

"A whole hour to convince you?" said Sam disgustedly. "You're still a greenhorn, if I'm not mistaken."

"Maybe so, but I passed the examination, didn't I?"

"The tryout? Yes, you did—but you wasted good time, too. It's not as dark as it was, and that guard is still watchin'."

Part of what Sam said was true; now there were occasional breaks in the clouds, and a little starlight filtered through. I looked over at the trees, and could see that Winnetou and his father remained in the same position against them. But even at this distance I could see that the guard's head was still resting on his chest. It was now almost an hour since I had cut the Apaches loose. Why hadn't they slipped away? They could have been far from the camp by now!

The reason was suddenly obvious to me—each of them waited for a sign from the other that he had also been freed. And now I saw Winnetou make a slight motion with the arm nearest Inshu-chuna, and an instant later the gesture was returned. I turned to reply to Sam's last words. We were both still whispering, but in urgent tones.

"We still have to try to cut them loose, regardless of the risk. That was the whole point of my tryout."

"Tryout or no, Bud, it'll only take one of us, and I'm gonna be the one, that's final! You proved you can move quiet-like, but I still have more spy-savvy than you, and—hello! What in tarnation!"

He'd cast a glance toward the Apaches, and now I did too, and saw that they'd disappeared. The Kiowa guard hadn't moved.

"What is it?" I asked. Sam didn't reply to me, but nudged the other two. "Dick! Will! Look over there and tell me if my eyes are goin' bad—can you see Winnetou and Inshu-chuna?"

They looked, didn't see the Apaches, and said so, after which none of us spoke for a minute or two, digesting this new development. Not new to me, of course, but I was silent too. And then the guard must have opened his eyes, for he sprang to his feet and let out a piercing yell. The sleepers woke, the guard shouted a string of words in their own language, and the Kiowas clustered around the trees from where the Apaches had vanished. The four of us ran over there too. The Indians, all two hundred of them it seemed, were shouting in anger and surprise. Tangua appeared and gave orders, and his braves ran off in every direction to find and bring back the escaped prisoners. I cast a silent prayer heavenward that the two wouldn't be found.

Tangua was foaming with rage. He slapped the inattentive watchman twice across the face, tore the medicine bag from his neck, threw it on the ground and stamped on it. This denoted utter dishonor for the poor devil, dishonor forever.

The "medicine bag" of the Southwest Indian tribes has little to do with *medicine*, nor with the "medicine bundles" of other tribes. The word was taken from the white man's language to describe the Indian equivalent of the palefaces' magic powers. The pills and salves used by the whites were unknown to the red men, but each of them had in his medicine bag some article, a talisman which he had dreamed about during the drug- and fast-induced hallucinations which were part of his coming-of-age ceremony. This article—it could be a stone, a shell, a feather, or even something with intrinsic value—was always with him, as precious to him as his soul, and its loss was a loss of his manhood. So now this Indian was an outcast, a dead man to his tribe.

The chief's rage was now directed toward me. He came to me and shouted in my face: "You wanted to have those two dogs for yourself! So now chase after them and bring them back!"

I started to turn away without answering, but Tangua grabbed my arm.

"Did you hear what Tangua ordered? Find the Apaches!"

I looked him in the eyes for a moment, and remembering his fear when Sam mentioned the explosives in our wagon, pulled the sardine can from under my shirt and held it before his face.

"Shall I answer you with this? This is my medicine bag, and it holds my giantpowder, enough to blow Tangua and his braves into many pieces!"

My dangerous bluff worked. Tangua jumped back a few steps and cried, "Ugh! Ugh! Keep your medicine to yourself—you dog like all the Apache dogs!"

That was an insult I wouldn't have taken lightly under normal circumstances, but considering Tangua's rage and the fact that we nineteen whites were overwhelmingly outnumbered, I let it pass. We returned to our camp area and discussed the disappearance of the Apache chiefs without being able to explain it. I said nothing about my part in it, not even to Sam, Dick and Will. It was rather a source of satisfaction to me to be the only one in the world to know the answer to the riddle. I kept the lock of Winnetou's hair through all my subsequent travels and adventures, and still carry it with me today.

CHAPTER EIGHT

Tangua's anger and the enmity of his braves made all of us feel insecure. For that reason, before we went to sleep we assigned watches for the few night hours remaining. The Kiowas took note of this and also took offense at it, for they acted toward us with even more rudeness than before.

The last watchman woke us at daybreak. There was some commotion among the Indians. They evidently hadn't been able to track Winnetou and Inshu-chuna until it got light, but now they'd found the trail, and it led right to the spot where the Apache warriors had tethered their horses, certainly with one or two of their number to watch them. Bao, with whom I'd smoked the peace pipe a couple of days earlier, told us that they'd found the tracks of three or four horses, galloping off to the south. Strangely, all the other Apache horses were still there. Tangua flew into another rage because his men hadn't found the Apache horses and guards during the night search.

Sam Hawkens came over to me with a sly look on his face, and asked, "Can ya think of a reason why Inshu-chuna and Winnetou didn't take *all* the horses, or stampede 'em away so the Kiowas wouldn't get 'em?"

I smiled at him. "Sure," I said. "I can think of a couple of reasons."

"Oho! The greenhorn's got it figgered out already! Lemme tell ya, Bud, it takes experience to be able to answer that question right."

"Well, I've got it,"

"What? Experience? You? Where and when didja get it?"

"Not actual experience, maybe," I answered, "but experience out of those books you're so down on, enough to be able to figure out why the Apache horses are still there."

"Books! Books again! All right, tell me the answer."

"Like I said, there could be two reasons. One, Winnetou and Inshu-chuna will be back soon with a larger force, to attack the Kiowas and free the captives. Those captives, whom they plan on setting free, will need horses—why should they take the horses away and then bring them back again?"

Sam threw up his hands. "You're right again, I gotta admit it. And the second reason?"

"That took a little thinking through," I said. "Suppose the Kiowas don't wait for the Apaches to return, but leave for their own villages with the prisoners, to torture them there, slowly. They'd want to travel fast so as to outrun possible pursuers, and if the captives had to walk, that would slow them down. So, if there were no horses for the captive Apaches to ride, they might decide to kill them fast, right here and now, and then race for home. The Apache chiefs surely decided to leave the horses for that reason, too, to lower the odds against their own braves."

"Hm-mm, that's pretty smart thinkin', if I'm not mistaken. I get fed up with you talkin' about your books, and then you tell me somethin' that makes me admit they're not so bad. But there's still another possibility you haven't thought of—horses or no horses, Tangua might decide to kill his prisoners here anyway."

"No," I said emphatically, "that's not going to happen."

"No? Why d'ya think it won't happen?"

"Because I'm here, and I won't let it happen."

Sam's small eyes squinted at me in amazement. "Oh, you're here, and you won't let it happen," he repeated. "Sometimes I can't believe my ears are hearin' the things you say, heeheehee! The Kiowas are two hundred men, and you, one man alone, a greenhorn to boot, are gonna stop 'em from doin' whatever they wanna do?"

"Well, Sam, I hope I won't be alone. I trust that you and Dick Stone and Will Parker will be standing by my side if I have to take steps to see that such mass murder doesn't take place."

"So, you trust us to stand by! Well, we're all grateful for the trust of such a man as you are, if I'm not mistaken!"

"Sam, I'm speaking in earnest. When we're dealing with the lives of so many human beings, the joking has to stop."

His eyes shot sparks at me. "Damn! You really are talkin' serious! Well then, I'll have to look at the situation serious, too. We can't count on the others, there'll be just us four. Against two hundred Kiowas! You think for a minute any of us can come out of it alive?"

"I'm not thinking about how it might end—I just won't let forty-odd men be killed like animals while I'm present."

"If Tangua wants it to happen, it'll happen. And us four 'll be killed too, maybe. Or d'ya think you'll put your new name Old Shatterhand to use—use your fists against the two hundred?"

"Nonsense! I didn't give myself that name, and don't plan to use violence, anyway. There must be a way to outsmart Tangua."

"Maybe. But till we know what he figgers to do, we don't know how to outsmart him, right? Now, suppose he does wanta kill the Apaches, what would you do, f'r instance?"

"I'd hold a knife at his throat till he changed his mind."

"And really cut his throat?"

"Yes, if he doesn't do what I say."

"Goddam, you're a hard man! I think you really would!" said Sam, shocked. "But if you can get that close to him without any of his braves to stop you, he really might have to do what you say, to keep from havin' his throat cut."

Bancroft came up then, and asked me surlily to go to work. I left with him immediately—we couldn't waste a minute, if we wanted to finish before Winnetou and his Apaches returned. If we'd worked with this urgency from the very beginning, we'd have been back in St. Louis weeks ago, a fact I should have needled Bancroft with, but didn't.

We worked quickly and efficiently until noon, with few words being exchanged. On the way back to camp for lunch, we met Sam, riding his mule. He pulled me aside; the others went on.

"I rode out to tell you," he said, "that the Kiowas are makin' ready for a torture party."

"When? Right now? Or later?"

"Now, natcherly, otherwise I wouldn't have rode out. They're cuttin' stakes, gatherin' firewood—and they've collected all the Apaches in one place, tyin' 'em to new trees."

"Where's Tangua?"

"In the middle of his braves, givin' orders."

We were almost back at camp, less than a quarter-mile away. It had been moved up along our survey line by Rattler's crew, and the Kiowas and their captives had moved with it, to the edge of a forested area, there being mostly grass and bushes between where we stood and the new campsite. I could see some bustling activity but not much detail at this distance. One larger bush was about halfway between us and camp.

"We have to separate Tangua from his braves. Will you take care of that, Sam?" I asked.

"Sure, but how?"

"Just tell him that I have something important to tell him—and to show him, that'll help—and I have work that I can't leave right now. I'd like to get him positioned on this side of that big bush, out of sight of his warriors. I hope he's curious enough to come."

"I hope so, too. What if he brings some men with him?"

"I'll leave that to you, Dick and Will; I'll have enough to do, taking care of Tangua. Have some rope ready to tie them. It will have to be done as quickly and as quietly as possible."

"Okay. I dunno if what you wanna do is the right thing, but I can't think of anythin' better, so I'll go along. Don't figger on dyin' just yet. But savin' the Apaches, if we can do it, will sure save us from gettin' killed by the Apaches who are comin'. Hope Dick and Will see it the same way, heeheehee!"

Sam left, and I busied myself pounding nearby stakes a little deeper, so any Indians watching would think I was working. A few minutes later Dick Stone and Will Parker walked out to me.

"This is asking a lot of you," I began, "but if you want to back out right now, I can try to—"

"Back out? What do you take us for?" Will broke in angrily. "Think we'd leave a fellow-Westerner to do a job alone, a job we can help him with?"

"Right!" Dick Stone nodded. "I wanna see if we're the very four who can stand off two hundred Indians! I'm goin' to enjoy hearin' 'em yell, and not bein' able to do anythin' but yell!" He opened his shirt to display a bundle of rawhide thongs.

I silently touched hands with each of them, and went back to looking busy, keeping my back turned toward the camp. A minute or two later, Will called, "Get ready, Bud! They're comin'."

I turned. Sam was approaching with Tangua. Unfortunately, there were three braves with him.

"One man for each of us," I said. "I'll take the Chief. But wait till you see me grab him, and then be quick to cut off their wind so they can't yell to the other braves."

I walked with leisurely steps to meet the group coming toward us, Dick and Will following right behind me. I'd mentally calculated the position, distance and timing so we'd meet where the big bush cut off the view from camp. The chief wore an enraged expression, and growled at me:

"The paleface named Old Shatterhand called Tangua to come to him. Did you forget that he is the Chief of the Kiowas?"

"No."

"Then you know that you should come to him, not call him to come to you. Speak quickly, Tangua has much to do."

"May Old Shatterhand ask what is it you have to do?"

"We want to hear the Apache dogs howl as they slowly die."

"When?"

"Now."

"Why so soon? We thought you would take the captives to your wigwams to kill them, so your squaws and children would also hear them howling."

"We wanted to, but we are on the warpath, and the dogs would be in our way. So we will kill them now."

"I ask you not to do it."

"Tangua does what Tangua wants to do, and what the paleface asks has as little power to change him as the wind in the trees." His voice shook with anger.

"They came into your hands only through our help, so we have the same rights over them as you have. We wish that they not be killed."

"Wish, wish, you paleface dog! Tangua spits at your words!" He spat on the ground in front of me and started to turn away. I swung my fist and knocked him down. But he wasn't out, his skull was harder than I thought, and he got up again. It took a second punch to put him away, and in that extra second or two my attention was diverted from the others. I looked to see Sam kneeling on one Indian, hands on his throat, while Dick and Will were tying the hands of a second. The third one was running toward camp, yelling. I jumped to help Sam, and we tied his Kiowa too.

"What happened?" I asked, looking to make certain Tangua was still out. "Why did you let the third one get away?"

"Dick and I both went after the same brave," answered Parker, "and the other one ran off before we could grab him."

"Don't make much difference," said Sam, "the picnic'll just start a little sooner. The red men'll be here in two or three minutes—let's get out in the open, where none of 'em can sneak up on us." We tied the still-unconscious Tangua and dragged all three Kiowas out onto the plain. "Let me talk to 'em," Sam went on, "what I can't say in Kiowa I can say in sign language. But watch careful for my signal—then hold the knife at the Chief's throat like you're gonna kill him."

He had no sooner said that than we heard wild angry howling, and a second later saw the horde of Kiowas rounding the bush where we'd overpowered the Chief and his men. Now they saw us and ran toward us with even louder screeching. Some ran faster than others, so they were strung out, not bunched together. This made it easier for Sam to halt them by running a few steps toward them, holding his arms wide in the universal 'STOP!' gesture. He also shouted something I couldn't understand. He repeated it, and the nearest Indians stopped, the others straggling to a halt behind them.

We saw Sam speak to them and make several signs. Suddenly he turned and pointed to us with a stabbing gesture, and we held Tangua upright. I put the knife to his throat. The Indians let out cries of rage.

Sam continued speaking to them. Presently Bao, the fox, left the others and came up to us with Sam, who pointed to our three captives and said, "You see I have spoken the truth."

Bao looked grimly at the three. "The two tied warriors are alive, but the Chief looks like he is dead."

He's not dead," said Sam. "Old Shatterhand's fist has put him to sleep. He'll come to in a minute, and we'll talk. But if any of the Kiowas lifts a weapon to us, Old Shatterhand's knife will cut Tangua's throat."

"Why do you act as enemies to us who are your friends?"

"Friends? You yourself don't believe that!" cried Sam.

"Yes, yes! Did we not smoke the peace pipe together?"

"Yes, and then your Chief insulted Old Shatterhand, so we can no longer treat the Kiowas as brothers—see, Tangua begins to move!"

Tangua, whom Dick had gently laid down on the ground again, opened his eyes and looked at each of us in turn, apparently trying to analyze the present situation. Then he seemed to return to full consciousness.

"Ugh! Ugh!" he began. "Old Shatterhand struck Tangua down. Why is he tied? I order that the ties be taken off!"

"You took no notice of my request, so now I take no notice of your command," I retorted quietly.

"Tangua demands to be set free! If you do not untie him, his braves will kill all of you!"

"There stand your braves," I said. "If any of them takes a step toward us, this knife will take your life." I held the blade against his throat.

He was silent for a moment, trying to decide whether I was in earnest. Then: "What do you want from Tangua?"

"Nothing more than what I asked you before. The Apaches are not to die on the stakes."

"You are asking that they not be killed at all?"

"Later you can do with them what you will. But they are not to be killed while we are still here."

Again he was silent, this time for several minutes, during which time, even through the warpaint, one could see expressions of rage, hate and helplessness pass across his face. Suddenly he gave in—with a stipulation.

"Tangua will promise not to kill the Apache dogs if you are willing to fight for their lives."

"Fight with whom?"

"With one of our warriors, one Tangua will choose."

"With what weapons?"

"Only a knife. If he kills you, then the Apaches will die. But if you kill him, they stay alive."

It was certain that he had some thoughts he wasn't revealing. He probably rated me as the most dangerous of all the white men present and wanted to render me harmless. It was clear as day to me that whoever he picked for me to fight would be a master in knife-fighting. But even knowing that, I didn't, I couldn't, hesitate.

"I accept," I said. "We will agree on the conditions, and together take an oath over the peace pipe. The fight can take place right afterwards."

"What're you thinkin' of, Bud?" cried Sam at this point. "I can't believe that you're stupid enough to take him up on it!"

"Sam, old scout, it's not stupidity," I replied.

"Oh yes it is! In an even fight you'd have an equal chance, but that ain't the case here! Have you ever fought with a knife before, fought for your life?"

"No."

"There you have it! You'll be up against a master of knife-fightin', if I'm not mistaken. And think about the unfair odds between winnin' and losin'! If you die, the Apaches die too; but if the man you're fightin' dies, then who dies? Only one man!"

"But the Apaches get their lives, for the time being, anyway."

"D'ya really believe that?"

"We're going to agree on it over the peace pipe, which is just like swearing an oath."

"The devil will swear an oath out loud, with a hundred silent noes and maybes behind it! And even if he did mean it honestly, you're still a greenhorn who doesn't have a chance—"

"Leave off with the 'greenhorn', Sam," I interrupted. "I've proven to you several times that this greenhorn usually knows what he's doing."

He continued to protest in spite of what I said, and both Dick and Will also tried to dissuade me. But I stuck with my decision, and they finally gave up.

"Okay, thickhead! But I'm goin' to see to it that everythin' goes fair and square, and I'll shoot anybody who tries to cheat our side, shoot him with my Liddy!"

Now the following was agreed: On a grassless spot nearby a figure eight would be marked in the dirt, or better described, two circles which slightly overlapped. Each fighter started in one of the circles, and during the fight could not step outside them. No quarter would be given—one of us must die—and no revenge would be taken on the victor by friends of the loser.

All this was agreed to with my knife still at Tangua's throat. Not until then did I cut his bonds and smoke the calumet with him. We released the other two, and the four red men returned to the Kiowa camp to tell the others what had taken place and what was about to take place.

The Chief Engineer and the other surveyors upbraided me for being a foolhardy idiot, but I paid them no mind. Sam, Dick and Will were also dead set against my plan, but they reproached me no more. Sam only said with concern:

"Tell me, what do you get out of it if you're stabbed in the heart? What's in it for you except dyin'?"

"That's all, simply dying, nothing more."

"Nothin' more? Don't joke about it, Bud. That's all there is. When you're dead, you're dead forever. I'm sick in my heart, 'cause it's almost sure that you're gonna be killed. What am I goin' to do out here in the West without a greenhorn to pick on, to quarrel with? In all my livin' days I'll never be able to find another greenhorn as easy to get along with as you."

"This fight might not end the way you seem to believe. There might be a way to end it with both of us still alive."

"Are you thinkin' what I think you're thinkin'? I know you have a good heart and wouldn't like to kill a man. I hope ya don't have a secret plan to just wound the man you're fightin'."

"Suppose I do just wound him? I mean, injure him so that he can no longer fight?"

"No, Bud, you agreed to the conditions; one of you must die. If he's only wounded and he can't fight, then you'll have to fight somebody else, and another and another, until one of you is dead. If you wound him, then ya gotta kill him. Don't let your conscience bother you—remember, all these Kiowas are thievin' scoundrels, and that they're to blame for everythin' that's happened, 'cause they tried to steal Apache horses! If you can kill such a one, you're doin' the world a favor—and you're savin' the lives of many brave Apaches besides. So don't think about sparin' him, he won't try to spare you. Look, here they come!"

All the two hundred Kiowas, except for a few guarding the prisoners, were now approaching. Tangua led them and us to the duel-field, where two circles had already been scratched in the ground. Then he gave a signal, and a warrior stepped out from the crowd of red men, a warrior as tall as me. Laying all his weapons aside except for his knife, he stripped to the waist, displaying the physique of a Hercules. Any other opponent, looking at those rippling muscles, would surely quake with fear; but I composed myself, for I knew it would not be simple strength that would win this fight, but guile and speedy reflexes.

Chief Tangua led him into the circle of spectators that had formed, our surveyors and the other whites among them, and cried loudly: "Here is Metan-akva, the strongest warrior of the Kiowas, whose knife has eaten every enemy who stands against him. He will fight with the paleface Old Shatterhand until one of them is dead! Tangua has spoken!"

"Damnation!" whispered Sam to me, "he's a real Goliath! And his name, Metan-akva, means somethin' like 'lightnin'-knife'. I better say goodbye to you, Bud; it's all up with you." He looked at me with moisture in his tiny eyes.

"Nonsense!" I replied, "of course Tangua would pit me against a strong skilled knife-fighter who's never been bested. But I'm smarter than he is, smarter than any of those he's killed. Don't say goodbye to me just yet, old Sam Hawkens, not just yet."

During this quiet conversation I'd also stripped to the waist and handed my revolvers and bear-killer to Sam. I felt calm and confident, and turned to face Metan-akva.

He swept me with a gaze of contempt, and said in passable English, "The paleface's body shakes with fear. Is the weakling afraid to step into his circle?"

As he finished this short speech, I quickly stepped into the southernmost circle, with the clear intention to have the sun at my back and in Metan-akva's eyes. Was that taking unfair advantage? I think not— I was angry under my calmness because he had lied about my shaking with fear. Now was no time for polite dueling ritual; one of us must die, and every slight advantage I obtained would help to determine that he would be the one. It was necessary to remain cool and cold-blooded, in spite of Metan-akva's name and appearance. Although I had never fought with a knife before, I was quite a good fencer; that lent me confidence.

"He's really going to risk it!" laughed the Indian derisively. "My knife will eat him. The Great Spirit took away his mind, and so gave him into my hands."

Among Indians these insulting exchanges are customary before a conflict, and I would have been considered a coward if I hadn't replied. So I answered him in kind:

"You fight with your mouth, but I stand here with my knife. Take your place in the circle, if you're not afraid!"

He took a great spring into the other circle and screamed in anger, "Afraid? Metan-akva afraid? Did you hear that, you Kiowa warriors? I'll take this white dog's life with the first stab!"

"My first stab will take yours!" I retorted. "Stop talking and fight! You should be named 'Boaster', not Metan-akva!"

"Boaster, boaster!" he roared. "This stinking coyote dares to call Metan-akva by that name! Watch! In two minutes the vultures will be eating his guts!"

It wasn't very clever of him to make that threat, downright stupid in fact, for it told me that he intended not to stab, but to disembowel me. I saw how he held his knife, the cutting edge upward, his thumb and forefinger near the blade, obviously ready for an upstroke.

So I knew what he intended, but not when. Timing was even more important than positioning, and it was vital to keep my eyes on his eyes rather than on his weapon. There is a signal called the "tremor of intent," a lightning-quick eye-flash or facial tic which occurs just before any abrupt action. I lowered my eyelids to give my opponent more confidence, but observed him sharply through my lashes.

"Stab, stab, you paleface coward," he challenged.

"Stop your chattering and start fighting, little boy," I returned. I wanted him to make the first move, and that was an insult which would surely trigger it. An instantaneous flash in his eyes warned me to get ready. In the next second he thrust forward and upward to slit my torso open. Had I been awaiting a thrust from above it would have been my finish, but I twisted to avoid his knife, and quick as thought thrust mine forward, cutting his forearm open from wrist to elbow as he completed his futile stroke.

"Scabby dog!" he roared, pulling his arm back in shock and pain, and letting his knife fall to the ground. I didn't reply, just lifted my arm and drove the blade up to the hilt into his heart, withdrawing it immediately. So exact was the stroke that a pencil-thin stream of blood spurted from the wound. Metan-akva swayed back and forth for a moment, tried to speak but could only sigh, and fell to the earth, dead.

The Indians raised a deafening, furious yowling, in which one of them, Tangua, did not join. He came over, kneeled by Metan-akva's body, felt the wound, stood up and considered me with an ominous glare which I remember to this day. It held a mixture of rage, shock, fear and admiration. Without a word he started to leave, but I held him back.

"Will you not say now who has won?" I asked him.

"You, you have won," he said, and took a few steps before turning again to look at me. "You are a white son of the Evil Spirit," he hissed, "and our medicine man will take away your magic. Then you will give up your life to us."

"The medicine man can do what he will," I answered, " but you must keep your word, your promise."

"What word?"

"That the Apaches will not be killed."

"They will not be killed; Tangua keeps his promise."

"Then I and my friends can untie them from the trees?"

"We will untie them when the time comes."

"Now is the time! I have won the fight, and—"

"Silence!" he spat out. "I will say when the time has come, and it is not yet. We did not speak of time. The Apaches will not be killed, but we can let them die without food and water."

"Liar! Cheat!" I shouted in his face. He stepped back and pulled the tomahawk from his belt. "Stay away from Tangua!" he warned, "or he will cut off your head."

I stared at him long and threateningly until he dropped his eyes, probably in fear of the evil magic in mine.

"I will talk with my white brothers about your promise"—I spat out the word—"and about your Apache prisoners. Do not try to betray us again with your lies. Remember that we can blow all the Kiowas to pieces with our giantpowder."

After these words I left the circle and went to Sam. He hadn't heard the exchange between Tangua and me because of the Indians' continuing howls of anger and dismay. He ran to meet me, shouting with delight:

"Welcome back, Bud, welcome back from the dead! Man, friend, greenhorn, what kinda man are you? Never saw a buffalo before, and kills two of the biggest; never saw mustangs before, and culls my Nancy out of a herd of 'em; never saw a grizzly, but kills one with only his knife, and with the same knife kills the biggest, baddest Indian knife-fighter I ever saw, without losin' a drop of his own blood! Dick, Will, come look at this young surveyor-lad from another country. What'll we do with him?"

"Well, for one thing," chuckled Will Parker, "we can stop callin' him 'greenhorn'. Think he rates pretty high as a regular Westerner, even without havin' the years of experience it usually takes." That was the longest speech I'd ever heard Will make.

"Not call him 'greenhorn' any more? I dunno, I'd have to twist my thinkin' out of kilter to change that. I simply gotta have a greenhorn to pick on, even if we all know he's learned a lot and learned it fast. But now, with our greenhorn's fist and knife, we've saved the lives of the Apaches!"

"I'm afraid that's where you're mistaken," I put in, "the Chief had some mental reservations when he gave his promise." I told them what Tangua had said, and Sam stamped on the ground in rage. He went off to talk to Tangua, and I took the time to wash off the sweat and stains of battle, dress again, and shove knife and revolvers back into my belt.

CHAPTER NINE

The Kiowas had been certain that I would be knifed to death by Metan-akva. They'd been disappointed by the quick and unexpected end of the duel, and were doubly angry with us whites because of it. They would have enjoyed nothing more than to quickly kill us all. Only one thing kept them from it—the fact that it had been ritually agreed by their Chief over a calumet that revenge would not be taken on the victor and his party.

Sam returned from the Kiowas, his anger changed to disgust. "They're holdin' a ceremony over 'Lightnin'-knife', and that red bastard Tangua wouldn't even talk to me. He thinks he's just goin' to let the Apaches die of thirst and starvation, does he? And he calls that 'not killin' 'em'. Well, we'll just keep a sharp eye open, and find some way to derail him, heeheehee!"

"Yes, if we don't get derailed instead," I said. "It's not easy to protect others when you need protection yourself."

Sam grinned at me. "I can't believe you're afraid of the red men."

"Bah! I retorted. "You know damn well, I'm just as little afraid of them as you are."

"'Course I know it, I'm just funnin'." His voice and manner turned serious. "What're you really thinkin' right now—is it givin' you shivers inside?"

"Is what giving me shivers?"

"The knife fight. The fact that you killed a man."

I mulled it over for a minute. "No shivers. It was something that had to be done, so I did it."

Sam shook his head. "Cold-blooded. Tell me, Bud, over there in the old country, didja ever kill a man? Didja ever kill a man before, anywhere?"

"No, never."

"Then today you killed your first man. What does it make you feel like inside, that's what I wanta know."

"Hm-mm. It isn't a very pleasant feeling, and it won't be easy to forget. I hope I don't ever have to kill another man."

"Ho! Don't get any fixed idee about that. Here in the West it could happen any day, even every day, that you'd have to kill a man to keep from bein' killed yourself. In such a case—hey, it's gonna be such a case right now! Here come the Apaches! Now there'll be buckets of blood! Get ready, Mesh-shurs, and try to keep any of that blood from bein' yours!"

From the direction where the captives were tied came a shrill ululation, a drawn-out "Hiiiiiiiiii," the Apache war cry. I'd heard it once before, when fifty ran into the Kiowa ambush, but this time it came from hundreds of throats, and it was a sound to curdle the blood, to terrify the bravest heart. Winnetou and Inshu-chuna had returned with their warriors sooner than expected. An instant later the cry came again, louder and shriller, and from all around us—we were encircled!

The four of us were still out on an open grassy area, but there were many bushes round about, and Apaches had taken cover behind them until the raid started. Now they were coming in from all sides, some toward us, some running past us. The Kiowas were shooting at them, and we could see some Apaches go down.

"Don't kill any Apaches!" I shouted to the three scouts, as hand-to-hand fighting grew thicker around us. We took no part in it, just tried to avoid being killed. In so doing, we had to dodge, punch and strong-arm those Apaches who attempted to attack us, lucky to escape being cut by flashing knives and tomahawks. We saw Bancroft and the other three surveyors run out and join the battle—the poor devils were only trying to protect themselves, but they were cut down immediately. It was shocking to see men die, men with whom I had been living and working for months, but now was no time for reflection.

Sam yelled: "Run! Run back there to the big bush!" He meant the bush where we had dealt with Tangua, and we all ran toward it, still dodging and punching our way past Apaches, or using our gunstocks as clubs. I'd hesitated a moment, looking back with a futile thought that I could help the whites, so I was bringing up the rear. The others had already rounded the bush, and suddenly, standing between me and it, was Inshu-chuna, holding the barrel of his Silver-rifle like a club.

"The land-thief!" he shouted in my face, and swung the rifle at me. I dodged, and shouted back that I was not his enemy, but he paid no heed, and kept trying to club me. There was no help for it; if I wanted to keep from being killed I'd have to resist. I threw down my bear-killer, with which I'd been warding off his blows, grabbed him by the throat with one hand and knocked him down and out with the other.

From behind me came a joyful shout: "It's Inshu-chuna, Chief of the Apache dogs! Tangua must have his scalp!"

I turned and saw Tangua, who'd chanced to run in the same direction, throw down his gun and pull the knife from his belt. He swept past me and knelt by the unconscious Apache Chief. I bent and grabbed his arm.

"Don't touch him!" I yelled. "I defeated him, he's mine!"

"Silence, paleface!," he hissed, and shook off my arm. "The Chief belongs to me!" He swept up the knife and stabbed me in the left wrist, but I was able to drag him a few feet away and throttle him with my right hand until he stopped struggling. I bent to look at Inshu-chuna, whose face was smeared with blood from my hand-wound. At that moment I heard a sound behind me and started to turn. That movement saved my life; I took a terrible blow on the left shoulder, one which would have split my skull had it landed there. The one who dealt it was Winnetou.

He'd been following his father, but wasn't near enough to see the lightning-swift events of the previous minute. He'd seen me kneeling by his unconscious blood-spattered father and had tried to club me on the head. Now he drew his knife and came at me like a madman.

I was in bad shape. The violent shoulder-blow had affected my whole body, and my left arm was useless. There was no time to explain, no time for a word. Winnetou stabbed at my heart; had I not moved slightly, that would have been my finish. The knife pierced my breast pocket, hit the sardine can where I kept my papers, and was deflected upward inside my jawbone into my mouth and through my tongue.

Winnetou withdrew it, grabbed my throat with his left hand and stabbed at me again. Mortal fear doubled my strength. I could use only my right hand and arm, and I seized his knife-hand and squeezed it until the pain made him release the knife. Then I quickly grasped his left arm by the elbow and twisted it upward to make him release his hold on my throat. I kept twisting, put one leg around his and tripped him face-down on the ground, now holding his left forearm up behind his back.

Now I must hold him down, for if he got up again I was lost. I put one knee on his forearm, the other across the backs of his thighs, and seized his throat with my now-free right hand, while his right hand felt around in vain for the fallen knife. He was wriggling and struggling, and it was all I could do to hold him down. Think of it, my opponent was Winnetou, supple as a snake, with iron muscles and steel sinews, Winnetou, who until then had never been bested in a fight, and since then never has been! Now there was time to try to say a word of explanation, but blood filled and spilled from my mouth, and when I tried to speak with my pierced tongue, only an unintelligible babble came out.

He tried with all his might to throw me off, but I held him down with all of mine. I pressed his windpipe with my fingertips to shut off his breath, but released it when he started to cough and choke, for I didn't want to strangle him. He raised his head and exposed his jaw, and I gave him a mighty blow with my fist. His head dropped. I had conquered the Unconquerable! The fact that I had laid him low once before didn't count, for that time there had been no battle between us.

I took deep, deep breaths, being careful not to breathe or swallow the blood that filled my mouth. I held my lips apart, to let blood out and let air in. Blood was also running from the external wound under my jaw. Head whirling, I tried to stand up, and heard an angry Indian yell behind me. I felt a blow on my head, and remembered nothing more.

It was early evening, still light, when I came to again. At first it seemed like I was dreaming: I was jammed between a mill-wheel and its abutment; my body prevented the wheel from turning, and the pressure of the rushing water, trying to turn it, was crushing me, crushing me . . . my entire body throbbed with pain, especially my head and left shoulder.

Little by little I realized that it wasn't a dream, it was reality, and that the sound of rushing water came from inside my own head, the result of the last blow I'd received. The pressure and pain in my shoulder was not from a mill-wheel, but from the blow Winnetou had given me. Blood was still running from my mouth and some trickled down my throat, choking me. I heard a fearful rattling and gurgling, and came to full consciouness; the gurgling sounds were my own.

"He's movin'! Thank God, he's movin'!" I heard Sam cry.

"Yes, I can see that." Will Parker's voice, quietly.

"He's openin' his eyes!" Dick Stone this time. My eyes were open but it took an effort to focus them, and the first thing I saw was not very reassuring. We all lay on the ground, tied hand and foot. Stone and Parker lay on my left; on the right I saw Sam Hawkens, his feet bound, his left hand tied behind him—his right hand was free.

Another man lay nearby, his body tied and folded together, head on knees, heels pulled up against his buttocks. It was Rattler; he was groaning weakly.

"Thank the Lord, you're back with us again, Bud!" said Sam, touching my face with his free hand. "What happened to you?"

I tried to answer but couldn't; I had a mouthful of blood.

"Spit it out!" Sam ordered. I did, but my mouth kept filling up with blood, and I could only squeeze out a few weak and scattered words. Sam bent his head to hear.

"Fought Inshu-chuna—Winnetou came—club on shoulder—stab in mouth . . ." It was an effort to speak; I fell silent. I felt that my head was lying in a small blood-puddle, and turned it away. Sam lifted and held it with his free hand, and now I could look toward the center of activity.

There were at least twenty campfires burning, and what looked like hundreds of Apaches moving between and among them. Nearer to us were two rows of dead men; they lay straight and still, so I assumed they were dead. Beyond them, closer to the fires, wounded Indians I assumed to be Apaches were being tended by their fellow-braves. Around us scores of bound Kiowas lay on the ground. All this I saw in the half-minute before Sam lowered my head gently to the ground again.

"Save your strength," Sam said, "don't try to talk any more, and I'll tell you our side of the story. We thought you were right behind us goin' around that bush, and when after a couple of minutes you didn't show up we looked back for you, and saw a howlin' bunch of Apaches around Winnetou and Inshu-chuna, lyin' on the ground like they were dead. Didn't see you for a minute, and then when the Chiefs both came to, saw you lyin' there like *you* were dead. We all came out of cover and ran to see if there was still life in you, and of course they grabbed us.

"I told Inshu-chuna that we were the Apaches' friends, and wanted to free him and his son last night, but he laughed in my face. Winnetou let me have this hand free to tend to you, and he had your jaw bandaged so you wouldn't bleed to death. Even then, we didn't know if you'd wake up again, if I'm not mistaken."

Now I felt that there was a bandage under my jaw. I spit out some blood and stuttered, "Tongue—too." Sam understood.

"Yes, I saw. That's bad—we can't bandage it. Just don't move it, and like I said, don't try to talk. I hafta tell ya that we five are the only whites alive. Dunno what they got planned for us, but they kept Rattler alive so they could kill him slowly, like I heard 'em sayin'. There's twelve dead Apaches and thirty dead Kiowas. All the rest of the Kiowas were caught, not one got away." He bent to me, and said with emphasis: "You know how big a war-party Inshu-chuna brought? Five hundred!"

Those were the last words I remember hearing.

When I came to life once more, I was moving. I heard the hoofs of many horses and I opened my eyes. I was lying on the hide of the grizzly I'd killed, which was slung like a hammock between two horses. I lay so deep within it that I could see only the sky, high tree-tops, and the two horses' heads. My mouth was swollen and full of congealed blood. I was terribly thirsty and wanted to call for water, but couldn't make a sound.

I fell into a dream-world, in which I fought with Indians and buffalo, bears and tigers—tigers?—rode for weeks across scorched plains, swam for months through shoreless seas . . . it was the delirium of fever, an endless delirium while I wrestled with death. Sometimes I heard Sam Hawkens' voice from far, far away; sometimes I saw Winnetou's dark-velvet eyes staring into mine. Then I died, was placed in a coffin and lowered into the grave. I heard the clods of earth being shoveled on the coffin, and lay motionless in the ground for an eternity, until one day the coffin-lid floated silently upward and vanished. I saw the blue sky above me, and the walls of the grave sank down and away. Could it be true? I raised my hand to my fore-head and—

"Hallelujah! He's woke from the dead!" I heard Sam cry joyfully.

I turned my head toward his voice.

"Look, look! His eyes are open, he can move his hand and his head!" Sam bent over me, his little eyes shining.

"Do ya know me, Bud, my good-friend-greenhorn Bud? You must be alive—you opened your eyes and moved. D'ya know who I am?"

I was too weak to answer, and couldn't anyway, for my tongue filled my mouth like a ball of lead. But I could nod, and I did.

"And can ya understand me?"

I nodded again. I saw Dick's and Will's heads next to Sam's, and tried to shape my lips into what I hoped was a smile.

"Are you hungry, Bud? Are you thirsty? Could you eat or drink anythin'?"

I moved my head slightly, side to side. I had no desire for food or water; I wanted only to lie quietly in this baby-weak, almost pleasant state.

"Nothin'? You don't want nothin'? D'ya know how long you've been lyin' here? Three weeks, three whole weeks! You had a fever we coulda fried pancakes on, then lockjaw—we had to pry your mouth open to pour in a little water—and then it looked like you stopped breathin'! My God! The Indians wanted to bury you, but I wouldn't believe you were dead, and made 'em promise to wait till you started to turn green! Got Winnetou to thank for that promise. I'm gonna go get him!"

I closed my eyes and lay still again, not unconscious this time, but in peaceful, almost blissful weariness. I wanted to lie like that forever. Then I heard footsteps. A hand touched me and shook my arm. I heard Winnetou's voice.

"Is Sam Hawkens mistaken? Did Selwiki-lata really wake up?"

"He did!" insisted Sam. "All three of us saw him open his eyes, and then he nodded when I asked him questions."

"Then a miracle has happened. But it would have been better had he died. He came back to life only to die again—he will be put to death with all of you."

"Why won't you believe he's the Apaches' friend—that all of us are?" I listened, still lying motionless, eyes closed.

"Friend? Twice Selwiki-lata knocked Winnetou down!"

"He had to!" Sam burst out. "The first time to save your life by keepin' the Kiowas from killin' you, and the last time he was just tryin' to keep you from killin' him!"

"Sam Hawkens speaks lies. He wants only to save all of you from death."

"No, it's the truth! Ask Old Shatterhand when he wakes again."

"He will lie just as you lie. Palefaces are all liars and betrayers. Winnetou has only known one white man who had truth in his heart, Kleki-petra, whom you murdered. When I first saw Selwiki-lata—Old Shatterhand—I thought he was also such a one. I admired his strength and bravery, I thought I saw honesty shine in his eyes. But he was the same kind of land-thief as the others, and with all of you he let us fall into the Kiowa trap. Why did the Great Spirit create such a strong, brave man and then give him the heart of a snake?"

When he'd first touched my arm I wanted to look at him, but my eyes wouldn't obey my will. But now, when I heard Winnetou's judgment, I mustered the strength to lift my eyelids, and saw him standing near me. He was wearing a white linen robe, and carried no weapons. A book was under his arm, and I could read part of the title "—OF HIAWATHA" in large gold letters. This son of the "savage" race of Indians could not only read, but had a taste for classic literature, in this case Longfellow's epic poem celebrating noble and romantic characteristics of his race. Poetry in the hands of an Apache Indian!

"He's opened his eyes again!" cried Sam, and Winnetou turned to look at me, a long searching look deep into my eyes.

"Can you understand me?" he asked. I nodded.

"When a man comes back from the dead, he should be able to speak only truth. So answer me: Did the four of you really want to save the Apaches from the Kiowas?"

I nodded 'yes' as best I could. But Winnetou made a scornful gesture, and said loudly, "Lies, lies, lies! Even on the edge of the grave, lies! We will make you well and strong again, so that you will suffer a long time while you die; to kill a weak, sick man is not punishment enough!"

He turned away, and I closed my eyes. If only I had been able to speak, to tell him about the fight with Metan-akva! Sam had the same thought, and spoke for me:

"We can prove that we were on your side. Tangua was goin' to torture the captives, but Old Shatterhand fought and killed their best knife-fighter to save Apache lives. He risked his life for your braves!"

"Which knife-fighter? You mean the famous Metan-akva?"

"Yes."

"Another lie! His body lies there with the other Kiowas we killed when we attacked."

"He was already dead when you attacked! Old Shatterhand—"

"Silence!" from Winnetou. "I will hear no more of your lies! If you had admitted your guilt, we might have spared your lives, for the Apaches learned about mercy and generosity from that good man, that teacher whom you murdered, Kleki-petra. His murderer will die a long death, and you four must share it, for not only did you betray us, you were his comrades. But we have no bloodlust against the Kiowas. They will pay for their evil deeds not with their lives, but with goods—tents and blankets, horses and weapons—and we will let them live, to return in peace to their village."

These were long speeches, among the longest I was ever after to hear from the usually taciturn Winnetou. I listened, alert but motionless and speechless, unable to react. I heard Sam make one last plea for Winnetou to believe we were his friends. Then:

"Enough! Winnetou sees that you are willing to die with lies on your lips. The sick man needs your help no more. Come with me—you will be held elsewhere."

"Please, Winnetou, let us stay! You can't part us from Old Shatterhand!"

"I can and will. Do you come quietly, or shall I call my warriors to tie you and drag you away?"

"We hafta do what you say," said Sam resignedly. "When will we see Bud—Old Shatterhand—again?"

"On the day of his death, and yours."

"Not before?"

"No."

"Then let us tell him goodbye before we go with you."

Sam took my hand in his, and I felt his beard on my face. He kissed me on the forehead, and then Dick and Will did the same. They left with Winnetou, and I was alone. A little while later some Apaches came and carried me away, and the motion of their carrying lulled me to sleep.

I don't know how long I slept, but it was a healing sleep, for when I awoke I felt stronger. Not strong, but rather less weak than before. I could open my eyes and keep them open, and I could move my tongue. I put my finger in my mouth and removed clots of congealed blood, then raised my head and looked around.

I was amazed to find myself in a room, a room with four stone walls. I lay in a corner on my own bearskin, with a Saltillo blanket thrown over me. Light came through an open doorway, to the right and left of which sat two Indian women, one of them old and wrinkled, the other a young girl with the most beautiful face I had ever seen. She wore a long gown, belted at the waist with a snake-skin, but no jewelry at all, no silver or turquoise like many Indians commonly wear.

Neither of them had noticed my awakening, so I had time to ob-serve and absorb this exquisite vision in detail. Her sole decoration was luxuriant blue-black hair, falling in two glistening braids to her waist. It reminded me of Winnetou's, and her features were also simi-lar to his. The same velvet-black eyes under long, heavy lashes, soft full cheeks and a dimpled chin, her skin a pale copper-bronze with silver highlights. She was speaking to the old squaw, softly, so as not to awaken me. They were both busy decorating white-tanned leather belts with red stitching. All this I saw before raising myself on my el-bows and so attracting their attention.

"Ugh!" cried the old squaw, and then some other words I of course didn't understand, but gathered to mean: He's awake! The girl rose and came over to me.

"You're awake at last," she said in perfect unaccented English. "Do you want anything?"

I opened my mouth to speak, remembered that I couldn't and closed it again, then decided to give it a try anyway.

"Yes. I want—several—things." It made me happy to hear my own voice, although I could barely recognize it. It was weak, slow and raspy, and it pained my throat to speak.

"Speak softly or just make signs. Nsho-chi can see that it's painful for you."

"You are—Nsho-chi? What does your name—mean?"

"Yes, I am. It means 'Lovely Day' in the paleface's tongue."

With each word it became easier for me to speak. I said: "It is the right name—for a lovely girl—on this lovely day when I have found my voice again."

A slight blush arose under the tawny skin. "You said you wanted several things."

"First tell me, are you here on my account?"

"Yes. My brother Winnetou sent me to tend you."

"I guessed you were his sister—you resemble that valiant young warrior."

"You tried to kill him!" It sounded like it was half assertion, half question. As she spoke she looked deep into my eyes, searching as her brother had done, as if she were trying to see into the very core of me.

"No." I returned simply.

"You struck him down twice, my brother Winnetou, whom no one has ever bested until now."

"Yes, I did—once to save his life, and once to save mine."

She was silent for a moment, her dark eyes scanning my face.

"He does not believe you. He believes you are his enemy, and Nsho-chi must also believe, for I am his sister. Are your mouth and throat less painful?"

"Yes. It's becoming easier to speak."

"Do you think you can swallow?"

"I'd like to try. Can you bring me some water?"

"Yes, to drink and also to wash with. I'll bring it now."

She and the old one both went out, and left me wondering. Winnetou took us for enemies, rejected our protestations that we were not, and yet sent his own sister to care for me. It didn't make sense then. Later, much later, I learned the reason.

After a time they returned, Nsho-chi with a small clay bowl filled with water, the old squaw with a hollowed-out half squash, also full. Nsho-shi held the bowl to my lips, and I tried to drink, with some success, though swallowing was painful. Painful, but the water was unbelievably refreshing. I finished the bowlful, and at once felt stronger.

"Nsho-chi sees that the water has done you good. Presently I will bring you more, and also something to eat. Now would you like to wash?"

"If I can."

"Try. I will help you." She held out a dampened cloth to me and I tried to wash, but I was still too weak to manage it. When Nsho-chi saw that, she took the cloth and began to wash my face and hands— me, the alleged deadly enemy of her father and her brother. When she finished, she said with a slight smile:

"Have you always been so lean and haggard as you are now?"

Lean? Haggard? I wondered what changes the long weeks of illness had wrought, that she should speak such words.

"I've always been strong and in good health," I said, "that is, until now."

"Look at your face in the water."

I looked down into the squash-bowl at the face of a ghost, a stranger with burning eyes set in a skeletal face covered with a thick beard, although not nearly as thick as that of Sam Hawkens. "—if I'm not mistaken," I thought silently.

"It's a miracle I'm still alive!" I said with wonder.

"Yes, Winnetou said the same. He was amazed that you survived the long ride here. The Great Spirit gave you a strong body—no one else would have lasted through those five days."

"Five days? Where are we?"

"In our pueblo on the Rio Pecos."

"You live in a pueblo? I thought the Apaches lived in tents or tepees."

"Different Apache tribes live in different kinds of houses. We Mescaleros live here in our pueblo."

"Nsho-chi—can you tell me where my three comrades are?"

"They are in a room like this one."

"Are they tied?"

She shook her head. "No, there is no need. Where would they escape to? They are well treated, as you are, because men must be well and strong to stand the long death."

"We are all going to die?"

"Yes, all of you are going to die."

Her voice held not a trace of regret. Could this beautiful girl have such lack of feeling that she could speak so matter-of-factly of the torture-deaths of other human beings?

"Before that day, will Winnetou come to see me? I want to talk to him."

"He does not wish to talk to you."

"I want to tell him something very important."

"Important to him?"

"No, to me and my comrades."

"Then he will not come. Do you want Nsho-chi to bring him the words you want to tell him?"

"No—if he is too proud to come and talk with me, then I am too proud to send him messages."

"You can talk with him on the day of your death. We must go now. If you want anything, blow on this,"—Nsho-chi handed me a small reed whistle—"and someone will come." She and the old one left, and I fell asleep again.

When I awoke I had a raging thirst and hunger. I blew on the whistle, and the old squaw, who must have been sitting just outside the doorway, stuck in her head and asked me something, using words I of course couldn't understand. I made eating and drinking motions and she disappeared. In a short while Nsho-chi came, bringing a clay bowl filled with the most delicious food I had ever tasted, or so it seemed then; a thick, meaty soup laced with cornmeal, which she fed to me like one feeds a child, a spoonful at a time.

It was still not easy for me to use my throat and tongue even to speak; chewing and swallowing were at first quite painful, but gradually became easier. I finished the soup, every spoonful.

"You are weak and sick now, but one can see that you are a strong man, one who can perform brave deeds." Nsho-chi contemplated me silently for a few moments. "If you had only been born an Apache, instead of a lying paleface."

"I do not lie. Soon I will prove that to you."

"I would so much like to believe that. But Nsho-chi has only known one paleface who spoke the truth; he was Kleki-petra, whom we all loved. One of you murdered him, and the murderer will be buried with him."

"You mean he hasn't been buried yet?"

"I know what you are thinking—his body is preserved in an airtight box which prevents decay. You will see it shortly before your own death."

She withdrew, leaving this cheerless promise hanging in the air like a cloud of noxious gas. I still couldn't seriously believe that I was going to be put to death; on the contrary, I was convinced that I would live, for I had incontrovertible proof that we were Winnetou's friends: the lock of his hair I had cut off when I'd freed him.

But—did I still have it? I panicked—the Indians customarily plunder the possessions of their captives! I was still wearing the same clothes I had on when we were captured. Soaked as they were with weeks of fever-induced sweat, I suddenly became aware of the stench of my own body's effluvia as I searched in all my pockets for the precious sardine can—and found it! I opened it with trepidation, and there was the lock of hair! I breathed a sigh of relief, put back the can, and slept again.

Day by day I became stronger in both body and mind. Nsho-chi came every day to bring me food and water. Soon I was able to get up and walk around the room, giving my wasted limbs much-needed exercise. One evening Nsho-chi came and said to me:

"Today I visited your three companions."

I smiled my gratitude. "Are they well? Did they ask about me? Please tell me what they said."

Nsho-chi smiled in return. "They are well, and I told them that you feel stronger and are almost well again. The one named Sam Hawkens asked me to give you something that he made for you."

"What is it?"

"I asked my brother Winnetou if I could bring it to you, and he gave permission. Here it is. You must be a strong brave man to have killed the gray bear with only your knife. Sam Hawkens told me about it."

She held out a necklace made of bear-teeth and claws. I took it and looked at it in astonishment. When did Sam make it, and where did he get the tools? Nsho-chi explained.

"He told Winnetou what he wanted to do, and Winnetou gave him back the bear-things and a knife and needle—whatever he needed to make the necklace. Put it on now, because you will not have the pleasure of wearing it much longer." She took it from my hands and slipped it over my head.

"Nsho-chi," I said, smiling, "I will wear it for many years."

"Oh, if I could only believe that was true," she said sadly. I could see unshed tears in her eyes.

"Believe it, it is true. If you see Sam Hawkens again, tell him not to worry—as soon as I have recovered completely, we will be free."

"Selwiki-lata, that is a false hope."

"It's not a hope but a certainty, you will see. And tell me, what does 'Selwiki-lata' mean? Your brother also named me so."

"It means 'hand that kills'—the Apache way of saying Old Shatterhand, your paleface name." She left without saying more.

I could look through the open doorway and see a cliffside not far away, so I guessed the pueblo was in an adjoining valley, not directly on the Pecos River. I knew the river valley must be far wider than the distance between my prison and the cliff. I would have liked to look the whole pueblo over, study the local area for escape possibilities in case my hair-lock didn't work. But this was impossible; two guards, whom I hadn't noticed till now kept constant watch just outside the doorway.

I slept on my bearskin, and when not sleeping, walked back and forth in the room. I asked Nsho-chi if I could have a stone to use as a chair. My request was transmitted to Winnetou, and he sent several stone blocks of various sizes; the largest must have weighed a hundred pounds. When no one was there to watch, I started exercising with the stones, first the lighter ones, then the heavier, until after two weeks I could lift the largest over my head several times. I kept improving, and at the end of the third week I knew that my former strength had entirely returned.

I had been here at the Pueblo for roughly two months, and had heard nothing about the approximately hundred and seventy Kiowas; it must have been a great burden on the Apaches to feed and house them while waiting for their tribute—or ransom—to arrive. Then one morning when Nsho-chi brought my breakfast, she sat down near me while I ate, not talking, just looking at me; I saw a tear roll down her cheek.

"You're weeping! Why, what has happened?"

"The Kiowa messengers came down the river last night, bringing all the articles to buy their comrades' freedom."

"And that saddens you? You should be happy about it."

"It isn't that. Today is your last day. The departure of the Kiowas will be celebrated by the death-by-torture of you and your three white brothers. Kleki-petra and his murderer will be buried also, but that is not what I am sad about."

I'd expected it for a long time and still it was a shock to be told that it was here at last. Today was the day, the day of decision, perhaps my last day. I composed myself, ate calmly, handed the empty bowl to Nsho-chi. She took it, walked as far as the doorway, stopped, turned, came back and gave me her hand.

"Nsho-chi speaks to you now for the last time. The daughter of the Apache Chief knows that she should not show sadness nor pity; she learned that from her father. But once she had another teacher, her mother, and she learned about tender emotions from her. And from

Kleki-petra Nsho-chi learned how to express those emotions in words, the words I say to you now."

"Once? Your mother is no longer alive?"

"No, the Great Spirit took my loving mother away. You, Old Shatterhand, are a brave warrior. Die bravely! If you let no sound pass your lips, Nsho-chi will be content and will remember you forever. Die as a hero—do that for me!"

She departed. I went to the doorway to see her go. Two gun barrels were trained on me. I shrugged and stepped back.

CHAPTER TEN

The word *pueblo* can denote several types of Indian villages and living quarters, but this one was typical of those built against a cliff, the rooms on terraces, each one set back from the one below. From the doorway I could tell that I must be high above the ground, perhaps on the seventh or eighth level. Each level could be reached only by ladder from those above and below; thoughts of escape were at this point futile. I would just have to wait and see what was planned for me and the others, and match my actions to the circumstances.

Keyed up as I was, the morning seemed to drag on forever, and it was almost midday when Winnetou appeared, accompanied by five of his warriors. He gave me a long, searching look and said:

"Old Shatterhand will tell me now whether he is well again."

"Not quite." I hadn't risen from the bearskin.

"But you can speak—you have recovered your voice."

"Yes, I can speak."

"And walk, and run?"

"Walk, yes; I haven't had much running practice recently."

"Do you know how to swim?"

"Ye-es." What kind of question was that, I thought silently. I didn't ask what he meant, and he didn't explain.

"Do you remember my telling you when you would see me again?"

"Yes. On the day I am to die," I answered evenly.

"You remembered well. This is that day. Stand up. Your hands and feet are to be tied."

I got up and held out my hands, and they were tied in front of me, not tightly but securely. My feet were tied together with a rope about two feet long, so I could walk slowly, or descend a ladder, but not run.

The 'ladders' down to each succeeding level were actually tree-trunks with staggered notches cut in them, but I had no trouble descending. Three warriors preceded me, Winnetou and the other two behind. We used six ladders to reach the ground.

It was as I'd guessed. The pueblo was in a narrow defile which opened immediately on to the broad Rio Pecos valley, the wide, slow-flowing river only a short distance away. We seven walked toward it through a crowd of what I estimated to be more than a thousand men, women and children; they parted to let us pass. I looked at none of them; my eyes were taking in all the visible geographical features and storing them in my memory.

There were trees far up- and downstream, and a few bushes. On this side there was a grassy stretch downstream, and I could see horses grazing. A broad strip of sand down to the river split the wooded area in two; it continued on the river's far side. There I could see a single tree, a tall cedar, in the center of the strip. A casual glance upstream gave my heart a lift; then I turned my attention to the scene and activity near us.

The surveying party's wagons were there, evidently having been used to transport some of the Kiowa tribute, for I saw goods piled near them, and Tangua and Inshu-chuna engaged in vehement conversation. All the Kiowa prisoners, free now, milled around. I turned away and saw Hawkens, Stone and Parker.

They were tied to three stakes driven into the ground, and I was now tied to a fourth one. So these were the torture-stakes, where we four were to end our lives in pain and torment! Bundles of firewood were piled nearby.

The stakes were not far apart, and I was tied near Sam. He gave me a rueful greeting. "I'd say 'welcome', Bud, but the word don't seem to fit. It's a miserable end they got planned for us, if I'm not mistaken." He had to speak loudly to be heard over the constant murmuring of the crowd of Indians.

"Have you given up all hope, Sam?" I asked, and raised my voice higher, "and you too, Dick and Will?"

Sam laughed derisively. "Dunno who's gonna come and rescue us. Been doin' lots of thinkin' the last weeks, but can't think of any way to keep us from dyin'. How've they treated you?"

"Very good."

"You look good, I see. They got our greenhorn all well again just to turn him into ashes. Injuries all healed?"

"All healed. But Sam, as bad as it looks right now, there's still a chance we'll come out of it. I've given you proof a few times that this greenhorn is different from most greenhorns."

He shook his head, puzzled. "What d'ya mean, a chance?"

"It's something I don't know the meaning of yet. Winnetou asked me if I knew how to swim."

"Well, happy day! Mebbe they're goin' to give you a chance to swim for your life! You do know how, don'cha?"

"Swimming has been my favorite sport since I was a child. I fancy myself to be a pretty good swimmer."

"Pretty good won't be good enough against these Apaches, Bud. They can all swim like fishes."

"Sam, I swim like an otter, that catches fish and eats them!"

"You're braggin'!"

"I hope to get a chance to show you I'm not!"

The spectators had closed into a half-circle around us, the children, girls and women in front, braves behind them. I looked and saw Nsho-chi, but she kept her eyes averted from us. Inshu chuna, Winnetou, and Tangua stood between us and the crowd, and now Inshu-chuna raised his hand for silence, and began to speak. It was in a strange mixture of spoken and signed language, and I heard an occasional English word, but Sam kept up a running interpretation for me in a low voice, and I got the most of it. It was mainly a recitation of the wrongs the palefaces had committed against the Indians, and it went something like this:

"The palefaces are enemies of the red men. Only one of them, Kleki-petra, has ever been our friend."

There was a chorus of "Howgh!"

"Kleki-petra was our teacher, and taught us many things. One of them was that the Great Spirit intended that the red men and the white men should live in peace together."

"Howgh!"

"But the white men came to do us evil, kill our buffalo, rob us of our land."

"Howgh!" It began to sound something like a church litany.

"Now they come to make a path for their fire-horse, to bring more palefaces here to steal and kill."

It went on and on like that for a good half-hour, until suddenly Sam said, "Hello! He just said somethin' about us not admittin' our guilt, and lettin' the Great Spirit decide if we were tellin' the truth! Mebbe you're right about that chance!"

As Sam finished speaking, Inshu-chuna turned to us, and said loudly in English so that all could hear, if not understand, "You have heard what Inshu-chuna said. Now you shall answer some questions, answer with the truth." He pointed at Sam.

"Do you belong to the band of white men who were measuring our land for a path for the fire-horse?"

"Yes," Sam replied, "but we three weren't measurin', we—"

"Silence!" Inshu-chuna broke in." Only answer my questions, nothing more. And the fourth man here, Old Shatterhand. Was he one of the measurers?"

"Yes."

"And you three guided and helped these people?"

"Yes."

"Then you are just as guilty as they are. And the murderer, Rattler, he was one of your band?"

"Yes, but he wasn't our friend, he—"

"Silence! And you added to your misdeeds by betraying us into the hands of our enemies, the Kiowas, is that right?"

"You were goin' to come back and kill us, and our plan—"

"Inshu-chuna has heard enough to call you guilty." He turned to Tangua. "They have said before that they wanted to protect us from your Kiowa braves. Is that the truth?"

"No!" cried Tangua, "they said we should show you no mercy!"

That was so far from the truth that I could keep silent no longer. I shouted: "That's a dirty shameful lie! If I had a hand free I'd knock you down for saying it!"

"Stinking dog!" he shouted back, raising a fist. "It's Tangua who should strike you down for saying he lies!"

"Strike away," I said evenly, "if you're not ashamed to hit a man who can't hit back." I turned my head toward Inshu-chuna. "You questioned us so that we could only answer yes or no, without letting us have a chance to explain. Is that what you call justice? Inshu-chuna is an unjust judge—the answers he lets us give are only those that condemn us. And then he listens to the lies of Tangua and believes them. Go ahead with the killing ceremony you've prepared—you won't hear a cry of pain pass the lips of any of us!"

"Ugh! Ugh!" from those Apaches who could understand. Courage is admired and respected, even the courage of an enemy.

I continued: "When I first saw Inshu-chuna and Winnetou my heart told me they were just and valiant men, whom I could love and trust. My heart was mistaken. They stamp on the truth, and listen to the words of a liar!"

"Dog, again you call Tangua a liar!" He leaped toward me, but Winnetou stepped between.

"The Chief of the Kiowas will remain calm. Old Shatterhand has spoken bravely, and there is some truth in what he says. My father Inshu-chuna, High Chief of the Apaches, will give him permission to say what he wants to say."

Inshu-chuna yielded to his son's wish. He stepped closer.

"Did you not strike me down with your fist?"

"Yes," I answered, "but I had to keep you from killing me. I tried to tell you that I was your friend, but you didn't listen to me. Then Tangua saw you lying there and wanted to take your scalp. He cut my hand when I tried to stop him, and I knocked him down also. Then—"

"The paleface lies!" screamed Tangua, turning to Winnetou. "My brother Winnetou should believe me, not this coyote!"

"Let him speak further. That much is true—you lay there senseless, and my father too. Old Shatterhand knelt by him. He may continue."

"Then Winnetou came up behind me and clubbed me on the shoulder. He stabbed me through the jaw and through my tongue, so I couldn't speak to tell him what happened, and that I wanted to be his friend and brother. I was injured and one arm was useless, but I was able to overcome him and strike him unconscious too. I could have killed both Winnetou and Inshu-chuna. Did I do so?"

"No, because one of my warriors came and clubbed you," said Inshu-chuna.

"No, I had time to kill you, but I wanted to protect you from harm. Didn't my three comrades come to you without weapons, to give themselves up?"

"They saw that it was hopeless to resist. But I admit that some of what you say may almost be believed. Some other words do not ring true. There was no reason for you to knock down my son Winnetou when the Kiowas ambushed us at your camp."

"Oh yes! We wanted to save both of you from being wounded or killed by the Kiowas, which would have happened had you resisted them. So I knocked Winnetou down, and my three friends kept you from fighting and so being harmed. I hope you can believe that."

"Lies, nothing but lies!" cried Tangua. "It was he who wanted to take your scalp, and Tangua who tried to stop him. An evil spirit must have helped him to strike Tangua down! If he was free I would battle him to prove which one of us is the liar!"

"I will remember those words," I said softly, "and you may have your wish come true."

"You, fight with Tangua?" he laughed scornfully. "You will have no chance. You will be burned, and your ashes scattered to the four winds."

"Don't be too sure. I'll be free sooner than you think, and will hold you to account." Winnetou looked at me inquiringly, trying to guess my secret thoughts, but Inshu-chuna put an end to the hostile word-exchange.

"Old Shatterhand speaks boldly about being free. He has said many words to defend himself, but has not been able to show proof that what he says is true."

"Didn't I strike down Rattler, when he shot at Winnetou and hit Kleki-petra? Isn't that some sort of proof?"

"You could have had other reasons; we know you were not a friend of Rattler's. Do you have any more to say?"

"Not now. Perhaps later."

"Better now. Later you will not be able to speak."

"We will see. Now I keep silent, because I want to know if the Apache Chiefs will change their decision."

Inshu-chuna turned away and gave a hand signal, whereupon several older Apaches came out from the crowd and gathered around him. They, and also Tangua, sat on the ground not far away and began conferring loudly, with much waving of hands. The Kiowa Chief's voice was loudest, accompanied by malevolent looks in our direction. The four of us had time to exchange a few words between ourselves.

"I wonder what they're cookin' up," said Dick. "I don't fancy dyin', but if I have to, I'd rather it was quick."

"That goes for all of us, if I'm not mistaken," Sam put in, "but mebbe what Bud said gave 'em somethin' to think about. You did pretty good, Bud—trouble is, once a redskin gets an idee in his hard head, it ain't easy to change it. Surprised he let you talk so much—he shut me up every time, heeheehee!"

Even in this desperate situation, Sam Hawkens was still able to emit that ridiculous giggle. I started to make some comment in return, but now the conference was over; Inshu-chuna stood, raised his arms, and spoke a few short sentences to the assembly. Sam interpreted.

"He says they already had somethin' planned for us, somethin' to do with the river, but on accounta what you said, he's goin' to let the Great Spirit decide—I didn't get all of it."

The Chief turned to us. "Selwiki-lata, the youngest of you, has spoken words which have a trace of wisdom and truth. So we have agreed to let the Great Manitou decide your fate." He paused to lend his words emphasis, and Sam asked me quickly:

"D'ya know what he means?"

"I have an idea it has something to do with swimming. Maybe a duel in the water."

"A duel! In the water! But who against who?"

Inshu-chuna went on: "The paleface Selwiki-lata, called by his companions Old Shatterhand, is also the highest-ranking among you, so he will represent you. His opponent must be the one who is highest-ranking among us, and I, Inshu-chuna, High Chief of the Apaches, am that one."

A chorus of "Ugh! Ugh!" from the spectators.

"Bud," said Sam, "it's a duel all right, but believe me, it's gonna be fixed so the white man loses."

Inshu-chuna continued: "Old Shatterhand will be untied and allowed to enter the river; he will have no weapons. Inshu-chuna will follow him, but he carries a tomahawk. If Old Shatterhand can swim to the other bank and reach the cedar tree, he is saved, and his comrades go free also. But if the Chief kills him before he reaches the cedar, so must his comrades also die. They will not be tortured, but they will be shot."

Sam laughed sarcastically. "Just like I said, it's fixed! You've already lost the duel. At least we'll die quick deaths."

"It's not lost if I can get close to him," I said.

"You'll never get close to him, Bud. Your fists won't be any help to you now. You prob'ly think the tomahawk is used just for hand-to-hand fightin'; it's a throwin' weapon, too, and an Indian could cut off the tip of your ear at a hundred yards with it. He won't aim at your ear, though. Don't matter how good you swim, you'll get it in the head, or even deadlier, in the neck."

"How about if I use a little cunning?"

"Cunnin'? Old Sam can't see what good cunnin' is against a well-aimed tomahawk!"

"It helps, Sam, you'll see. Or rather, you won't see. I'll just tell you that I have a plan."

"A plan! The only plan I can see is to swim to the other bank and reach that tree—and the tomahawk'll get you first."

"No. Listen carefully, Sam, and remember these words: *If you think I've drowned, we're saved.*"

"Drowned? Saved? Don't make sense."

"It will. Remember, if I drown, we've nothing more to fear."

I spoke the last words hastily, for now Winnetou and Inshu-chuna approached, and my bonds were untied. I stretched, and flexed my arms and legs to check their strength and muscle-tone. The next words I spoke were the first steps in my plan.

"It's a great honor for me to swim for my life in a contest with the High Chief of the Apaches. But it's no honor for him."

"Why not?" It was Winnetou who asked.

"Because I'm not an even opponent for him. I've swum some in shallow creeks, but even then was afraid I'd go under. I doubt if I could swim across such a wide river."

"Ugh!" said Inshu-chuna. "I am the best swimmer of our tribe. A swimming match with you would have no meaning!"

"And," I went on, "you have a weapon, and I don't. So I'm going to sure death, and my comrades too. Still, I would like to know the details of how you have planned this event. Which one of us goes into the water first?"

"You do! Then I follow you."

"And when do you attack me with your tomahawk?"

"Whenever Inshu-chuna feels like it," he answered, with the contempt of a master speaking to his apprentice.

"So, you can kill me. Can I kill you, too?"

His face assumed an expression of ridicule and impatience combined. "It is a swim and a fight for life and death. Yes, kill Inshu-chuna if you can. But whether you do or not, you must be able to reach that cedar tree."

"And if I kill you I will not be punished for it?"

"No, no! If the Apache Chief kills you, your companions must also die, and if you kill him, you must then reach the cedar, and you will all go free! Have I not said it once before? Come!"

He turned and walked to the river bank, and I removed my boots, my jacket and shirt, and stood bare to the waist. I laid aside what I'd had in my pockets and belt. I heard Sam shout:

"It's all up with us, Bud, all up with us! I'm tellin' you goodbye, this time for real, for the last time!"

I couldn't answer to reassure him, because I didn't want the red men to hear. The quibbling and complaining was part of my plan; I wanted Inshu-chuna to be confident of victory, so he'd be sure to fall into my trap. And it was working!

"One more question. If we are set free, will we get back all of our possessions?"

Inshu-chuna let out a snort of irritation—to him this question was absurd. "Yes, I promise."

"Our horses and weapons, the wagons, the instruments?"

He shouted at me angrily, "Yes, everything! Didn't you hear Inshu-chuna say it? A frog wants to race an eagle, and asks him what he will get if he wins! If you swim as stupidly as you ask questions, I should have you swim against a squaw instead of the Chief of the Apaches!"

It was clear to me that I was in the utmost danger. Whether I swam straight, at an angle or zigzag, it would be next to impossible to avoid the Chief's tomahawk. Diving and staying under was my only chance.

But I had to come up for air sometime, and then I would be a target. Unless—unless I could come up where no one would expect to see me. I glanced up-river again to verify that first hint that the landscape and riverscape were in my favor.

Upstream about a hundred paces distant, the river had washed away sand and dirt to make an overhang. From this position the space under the bank was dark, so it would be perfect for a short rest stop; no one would be looking for me upstream anyway. Beyond was a floating tangle of leafy twigs and bushes caught in an eddy against the bank. Still further, where the forest began, the river made a bend, and the far bank was no longer visible. If I jumped in the river and didn't come up again, they would think I had drowned, and they'd search for my body. Where? Here. And downstream, of course. But now— now it was advisable to act a little nervous and cowardly.

Inshu-chuna had disrobed to a belted loincloth; the handle of his tomahawk was held in the belt. He motioned to me.

"It is time to begin! Jump in!"

"Can I look first to see how deep it is?" I asked, with doubt and trepidation in my voice.

With a scornful smile he called for a lance. It was handed to me, and I couldn't touch bottom. That was just fine. Behind me I heard a low murmur, probably of contempt, from the Indian audience. That also suited me just fine.

Suddenly I wondered what Nsho-chi must think of me. I looked for her, and saw that her eyes were downcast; in shame, probably. On Tangua's face was a sneer. Winnetou's upper lip was drawn back in an expression of disdain. He was angry with himself for ever showing interest in or sympathy for me. Inshu-chuna yelled:

"Jump! Jump, or I'll kill you with the tomahawk right here and now!" He gave me a push, I fell into the river arms a-flap, and now my performance was over.

I touched bottom, put my head down, and swam upstream along the bank with all my strength and skill. I heard a splash behind me; Inshu-chuna. As I later learned, it had first been his intention to let me take a good lead and then kill me with the thrown tomahawk when I reached the other bank. But due to my obvious cowardice he had abandoned this plan, springing in right after me to kill me as soon as I emerged for air. One should make short work of cowards, and I was certainly a coward.

I soon reached the overhang, swam back in as far as I could, and came up with my mouth just above water level. Invisible to the Indians, the only one who could have seen me was Inshu-chuna, had he been looking in my direction. But he was looking everywhere else, his tomahawk held high, waiting for me to surface.

I took a few deep breaths, held the last one, submerged again and continued upstream to the tangle of trapped branches. I came up inside of it and could breathe at leisure. My head was so well hidden that I stayed for a minute or so, looking through the interstices at Inshu-chuna swimming randomly back and forth, searching for me frantically.

The last stretch was ahead of me, to where the woods began, and reeds and bushes grew down to the water's edge. I reached it with no trouble, and concealed by the bushes, climbed up on the riverbank.

Now I wanted to reach the river-bend, so I could swim across unseen; a short run through the woods would bring me to a good spot. But first I took another look through the foliage at those I had deceived. Many stood on the bank shouting and waving their arms, and the Chief still searched back and forth, although it would have been impossible for me to have stayed under water this long. I wondered if Sam thought about my last words: *If I drown, we've nothing more to fear.*

I ran to the river-bend, and completely out of sight of the gathering, swam across with ease, and ran back through the trees on the opposite side until they ended. I looked across and saw that several Apaches were in the water, probing with lances for the drowned body of Old Shatterhand. Inshu-chuna still swam near the bank, back and forth and around. It occurred to no one to cast his eyes across the river, to the other bank.

I could have walked leisurely over the sand to the cedar and to easy victory, but I didn't want that victory to be based on cunning alone; I wanted also to teach Inshu-chuna a lesson, and obligate him before all eyes to retract his low opinion of me. I slipped into the water, lay on my back with only my face exposed, and floated downstream until I was opposite the agitated activity on the other bank. Then I stood upright, treading water, and shouted across:

"Sam Hawkens, Sam Hawkens, we've won, we've won!"

A great howl of amazement and frustration went up from the Apaches. Inshu-chuna started to swim rapidly toward me, and I left the water and stood on the bank as if waiting for him.

"Run, Bud, run!" Sam yelled to me, "get to the cedar tree!"

I could have done so easily, there was nothing to hinder me; but I waited until the Chief was about thirty yards from shore before turning to lope lazily toward the tree, still a good two hundred paces away. When I'd covered half the distance, I stopped and turned to see Inshu-chuna climbing out of the water.

He couldn't overtake me, but he could throw the tomahawk, and I wanted to be able to see it coming so I could evade it. He would probably want to throw it from a standing position while I was running with my back to him. I ran, looking back out of the corner of my eye and letting him get close enough to hear the pat of his feet on the sand. When I heard his footsteps stop, I also stopped and turned, to see the tomahawk coming toward me. I stepped aside; it flew past me and buried itself in the sand.

That was just what I wanted. I ran and picked it up, but instead of hurrying to the tree, walked calmly toward the Chief. He gave a roar of fury and ran to meet me. I swung the tomahawk and warned him:

"Stop, Inshu-chuna! Once again you've been mistaken about Old Shatterhand! Do you want your own hatchet in your skull?"

He stopped short. "Dog! How did you escape from me in the water? The Evil Spirit must have helped you!"

"No," I answered, "it was the Great Manitou who helped me."

I saw his fingers clench and his eyes flash a signal, so I was ready when he sprang at me. I avoided his hands and tripped him so that he fell heavily in the sand. I was on him in an instant, pinioning his arms and legs with my own. I held up the tomahawk and cried:

"Inshu-chuna, do you ask for mercy?"

"Kill me, dog!" he shot back, while struggling to get loose.

"No, because you are the father of Winnetou, whom I love like a brother. But you force me to put you to sleep for awhile."

I slapped him on the temple with the flat of the tomahawk, an impact well-gauged to knock him unconscious but not inflict permanent damage. To those watching it must have looked as if I'd killed him, and cries of shock came across the water. I put his belt around his arms and body, carried him to the cedar and laid him gently at its foot.

Now I ran quickly back to the riverbank, for many warriors had dived into the water and were swimming toward me, Winnetou in the lead. I cupped my hands and called:

"Stay back! The Chief is alive, but if you come closer I will kill him! Only Winnetou may come, the others not!"

They came on, perhaps not hearing nor understanding me, but Winnetou turned and shouted at them, and they all turned back. He swam on alone and I met him at the riverbank.

"Is my father really still alive?"

"Yes, of course he is. But he was too proud to surrender, so I had to stun him."

"You could have killed him, he was at your mercy!"

"No. I honor and respect him because he is your father." I handed him the tomahawk. "Here is his weapon. Now you must decide whether I have won."

He took it, and looked at me for a long moment. His expression grew softer and more amiable, began to exhibit admiration, and finally he burst out:

"What kind of man is Selwiki-lata! Who can understand him?"

I smiled. "You will learn to understand me."

"You have given me this tomahawk without knowing if we will keep our promises to you. You have put yourself in my hands!"

"Yes, because I know that Winnetou is not a liar, but a noble warrior who would not break his word."

He held out his hand to me. His dark eyes shone.

"You are right. You are free, and the others too, except Rattler, who must die. You have given your trust to Winnetou; he should give you trust in return."

"In a short while you will trust me as completely as I trust you. Now come with me to your father, to see that he's alive!"

We walked to the tree and I removed the belt from around the Chief's body. Winnetou examined him and said: "Alive, but with terrible head-pain when he awakes! I will send some men to bring him back. My brother Old Shatterhand may swim back with me."

That was the first time that Winnetou called me by the name *brother*. How often in later years did I hear that word from him, and how earnest and true its meaning has remained!

We swam back side by side. The Indians on the bank watched us tensely, probably realizing how wrong was their previous estimate of me, how unjust their scorn and derisive laughter. We climbed out on the bank. Winnetou took my hand and cried loudly:

"Old Shatterhand has won! He and his comrades are free!"

"Ugh! Ugh!" from a thousand throats.

He sent two braves to fetch Inshu-chuna. I still had a score to settle with Tangua, who stood there silently, casting me black looks. He must be punished for his lies, for his efforts to send us to our deaths. We walked past him to the stakes, and Winnetou picked up his knife from the ground and handed it to me.

"You, who saved them, should be the one to cut their bonds."

I cut the ropes from all three, while Sam Hawkens shouted:

"Hallelujah, we're free, rescued, saved! Saved by our dear friend Bud, our greenhorn who's like no other greenhorn, if I'm not mistaken!" Dick and Will echoed his cries of delight, and they all hugged me till I couldn't breathe.

"How didja do it?" asked Sam. You acted so afraid of the water, and when you disappeared, everybody thought you drowned!"

"I told you, Sam, if I drown, we're saved."

"Didn't know what you meant, but I sure do now, heeheehee!"

"Old Shatterhand said that?" asked Winnetou, "Then it was all make-believe. Now I see that you must have swum upstream, and crossed the river out of our sight. My brother is not only as strong as a bear, but also sly as a fox. Woe to the man who has him for an enemy."

"Winnetou was such an enemy," I said.

"He was, but no more. Now he is your brother."

"Now will you believe me, and not the liar Tangua?"

"Winnetou believes you."

I had put my clothing on again, and now I took the sardine can from my jacket pocket and opened it. "My brother Winnetou has looked into my heart, and seen how I cherish him. Now I will show him proof that he has judged me rightly." I took the lock of hair and held it out to him.

He started to reach for it, then pulled his hand away and stepped back.

"That is hair from my head! How did you get it?"

I smiled. "Your father Inshu-chuna believes that the Great Spirit had sent an invisible rescuer to free you and him from captivity. Yes, he was invisible, because he couldn't let himself be seen by the Kiowas. But now it is no longer necessary to remain invisible—now Winnetou will know for certain that I was never his enemy, but have always been his friend."

"You—you were the one who cut us loose? Then you are the one we have to thank for our freedom—and for our lives!" He took me by the hand again and pulled me over to where his sister Nsho-chi stood. Thrusting me in front of her, he said:

"Nsho-chi sees here the valiant warrior who freed her father and brother from the trees where the Kiowas had tied them. She should thank him, thank him with all her heart."

Nsho-chi looked into my eyes, then dropped her head, held out her hand to me, and said only, "Forgive me."

Why did she think it more important to ask my forgiveness than to thank me for her father's and her brother's lives? I could guess—it was because she, as my nurse, should have known me better than the others, should have known I was honest and clever and her brother's friend. She had told me I was brave, and then my acting the coward had made her doubt me; of that she was ashamed—she was asking forgiveness for that doubt.

I pressed her hand and said, "Nsho-shi will remember all the things I told her would happen. Now does my sister believe me?"

"Nsho-shi believes in her white brother!"

Tangua stood nearby; I went to him and looked him in the eye.

"Does Tangua remember what he said when I was tied?"

"Tangua said many things."

"You said that if I were free you would fight me to prove which one of us is a liar."

"Tangua does not remember those words. Old Shatterhand must be mistaken."

Winnetou spoke: "No, Old Shatterhand is not mistaken. Winnetou was there, and he heard Tangua make that statement."

"You see," I said, "that you did say those words. Now I am free—do you stand by your challenge?"

"No! The Chief of the Kiowas fights only with Chiefs!"

"I say that I am a Chief. And if you do not want to take back your insults nor admit your lies, I will take a rope and hang you from the nearest tree."

To threaten an Indian with hanging is an insult of the worst kind, and I had said it with deliberate intent. Tangua drew his knife. "Dog, Tangua will cut out your tongue!"

Winnetou stepped between us. "My brother Old Shatterhand is right; he has been insulted, called a lying dog, and you said you would fight him. If you do not, the Kiowa tribe should cast you out as a liar and coward."

Tangua, before he answered, looked around at the gathering; there were three times as many Apaches as Kiowas, and he was in enemy territory. They had paid their tribute, but were still semi-prisoners. He had no recourse but to say:

"I will fight him. Who will choose the weapons?"

"Old Shatterhand, because you insulted him."

"Let Tangua choose," I put in, "it makes no difference to me which weapon I use to conquer him."

"You will not win!" cried Tangua. "Do you think I'll choose fists, fists that gave you your name, or knives, like you killed Metan-akva with? No, we will fight with rifles!"

"I agree," I said immediately, "but, Winnetou, did you hear what he said about Metan-akva? I fought and killed him to save all your Apaches from the torture-death. Tangua denied this—now another one of his lies is exposed."

"Tangua a liar! You'll pay for that with your life!"

A duelling-strip was measured—Tangua wanted two hundred paces between us, and I agreed—and it was also decided that we would each shoot in turn until the other lay dead or wounded on the ground. Over Winnetou's protests, I gave Tangua first shot.

"You had better kill me with that shot," I said, "because my bullet will not kill you. I will shoot you in the knee."

"Ugh!" he sneered. "At two hundred paces you will be lucky to hit me anywhere!" He laughed loudly, although no one else did.

They brought me my bear-killer and I checked it over; it was in prime condition and still loaded. Just to be sure, I emptied both barrels into the air and reloaded it. While I did, Sam and Will and Dick bombarded me with questions.

Sam: "I've got a hundred questions to ask ya, but there's no time for 'em all, so I'll just ask a couple—One: are you really goin' to just hit him in the knee, not kill him?" *Yes.* Two: what was that thing you showed Winnetou back there? Looked like a hank of hair." *It was.* And I explained,to their amazement and admiration, how I'd cut it off when I freed Winnetou and Inshu-chuna from their bonds those many weeks back.

Now the duel was to begin. I faced Tangua full-on, two hundred paces away, Winnetou counted—one—two—three! — and Tangua's bullet flew past my ear. I had counted on the fear and agitation he exhibited to spoil his aim, and luckily it did.

Tangua turned sideways to present a narrower target, and I shouted a warning, "Tangua, turn to face me, like I did you! If you stand so, both your knees will be destroyed, not just one!"

He paid no heed, and I shot on Winnetou's count of three. The Kiowa Chief let out a scream, let his weapon fall, threw his arms in the air and fell to the ground. Indians rushed to see where my bullet had struck, and they exclaimed in amazement.

"Both knees, both of them!" they were crying as I walked up.

Both Tangua's kneecaps were smashed, but I had to admire him for the fact that after that scream no sound of pain passed his lips.

"Tangua is wounded and cannot go home," he said, "he must stay with the Apaches."

Winnetou shook his head and answered, "You must go home, for we have no place here for one who steals our horses, murders our warriors. We took no revenge with blood, but with goods; you can ask no more of us."

"But I cannot ride!"

"Old Shatterhand's wounds were much worse, and he rode for five days and nights. You must leave. Winnetou has spoken!"

Winnetou took my hand and led me away. We saw his father and two braves emerging from a swim across the river, and Winnetou went to them to tell Inshu-chuna what had transpired. I and Sam and Dick and Will held our own private powwow, and I told them all the details of how I had contrived our deliverance.

Presently Inshu-chuna came, looked deep into my eyes as his son had so often done, and said:

"Inshu-chuna has heard everything from Winnetou. You are all free, and we have judged you wrongly. You, Selwiki-lata, are a valiant and skillful warrior, and will conquer many enemies. Will you and your comrades honor us by being our guests for a time?"

We assented, we shook hands paleface style, and then we four ascended as free men the ladders we had descended that morning to go to our deaths.

CHAPTER ELEVEN

We were all housed on the third level this time. Nsho-chi led me into a large empty room, windowless as all of them were, but with a tall open doorway to admit light. She disappeared for a few minutes, but returned with fur rugs, blankets, short reed tables, baskets and other miscellaneous articles, making several trips. The room was soon fitted out almost luxuriously.

On the last trip Nsho-chi brought me a beautifully carved calumet and tobacco, real tobacco this time, not the nauseating mixture I had smoked with Bao. She filled and lit it for me.

"My father Inshu-chuna sends you this calumet. He himself made the long ride to the sacred quarry and brought back the stone, and Nsho-chi carved it. It has never been in the mouth of another, and we want you to have it and think of us whenever you smoke it."

"You are very kind, and I am honored," I said. "I am rather ashamed that I have nothing to give you in return."

"You have already given us so much that we can never repay—the lives of my father and brother."

"I am happy and proud that it was in my power to do so; your father Inshu-chuna is a famous Chief and warrior, and Winnetou I have admired and cherished from the first moment I saw him."

"If you allow it, we want to consider you as if you were born an Apache."

"I am thankful and grateful; no more need be said. But this pipe-bowl is a work of art. How skilful your hands are!"

At this praise she blushed under the bronze and turned away.

"I know that the wives and daughters of the palefaces are much more artistic and skilful than we are. Now I will bring you some other things."

She returned with my revolvers, knife, and all the other articles that I hadn't kept in my pockets. Everything was there, even several worthless items I would have discarded. I asked:

"Will my companions also get back all their possessions?"

"Yes, everything. Inshu-chuna has already brought their guns to them, and all the other things of theirs."

"Do we still have our horses?"

"Your horses are here too. Also Nancy, Sam Hawkens' mule."

"Oh, you know his mule's name."

"Yes, and also the name of his old rifle, Liddy. During the weeks you were recovering I spoke with him often. He is a very amusing man, and I think he is also a skilled hunter and scout."

"He is that and more, namely a loyal and dependable traveling companion. But there is something else I want to ask you. Your warriors took from them all the booty the Kiowas were carrying, also what had belonged to my comrades. Is that right?"

"Yes."

"But why not mine? My pockets were not emptied."

"Because my brother Winnetou so ordered."

"Do you know why he gave such an order?"

"Because he had affection for you."

"Even though he considered me his enemy?"

"Yes. You just said that you cherished and admired him from the first moment you saw him. He had the same feeling for you, and it pained him to have to consider you an enemy—not only an enemy, but also—"

"Go on."

"No!"

"I'll say it for you. It's possible to respect an enemy, but he also believed I was a liar, a deceitful rogue, a coward—and a land-thief to boot. That is what pained him, right?"

"You are saying it."

"Well—happily, all that is behind us, and now Winnetou and I have each have the other's true measure. One more question: What will happen to Rattler, Kleki-petra's murderer?"

"They are now making him ready for death."

"Now? Why haven't I been told?"

"Winnetou wanted it so. He believed it was not a sight for your eyes, nor sounds for your ears."

"Where is the place of execution?"

"Downriver a little way, so it would be out of your sight and hearing. You should not go there."

"But I want to be there! How will Rattler be killed?"

"With all the pain we know how to inflict, for he is the most evil paleface we have ever had in our hands. He shot our white father, our teacher Kleki-petra whom we loved and respected. So he must die slowly and in agony."

"That should not be, that is barbarous, inhuman!"

"It is what he deserves."

"Are you allowed to be there and to watch him dying?"

"Yes. Does that surprise you?"

"A woman should not witness such things."

"Is that how it is where you are from?"

"Yes."

"If you believe so, you are mistaken."

"If I am wrong, then you must know our women and girls better than I do."

"Perhaps you don't know them at all. Nsho-chi has heard that when a criminal is put on trial, there are often more women in the courtroom than men."

"That may be true, but—"

"—and when a murderer is executed, when he's hanged or beheaded, are there no white squaws there to watch?"

"Once it was like that. But now no one but the executioner and guards are present."

"So, now no one watches. But if it were still allowed, the white squaws would be there in the crowd. Oh, the paleface women are not as soft and tender-hearted as you think!" Nsho-chi's eyes shot sparks. "They can stand pain very well, the pain of others, men or animals! I have not been where 'civilized' people live, but Kleki-petra told us about them. Aren't women present at bullfights, when maddened bulls are let loose against men and horses; and when the blood flows, don't they shout and clap just like the men do?" She paused to draw breath.

"I must admit that it never occurred to me, but—"

Nsho-chi cut me off with another outburst. "Wait! I have more to say about your tender white squaws, who can hear screams of pain without a shudder—who can see slaves in chains on the auction block, who can stand by with a smile while an innocent black servant girl is whipped to death!

"But here we have a criminal, a murderer. He will die as he deserves. I want to be there to see and hear it, and you believe that is not womanly? Is it wrong that I can stand calmly by and watch such a man die? And if it is wrong, who is really guilty—the red men who have become used to such cruelty, or the palefaces who have forced us to return their cruelties with our own?"

There was much truth in what she said, but still I felt that I should protest, say some words of justification. "A white judge would not condemn an Indian to death by torture."

Nsho-chi laughed scornfully. "Judge! Do not be angry with me when I use that word I have often heard from Hawkens: *Greenhorn!* You do not know the West. Where is he whom you mean when you say 'judge'? Here the stronger is the judge and the weaker is the one to be judged. You should learn how many Indians, overcome in battle against greater numbers of white invaders, were tortured to death at the paleface campfires! And they had done no more than assert their rights, try to protect their lands! And I, because I am a woman, should turn my eyes away when a murderer is put to death?" She paused and slowly shook her head. "Once we were different, a peaceful people. But you taught us, taught us how to see blood flow without turning a hair. Now I will go to see Kleki-petra's murderer suffer his sentence."

I had learned to know this beautiful young Indian maiden as a sweet, gentle human being. Now she stood before me with venom in her voice and lightning in her eyes, the living picture of a merciless goddess of revenge. This facet of her personality was so different from the one I knew, and yet she seemed to be as beautiful as before, perhaps even more beautiful. Could I judge her, condemn her? Was she wrong, unjust?

"Go, but I am going with you."

"It is better if you stay here," she pleaded, in a tone suddenly grown soft again. "Inshu-chuna and Winnetou would not be pleased if you came."

"Would they be very angry?"

"No. They would rather you were not there, but they have not forbidden it. You are our brother."

"I'll come, and they will forgive me."

We walked out on the platform and Sam was sitting there smoking; he'd also gotten a pipe and tobacco. He greeted us.

"Things are sure different for us now, Bud. From prisoners to guests—a much better feelin', if I'm not mistaken. The Chief himself gave us pipes and other things."

"Do you know where he is now?

"Down by the river, seein' off the Kiowas."

"Know what else he's doing there? He's conducting Rattler's death by torture."

"Rattler? Now? C'mon, let's go down, I wanta be there!"

"Easy, Sam! Can you watch that kind of ceremony without a shudder?"

"Shudder? Bud, you're still a greenhorn, even with your new Westerner's name, Old Shatterhand. When you've been out here in the West awhile longer, you'll see lots worse than that without a shudder. The bastard deserves to die, and he's gonna be executed Indian-style, that's all."

"But it's absolute cruelty for him to die by torture!"

"Ha! Don't talk 'bout cruelty, that's just a detail. He's gotta die, die, die, and how he does it ain't important!"

"Yes, he has to die, but the Apaches could make it short. He's a human being, after all."

"A man who shoots down another one for little or no reason ain't no human being—he's an animal. No, he's worse than an animal—animals don't kill for no reason."

"He was drunk."

"Don't make me laugh! For bein' drunk, they oughta kill him twice! He's gotta pay for whatever he does, drunk or sober, and a man who can't control his drinkin' is double-guilty!"

"Still, I'm going to try to get him an easier death."

"Bud, don't do nothin' that'll get us all in trouble."

Nsho-chi had left while we were talking. Sam called Dick and Will, we descended to ground level and walked downriver to the killing ground. The Kiowas were gone, taking their crippled Chief, their horses, and not much else. About half the village was there; all the warriors, but few women and children. From what Nsho-chi had said, I guessed their absence was due more to disinterest than to horror or pity.

The crowd had formed a half-circle, leaving a large clear area around our wagon. Inshu-chuna and Winnetou were there, and also Nsho-chi, talking to them earnestly. When she saw us, she retreated, melting into the group of women. The three scouts remained with the warriors, but I entered the half-circle and walked toward the Chiefs. Winnetou met me halfway.

"Why haven't my white brothers remained in their rooms at the pueblo?" asked Winnetou. "Are they not comfortable there?"

"They are comfortable, and we thank our red brother for his hospitality. We came because we heard that Rattler was to die."

"That is correct."

"I don't see him."

"He is in the wagon with the body of the one he murdered."

"Is he to die the long death?"

"Yes."

"I beg of you to let him die quickly!"

"The decision has been made, I cannot change it."

"Can I? Is there nothing I can do or say to change the verdict, to have Rattler die quickly without suffering pain?"

"Why does my white brother insist? Was not the murderer your enemy also?"

"I dislike seeing any living being suffer, especially a human being, no matter how evil he was or how foul his crime."

"I thought as much. That is why I wanted Old Shatterhand to remain at the pueblo." Winnetou stopped and pondered silently for a moment, his eyes on the ground. "There is a way you can have your wish. But I beg my white brother not to take that way, for it will cause our warriors to look down upon him."

"What could I do so dishonorable that the Apache braves would change their opinion of me?"

"You must ask us, my father and me, to thank you for saving our lives, and you must do so before all here assembled. When we give you that thanks, we must also grant your wishes. But by the red man's standard, gratitude must be freely given, and one who requests it is despised. You would be cast out, no longer our brother, and all your valiant deeds as if they had never been. Is Rattler worth that sacrifice?"

"Certainly not!"

"Winnetou can understand the thoughts and feelings in his brother's heart and mind; but our warriors have had only hostile contact with palefaces, and can make no sense of those emotions. Should Old Shatterhand, who could be the greatest and most famous warrior of the Apaches, leave us in disgrace because of his pity for one who does not deserve it?"

It was hard for me to answer. I was torn between my desire to intercede for Rattler and my pride in being accepted as a full-fledged warrior of the Mescalero Apache tribe. Winnetou saw the indecision in my expression, and said:

"Winnetou will talk to his father Inshu-chuna. My brother may wait here with his comrades." He left.

"Don't do anything stupid, Bud," begged Sam in a whisper. "You don't know how much is hangin' on how you act. Remember it ain't only you—me and Dick and Will are in the same boat."

Inshu-chuna and Winnetou were conferring earnestly together. Presently the Chief came to us and spoke to me:

"If Kleki-petra had not told us so much about the paleface world, your feelings would be puzzling to me. Although I cannot agree with them, I can understand them. So Inshu-chuna has decided on a way to grant your wish without bringing you shame. The murderer is an evil man, and was also your enemy. But we will see if there is still a trace of good in him. If he will ask your forgiveness for his deed—your forgiveness, not ours, for we cannot give it—he will die a quick death."

"May I tell him all of what you said?"

"Yes." He returned to Winnetou, and I sat down to wait.

"I can't hardly believe it!" said Sam. "The Chief is goin' to let you have your way. Me, I never would've made a fuss. Hey, now somethin's happenin', if I'm not mistaken!"

The wagon's canvas cover was removed, and several braves slid out a long coffin-like box. As they stood it upright we saw that Rattler was tied fast to its one flat side, a gag in his mouth.

"My God!" I exclaimed. "Is the body inside that box? Kleki-petra was killed weeks ago!"

"They burn a log hollow," Sam explained, "put in the body and cover the openin' with a slab. Then that's covered with a wet hide, and when it dries it stretches so tight that no air can get in or out. The body's prob'ly still in pretty good shape. As good shape as it can be when it's dead, heeheehee!"

Not far away was a side valley with a sheer cliff, the rear of the formation on which the multi-story pueblo was built. We all followed the crowd of Indians as the coffin-plus-Rattler was carried there and leaned against the cliff face, where a crypt made of stone blocks had been built. The front was open and more blocks lay nearby. There was deep silence.

Until Inshu-chuna gave a sign, and Rattler's gag was removed. He drew a deep breath and screamed, then loosed a flood of invective at us, garbled and unintelligible, but obviously curses. I stood in front of him, and he fell silent and eyed me with hate. He saw that I was free, evidently friendly with the Indians, and I thought perhaps before I even spoke that he would ask me to help him. The Chief motioned for me to proceed, and I said:

"You know that you've been sentenced to die, Rattler, and the Apaches want to kill you slowly, as penalty for shooting their friend and teacher, Kleki-petra. But—"

"Go to hell!" he shouted. "Damn redskin-lover!"

"Let me finish," I said quietly. "You have to die in any case. They say that if you ask my forgiveness for what you did, they will let you die quickly, not by torture."

"Forgiveness! I said to hell with you!"

"You won't have a chance to change your mind," I warned.

Another string of curses. I stepped back. Inshu-chuna took me by the hand and led me away. "My young white brother sees," he said, "that this man asks no forgiveness, for he feels no remorse, only anger. Now we will begin." He gave a signal.

Several younger braves stepped forward, their hands full of throwing knives. The spectators settled themselves to watch, as if it were a circus performance, and in truth it started like one. Knives were thrown at Rattler, the braves taking turns. None of them hit him, but they were thrown so accurately, from a distance of about ten paces, that his body was soon outlined against the coffin cover.

Now one could see and hear Rattler's fear. Bound tightly, he couldn't dodge or cringe, but he gasped and sobbed as each blade 'chunked!' into the coffin lid. They had started throwing at his feet, moving slowly upward, and when they reached his upper body and then his head, his sobs turned to screams of terror.

The knives were pulled out, the young braves sat down, and this preliminary entertainment was over. Inshu-chuna pointed to several adult warriors, who lined up about thirty paces from the target. The Chief stood close and pointed to Rattler's upper arm. A knife flew, pierced the muscle and pinned his arm to the wood. Rattler howled. The Chief pointed to the other arm, and as the knife struck, Rattler's cries increased in pitch. Thighs, forearms, calves, wherever Inshu-chuna pointed. No blood was seen to flow; Rattler was still clothed, and the knife-throwers' accuracy was so great that each throw hit the exact spot the Chief indicated, striking no vital area.

Perhaps the condemned man had until now not been able to believe that he actually was going to die; now he saw that death was imminent, and knew that it would be painful. He began to sob with pain and terror, and the watchers saw and despised him.

An Indian prisoner bound to the torture-stake will never let a sound of pain pass his lips. Instead, when the torture begins, he may start to sing his death-song, in which he boasts of brave deeds in his life, and derides his tormentors. The more pain inflicted on him, the more he insults the torturers. When he dies, his bravery is proclaimed, and he is buried with honor and ceremony. The spectators also consider themselves honored.

It's altogether different with a coward, who cries and begs for mercy. To torture him is no honor, but shameful—shameful both for him and for those present. Rattler was such a coward; the wounds inflicted so far, though painful, were minor and not life-threatening, yet he howled as if he was undergoing the torments of Hell; he began to call my name repeatedly.

I looked inquiringly at Inshu-chuna; he said, "My young white brother may go and ask him why he cries. The knives can not have hurt him enough to cause him to complain so loudly."

"Come here, Bud, come here!" Rattler called between sobs.

I went to him and asked, "What do you want from me?"

"Pull out the knives from my arms and legs!"

"That I cannot do."

"But I'll die from these cuts, bleed to death!"

"Did you really think you weren't going to die?"

"But you're alive!"

"I haven't killed anybody."

"I didn't know what I was doing! You know I was drunk!"

"The deed was done nevertheless, and you have to die for it."

"Say something to the Indians for me!"

"I did. I offered you a chance to die quickly and without pain, and you rejected it. Now I can do no more for you."

"Die quickly! But I want to live, to live!"

"That's not possible."

He began to scream and sob so loudly that I could bear it no longer, and turned away. Inshu-chuna then went to him.

"Stop your howling, dog! You're a stinking coyote that no warrior would shame himself to touch!" He turned to the crowd and asked loudly, first in Apache, then for my sake in English:

"Which brave Apache warrior will continue with the ceremony of slaying this coward?"

There was no response.

"Ugh! This murderer isn't worth being killed by warriors. He should not be buried with our beloved Kleki-petra—how could we think of sending a snake to the Happy Hunting Grounds with a swan!" He signalled to two boys who looked to be about nine or ten years old. "Cut him loose!" The boys ran to do his bidding.

"Tie his hands behind him!" They did. Rattler made not the slightest resistance. I felt ashamed to be a paleface.

"Take him to the river and push him in! If he can reach the far bank alive, he can go free!"

Rattler gave a cry of jubilation as the boys led him to the riverbank and pushed him in. He went under for a moment but surfaced and started swimming on his back. He could use only his legs to swim, but he was moving away slowly and steadily.

Was the Chief going to let him get away, perhaps to commit more murders in the future? My unspoken question was soon answered.

"Fetch rifles and shoot him in the head!"

The boys ran to the braves and took two rifles from them, ran back to the riverbank, kneeled and aimed. One could see they had already been trained to handle weapons with skill and care.

Rattler, on his back, could see them. "Don't shoot, for God's sake, don't shoot!" he called. They let him get a little further away before shooting. Bullets struck his head. He disappeared.

No cheer went up from the Indians, which would have been the case at the a heroic death of a captive warrior. They turned their attention to Kleki-petra's sarcophagus; no one looked back to see if Rattler's body was floating downstream.

"Today," said the Chief to me, "you have seen the difference between a valiant red warrior and a white coward. The palefaces are ready to do every evil deed, but when it comes time to show courage, they howl with fear like a dog being beaten."

"The Apache Chief must not forget," I said, "that there are brave and cowardly, good and evil men everywhere."

"You are right, and Inshu-chuna does not mean to insult you. No one is better or worse than another because of skin color."

I asked, "May I and my companions remain while Kleki-petra is laid to rest?"

"Yes. Had you not asked, I would have requested it. When my son and I returned with the horses on that black day of his death we saw that you were walking together, and knew that you had been speaking with him. May Inshu-chuna ask what you spoke about?"

"Of course. He told me how he had come to the Apache tribe so long ago, and had grown to know and love you. He loved your son Winnetou as if he were his own, and said that he had seen a flash of—of recognition, if I can call it that—pass between Winnetou and me when we first saw each other. He said that he would give up his life for Winnetou, and alas, the Great Spirit granted him that wish a few minutes later."

Winnetou had come up as I was talking. "Why did he hold out his hand to you, asking you to stay by me and be my friend?"

I smiled and held out my hand to him. "You know the answer as well as I, Winnetou. He saw at once that we were brothers. I answered him silently, in my heart, promising him that I would do as he asked. It has taken some time for me to be able to keep that promise, but now, and from now on, it will be kept."

Winnetou took my hand, and said, "My brother!"

I answered, "With all my heart!" He smiled, and said:

"Here at Kleki-petra's grave we will tie the bond in blood. A true heart has gone from us, but left another in his place. My blood shall be yours, Shatterhand, and yours mine. My father, Inshu-chuna, High Chief of the Apaches, will allow it!"

The Chief held out his hands to us. "Inshu-chuna allows it. You will be more than brothers—you will be one brave warrior with two bodies! Inshu-chuna has spoken!"

The ritual Indian ceremony for the dead had already begun. The coffin was inside the stone crypt, and the opening was being filled with stone blocks. From the assembled Indians, both warriors and squaws, came a haunting, keening song of lament, now and again punctuated by a high shrill cry of grief. In front of the crypt a masked and costumed figure, the tribe's medicine man, danced with slow steps, while shaking a handful of rattles.

I hadn't noticed Nsho-chi's absence, but now saw her coming from the pueblo holding two clay bowls, which she took to the river and filled with water. She brought them back and placed them in front of us. I was soon to know the reason why.

The keening and dancing was over, and now Inshu-chuna stood in front of the crypt and spoke a dirgelike requiem. It was in Apache, but Sam translated the most of it. It was a eulogy to the deceased, how he was loved and honored in life and how his memory would be honored forever. The Chief paused from time to time to wait for a "Howgh!" response from the assembly, again strangely reminiscent of the "Amens" at a Christian ceremony.

When he finished he turned to me and said in English: "It was Kleki-petra's last wish that Old Shatterhand take our teacher's place with the Apaches, and Old Shatterhand has agreed to do so." That wasn't exactly what had been said and agreed to, but I let it pass without objecting—it was after all a great honor for a paleface to be accepted into an Indian tribe, into red society. Inshu-chuna continued: "Instead of the calumet-smoking ceremony to take Old Shatterhand into our tribe, he will become the blood-brother of Winnetou. They will drink each other's blood." Then in Apache, what was apparently, "Do the Apache warriors agree?"

A chorus of cries of assent.

Inshu-chuna made a small cut in his son's forearm, and a few drops of blood were let fall into one of the bowls. Then he did the same to me, and drops of my blood fell into the other bowl. I took Winnetou's bowl and he took mine, and the Chief intoned:

"The spirits of these two young warriors shall join in their blood and become one spirit. What Old Shatterhand thinks will be Winnetou's thoughts, and what Winnetou desires shall also be the will of Old Shatterhand. Drink!"

I emptied my bowl and Winnetou emptied his. I could taste no blood, only river water, but the blood was there and our unity was sealed for all time. Inshu-chuna gave me his hand.

"Now you are the son of my body and a warrior of our tribe, just as is Winnetou. Your brave deeds shall soon be known everywhere, and no other warrior shall overtake you. You are a chieftain of the Mescalero Apaches, and all the tribes of our people shall honor you!"

That was a speedy ascent in rank! From a children's tutor in St. Louis to a railroad surveyor to an Indian chieftain, honored and accepted by these 'savage' heathen. But these savages were better and nobler in my sight than the white men I had recently known and lived with.

Today's ceremonies, Rattler's death, Kleki-petra's interment and my and Winnetou's blood-brothership were now at an end, and the gathering dispersed. We, Inshu-chuna, Winnetou and I, ate in silence a simple evening meal served by Nsho-chi, after which Winnetou asked me:

"Does my brother want to rest now, or will he come with me?"

"I'll come, "I said, without asking where or why. We climbed down the ladders, walked to the riverbank and sat on the ground. I waited for Winnetou to break the silence. Finally he said:

"Will my brother Old Shatterhand ever forget that we were once his enemies?"

"It is already forgotten."

"But one thing you cannot forgive: my father's deadly insult to you on that day we first met."

"You mean when he spit in my face?"

"Yes."

"I have forgiven—why do you say I cannot?"

"Because such an insult can be washed away only by the blood of the insult-giver."

"Winnetou should not be concerned about it—really, it is forgotten. I washed it away with water, and that was all."

"We wondered why you did not strike him. No warrior accepts such an insult without reacting."

"You know what I felt about you, my brother; and Inshu-chuna was your father. I would not strike him in anger, then or now."

"For you it is over and done; but you must understand the customs of our tribe. My father knows he did you a wrong, but just as no Apache may ask for thanks, he may also not ask for forgiveness. That is why I have now asked you in his name. And you have already answered, for which I, Winnetou, thank you."

"Over and done! Let's talk about other things. Today I have become an Apache. What about my three comrades?"

"We cannot make them tribesmen, but we can accept them as brothers. Tomorrow we will smoke the pipe of peace with them. Is there not some such ceremony among the white men? Kleki-petra told us that all palefaces are brothers, but yet there are wars between your countries. How can that be?"

"That is a question to which I have no answer."

"Then Winnetou wants to know more about you, his new brother. Why did you leave the land where you were born?"

It is not Indian custom to ask such questions. Inquisitiveness is a breach of manners; information not freely given is not to be asked for. But this case was different—Winnetou and I were brothers, and his curiosity was understandable.

"It was from a desire for adventure," I replied, "to seek my fortune here on this side of the Big Water."

"Kleki-petra taught us many English words that I do not know the meaning of," said Winnetou. "To seek your fortune, you say. What is fortune?"

"Riches," I replied, "riches with which I—"

"Riches!" he broke in. "That desire for riches has caused nothing but misery for the red man. In their greed for gold the palefaces have driven us from plains to mountains, from prairie to forest, slaughtering our buffalo, laying waste to Indian villages—*Gold!* Gold means the Indians' death! And you, brother, are searching for gold, for riches?"

"No, no, my brother, that is not what I meant! Riches may come in many forms—gold is but one of them, and that is not my principal goal; wisdom, experience, health, honor, glory, and the respect of my fellow human beings—those are also riches!"

"I see. And for which of those do you search?"

In my mind I went down the list I'd just named. "All of them, I suppose. All of them are part of the adventure of being in a new land, and in a new part of that land, the West."

"I begin to understand. But how did it happen that Old Shatterhand, my brother, joined a band of land-thieves? Did he not know that what he did was a crime against the red men?"

"No, I didn't know. It never occurred to me that the rail line we surveyed crossed land which belonged to others. I was only working as a surveyor, and being paid well for it."

"Well paid? But your work has not been completed!"

"True. I received a small amount in advance; the rest would have been paid when the work was finished."

"Is it much money?"

"In my situation, yes."

He was silent for awhile. Then:

"I am sorry that my brother will suffer such loss because of us. In your own country, are you rich?"

I smiled. "With respect to gold, I am poor."

"How much longer would it have taken to finish to the end of your land-measuring?"

"A day, a day-and-a-half. We were almost finished."

"Ugh! Had I known you then as I now know you, we would have raided the Kiowas a day or two later, for your sake!"

"You mean you would have let us complete our land-thievery?" I asked, astonished.

"Not the thievery, only the land—the surveying, you call it. Lines and numbers that you draw on papers do not harm us, nor do the stakes you drive—they are only making ready for the thieving. That begins when the paleface workers come to build the path for the fire-horse. I would—"

Winnetou stopped in mid-sentence, as if a new thought had suddenly entered his mind. Then he continued:

"In order to be paid your money, you would need to have those papers I just spoke about. Is that right?"

"Yes."

"Then you would not have been paid anyway, for we destroyed all the papers with your numbers and drawings."

"And what was done with our instruments? When I asked your father whether we could have them back if I survived, he said yes, but I didn't know if they actually still existed."

"The braves who found them in the wagon wanted to destroy them, but I knew that they must have some value, so I ordered that they be wrapped carefully and taken with us. I will give them back to my brother Old Shatterhand."

"I thank you. Although I can no longer make use of them, I can return them to my employer."

"You cannot use them? Why?"

"They would be useful only if I could use them to complete the surveying of our section."

"But as I told you, all your papers were destroyed!"

I put my hand on Winnetou's shoulder and smiled. "You were also thoughtful enough to order that nothing be taken from me, even though I was an enemy. And I had been careful enough to copy all my sketches and measurements." I took the log-sheets from my jacket, crumpled and sweat-stained but still legible.

He gave an exclamation of satisfaction, but spoke no more of surveying or land-thievery, only, "I will try to make amends." We returned to the pueblo, and exhausted from the day's events, I quickly fell asleep.

The next morning, with much ceremony and the customary long oratorical speeches, Sam, Dick Stone and Will Parker smoked the calumet with the Apache warriors. Sam's speech was the longest and most elaborate, and some of the things he said elicited peals of laughter from the usually impassive braves. His talk was in a mixture of Apache, English, and hand signs, a hybrid language which was then unknown to me. In later years I learned to use it skilfully, although never with Sam's unique brand of humor.

We four had some time to ourselves afterwards, and I complimented Sam on his eloquence. We were sitting at the riverbank.

"I'm amazed, Sam! You always come up with some new ability I never dreamed you had. Sometimes I wish I was able to do some of the things you do, have some of your qualities."

"Now that would really be somethin'!" he snorted, "a greenhorn like you havin' some of the qualities of Sam Hawkens! Impossible! That'd be like a frog tryin' to be a opera singer—"

"Stop!" Dick Stone broke in, laughing. "You just go babblin' on forever, and turn everythin' around backwards! You oughta be the one to wish you had some of the qualities of our greenhorn. If I were Old Shatterhand, Sam, I wouldn't stand for bein' called by the name 'greenhorn' anymore."

"But it's true! He still is!"

"Not true! He's saved our lives! Of all the Westerners you know, plainsmen, trappers, scouts, can you think of one who could have done what he did? Wasn't for him you'd be underground, and there'd be grass growin' up through that false wig of yours!"

"False wig? Have you know this is a genuine 24-carat wig! Insult my wig, you insult Sam Hawkens too!" He left in a huff, although we knew he was shamming, and our laughter followed him as he walked back to the pueblo.

CHAPTER TWELVE

Now was the time for us, as honored guests of the tribe, to recover from the recent violent events and to regain our self-assurance, we who had come so close to dying. For the three scouts this meant hours of leisure, with an occasional day-long ride to explore and learn more about the surrounding territory.

But for me it was a time of strenuous activity. Winnetou founded an 'Indian School', in which I was the only student. We also were often absent from dawn till dusk, on far rides during which I learned much about hunting, trapping, fighting, tracking, and lore of the forest and plain. We crept through trees and brush while he schooled me in stalking, and I added to the instinctive talent I had shown when I freed him and his father from Kiowa captivity.

Often we separated, and Winnetou set me the task of finding him. He made every effort to move without leaving a trace, and I made every effort to track and find him nevertheless. Sometimes he hid in thick undergrowth or immersed up to his chin in reeds near the riverbank, and watched me as I searched for him.

He pointed out my errors and showed by example how I should move and what I should do or not do. It was excellent education and I took to it with joy, and with admiration for my brother's skill and knowledge. No word of praise ever passed his lips, but there was also no word of criticism. He was not only a master of proficiency in everything that had to do with Indian life, but he was also a master teacher.

Even though I often came home pleasantly exhausted, there was no rest for me; my education would continue, with new subjects to learn and two new teachers. Nsho-chi was teaching me the Mescalero Apache tongue and Inshu-chuna the Navajo speech. As these two languages were closely related and neither required an extensive vocabulary for ordinary conversation, I learned fast.

On days when Winnetou and I ventured not far from the pueblo, Nsho-chi would accompany us. It apparently made her happy to watch me learning or to see me solve a problem. One time in a forest clearing Winnetou asked me to leave, go some distance away and return to the clearing in fifteen minutes. I was then to track and find Nsho-chi. When I returned in the specified time, the tracks of both of them were easily seen, and I followed them for a short while when suddenly Nsho-chi's tracks disappeared!

I knew she walked with an exceptionally light tread, but there was moist moss underfoot and her steps should have been easy to follow. Winnetou's tracks were plain to see, but it was his sister I was to find, not him. I thought he might be in concealment nearby, watching to see what I'd do.

I circled the spot where her tracks had ended, but found no clue to her disappearance. Strange. She must have left some trace, for every step that touched the ground—aha! Suppose her steps hadn't touched the ground! I examined Winnetou's footprints closely and saw that they were slightly deeper from that point on. He was obviously carrying his sister.

And Nsho-chi must have left traces of her passage, even held in her brother's arms. I looked carefully and saw broken twigs and damaged leaves. Had Winnetou been traveling alone with his hands free, he would not have left such traces, but Nsho-chi could hardly avoid leaving them. The trail led beeline-straight to another much smaller clearing, which I saw but did not enter; I was sure the two of them were hiding somewhere not far beyond.

Quietly, very quietly, I stole between the trees and bushes, making a wide circle around the clearing and watching the ground for traces of either of them. I knew they had come to rest, and that their trained ears would pick up the slightest sound, so I was especially careful not to make one.

Then I saw them. They were sitting close together under a leafy hazel bush with their backs to me, facing toward the clearing. If I had been able to trail them, they thought, I would appear from that direction. They were holding a whispered conversation, much too low for me to overhear.

I grinned with delight, and moved nearer, slowly, quietly, until I was so close I could almost reach out my hand and touch either of them. I was about to do so but hesitated, for now I could hear what they were saying. They spoke in Apache.

Winnetou: "Shall I go and find him?"

Nsho-chi: "No, no. He will come, you'll see."

"I don't think he will; he's learned tracking well, but how can he find your trail when it goes through the air?"

"He'll find it. You said he no longer makes mistakes."

"But this time I gave him a difficult problem. His eyes will read my trail easily, but yours he'll have to read with his mind, and he hasn't learned to do that yet."

"He'll come, he'll find me, because Selwiki-lata can do anything he has the will to do."

These words were whispered, but with such admiration and assurance that I felt a thrill of pride.

"That's true. There remains but one thing I wish he had the will to do."

I had been about to make my presence known, but stopped once more. What was it that Winnetou wished I had the will to do? What wish of my brother had I not fulfilled?

"Has my brother Winnetou spoken to him about it?"

"No."

"Has my father?"

"No. He says it must come from Selwiki-lata's heart."

"But Nsho-chi loves this paleface very much. Perhaps he thinks it would be too forward of him to speak, because Nsho-chi is the daughter of the High Chief of all the Apaches."

"Yes, you are that and much more. There is no warrior who would not be happy to have you as his squaw. Nor any paleface who saw you and learned to know you. Except Selwiki-lata."

"How can my brother Winnetou say that, when he has not spoken to Selwiki-lata about it?"

"I say it because I know him. He's not like other white men—he wants someone on his own level or even higher; he would not take an Indian maiden for his squaw."

"Does his heart belong to some white girl?"

"No. We've spoken of women, of course, but there is no one wait-ing for him. When he does choose one, she would have to be a woman among women as he is a man among men."

"Am I not such a one?"

"Among Indian women, yes; my beautiful sister is above them all. But compare yourself with the daughters of palefaces. What have you seen and heard, what have you learned? You know what red women know, but not what a white squaw has learned and what she must know to fit in paleface society. Selwiki-lata looks at you and finds you beautiful; but he seeks more than beauty, he wants qualities he can-not find in an Indian maiden."

Nsho-shi lowered her head and was silent. After a moment Winnetou touched her tenderly on the cheek and whispered:

"It hurts me to say things that grieve my sister, but I must speak truth even when it is unpleasant. However, perhaps I know another way to help Nsho-chi gain what she desires."

She quickly raised her head. "What way is that?"

"The way to the cities of the palefaces. Where you can learn what you must know for Selwiki-lata to love you and need you."

"Oh, yes, yes! Please ask our father if I may go!" Still spoken in a whisper, but with urgency. I listened no more, but silently retreated, feeling ashamed that I had eavesdropped on a subject so close to their hearts, even though the subject was me. When I was safely out of earshot I circled quickly back to the other side of the clearing until I came to their trail again. I entered the clearing and called:

"My brother Winnetou may come out of hiding!"

No response, no sound or movement. I called again:

"I see my brother! He sits there in that hazel bush!"

The foliage moved and Winnetou stepped out, alone.

"Has my brother found Nsho-chi?" he asked.

"Yes, I have."

"Where is she?"

"In the same bush where your trail led me."

"But her trail, did you see it? I'm sure my sister was careful not to leave one."

"Ah, but she did! Broken twigs and bruised leaves, while you were carrying her."

"How do you know I was carrying her? I could have left those traces myself."

"Not if your hands had been free. Then I saw that your footprints were deeper, so you must have been carrying her. And as I find no other traces of Nsho-chi on the ground, she must be in the same bush from where you emerged. Come out, Nsho-chi, come out!"

She came out, smiling. "See, my brother! I told you that Old Shatterhand would find me, and I was right."

"Yes, you were right, I was wrong. My brother Selwiki-lata can track anyone not only with his eyes but also with his head. I think there is not much more I can teach him about tracking."

That was the first time Winnetou had said anything resembling praise, and I felt proud that I had earned it. We returned to the pueblo, I, Old Shatterhand, serene, the other two pensive.

That same evening Winnetou brought me a superbly-cut hunting outfit made of soft white-tanned leather, nicely decorated with red stitching in Indian style. It was so elegant that I couldn't find the right words—I stuttered my thanks.

"The clothes you have been wearing are too worn and soiled for a warrior like Old Shatterhand," he said. "My sister Nsho-chi has made these, and begs you to accept and wear them."

True, the clothing I'd been wearing since I left St. Louis was no longer wearable. Ragged and filthy, it would have branded me a tramp had I appeared in it on the streets of that city. I emptied the pockets and discarded it, then put on the new outfit. It fit me as if it had been professionally tailored. I finally found words and thanked Winnetou effusively, and Nsho-chi also, when I saw her at the evening meal.

After we had eaten, they left me alone with Inshu-chuna. It seemed as if Winnetou and Nsho-chi had spoken of the subject I'd eavesdropped on, and he wanted to feel me out. He came right to the point.

"What does my younger brother Old Shatterhand think about the joining of a white man with an Indian woman?"

That question had occupied my mind almost entirely since I'd overheard the conversation between Nsho-shi and her brother, but I'd come to no conclusion, and was not really ready to answer it. After a pause to choose my words, I tried nevertheless.

"It depends on who the man is and who the woman is. The two should have much in common—the same desires, similar knowledge about customs and language, how to fit into the society where they live. White and red societies are very different, but if those basic parallels exist, I see no objection to such a union. The fact that their skin colors are not the same should make no difference at all. And of course they must love each other."

Inshu-chuna nodded. "My younger brother has spoken from his heart, and his heart has spoken well. Your answer to my question will help me decide another question which has arisen."

I already had a clue to what that question was, but said no more and took my leave, wondering whether I had worded my reply correctly. I looked deep into myself and realized that I did love Nsho-chi, and I knew that she loved me. But the thought of marriage was a new one to me—I had never even thought about wedding a white woman, let alone a red one. I wasn't ready for home and family, here or elsewhere. There were too many adventures still to be experienced, and having a wife would put a dead stop to further adventuring.

That short question-and-answer conversation with Inshu-chuna apparently set wheels to turning. The next morning he brought me to a room on the second level where I hadn't been before, and showed me all the surveying instruments, carefully wrapped in blankets.

"These belong to you, younger brother," he said. "Look to see if anything is missing." I checked. Everything was there.

"These things were looked upon by our warriors as 'medicine', and good care taken of them for that reason. What will you do with them?"

"I will take them back to St. Louis with me, and return them to their owner."

"Then you intend to leave us? We thought now that you are a Chieftain of the Apaches and Winnetou's blood-brother, that you would stay here with us on the Rio Pecos."

"Brothers do not stay together always—they often go their separate ways, when they have different things to do, different goals. But they always remain brothers. Winnetou will always be my brother, and Rio Pecos will always be the home I return to."

"My ears hear your words with joy. But what will you do in that city of the palefaces? Will you go back to the people who set you to measuring a road for the fire-horse?"

"No! I will give them back their instruments, that is all."

"You are right to do that. Now you are a brother of redmen, and must no longer help the palefaces to take our land. But my son and younger brother Old Shatterhand cannot live there as he does here, by hunting. You must have money, and Winnetou has told me that you are poor. You would have been paid had we not interrupted your work, so my son has asked me to make it up to you. Would you accept some gold from me?"

He looked at me so sharply as he asked this question that I knew I was being tested, and avoided answering affirmatively.

"Gold?" I asked. "You have taken none from me, and so I can not accept any from you."

"No, we have not robbed you, but because of us you will not get paid for your work. In the mountains there is much gold, and the red men know where it may be found. Do you wish Inshu-chuna to bring some back for you?" He looked at me in anticipation of a 'yes' answer, and so I refused.

"I thank you, but it is not right to receive wealth as a gift when one has expended no effort for it. Only something one has worked for has real value. Even though I am poor, I am capable and resourceful, and I will not die of hunger when I am back in the cities of the palefaces."

The tension in Inshu-chuna's expression relaxed. He took my hand and said with obvious deep feeling:

"Your words tell me that we will never regret taking you into our tribe as an Apache Chieftain and as Winnetou's blood-brother. The gold nuggets, the gold dust that the white men seek is the dust of death. It kills not only the body, but also the spirit, the soul! Inshu-chuna wanted to test you. He will not give you gold, but he will see that you get the money you have earned."

"That is not possible."

"Inshu-chuna will make it possible. We will go to the place where our attack stopped your measuring, and you will finish your work. Then you will get the money you worked for."

I looked at his face in silent amazement. Was he joking? No, an Indian wouldn't joke about so serious a matter. Or was he still testing me? That seemed just as unlikely.

"My young white brother does not speak," he continued. "Is my decision not agreeable to him?"

"Oh, yes! But it's hard for me to believe that you speak in earnest. You'll let me finish the work that my fellow-surveyors were killed for doing? At our first meeting you said, 'I forbid you to continue measuring our land'."

"There is a difference. You were measuring without my permission. Now my permission is given. My son Winnetou has told me that completing your measurements will bring us no harm. It is the next work, the road for the fire-horse, that will harm us!"

"You know that whether I or other men finish measuring, the road will be built. The white men will come. There is no way to stop them, whatever you do."

"You are right," the Chief answered sadly, "we cannot stop them. First they will come in small numbers, like your group. Those we can kill or drive back. But then come soldiers, and crowds of settlers, and we must give way. We know it will happen and yet we resist, because there is nothing else we can do. I know the fire-horse will come. At least I can let my younger brother finish his work so that he will be paid."

"I thank you, Inshu-chuna, my new father and older brother. But I cannot finish that work by myself." I thought a moment. "There isn't much more to do; perhaps I can show Sam and—"

"Inshu-chuna has not told you all of his decision," he broke in. "You will not ride alone. I and my son Winnetou ride with you, and also thirty warriors. They will be for your protection while your work is being done. Then the thirty braves will come with us until we reach the river. There we will ride the great boat that goes by steam until we come to the city St. Louis."

I was astounded. "What is my older brother saying? Will you come so far East with us?"

"Yes, with you, Winnetou and Nsho-chi."

"Nsho-chi is coming too?"

"Yes, my daughter will also come. She wants to see the great cities of the palefaces, and remain there as long as it takes for her to learn all the things she must know to be accepted and respected as if she were a white squaw."

I must have had a stupid, mouth-open look on my face during the half-minute or so it took to digest this new information, for Inshu-chuna had a smile on his as he watched me.

"My younger brother seems surprised. Would he rather that we did not go with him?"

"No, no, just the opposite! Your plan gives me great happiness! With a group so large we can travel in safety, and most important, I will not be separated from those I love."

"Good! You will finish your work and then we will travel to the East. Will Nsho-chi find people with whom she can live while she learns the paleface ways?"

"Yes, I will be glad to arrange it. But the Chief of the Apaches must realize that the palefaces do not offer the same generous hospitality that the red men do."

"Inshu-chuna knows that. We Indians give food and shelter to our guests and ask nothing in return. But Nsho-chi must pay for the pale-face—hospitality, you call it?—and she will do so."

"But I want to take care of her, she is my sister! Because you are letting me complete my work, I will be paid much money. Nsho-shi will be my guest while she is in the paleface world."

"Ugh! Ugh! What is my younger brother thinking! Have I not said that the red men know where gold is to be found. We leave it there, we have no use for it. But because Nsho-shi will need to pay for living in the white world, I will give her gold which she can sell for money. One such gold vein is on our way, and we will stop there and gather some. When will my younger brother be ready to leave?"

"Any time, as soon as you are ready."

"Then we will not delay, for it is late autumn, and winter will soon be here. Red warriors need take nothing with them; as we travel, we hunt for food, and build our own shelters in case of bad weather. We can leave tomorrow morning, if you wish."

"I will be ready. I will see about horses, to ride and to carry our instruments and—"

"Winnetou has already taken care of those things. He has thought of everything, and you need not worry."

I climbed the ladders up to my room, and Sam Hawkens was waiting there for me.

"Got some news for you, Bud, somethin' you prob'ly don't know about yet, if I'm not mistaken."

"Let me guess. We're going to leave tomorrow."

His mouth fell open, what I could see of it under the beard.

"Guess! That was no guess, you already knew about it!"

"So, you were mistaken. Yes, I know all about it. Nsho-chi is coming, too. Winnetou and Inshu-chuna, and thirty warriors, you, me, Dick Stone and Will Parker. Let me see, that makes, ah, thirty-seven of us altogether. If I'm not mistaken, heeheehee!"

My Hawkens imitation was not nearly as good as the original, and I decided never to repeat it, for Sam looked a little upset.

The next morning after a short breakfast we were ready to go. Only one ritual remained before our departure, the medicine-man's ceremony to wish us well on the journey. We, and all the pueblo residents, gathered by the river. There the medicine man had expropriated the supply wagon which we'd decided to leave behind, and had hung the outside with feathers, herbs, signs and symbols painted on bark, and other magical and mystical paraphernalia.

Strange sounds came from within the wagon, growling, hissing, clanking, and went on for a good five minutes before the medicine man made an appearance. I spent this time looking our company over. Nsho-chi was dressed in male clothing like her brother's, like mine, for that matter—a similarly decorated white-tanned leather suit, long hair down her back interlaced with snakeskin. I was struck anew by how closely they resembled each other. The three of us, costumed alike, although I wore paler skin, could have been taken at first sight for members of the same family.

Suddenly the medicine man sprang out of the wagon and started to dance in a circle, chanting in time to his steps and shaking a bundle of gourd rattles. As he danced, Winnetou said to me:

"My white brother may think this is nonsense, but each of the medicine man's sounds and motions has a meaning to those who understand them. He is brushing away all the dangers that lie on our path to the East. Or, as Kleki-petra would surely say, he believes he is."

"I do not think any religious ceremony is nonsense," I said. "Even though I myself may not believe in it, others do, and I respect their belief and their right to believe as they will."

The dance and chant was over, the medicine man retired, and we made ready to depart. Our horses were brought, saddle horses and also several pack horses to carry the instruments and those few of our own personal possessions and supplies that had been salvaged from the Apache raid on the Kiowa camp.

And of course Sam Hawkens rode his mule Nancy. He had ridden her often during our time at the pueblo, and they had obviously become more and more attached to each other. I had my roan back, and we were also happy to be together again; I hadn't ridden him as often as I'd liked, for schooling by Winnetou, mainly on foot, had taken up most of my daylight hours.

We rode strung out, not bunched together, for after leaving the Rio Pecos valley there were few open stretches. Several of the braves rode on ahead, Sam, Dick and Will next. Inshu-chuna, Winnetou, Nsho-chi and I followed the three scouts, and the rest of the Apache warriors, some leading the packhorses, brought up the rear.

The Apaches, with their prisoners and wounded, had taken five days to cover the stretch from the raided camp to the pueblo. We were not so burdened, and reached that spot without incident in the afternoon of the third day. I had intended to continue the surveying immediately and get it over with as soon as possible, because it was not only a time-delay, it was a distance-delay. That is, we would have to survey westward until we reached the spot where White's party had started surveying.

But first there was some other necessary, but very unpleasant work to do. Namely, burying decomposed human bodies and bones scattered by vultures and carrion-eaters. It hadn't occurred to the Apaches to do so before they rode for home; the dead, both red and white, had been left lying in rows, the rows I'd seen when Sam had raised my head from the blood-pool many months ago. The four of us buried the fragments in a common grave.

That occupied the rest of the day and all the next morning. None of the Indians offered to help, and we didn't ask them. In the afternoon I unpacked the transit, leveling rod and the other surveying gear, and gave Sam, Dick and Will a few basic instructions. It wasn't necessary for them to become trained surveyors in order to help me—I operated the transit, and they only had to learn how to lay out the measuring tape, hold the leveling rod vertically, and drive stakes. I recorded data on the stained and wrinkled sheets I had kept, having no other paper.

Still, the work that could have been finished in a day or so with an experienced diligent crew took us three days. I recalled the information Mr. White had given me, and was able to join the end of our stakeline to the beginning of his with accuracy.

The Apache braves kept us supplied with meat, and Nsho-chi gathered nuts and wild edible greens. But it was not a leisurely camping-out vacation; we broke camp as soon as the last stakes were driven, and resumed our journey east.

Two days later, after a long wooded stretch, we came out on a wide grassy plain, dotted here and there with bushes. We liked that better, for we had a good long view, and could see possible dangers before they were upon us.

We saw four riders, white men, coming toward us, and they approached us cautiously; it could be dangerous in this part of the West for a small white group to meet a party of thirty red warriors, not knowing whether they were of a friendly or hostile tribe. But then they saw that there were whites among us, and that assured them that there was no need to detour around us.

They were dressed like cowboys, and armed with rifles, knives and revolvers. When they came within hailing distance they stopped, rifles ready in their hands, and one called:

"Good day, sirs! Should we keep fingers on our triggers?"

"Good day, gentlemen," Sam answered. "No, you can put your shootin' irons away—we're peaceful people. Can I ask where you're comin' from?"

"We're from Mississippi," one answered as they rode nearer, "and we're goin' to New Mexico, lookin' for range work. Heard cowpunchers get better pay out there than where we come from."

"You could be right. You still got a long way to ride. We come from thereabouts and we're on our way to St. Louis. Is the route clear—did'ja run into any kind of trouble?"

"No, all clear. But you wouldn't have to worry about trouble anyway—you got enough fighters with you. Or ain't they goin' the whole way?"

"Just the two warriors here, Inshu-chuna and Winnetou, Chiefs of the Apaches, and their daughter and sister, Nsho-chi."

"What! A red squaw goin' to St. Louis?" He shook his head in disbelief. "Can I ask your name, sir?"

"Sure, it's an honest name—it's Sam Hawkens, if I'm not mistaken. These two alongside are Dick Stone and Will Parker; the three of us are scouts. And my other pardner, Bud, is also known as Old Shatterhand, 'cause he can knock any man down and out with one punch. So, now you know all about us, and you can tell us your names."

"Glad to. We've heard of Sam Hawkens, but don't know any of the other names. My name is Santer, and you've never heard of me, because I'm just another plain, poor cowboy." He told us the quickly forgotten names of his three companions, asked a couple of questions about the best route west, and they rode on. None of the rest of us had spoken a word. Winnetou asked:

"Why did my brother Sam give those men so much information?"

"Well, they asked polite enough. Think maybe I shouldn't have told 'em our names and where we're goin'?"

"Yes, I think it was a mistake. I don't trust the politeness of the palefaces. They were polite because we had thirty braves with us. I am sorry that you told them who we were."

"I'm sorry, too. Guess mebbe I did talk too much."

"I didn't like the look of those men. The eyes of the one you spoke with were never still—not once when he spoke did he look directly at you."

"I didn't notice. But even if you're right, they can't do us no harm. They've gone their way and we'll go ours. They'd be crazy to turn around and attack us—four against thirty-seven!"

"Still, I would like to follow them to see what they do. My brother Old Shatterhand and I will ride behind them for a little while; the rest of you can continue slowly east, and we will come after you." Winnetou and I rode off on Santer's trail.

I must say that I also didn't like Santer's looks, nor the looks of his three fellows. They didn't have the raw, weather-beaten, hard-working appearance that genuine cowboys have, and I suspected they were the sort who confused the possessions of others with their own.

"If they are thieves," said Winnetou, as we rode, "they will not try anything as long as we're together. But they may follow us in the hope that those whom they have their eyes on will separate from the others, and be easier prey."

I was puzzled. "My brother is thinking faster than I can," I said. "Which of us do they have their eyes on, and why?"

"On my father, my sister, and I, because they surely suspect that we are carrying gold. They have only to think, 'here is an Apache Chief and his son and daughter, going to St. Louis. They must have gold with them, to pay their way'. Sam was careless to tell them anything about us."

"Oh, now I see what my brother means. When Indians go to the paleface cities they need money. As they don't have minted coins they take gold with them. And if they're Chiefs, they know where that gold is found."

"Selwiki-lata is right, but what those four do not know is that we have no gold with us."

"No? You're going East with neither money nor gold?"

"Why should we carry it with us when we have no use for it? Until now we've not had to buy anything. But tomorrow we will gather some gold, to pay for food and lodging at the towns and forts we come to, and for Nsho-chi's expenses in St. Louis."

"Do you know of gold deposits nearby, along our route?"

"My father does. It's on a mountain, an outcrop called by us 'Nugget Peak'. The whites have another name for it, because they do not know that gold is there. By this evening we will be near to it, and tomorrow we will take what gold we need."

We were riding speedily but cautiously, taking cover whenever possible; Santer should not know we were following him. In about a half-hour we caught up with the four. They were still traveling westward at a moderate pace, with apparently no intention of returning to waylay our party. We halted and watched as they rode on and out of sight.

"It looks as if they have no evil intentions," Winnetou said, "so our minds can rest easy. We will return and join the others."

I thought the same, and both of us were wrong, so wrong—they did have evil intentions. But they were exceptionally sly; they suspected that we'd observe them for a stretch, so Santer kept them riding west. Later, however, they'd turned and made a wide sweep to follow, watching us from a parallel course.

Winnetou and I galloped back and rejoined our party, and at dusk we made camp. There was a freshwater spring, and plenty of grass for the horses, an ideal spot. The surrounding area was thickly wooded, with bushes and undergrowth where an enemy could easily take cover to spy on us, so Inshu-chuna had his braves make a thorough check for a half-mile around before we settled down to build a fire and prepare some food.

We conversed, as we sometimes did, before turning in. Inshu-chuna mentioned in the course of our conversation that we would break camp later than usual next day, namely at noon. When Sam asked him why, he replied with frankness which I later deplored:

"It is really a secret, but if my white brothers will promise never to repeat it to anyone, I will tell you."

We all promised, hands on hearts. I, of course, already had an inkling of what the secret was, but said nothing about my conversation with Winnetou.

"We need money," said the Chief, "so early tomorrow morning my children and I will leave you for a little while to go to a secret place I know of where gold can be found. We should return here about midday, and then we will continue our journey."

Stone and Parker emitted expressions of astonishment, and Sam asked with similar surprise in his voice:

"Gold in this area? First I ever heard of it!"

Inshu-chuna smiled. "That is because, as I said, it is a secret place. I know where it is from my father, and he from his father before him, and tomorrow I will show it to Winnetou and Nsho-chi. Not even my warriors know where it is, although they know that it exists, as you do. But I trust you not to follow us, not to leave this spring until we return." This last was spoken without the smile and with a warning intonation. The subject was quickly abandoned and we talked of other things.

We were sitting around the waning campfire, the Chiefs, Nsho-chi and I on one side; Sam and the two scouts sat opposite us, so could see past us to the bushes at our backs. Suddenly Sam let out an oath, jumped to his feet with revolver drawn, and emptied two chambers over our heads.

The reports set the whole camp in an uproar. The Apaches all came running, and the rest of us shot shocked questions at him.

"I saw a pair of eyes shinin' outa that bush! Wasn't sure at first, but then Winnetou moved his shoulder outa the way, and the fire made 'em shine brighter. Ain't none of our own braves a-spyin' on us for sure, so I figgered it was no friend of ours."

Some of the Apaches grabbed brands from the fire to use as torches, and scattered, searching through the trees and bushes but finding nothing. We composed ourselves and sat down again.

"Sam Hawkens must have been in error," said Inshu-chuna. "A flickering fire can be confusing, make shiny leaves reflect light like a pair of eyes."

"Maybe," Sam replied, "but they sure looked like eyes. If they wasn't, then I just killed some innocent leaves, heeheehee!"

Almost everyone was reassured after the futile search that no spy had been in the vicinity. But Winnetou was still uneasy; he rose after awhile and left, returning more than an hour later.

"Nothing, no one," he said. " But, brother, I wish you would check again by daylight, after we have gone, to see if there are traces of an intruder. Will you do that?" I assented.

I slept fitfully, sleep interrupted by short dreams in which Santer and his companions played leading roles. Even after I'd awakened I couldn't push him out of my mind. His name took on a significance in my thoughts entirely out of proportion to the brief encounter we'd had with him.

After a meagre breakfast of dried venison and cornmeal gruel, Inshu-chuna and his son and daughter departed. They were afoot, so I guessed that the distance to Nugget Peak could not be great. The peak itself could be any one of several heights visible from our camp through the trees; I honestly had no desire to discover its location by secretly following them. Instead I did as Winnetou had asked, and started checking the area.

First I walked to the rear of the bush where Sam had "killed some innocent leaves," and immediately found evidence to confirm our suspicions. There were broken twigs and leaves in line with Sam's bullets, but there were also bruised leaves, and branches pushed carefully aside, which proved that someone had been inside that bush, watching and listening to us. Unfortunately there was no sign that either of Sam's bullets had hit that person.

Based on no reason other than his shifty eyes and my dreams about him, I was certain that the someone was Santer, and that he knew that Inshu-chuna was on his way to obtain gold. What should I do? I had promised not to follow them, yet I knew that they would be in deadly danger if ambushed by Santer and his men.

They had set off to the south, and assuming that was to mislead anyone watching, I took my bear-killer and started north. Sure enough, a scant twenty minutes later their tracks came in from the side and continued in the same direction, north. I followed, and in a few minutes met tracks of four persons, intersecting and following the now-upward trail I was on.

I heard a horse's whinny, and backtracked on the new trail for only a couple hundred yards before coming upon four horses tethered to trees. Santer's gang! I knew now that the danger was real and that time was critical, so I took one of the horses and rode as fast as the terrain would allow, following the plain traces left by seven pairs of feet. This rapidly became more difficult as the incline grew steeper and the ground cover turned to broken rock and shale. I had to dismount; I tied the horse to a tree and continued uphill on foot.

There were no longer footprints to follow, but I didn't want to slow down for closer examination of the stones underfoot, so kept running, running straight uphill. Suddenly the incline leveled out; I was in a dry gully, with a stand of pine trees on my left. I stopped to catch my breath and decide which direction to take, when I heard several gunshots and a scream, an Apache cry which vibrated through my every fiber; the shots and cry came from the pine trees, and I sped toward them, not merely running, but leaping like a predatory animal.

Another shot, and another—I recognized Winnetou's double-barrelled rifle. Thank God, he was alive! Through the trees to a clear area beyond, and I stopped, for what I saw riveted my feet to the ground. In the center of the clear spot lay Inshu-chuna and his daughter. They didn't move, I couldn't tell if they were still alive. Not far beyond was a large boulder, and I could see Winnetou's white-clad arm desperately reloading his rifle. Two men stood on my left with their backs to me, shielded from Winnetou by tree-trunks, rifles at the ready to shoot at him as soon as he showed himself. On my right a third man was slipping through the trees to get around behind Winnetou. A fourth man lay on the ground almost at my feet, dead. I took in the whole scene in less than a second, and reacted a second later.

The two on my left were the immediate danger to my brother; I lifted the bear-killer and with no compunction shot them both in the back. Not taking time to reload, I sprang after the third one, who had heard my shots, stopped and turned, saw me coming, shot at me, missed, turned again and ran out of sight.

The man was Santer. I ran a few yards through the trees after him, but saw that chase was futile; he could have taken any of several different directions. I returned to the clearing.

Winnetou knelt by his father and sister, anxiously searching for signs of life. He turned when he saw me coming. There was a violent, almost insane, look in his eyes which I will never forget, a projection of rage, grief and pain.

"My brother Old Shatterhand sees what has happened," he said, choking back tears. "Nsho-chi, the best and most beautiful of all the daughters of the Apaches, will never go to the cities of the palefaces. She lives yet, but she will not open her eyes again."

I was unable to speak a word. What could I say, what could I ask? They lay next to each other in pools of blood, Inshu-chuna shot in the head, Nsho-chi in the breast. He had died instantly; she was still breathing raspingly, the glow beneath the bronze sheen of her face fading, slowly fading . . .

She moved her head, and her eyes did open. She lifted her hand and put it to her breast, felt the warm blood seeping from the wound and sighed a deep, bubbling sigh. I knelt by her side.

"Nsho-chi, my beautiful, beloved, my only sister!" Winnetou cried, with indescribable despair in his voice.

She looked at him. "Win-ne-tou—my brother—revenge . . ." Her eyes went past him to me, and the ghost of a smile came to her lips. "Old Shat-ter-hand," she coughed, "you—are—here. Now I can—die—oh!" Blood flowed from her mouth, and her eyes closed forever. I felt as if my heart would burst. I sprang to my feet, drew breath, and screamed until echoes returned.

Winnetou stood up also, stood as if he were a hundred-year-old man lifting a hundred-pound weight. He put his arms around me.

"Now they are dead! The greatest, noblest Chieftain of the Apaches and Nsho-chi, my sister, who gave you her heart and soul! She died with your name on her lips. Never forget that, my beloved brother!"

"Never!" I cried. "I will never forget!"

Then his face hardened, and his voice sounded like the rolling of thunder.

"Did you hear her last word to me?"

"Yes."

"*Revenge*, she said! Yes, I will revenge her as no murder has ever been revenged before! You saw who the murderers were. Palefaces to whom we had done no harm. It has always been, and will always be that way, until the last Indian has been murdered. Even should he die a 'natural' death, it is murder nevertheless, murder committed by the white men, with the red men the victims. Nsho-chi wanted to go to the cities of the madmen, the cities of the palefaces, there to learn their customs and knowledge so she could become as a white squaw and win your heart. She has paid for that desire with her life. Remember, brother, *revenge!*"

CHAPTER THIRTEEN

After that outburst Winnetou grew calmer, but there was still steel in his voice as he continued:

"All the Apache tribes will lament, and a cry of anger and vengeance will travel from one to the next, wherever they may be. The eyes of every Apache will be on Winnetou, to see how he exacts revenge for the murder of his father and sister. Listen, my brother Selwiki-lata, what I swear here by the bodies of the ones I loved. I swear by the Great Spirit and by all my valiant forefathers, there beyond in the ever-green savannah, that from this day on, every paleface I meet will find death by a bullet from the Silver-rifle I now take, fallen from my father's hand—"

"Stop! Stop, my brother!" I cried. He glared at me.

"Does Old Shatterhand want to hinder me from doing my duty?"

"No, I would not do that. I want revenge on the murderers as you do. Three of them lie dead—only one has escaped, but not for long; I, Old Shatterhand, now swear that to you." I took him by the hand and said:

"You will do what you have to do. But before you swear revenge I ask one favor of you. By the love Nsho-chi and I felt for each other, by the love between you and these two lying here, I ask you not to swear your oath of revenge until the last stone is placed over the grave of the noblest daughter of the Apaches."

He looked earnestly into my face with those piercing velvet dark eyes, then dropped them to the two bodies. I saw the hard facial muscles soften, and he said no more for a minute or two.

Then: "My brother Old Shatterhand wields great power over the hearts of all those near him. Nsho-chi would have done anything he asked of her, and Winnetou, her brother, will also do as he asks. Not until I no longer see the bodies of these, my loved ones, will it be decided if the Mississippi will flow red to the Great Water, red with the blood of red men and white men alike. Winnetou, now High Chief of all the Apaches, has spoken!"

"Thank you, brother. Now—the last guilty one must not have time to escape the death he deserves; tell me how you wish to organize the hunt for him."

"I must leave that to you, my brother, for by the custom of my people I must stay by the bodies of my family until they are buried with all the proper ritual. Only then may I start on the path of revenge."

"When will the ceremony take place?"

"I will confer with my warriors. We will either entomb them here on the spot where they died, or bring them back to the Rio Pecos pueblo, where they will rest with their own. But even if they are laid to rest here, many days will pass before all the requirements for the burial of a noble Chief are met."

"Then the hunt for the murderer Santer is my hunt. If I am able to capture him alive, I will bring him to you for proper punishment, wherever you may be."

By now Winnetou had control of his emotions, and his features had regained their normal composure. He asked me curiously:

"My brother arrived in time to save me, if not my father nor my sister. Will he tell me how he came to be here?"

I told him of the spy's traces I had found, and the logical sequence of thoughts and actions which had driven me to find and try to protect him and his father and sister. As he bent his head in silent understanding, we heard a low gurgle from one of the two bandits I had shot and thought I had killed. We walked over and saw that one was shot through the heart. My bullet had also gone through the other, back to front, but it had missed that organ. He still had a little life in him, enough to bring him to semi-consciousness. I bent over him.

"Look at me, man! Who are you?"

It was an effort for him to focus his eyes, let alone to try to speak. He asked softly, "Where is—is—Santer?"

"He's run away and left you to die."

"Where—where did—he go?" I had to strain to hear.

"We hoped you could tell us, for your other mates are dead. Where did Santer come from?"

"Don't—know."

"Where were you going?"

"Out West—gold—easy pickin's . . ." His eyes closed. I started to ask another question, but Winnetou touched me on the arm and said, "No use—this paleface dog will answer no more questions; he's dead. They wanted to learn our secret, but they came too late, we were already returning. They heard us coming, hid behind trees and shot at us without warning. They killed my beloved father and sister, but the bullet meant for me only went through my sleeve. I killed one, but my other shot missed. I jumped behind the boulder to reload, but if my brother Old Shatterhand had not appeared, I too would have been among the dead, for the last one, Santer, was racing to shoot me from behind, where I had no cover. When I heard the reports of my brother's bear-killer, I knew I was saved. Now you know everything, and we will plan our next moves."

"I can follow Santer's trail, but I will have to travel much slower than he does. What does Winnetou advise?"

"No trail—go quickly to where they left their horses. He will surely have been there before you, unless he took the horse you left tied beside the trail. But from where the other three horses were tied, you can backtrack to where they camped last night. The search for Santer will start there."

"Good—what then?"

"Take ten of my braves with you, to help you follow and capture him. Send the other twenty to me here, to sing with me the song of lament for the dead, and to prepare for the interment."

"It will be done as you say. I am proud that my brother has so much confidence in me."

"I know that Old Shatterhand will do everything exactly as I myself would do it. Go then, and may the Great Spirit guide you!"

He held out his hand to me. I shook it like friends do, and then we embraced, as blood-brothers do. I went back and kneeled by the two dead loved ones for the last time, kissed Nsho-chi on both eyelids, arose and went. At the edge of the clearing I turned my head for a final look. Winnetou was kneeling by the bodies, starting to sing that Apache song for the dead, a heart-tearing lament in minor key. My eyes misted over and I left.

I ran downhill, and when I came to the place where I'd left the horse, saw that it was gone. I didn't stop, but continued running to the place off-trail where I'd found the other three horses; they were still there. I knew then that Santer must be so fearful of pursuit that he wouldn't stop running for any reason except sheer exhaustion.

I took the reins of the three horses and led them back to our camp by the spring. It was past noon, and the three scouts were eating. Through the trees I could see our Apaches at their camping-place not far away. Sam jumped up in amazement.

"What the hell! You left here on foot, and you come back with three horses! Didn't steal 'em, I hope!"

"No, but they belong to us now," I said. "Their former owners are dead." And I told them what I'd done, what I'd found, and the tragic end to the morning's events.

"Terrible, terrible!" cried Sam, almost sobbing, "that sweet young Indian miss! And her father, the High Chief, who—"

"Yes, Sam, I'm broken up, too," I said, "but we can't stop to grieve. The first priority is to catch the murderer, Santer. I have to tell the Apaches now, and give them Winnetou's orders—I'm sure they're not going to take the news calmly."

I called the braves to us, and told the troop leader of the deaths of their Chief and his daughter. At first there was deep silence; they just couldn't believe it, couldn't grasp it; then a howl of grief and rage went up from them in unison, so loud and penetrating that tree-branches swayed as if blown by a gale. It was several minutes before I could make myself heard again.

"The Apache warriors want revenge, as we all do," I said to them, "but we must act quickly—the murderer must not escape. Winnetou wants twenty of you to come to him, the other ten will stay with us to track Santer." The leader, Akana, counted off the twenty, and I told them how to find Winnetou, and that they would have to lead their horses on the steep part of the trail. They led Winnetou's horse with them. Akana stayed with us.

"Where do we start?" asked Will Parker. "Have you any idea at all how we can pick up his trail?"

"Yes," I answered. "First we go to where I got these horses, and from there follow their tracks back to wherever they camped last night. Santer was in a desperate hurry, but he may have stopped at the campsite to pick up his gear—notice that none of these horses had saddlebags, just saddles. If he did stop, we can trail him from there. This was Winnetou's idea."

"And a good one," put in Dick Stone, "seein' as it's the only one we got. We won't be comin' back here, so let's collect our stuff and start off."

"My thoughts exactly," I said. We took but a few minutes to make ready, and we were on our way. Besides the pack animals, we now had five extra saddle horses; taking them with us would be a handicap to a speedy search for Santer. It would be best to find some spot to use as a base camp and leave them there.

Santer's campsite was found with no difficulty. There were three rifled saddlebags, and a miscellany of clothes and personal articles strewn about. Santer had been there and gone. But the spot was ideal for our base camp. I left two braves there with the extra horses and supplies, and sent a third to tell Winnetou where our base was and that we had found Santer's trail.

Actually finding it took a little while. We could see no single set of hoofprints going off in any direction, only the multiple prints the four had made arriving, and those made when they'd set off to ambush the Apache chiefs and Nsho-chi. The first set, very faint on hard ground, came from the west. Akana followed them for a spell, and returned with the information that he'd found a single set overlaying them with the prints pointing the other way. That was our man!

We started off, seven redmen and four palefaces. We were no longer slowed by riderless horses, but still had to move at a moderate pace; we were all watching carefully for a single track branching off from the multiple one.

We found it about a half-hour later, leading south. The four early hoofprints were the ones made when they'd come back to spy on us, and they went on to the west. Now we had only one trail to follow, and we made better speed during the several hours of daylight left to us. Winter was closing in and the days were shorter, the nights colder. We had to wait for dawn before we could pick up the trail again, so we rolled up in our blankets and slept. We woke at dawn and rode right off. Sam said:

"He had a little moonlight last night—he could've just kept goin', to put more distance between us. He knows for sure that we wanta catch him, but 'course he don't know that we found his trail. He's just gonna keep movin' fast as he can. What he also prob'ly don't know is that he's headin' for the Salt Fork."

"Does that make any difference to us?" I asked.

"Well, yes. That's all of it Kiowa country. Their huntin' grounds are all along both sides of the Salt Fork, and their main village is where it joins the Red. Maybe Santer don't know it, but that's where he's goin', and looks like we are too."

I shrugged. "Just hope we catch him before he gets there."

An hour later we found where Santer had stopped to rest. His horse had flattened a patch of grass; both horse and rider must have been exhausted. But his rest stop had brought us closer to him; the ongoing trail was not more than two hours old. It still led due south, alternating between forest and grassland, and he had made no detours to avoid hills or rough terrain.

About noon we started riding more cautiously, holding guns ready, expecting to come upon Santer at any minute. I could see the murder victims lying before me, and wanted their murderer, wanted him here in my hands. We were riding through trees, and suddenly came out on the bank of a dry creek. I saw the trail leading down the bank and across the gravelly creek-bed, raised my eyes, and instantly pulled my roan back into the shadows of the trees, bringing the three scouts up short behind me, and our seven warriors behind them.

"What is it, Bud?" Dick asked.

"Kiowas."

Sam looked out from the shadows. "Right, Kiowas! Damn Santer must have the devil helpin' him, to let him slip through our hands at the last second. He'll hafta tell 'em what he's runnin' from, and when he does, they'll make a hero out of him!"

Directly across from us but away from the creek-bank, about two hundred paces distant, a dozen Indians were working busily among their horses. I could see posts in the ground with cords strung between them from which meat hung, and fires where it was being dried and smoked. There was no hue and cry; apparently no one had been looking in our direction. Santer was not in sight.

"It's not a very large group," I said.

"Ho! We're only seein' those that're this side of the trees; there's sure to be lots more of 'em beyond. It's a huntin' party gettin' their meat ready to take back to the village."

"What should we do, men, retreat a little way?"

"Hell, no! We'll stay here."

"But that could be dangerous! Some of them might take a notion to come over to this side."

"Why should they? They're kinda busy over there, if I'm not mistaken. And they don't know we're already here, though Santer has for sure told 'em we're after him."

"Well, Sam, you're the expert. What do you suggest we do?"

"That's easy. I suggest you all stay right here under cover, and as soon as it gets dark I'm goin' to suggest myself right over there on the other side and find out where Santer is."

"I want to go with you!" I said.

"No, Bud, no. This ain't fightin', just scoutin', and I'm the scout. I guaran-damn-tee ya, I won't let myself be caught. It's either one of two things: Santer might still be there, or they might've brung him to the main village. I'll find out which and then we can make plans accordin'ly."

I let him have his way. We pulled back into the forest a few hundred yards before dismounting, invisible from the creekbed and well out of earshot, and ate some "iron rations." I was getting a sour stomach on our diet of beef jerky and cold corncakes, but there was no help for it—a cooking campfire could have shown a casual watcher that we were there. At dusk Sam slipped away; he took his knife and one revolver, leaving his Liddy behind.

The hours of darkness passed slowly. All of us were exceptionally alert, listening for shots or shouts that would tell us Hawkens had been discovered. They didn't come, and Sam returned shortly before midnight, as silently as he had left.

"We were a little worried about you, Sam," I said, "and were about to send out a posse. We're real happy to have you back."

"And I'm happy to be back, heeheehee! Although I dunno if I'm bringin' good news or bad news. The news, good or bad, is that Santer was there, but he ain't there anymore. They've sent him downriver to Tangua at the Kiowa village. With a couple of braves as guides or guards, I don't know which."

This was a new development, and I chose to sleep on it. We could do nothing until daylight anyway, whatever I decided. And we all needed to get some rest—we'd had few hours of sleep.

In the morning I held a conference, all eleven of us present. Some of it was in Apache—among the seven warriors, only Akana understood English.

"Capturing Santer is our only reason for being here," I said, "and I want all of you to go to the Kiowa village and keep it under observation, making sure that Santer doesn't leave it. If he does, grab him and bring him to our base camp, and send someone uphill to tell us you're there. If Winnetou and I return to the base camp and don't find you, we'll know that you still have the murderer bottled up at the village, and we'll come to reinforce you—let's see, there'll be twenty-three, no, twenty-four more of us. Now if—"

"Wait a minute, Bud!" Sam broke in. "You're goin' too fast for my slow thinkin'-cap. Where're you goin' to be while we're down there at the village?"

"I'm riding back alone, to be there at the burial ceremony of Inshu-chuna and Nsho-chi. I owe them and Winnetou my presence. I trust you, all of you, to keep Santer, their murderer, from escaping his death sentence."

There was a short silence while all thought it over, and they accepted my decision with no dissent. I put Sam in charge of the operation, with Akana, a loyal and efficient warrior, to dispose his braves as Sam ordered. My roan had had time to graze and to get some sleep, and I set off after a short farewell. I figured that if I rode without sleep it would take me a full twenty-four hours to reach the murder—the burial—site. But I'd surely need a short nap; say, thirty hours elapsed time at the very most.

Nap and all, I believe we did it, my untiring roan and I, in only twenty-four hours. For when we reached the foot of the steep trail, the sun appeared to be in the same position as it had been when we'd left the day before. I tethered the roan and began to climb.

A sentry stood at the edge of the clearing; he greeted me with a silent wave of the hand. I saw at a glance how diligently the twenty Indians had been working to prepare for the burial of their Chief and his daughter. Many slim trees had been felled for scaffolding, and an enormous pile of stones gathered.

To one side of the clearing a makeshift hut had been built, in which the bodies reposed. Winnetou was within. He was told that I had arrived and he came out. His face was gray—never before or since had I seen him looking like that. His normal demeanor was serious; seldom did he even smile, let alone laugh. But through his earnest, grief-drawn, and now stone-hard expression shone the good heart and the good will of the man inside.

He came to meet me walking slowly and heavily, took my hand, then embraced me before saying a word. Then he asked:

"Has my brother Old Shatterhand caught the murderer?"

I cast my eyes downward, ashamed to speak my answer.

"He escaped us."

Winnetou also looked down. "Did you lose the trail?"

"No, we know where he is. He is with Tangua in the village of the Kiowas, and his escape is only temporary." Then I told him all that had transpired since we parted, and the orders I had given the others.

"My brother could have sent me this information."

I looked up and our eyes met. "Winnetou, my blood-brother," I said, my throat constricted with emotion, "I wanted to be with you when the bodies of our father and sister are laid to rest."

Winnetou took both my hands in his. I could see that he was too moved too speak, but he nodded and smiled a faint smile. In a minute or two he recovered his composure and said:

"When you left I was ready to swear vengeance on the entire white race. Your presence here has saved the lives of many palefaces I would have killed, obeying the Apache law of blood for blood. I have had time to think on what you said to me at that time, and I take back the oath I was about to make. There will be no holy war of redmen against white men. Your words have made my heart soft, Charlie, my brother."

His eyes were wet, though no tears fell. He was ashamed to show such emotion before his warriors, so turned and reentered the hut. That was the first time he had ever called me by my first name, or rather its diminutive. He has used it often, al- though not always, from that time on.

The burial, if one can call it that, took place the next day with all the customary Indian ceremony. I could describe it in detail, but when I think back on that day my heart fills with grief again, and to give a step-by-step detailed report would be a desecration. This much I will relate:

Inshu-chuna's body was placed upright on his horse, which had been dragged, almost carried, up the steep slope by many braves. Earth was piled up around and over both of them until the animal could no longer move; then he was shot in the head. A pyramid of logs was made, and more earth piled on till it made a great mound a good six feet higher than the rider's head. Then the mound was covered with a layer of stones all the way to the top.

At my request Nsho-chi's body was not covered with earth. We sat her against a short dead tree, and built a hollow pyramid of stones to the top of the tree, completely hiding it and her.

We have visited there a number of times. All remains as we left it.

CHAPTER FOURTEEN

O ur two braves were still at the base camp, obviously bored and restless, and they weren't too pleased when we ordered them to return to Rio Pecos with the pack animals and extra saddle horses. They had hoped to participate in whatever action was planned against Santer, and against their enemies the Kiowas. There was no point, however, in maintaining a base at that spot, and Winnetou and I wanted to travel light. We no longer had use for the extra clothing and supplies which were intended for my poor dead Nsho-chi during her stay in St. Louis.

We rode over the same trail I had taken to return, now well-marked by many hoofprints, and it required almost the same thirty hours I had expended to reach the spot on the dry tributary creek across from the Kiowa hunting campsite. We encountered no one— the campsite was deserted—and so assumed that Sam Hawkens and party still had Santer bottled up and under observation at the main Kiowa village. We continued onward.

The area was all so-called Indian Territory, and besides the Kiowa, Osage, Comanche and other tribes which had lived there for generations, was filled with tribes and splinters of tribes which the government had forcibly uprooted from their settlements east of the Mississippi and resettled in this area over thirty years earlier. Among these were Cherokee from Carolina and Seminole from Florida. We were lucky not to meet a war-party—they were all in a constant state of hostility, not only to palefaces, but in the eternal competition for hunting-grounds, to each other.

The Salt Fork was now running almost due south, and we stayed on or parallel to the left bank. Winnetou knew the area well, and said that following the Fork's winding course would have wasted time and lengthened distance, so we kept a fairly straight route, even when the river was lost to sight for several miles.

One of these "detours" took us out onto a stretch of prairie, and there we saw two riders in the distance, one before and one behind a line of a half-dozen loaded pack-horses. They came from the direction we were heading, and although we couldn't see their features, their clothing identified them as whites even from a half-mile away. They saw us too and stopped, although if we'd kept to our routes we would have passed each other with a good quarter-mile between us.

"Shall we go over and talk to them?" I asked Winnetou.

"Yes, let's. They're paleface traders, and have probably been doing business with the Kiowas—maybe we can get some information from them. But it would be better if we don't let them know who we are."

I thought fast. "Good! I'm a minor official of the Bureau of Indian Affairs on my way to confer with the Kiowas. And as I can't speak their language, I have you along as interpreter. You can be a—a Pawnee."

"That sounds reasonable. You do all the talking."

We rode toward them. As most riders in the West do at such encounters, they held their rifles at the ready and watched our approach warily.

"Put away your guns, sirs," I said, "we're peaceful people."

The lead rider looked us over. "That may well be," he said, "but we're some suspicious of everybody, and you two don't ease our minds with a few peaceful words."

"Suspicious of us? Why?"

"Well, when we see two horsemen, one red, one white, ridin' on the prairie together, they could be bandits. 'Specially as the white one is dressed like an Indian."

I laughed shortly. "That's stating it plain as day—it's always nice to know what other people think of you. But I assure you that your suspicions are unfounded. I'm with the Bureau, on my way to confer with the Kiowa Chief Tangua. And being as I don't speak Kiowa, this Pawnee is with me as interpreter. About the Indian outfit—well, I work with Indians, why shouldn't I dress like one? These clothes look good and feel comfortable."

The two lowered their rifles. "Fair enough—our minds are eased, so to speak. Now I can feel free to give you a few words of advice: *Stay away from the Kiowa village!* We've just come from there, and we know Tangua, have traded with him for years—he speaks English, incidentally, so no interpreter is needed—but there's all hell breakin' loose there, and you could be in deep danger. They're wild men these days, the Kiowas, never seen 'em like that before."

"Hm-mm. Do you know why?"

"Well, yes, for several reasons. For one thing, the Apaches just stole a couple hundred of their horses. Tangua chased after them, but the Kiowas were outnumbered and got beaten back. Then, the Apaches were helped by some whites, one of whom shot Tangua in both knees and crippled him. He's foamin' at the mouth, says he's going to find and kill this Old Shatterhand, he calls him, and Winnetou, too." And all other Apaches and palefaces."

"Winnetou—who's that?"

"He's a young Apache Chieftain. His father was killed by a white man who's there with Tangua, an unsavory-looking rascal. And by the way, there's another white man there as a prisoner, one of that group who was with the Apaches."

I steeled myself to show no overt reaction, and didn't turn to look at Winnetou. "Another white, a prisoner?"

"Yes, a small man with a big beard, and with a strange sense of humor. They keep him on the further one of the two upriver islands, tied up and well guarded. Tangua let us go over and talk to him, and when I asked him if there was anythin' I could do for him, you'll never believe what he said."

"Tell me—I'll believe it."

"He said he had a hellish cravin' for buttermilk, and would I ride over to Cincinnati and fetch him a glassful."

So Sam had most likely gone across the river to spy on them, and this time got caught! In that case they knew or suspected that there were more of us in the vicinity. I didn't want to seem too inquisitive about him, so changed the subject.

"He must be a strange person. But you said Tangua wants to kill palefaces, too. How did he let you two get away?"

"Oh, we've been tradin' with him for years, and we treat him honest, though he's a pretty sharp bargainer. We bring cloth and tools, and trade 'em for beaver pelts and deerskin."

"Well, thanks for the information, it's all very interesting. But as I'm from the Bureau, I don't think I'll have any trouble with the Kiowas."

The trader let out a shout. "Ho! It's 'specially dangerous for you. Tangua hates the Bureau of Indian Affairs like poison; told us how you people have been cheatin' and betrayin' him."

I had no idea what he was referring to, but made a quick recovery. "Well, yes, there were some administrative mistakes. I'm here to tell him that we're going to make it right with him."

"Hm-mm. Then, I guess you'll be safe." He seemed to want to talk some more, probably starved for conversation in English with another white man, but we'd heard enough and I wanted to find and join the rest of our party, so I said farewell and we rode on. Winnetou, as agreed, had kept silent throughout, as had the other trader. No names had been exchanged.

About two hours later, as we approached the Salt Fork's confluence with the Red River, we moved even more cautiously than before. Suddenly an Apache sentry emerged from a thicket, greeted us silently and guided us to where our group was camped.

Will Parker grabbed my hands. "Bud, Old Shatterhand, are we glad to see you! And Winnetou! Afraid there's bad news, though—old Sam, he tried to sneak over to do a little spyin'—"

"We know, Will, "I interrupted, "we met a couple of traders who told us he was there. He's not been harmed; they have him under guard. What worries us, though, is the fact that if they have Sam, they must know we're nearby. Have they been sneaking around, and have you seen any signs of Santer?"

"We haven't," Dick Stone said, "but this was Sam's second trip, and on his first one he found out that Santer's tent is upstream on the Red River side, second or third from the end. We been sneakin' around too. Went downstream aways and crossed the Red, then came up on the other side. We could see those tents through the trees—'course we didn't show ourselves. There's a coupla islands still further upstream—might be we could get a closer look from one of them."

"That fits the trader's story, brother," Winnetou said. "Sam is on one of those islands, and Santer is also on the far side of the Kiowa village. Sam Hawkens must be freed, but forgive me if I say that Santer is more important to me than Sam."

"I understand, my brother. Perhaps we can plan how to take Santer and free Sam at the same time. But I think our present location, on this side of the Salt Fork, is dangerous. I suggest that we cross the Red like Will and Dick did, come back up on the south side and settle in there."

Dick: "Why do you think it's dangerous here?"

"Because Sam, and you too, scouted from the south bank and returned safely; but he got caught coming from this side of the Salt Fork, right? They must know there are more of us, and when they look for us or send out a raiding party, it will be on the side Sam approached from. Doesn't that sound logical?"

Dick raised his eyebrows. "You've got more Westerner savvy than the man who's been teachin' you. When we get him back—and 'course we will—he's got to stop that 'greenhorn' talk."

"It has nothing to do with being a Westerner," I laughed. "Any Eastern greenhorn could have figured it out, even if he was never outside New York City."

Winnetou went to assemble his warriors, and we all gathered up our sparse gear and went downstream to where Will and Dick had crossed, made the crossing, slipped upstream again and settled in as planned. We had good cover here, trees close together, many bushes and thick undergrowth, so we could stay close to the river and watch the village without being spotted.

It was early evening now and a waxing moon was up, obscured much of the time by scudding clouds. There was activity at the village, cooking fires and bustling about; we wanted to wait till it was quieter before acting, so lay down for an hour's rest.

I had never been a deep sleeper, and these nights of spying, counterspying, and the proximity of enemies had made my sleep so light that I was always on the edge of wakefulness. I was lying further from the riverbank than the others, and a slight rasping sound beyond me snapped my eyelids open. I didn't move, and now it came again. Not rustling, not crackling, but *rasping*. Could it be an animal? What would make a sound like that? The moon was hidden at the moment, so nothing could be seen.

I yawned, stretched, got slowly to my feet and shambled off to the side as if I was going to answer nature's call. I circled around and approached my resting-place from the far side, where whatever was making rasping noises was between me and the dying fires across the river. I crept closer, silently closer.

Now I could see a faint silhouette, a human body slowly trying to extricate itself from a thornbush just behind the spot where I had been sleeping. It wasn't one of ours—would one of our own Apaches be spying on us? He was almost free; one arm and shoulder was still held by thorns, which rasped as they released their hold. I took good aim, and as the last thorn rasped free, swung my fist at his head and knocked him out.

"What was that?" I heard Will say. "Did you hear somethin'?"

"One of the horses, mebbe," Dick answered.

"Hey, Old Shatterhand's not here! Where'd he go? Hope he's not goin' to take on the Kiowas without our help."

"I'm here," I said softly through the thornbush. "Be back in a moment." I lifted the dead weight to my shoulder, walked around the bush and deposited it on the ground. It was an Indian, obviously a Kiowa.

"I'll be damned! Where'd he come from?" Dick whispered.

"Whew!" from Will, "is he dead?"

"No, just knocked out. Help me tie him up before he comes to. And we'd better gag him so he doesn't yell for help."

The noise and low voices had awakened Winnetou. When he saw our prize he was elated.

"Good work, brother. Now we also have a hostage, just as Tangua does. And he won't get back to report our position. It's time, I think, for us to start."

"All of us?" asked Will

"No," answered Winnetou, " you two, and my warriors, remain here on call. But stay awake, we may need help at a moment's notice. Old Shatterhand and I will swim across and see how things stand and where everybody sleeps, so we can plan our next step."

We removed all clothing except loincloths and a belt to hold our knives, no other weapons. Before entering the water we took a walk along the south bank parallel to the village for its entire length, to see how it was laid out. We crossed the river upstream, above the village but below the islands, only one of which was visible to us.

We didn't climb out on the bank, just drifted down with only our heads exposed until we came to where we had a good view of the entire central area of the village. A fire burned in front of almost every tent, its dwellers sitting around it eating. A larger tent stood in the center, with decorations and symbols painted on and hanging from its cover flap. Tangua, the Kiowa Chief, sat there with a young brave perhaps sixteen years old, and two younger boys of ten or twelve.

"Those are his three sons," said Winnetou. "The oldest is his pride and joy, and will be a valiant warrior if he can rise above the corrupting influence of his father. He runs like the wind, so was given the adult name Pida, which means deer."

I absorbed this information silently. I saw women walking about, cooking, serving the men but not eating with them. Winnetou answered my unspoken question:

"The Kiowa women eat later, if there is any food left. They do the hardest work, but receive little benefit from it."

The half moon came out, and I looked upriver. From this angle I could see both islands, the near one and also the one further upriver, the one the trader said Sam was being held on.

"What's our next step?" I asked Winnetou.

"We separate now; Santer must be in his tent, and I want to know which one of those it is. We only know it's near the end of the row. My task has to do with the murderer of my father and sister, while yours has to do with your comrade Sam Hawkens."

"Good. Where shall we meet?"

"Right here where we separate."

"All right, if nothing unexpected happens. But if either one of is seen and caught, or seen and not caught, there'll be an uproar. We'd better pick an alternate meeting-place, one not so close to the village."

"Your project is more difficult than mine. You have to swim to the island, where you might easily be seen by Sam's guards. If you are discovered, I'll come to your aid. But if you get away without my help, I'll meet you on the other island, the near one. But get there by some roundabout route, don't swim directly to it. Take a run on the far bank first, perhaps."

"But in the morning they'll find my tracks!"

Winnetou looked up at the clouds. "I doubt it—It's going to rain, and your tracks will be washed away."

"All clear. Now if you get caught, I'll come to your aid."

I couldn't see his smile but I could feel it. "Not likely—look, one of those huts has no fire in front of it, and that's sure to be the one where Santer is sleeping. Goodbye, brother."

He swam away, not up toward the tents, but out into the middle of the stream. I swam upstream, near the bank but mostly under water until I was opposite the upper island, then surfaced and—hello!—what's this? A row of canoes!

There were about thirty or forty of them lined up against the bank, in a curve which gave them some shelter from the pull of the current, and hid them from me until I came on them suddenly. The current wasn't very strong in any case, although stronger than that of the Rio Pecos; this river was even wider.

I could see that the prison island was covered with bushes and had but few trees; it was a small island, but I couldn't make out any details, and was wary of coming up under the nose of one of the guards. Still, I was about to strike out for it when I heard someone approaching. I ducked behind a canoe. The wrong canoe—it was being boarded! I submerged under it and came up behind the next one, peeked out from its shadow and saw that the someone was Tangua's favorite son, Pida the deer.

He untied the craft and started paddling to Sam's island, which was only about fifty feet away. I thought it prudent to wait. A minute later I heard voices.

"My father wants to know!" Pida.

"Think I'm goin' to tip you off to my friends?"

"If you don't tell where they are, you'll suffer ten times as much torture!"

"Don't make me laugh! Sam Hawkens suffer torture? Your pop was lookin' forward to that once, there on the Rio Pecos. And what happened, tell me that, heeheehee!" They were speaking a mixture of English and Kiowa.

"I know. That devil Old Shatterhand crippled him!"

"Well, somethin' like that, somethin' you don't expect, is goin' to happen here. You'll soon see it, if I'm not mistaken."

"You're crazy if you think so! You can't get away!"

"Not right now, you got me tied pretty tight. With these four stone-faced Kiowa braves, who won't even tell me the time!"

"If you tell me where they went or where they are, we'll let you go free."

"All right. They went to Nugget Peak, that place that Santer is wild to find. Now untie me."

"I know you're lying, and I know you're feeling pain right now. But that's nothing to the pain you're going to feel."

"Look, young 'un, you'll never catch Old Shatterhand—he's my pupil, and I taught him how to keep from bein' caught."

"But look at you, the teacher—you were caught!"

"Why, no, I just stopped by to pass the time. A little vacation here with you nice people because I like you so much."

Suddenly there were loud cries from the village below. I heard Winnetou's name being shouted, and general sounds of alarm. I could hear Pida getting back into the canoe. I retreated to the spot where it had been tied, and waited for him to return. I couldn't very well free Sam right now; I only had a knife, and four braves to contend with. But what I could do was to take Pida, Tangua's pride and joy, hostage, and trade him for Sam.

The situation was favorable. Winnetou had been seen, but I was fairly sure he wouldn't be caught. And the guards' attention was probably concentrated on whatever they could see of the village hullabaloo. I pulled myself up on the bank, waited till Pida had debarked and secured the canoe, then swatted him behind the ear. He fell like a log. I lifted him, trotted to the canoe furthest upriver, tossed him in and paddled around *upstream* of the island.

Mist had started rising on the river, and while that was fine for avoiding discovery and pursuit, it made navigation difficult. I was to meet Winnetou on the lower island, and I found it more by feel than by sight. I lay Pida in the grass, cut away all the rope I could find in and on the canoe, and set it adrift so it would give no clue to my location. Then I tied Pida with the rope, finishing just as he was coming to.

He shook his head to clear it. "Who are you?" he asked angrily, seeing my face in the clouded moonlight. "A mangy paleface who my father will catch and kill!"

"Your father can't catch me," I retorted cruelly. "He can't even walk, let alone run."

"But he has many warriors he can send to find me."

"I laugh at his warriors. They have as much chance against me as your father had when I fought him and crippled him."

"You fought him? Then you are Old Shatterhand?"

"Need you ask? I put you to sleep with one blow—only Old Shatterhand and Winnetou can do that. And who else but us could kidnap the Chief's son out of his own village?"

"Ugh! So I am going to die! You won't hear me make the least sound of pain."

"We're not going to kill you—we're not murderers like the Kiowas are. We want to trade you for the two palefaces. If your father will give them to us, you will go free."

"Santer and Hawkens!"

"Right you are!"

"He will give them to you. The Chief's son is worth a hundred of Hawkens, and my father doesn't like Santer."

It began to rain, and some of the mist was washed away, but I still couldn't see the right bank, to spot where it lay in relation to our camp. I carried Pida under the imperfect shelter of a large tree, and set myself to wait until the rain stopped or daylight arrived, or both. But where was Winnetou?

Pida and I had no more to say to each other; it was a long monotonous wait, and the rain was icy cold. Finally day broke, the rain stopped, and I gave a low hail toward the right bank.

Winnetou's voice: "Is it my brother Shatterhand?"

"Yes."

"Swim over. Don't call any more, it's dangerous."

"I have a prisoner. You swim over here and help me bring him to that side."

How relieved I was to hear his voice and know that he hadn't fallen into the hands of the Kiowas. He arrived a minute later.

"Ugh! Pida! How did you capture him?" I told him.

"Did you see Hawkens?"

"No, but I heard him talking to Pida, and when the cry went up after you, it gave me an opportunity to catch Pida."

Yes, that was a chance accident. I was almost to Santer's tent when some Kiowas came by, stopped and talked. I stood over at one side, still as a rock, but a stray beam from one of the fires lit my face just as one of them turned toward me. I dove in and swam upstream—I learned that from you, brother—and as they were searching for me downstream, I got away. But of course I didn't see Santer."

"You'll see him soon! This young warrior told me that his father would gladly give up both Santer and Sam Hawkens to get his beloved son back. Anyway, Tangua doesn't like Santer."

"Ugh! That's good, that's just fine! My brother Shatterhand always makes everything come out right. Now let's swim over to our side. Keep Pida's hands tied, but release his feet. We'll keep him between us and he can help swim by kicking." We entered the water, Pida still silent and unresistant. I had said that Winnetou would see Santer soon, but I didn't realize how soon. For we heard the faint susurrus of a canoe paddle, stopped to tread water, and saw Santer paddling toward us at the same time he saw us. The canoe was about thirty feet away.

It was mutual shock! "—be damned!" shouted Santer, at the same time as Winnetou yelled, "It's Santer, getting away!" Santer pulled in his paddle and picked up his rifle as Winnetou left Pida and me and swam with mighty strokes toward the canoe. Santer's shot at Winnetou missed, and my brother submerged, obviously to come up under the canoe and upset it and its occupant. But Santer saw him disappear, frantically picked up the paddle again and paddled furiously away into the mist.

Winnetou came up where the canoe had been a second earlier and made a few desperate strokes after it, but to no avail. The fastest swimmer in the world could not overtake a canoe where the downstream current and powerful paddle strokes add together to increase the distance between them.

The whole event took place within a space of fifteen seconds, and a quarter-minute later a dozen Apaches appeared on the near bank, drawn by the shouts and the shot. We swam toward them.

Before we'd even reached the bank, Winnetou shouted to them in Apache: "Fetch our horses and get ready to leave! Santer is going downriver by canoe and we must follow and catch him!" He was more agitated than I had ever seen him before. Or since.

"Yes!" I chimed in, "after him—every minute counts! But what about Sam, and our two hostages?"

"I'm going to leave that to you, brother," replied Winnetou.

"Then we must separate. When and where will we meet again?"

He thought a moment. "Where and when I cannot say; only the Great Manitou knows. I believed we would remain together for a long time, but it seems the Manitou has willed it otherwise. Do you know why Santer left so suddenly?"

"I can guess. We didn't get caught in any Kiowa trap, and we were seen, that is you were, yesterday. So it's known that we're in the area and won't rest until we grab Santer and free Hawkens. Santer got panicky and decided to leave."

"Yes, and I can think of another reason. The Chief's son has disappeared, and naturally the Kiowas assume we have something to do with it; they guess that he's fallen into our hands. Tangua's anger is directed at Santer, the cause of it all, and has driven him away."

"Very probable. Santer probably heard that he was no longer under Kiowa protection, and decided to flee. But why did he go by water and not by land?"

"From fear of us. On land he might meet up with us, but if he puts a long stretch of river miles between us before going ashore, he has a much better chance of avoiding us. He can probably trade the canoe for a horse. However, now he knows that we saw him escaping via the river, and he may go ashore sooner."

"Yes, but on which bank? You'll have to ride along both sides of the river to find the spot where he went ashore. And you'll have to ride near the banks to pick up his tracks. Sam once told me that the Red River is the crookedest one he knows."

"With that in mind, my brother Old Shatterhand, Selwiki-lata, we had better get started. I hear my warriors coming with our horses."

"You can't know how badly I want to ride with you, my brother Winnetou. But I must stay to get Sam Hawkens free."

"I am certain you will do so without trouble. If we do not meet in the next days or weeks somewhere on or near this river, go to the people in St. Louis, the palefaces who employed you to survey for the fire-horse road. I will leave a message for you there, or if there is none, you will leave one for me.

"But I beg you to come back to us in the pueblo on the Rio Pecos. You will always be welcome there, for it is your home. If I am not there, you will be told where to find me."

While we spoke the Apaches had returned with the horses, and had brought Will Parker and Dick Stone with them. Winnetou gave each of the scouts his hand in a farewell clasp, turned to me again and said:

"Remember how happy our hearts were when we began our ride at the Rio Pecos. It brought death to my father and sister. When you return you will not hear the soft voice of the most beautiful daughter of the Apaches, Nsho-chi, who has gone to the ever-green savannah-land instead of to the cities of the palefaces. Revenge now tears me away from you, but love will always lead you back to us. You know that you must replace Kleki-petra in our hearts; so promise to return soon, my beloved brother Charlie."

"I promise, as I promised Kleki-petra when he lay dying. My heart goes with you, my beloved brother Winnetou."

We embraced, he mounted his horse, gave his warriors a command, and they rode away through the trees.

Pida, still tied, still wet, had stood by silently during this exchange, and Dick and Will were looking him over curiously.

"Where did you catch this fish, Shatterhand?" Dick asked.

"He's not a fish, he's trade goods," I said, "and we're going to trade him for our dear friend and well-wisher Sam 'Westerner' Hawkens. Pida is Chief Tangua's son, a valuable property."

"Whew!" said Will. "He *is* valuable! How do you think we ought to go about it? We have still another hostage, remember."

"Well, advise me. How do you think we should do it?"

Will stroked his beard. "I reckon the simplest way would be to send the Kiowa spy to Tangua to tell him where we're holding his son and we'll trade him for Sam. Or is that too simple?"

Dick growled. "Simple? It's worse than simple, it's simple-minded! If we tell Tangua where we are, he'll just send a bunch of warriors to take Pida and wipe us out. And no Sam!"

"Well, wise man, how would you do it?"

"All right—we leave here and go beyond the woods a fair piece onto the open prairie, where we have a good view for a half-mile or so in all directions. Then we send the messenger to the village to tell Tangua to send two warriors, no more, to bring Sam to us. Then they can have Pida. If they send more than two, to overrun us, we can see them comin' from far away, and we just ride off. What do you think of that, Bud?"

"I think there's a surer way, without sending a messenger."

"No messenger? How will Tangua find out that—?"

"He'll find out. I'll tell him myself."

"What! You'd go right into the village? They'd grab you right off!"

"No they wouldn't, because then they'd lose Pida. It's just that we now have two hostages, and I don't fancy losing one of them just to send a message."

"But think how Tangua hates you!" said Will. "Maybe if I go to him he'd accept your conditions, and we'd get Sam anyway."

"But it's because of that hate that I want to go. Think how furious he'll be that I dare to come to him in person with an offer to exchange hostages, an offer he can't very well refuse. If I send someone else he might think that I'm afraid of him, and I can't let him get that ridiculous idea."

"Then do it your way, Bud. When do you wanta go?"

"Tonight."

"Not until then? If it all goes well, we could make the trade by noon. Then we could follow Winnetou sooner."

"And have a hundred Kiowa braves on our tail! No—Tangua will be glad to give us Sam and get his son back in return. But after the trade is made he'll use every means to find us and wipe us out. If the trade is made in the evening, and then we ride away during the night when they can't track us, we can put a lot of miles behind us before it's light enough for them to start the chase. Waiting until evening is better for still another reason—by that time the Chief's worry about Pida will have increased tenfold." I laughed. "Or perhaps even elevenfold."

I watched Will's face as the wheels went around in his head. "But suppose," he said earnestly, "they send a search party and find us and Pida here while you're in the village."

"We can make that unlikely, like this: Go fetch our horses, Sam's Nancy, our guns and gear; and our other hostage, of course. Take them south, away from the river a good way, say to where the trees thin out, then in an upstream direction, west, for a half-mile or so— pick out a good spot. That's not where we'll make the exchange, we'll do that right here. The point is, when they cross the river, either before we have Sam back or after, the first thing they'll see will be the tracks made by Winnetou and his warriors, twenty-nine sets of hoofprints heading east along the river. Think they'll be able to tell whether or not ours are among them?"

Will: "Hmm-mm. If Sam ever calls you greenhorn again, I'll break his Liddy over his head." He and Dick left.

I heard voices through the fog, and pulled Pida back under the trees, my hand over his mouth. What I'd just said in theory was already happening—a group of braves was jabbering with excitement, below us where Winnetou and his party had milled around and ridden away. No heads were turned in our direction.

They returned to the village; about an hour later a group of mounted warriors swam across the river and took off after our

Apaches. It worried me a little—Winnetou's braves had a good start and surely expected pursuit, but tracking Santer would slow them.

I waited and the hours crept by. But happy day! Just after midday a canoe came drifting slowly along the bank. It was the same one I'd transported Pida in and cast adrift upriver at the island the night before. It must have hung up somewhere, and had been released and sent to me by a benign providence. Or by the Great Manitou. I pulled it ashore.

Will and Dick returned, bringing some beef jerky and crumbled corn cakes. We ate, and I fed Pida, hesitant to untie his hands. Will described the route to our new headquarters.

As soon as it was dark I pushed the canoe into the water and paddled upstream a good distance above Sam's island, crossed to the village side and let the canoe drift with the current close to shore till I came to the canoe harbor. I stole a piece of line from another canoe and tied mine fast.

The village scene was just as it was the night before. Fires burned, men ate, and the women went about their menial tasks. I thought the village would be well guarded, have sentries posted, but this was not the case. The reason was probably because they had already sent a party after their enemies and felt secure.

Tangua sat before his tent with his two younger sons. His head was bowed, and he stared sadly into the fire. I ducked behind the row of tents and came up at the rear of his. Luckily no one saw me. I lay flat on the ground, crawled along the side of the tent, rose up, and suddenly stood next to the Chief.

Tangua's shock at seeing me was indescribable. He tried to speak, but couldn't—his lips moved but no words came out. He wanted to rise but his broken kneecaps made that impossible. He stared at me as if he were seeing a ghost, and finally:

"Old—Old—Shatter—Shatterhand! Ugh! How—how can you—be here? You are—still here, not—gone away?"

"As you see, I am still here. I came to talk with you."

"Old Shatterhand!" He finally got my name out in one piece. His young sons heard it and ran into the tent.

"Old Shatterhand!" he cried it again, and his face took on such a look of fury I thought it would burst. He yelled out a long string of words aimed at the adjoining tents, in which I heard my name mentioned again, and in a few seconds a crowd of howling warriors made a circle around us. Several of them advanced at me with weapons drawn.

I drew my knife and held it at Tangua's throat. I shouted in his ear, "I have Pida! He sent me to you!"

He heard my words through the deafening howls and held up his hand. The noise subsided to a muttering and died away, but the threatening ring of Kiowas drew closer. I sat down on the ground facing Tangua and said:

"There is deadly enmity between Tangua and Old Shatterhand. I am not to blame for it, but I accept that it cannot be otherwise. Tangua can see that I do not fear him, for I am here in his village, where every Kiowa is also my enemy. I'll say it quickly: Pida is our prisoner, and he will be hanged from a tree if I do not return in a short time."

There was no sound nor motion from the circle of redmen, many of whom understood some English and all of whom had heard me say Pida's name. Tangua's eyes blazed with fury and frustration. He spoke through clenched teeth: "How did you capture him?"

"I was there at the island when he spoke with Sam Hawkens; I knocked him out and took him with me."

"Ugh! Old Shatterhand is favored by the Evil Spirit! Where is my son?"

"He is in a safe place; he will tell you when you see him. You can know by these words that I do not intend to kill Pida. We hold another Kiowa brave prisoner; both he and your son will be returned to you when you give me Sam Hawkens."

"Ugh! You can have him! But first bring me Pida and the other Kiowa warrior!"

"Bring them to you? No—I know that Tangua can not be trusted. I am giving you two men for one, a good bargain, so the exchange must be made my way."

"And what is your way?"

"First show me Sam Hawkens. I want to hear from his own lips that he has not been mistreated."

Tangua spoke an order and I was led to a nearby tent, where Sam had been moved from the no-longer-secure island. As soon as he saw me he cried jubilantly:

"Heighday, Old Shatterhand! I knew you'd be comin' for me!" His face fell. "Or are you a prisoner too? No, your face looks too happy!

So, you want to have old Sam back again!" He greeted me by holding out his hands, still tied.

"Yes," I said, "the greenhorn has returned—the student has come back to pull his teacher out of trouble. I thought you were a master at slithering around without getting caught."

"Well, it was thisaway—never mind, I'll tell you later. Have you still got my Nancy?"

"Yes, she's with us."

"And my Liddy?"

"Yes, but you'd better be careful. Will Parker has promised to break Liddy over your head if you keep calling me greenhorn."

"It's a habit I'll find hard to break, heeheehee! Now, untie my hands and let's get away from here!"

"Patience, Sam, patience. Tangua is conferring with his elders, trying to figure out some way to get the best of us. But there's no way he can—we've got all the aces."

I went out and told Tangua that I would wait no longer, that if I didn't return soon my companions had orders to hang Pida from a tree. As I once related, hanging is the most disgraceful way for an Indian to die, and repeating this threat scared him. He quickly agreed to terms I suggested, that Sam and I would take a canoe, and two unarmed braves would follow us in another canoe; of course I didn't say where to. If more warriors secretly followed behind, I warned Tangua that Pida would die.

Sam's hands were untied, and he shouted, "Free! Free again! I'll never forget, Bud, Old Shatterhand! How many times have you saved me, saved my life, saved my good name even!"

As we boarded the canoes, a hostile murmuring arose from the assembled Kiowas. They were enraged to the edge of violence that we were slipping out of their hands. Powerless to prevent it from happening, they sent us a goodbye howl of anger and frustration.

Tangua called after me: "You are safe until my son returns! But then the whole tribe will be after you to kill you! We will find your trail even if you fly through the air!"

I didn't think it necessary to reply. As we paddled I told Sam of all that had happened in his absence, and that Winnetou and the Apaches were on Santer's trail. The moon was obscured by clouds, but we landed safely in the dark, and were received with joy by Dick Stone and Will Parker. The hostages were released, no word of farewell being uttered. We waited until we could no longer hear the paddles of the returning canoes, then slipped through the trees to our horses and rode away. We had many miles to cover that night, but Sam knew the area well. He turned and shook his fist in the direction of the Kiowa village and yelled:

"I know you Kiowas are plottin' back there how to trail us and kill us! But you'll never be able to catch old Sam and his crew, if I'm not mistaken!"

THE END
OF WINNETOU I

THE TRANSLATOR

DAVID KOBLICK was born in 1916, and attended schools in San Francisco. In early adulthood, he became an electrician and was working on a U.S. Navy project at Pearl Harbor, Hawaii, when the Japanese attacked, December 7, 1941. Returning to the mainland, he joined the Navy Seabees and spent World War II in the South Pacific.

After taking undergraduate studies in Electrical Engineering at the University of California, Berkeley, Koblick returned to the electrical construction industry. In 1961, he met his wife, Berta, on his first visit to Europe. He started translating in 1969—beginning with a translation into English of a biography of the ancient-astronaut theorist Erich von Däniken.

The Koblicks have traveled widely and circled the globe twice, the first time taking a year to do so. They traveled unescorted in China and Japan, and have visited every country in Western Europe.

After Koblick's retirement in 1981 and a one-year camping tour of North America, he settled with his wife in Steyr, Austria, living in the very house in which she was born. He has continued a second vocation translating an array of items in German and English—in the arts, history, travel, medicine, and business. Included among these are books, brochures, catalogs, technical manuals, computer programs, legal documents, and contracts. He is a lifetime member of Mensa and of the American Translators Association.